TYPHOON FURY

TITLES BY CLIVE CUSSLER

DIRK PITT® ADVENTURES

Odessa Sea (with Dirk Cussler)

Havana Storm (with Dirk Cussler)

Poseidon's Arrow (with Dirk Cussler)

Crescent Dawn (with Dirk Cussler)

Arctic Drift (with Dirk Cussler)

Treasure of Khan (with Dirk Cussler)

Black Wind (with Dirk Cussler)

Trojan Odyssey

Valhalla Rising

Atlantis Found

Flood Tide

Shock Wave

Inca Gold

Sahara

Dragon

Treasure

Cyclops

Deep Six

Pacific Vortex!

Night Probe!

Vixen 03

Raise the Titanic!

Iceberg

The Mediterranean Caper

SAM AND REMI FARGO ADVENTURES

The Romanov Ransom (with Robin Burcell)

Pirate (with Robin Burcell)

The Solomon Curse (with Russell Blake)

The Eye of Heaven (with Russell Blake)

The Mayan Secrets (with Thomas Perry)

The Tombs (with Thomas Perry)

The Kingdom (with Grant Blackwood)

Lost Empire (with Grant Blackwood)

Spartan Gold (with Grant Blackwood)

ISAAC BELL ADVENTURES

The Cutthroat (with Justin Scott)

The Gangster (with Justin Scott)

The Assassin (with Justin Scott)

The Bootlegger (with Justin Scott)

The Striker (with Justin Scott)

The Thief (with Justin Scott)

The Race (with Justin Scott)

The Spy (with Justin Scott)

The Wrecker (with Justin Scott)

The Chase

A Novel of the Oregon® Files

TYPHOON FURY

CLIVE CUSSLER
and Boyd Morrison

G. P. PUTNAM'S SONS | NEW YORK

G. P. PUTNAM'S SONS
Publishers Since 1838
An imprint of Penguin Random House LLC
375 Hudson Street
New York, New York 10014

Copyright © 2017 by Sandecker, RLLLP
Penguin supports copyright. Copyright fuels creativity, encourages diverse voices,
promotes free speech, and creates a vibrant culture. Thank you for buying an
authorized edition of this book and for complying with copyright laws by not
reproducing, scanning, or distributing any part of it in any form without
permission. You are supporting writers and allowing Penguin to
continue to publish books for every reader.

Library of Congress Cataloging-in-Publication Data

Names: Cussler, Clive, author. | Morrison, Boyd, author.
Title: Typhoon fury : a novel of the Oregon files / Clive Cussler and Boyd Morrison.
Description: New York : G. P. Putnam's Sons, [2017] | Series: The Oregon files ; 12
Identifiers: LCCN 2017012116| ISBN 9780399575570 (hardcover) |
ISBN 9780399575587 (ebook)
Subjects: | GSAFD: Suspense fiction. | Adventure fiction.
Classification: LCC PS3553.U75 T97 2017 | DDC 813/.54—dc23
LC record available at https://lccn.loc.gov/2017012116

International edition ISBN: 9780735218376

Printed in the United States of America
1   3   5   7   9   10   8   6   4   2

Book design by Lauren Kolm

This is a work of fiction. Names, characters, places, and incidents either
are the product of the authors' imaginations or are used fictitiously,
and any resemblance to actual persons, living or dead, businesses,
companies, events, or locales is entirely coincidental.

CAST OF CHARACTERS

SECOND BATTLE OF CORREGIDOR 1945

Sergeant Daniel Kekoa Soldier in the 24th Infantry "Hawaiian" Division.

Captain John Hayward Biochemist in the Research and Analysis Branch of the Office of Strategic Services (OSS).

THE CORPORATION

Juan Cabrillo Chairman of the Corporation and captain of the *Oregon.*

Max Hanley Vice president of the Corporation, Juan's second-in-command, and chief engineer of the *Oregon.*

Linda Ross Vice president of Operations for the Corporation and U.S. Navy veteran.

Eddie Seng Director of Shore Operations for the Corporation and former CIA agent.

Eric "Stoney" Stone   Chief helmsman on the *Oregon* and U.S. Navy veteran.

Mark "Murph" Murphy   Chief weapons officer on the *Oregon* and former U.S. military weapons designer.

Franklin "Linc" Lincoln   Corporation operative and former U.S. Navy SEAL.

Marion MacDougal "MacD" Lawless   Corporation operative and former U.S. Army Ranger.

George "Gomez" Adams   Helicopter pilot and drone operator aboard the *Oregon*.

Hali Kasim   Chief communications officer on the *Oregon*.

Dr. Julia Huxley   Chief medical officer on the *Oregon*.

Kevin Nixon   Chief of the *Oregon*'s Magic Shop.

Maurice   Chief steward on the *Oregon*.

PHILIPPINE NATIONAL POLICE

Luis Navarro   Inspector in charge of prisoner transfer.

Captain Garcia   Captain of prison transport vessel.

CHINESE MINISTRY OF STATE SECURITY

Zhong Lin   Field agent.

NATIONAL SECURITY AGENCY

Abby Yamada   Chief computer cryptanalyst.

CENTRAL INTELLIGENCE AGENCY

Langston Overholt IV   The Corporation's CIA liaison.

PHILIPPINES COMMUNIST INSURGENCY

Salvador Locsin Leader of the insurgents.

Nikho Tagaan Locsin's second-in-command and marine engineer.

Stanley Alonzo Interior Ministry bureaucrat and mole for the insurgency.

Mel Ocampo Biochemist hired by the insurgency.

Maria Santos Biochemist hired by the insurgency.

Dolap Insurgent soldier and Locsin's cousin.

THAILAND

Beth Anders Art theft investigator and appraiser.

Raven Malloy Beth's bodyguard and former U.S. Army Military Police investigator.

Udom Leader of drug gang.

Alastair Lynch Interpol duty station official in Bangkok.

Gerhard Brekker Leader of South African mercenary squad.

Altus Van Der Waal Brekker's second-in-command.

UNITED STATES ARMY

Greg Polten Civilian biochemical weapons expert.

Charles Davis Greg Polten's assistant.

General Amos Jefferson Director of biochemical weapons testing at Dugway Proving Ground.

TYPHOON FURY

PROLOGUE

WORLD WAR II
THE SECOND BATTLE OF CORREGIDOR
THE PHILIPPINES
FEBRUARY 20, 1945

The tunnel exploded.

Sergeant Daniel Kekoa dropped to the ground and covered his head as the M4 Sherman tank that had fired on the ragged entrance was thrown backward a dozen yards by the gigantic secondary blast from inside the tunnel. The thirty-ton tank flipped over and landed on its turret before a loose shell inside tore it apart in a fireball.

When debris stopped raining down around him, Kekoa staggered to his feet, his ears ringing from the deafening explosion. Dozens of American soldiers lay dead or writhing in pain. He turned over the nearest man down. The vacant eyes and chunk of shrapnel protruding from the soldier's chest showed that he was beyond help.

Kekoa shook his head in disgust at the deadly foul-up. The briefing from Army Intelligence indicated that this particular tunnel sheltered enemy soldiers defending the island fortress strategically located at the mouth of Manila Bay. Kekoa had called in the tank to prevent a suicidal banzai attack, which had become commonplace with the fanatical Japanese. But there had been no indication that the tunnel might also contain large quantities of explosives close to the entrance.

Captain John Hayward crouched nearby in one of the many craters created by the American pre-invasion bombardment, his hands still over his ears. Kekoa reached down to haul him to his feet. The slight man, with brown hair and circular-framed glasses, was shaking.

"All clear now, Captain," Kekoa said. "I told you I'd get you through this battle in one piece." Of course, Kekoa could make no such promise, but what else was he going to tell this officer whose safety the Army had entrusted to him?

"Thanks, Sergeant. I appreciate that." Hayward took in the carnage with wide eyes. "What happened?"

"Must have been an ammo dump inside the cave. Your boys in the OSS told us the ammunition would be stored farther down the tunnels."

"They're not my boys. That intel came from a different part of the Office of Strategic Services. I'm not a spy, Sergeant Kekoa. I'm a scientist in the Research and Analysis Branch."

"I can't say I'm surprised, given the way you carry that carbine."

The mission briefing had been just that: brief. The battalion commander had specifically asked for Kekoa to babysit Captain Hayward and follow his orders while keeping him alive. Everything else was on a need-to-know basis only, and as a grunt in the 24th Infantry "Hawaiian" Division, Kekoa apparently didn't need to know anything. All Hayward had told his unit was that he needed to get inside the underground fortress before the Japanese could destroy it.

The tadpole-shaped island of Corregidor and its howitzers guarded the entrance to Manila Bay, one of the largest harbors in the Pacific. The strategic outpost, also known as The Rock, was four miles long and little more than a mile across at its widest. As a

U.S. commonwealth, the Philippines had been the last bastion to fall during the initial Japanese onslaught at the outbreak of the war, holding on until the island's forces surrendered in May of 1942, two months after Douglas MacArthur had been evacuated.

Kekoa was leading his unit as part of the operation to retake Malinta Hill on the island's tail. Its vast grid of tunnels was bisected by a twenty-four-foot-wide main passageway that had served as a hospital and MacArthur's headquarters. Dozens of smaller tunnels branched out from the main one, a bomb-proof network so large that it not only housed munitions, food, and water for a huge garrison that could withstand a siege for months but also had room for the thousand-bed hospital. In the three years since the Japanese conquered Corregidor, they had fortified their positions, digging out additional tunnels to augment the extensive system built by the Americans, some of which had been collapsed intentionally before the 1942 surrender.

Hayward's target was inside one of those tunnels.

Kekoa took stock of the dozens of casualties and found out that two of the men who had died were in his platoon. Kekoa had served with both of them in the National Guard in Honolulu before joining the Army after the attack on Pearl Harbor. He then fought side by side with them during the invasions of New Guinea and the Filipino island of Leyte. They weren't the first men he'd lost, and judging by the insanity of this mission, they wouldn't be the last, either.

The explosion had closed off the entrance. They had to find another way in. Under Hayward's direction, Kekoa gathered his platoon and headed toward the south side of Malinta Hill. The sound of rifle fire and artillery blasts continued nonstop from around the island, and Kekoa was bathed in the stench of gunpowder and burnt flesh.

When they reached their new position, Kekoa and Hayward crouched in a foxhole to plan the assault.

When he asked Hayward for orders, the captain hesitated and then asked, "What do you suggest?"

"Have you ever been in battle before, sir?"

"I think you know the answer to that. My office is in the new Pentagon building. This is the first time I've been outside the United States, let alone under fire."

"What do you do in Washington?"

"I'm a biochemist."

"I don't even know what that is. What I do know is that it's suicide to go into those tunnels before we've cleared them out."

Hayward gave him a halfhearted grin. "I thought you promised to get me through in one piece."

"I'll do my best, sir. But these defenders are fanatical. I've heard from soldiers in some of the other battalions that they're strapping bomb vests to their chests and running at us kamikaze-style. The battle plan is for our troops to get close enough to the tunnels to dump gasoline down the openings, light it on fire, and then seal the entrances up to burn through all the oxygen."

"That's exactly why we need this mission to succeed," said Hayward. "We need to get inside before that's done." He looked around, then lowered his voice so the other men couldn't hear. "Do you think I want to be here, Sergeant? I have a wife and two children in a nice house in the Virginia suburbs. I was a college professor at Georgetown before this all started. I am not a warrior."

"Then why are you here, sir?"

Hayward sighed with resignation. "I can't tell you much, but you deserve to know the stakes if you might die for my sake. You can see where this war is going, right? The way we're hopscotching islands northward?"

Kekoa nodded.

"The war is nearly over in Europe. It's just a matter of time until Germany gives up, which means the U.S. will turn all its resources to this side of the world. Our government has said we'll accept nothing less than unconditional surrender, so what do you think the ultimate goal in the Pacific is?"

"The invasion of Japan."

"Right. Look around you. We're fighting like mad for every yard on this tiny rock. Now imagine what it will take to conquer the home islands with every citizen willing to fight to the death for their beloved Emperor."

Kekoa frowned. "I don't want to land on the beaches of Japan any more than the next guy, but if that's what it takes to end the war, I'm willing to do it."

"My research group believes there is something in these tunnels that could make the cost of taking the home islands too terrible to conceive."

Kekoa stared in disbelief at Hayward and waved his arms at the destruction around him. "Worse than this?"

Hayward nodded solemnly. "You've heard the rumors that the Army is manufacturing half a million Purple Hearts in anticipation of the invasion of Japan?"

"That's the scuttlebutt."

"It's true." The captain scientist pointed toward the tunnel complex. "But if we're right about what's in there, it won't be nearly enough."

Kekoa grimly nodded at Hayward. "We'll get you in there. Where do you need to go once we're inside?"

"Thanks, Sergeant," Hayward said. "I'm looking for a lab in one of the Navy Tunnels. It may have collapsed in the original Japanese invasion, but the enemy could have dug it out since then. There should be a small entrance on the south side of the hill." He pulled out a map and showed Kekoa the spot he was talking about. Kekoa frowned and checked his own map.

"Mine doesn't have an entrance there."

"Trust me," Hayward said. "It's there. That is, if the Japs didn't seal it."

Kekoa assumed the captain had read his file and knew his mother was Japanese, like the parents of many of the men in his division. But Hayward didn't seem at all concerned that Kekoa was a potential traitor, which boosted the captain a few notches in his eyes.

Kekoa cautiously guided his men to the place Hayward had pointed to on the map, and, sure enough, there was a tunnel opening concealed by the remaining shrubbery that hadn't been destroyed by the bombardment. If the captain hadn't led them here, they never would have seen it.

Kekoa called for more tank support and was surprised when he got an instant response in the affirmative. Obviously, Hayward must have had more pull than he realized.

Another Sherman trundled its way to the tunnel entrance. This time, Kekoa ordered everyone to cover before it fired. The tank blasted the tunnel with a high-explosive round. There was no secondary explosion. Anyone inside had to be dead, but Kekoa ordered the tank to fire three more shells as insurance.

He called his flamethrower team forward and ordered the platoon to follow them in. Every twenty feet, a jet of fire would shoot forward to clear the path of hiding Japanese Marines, illuminating the otherwise darkened tunnel.

Kekoa didn't like having daylight framing him in silhouette as he moved into the tunnel. He glanced behind him to see Hayward clinging to his carbine as if it were a talisman.

"Should be two intersections down," Hayward whispered. "On the right."

Kekoa motioned for his team to keep going until they reached the intersection and turned. They got another twenty feet when banshee-like screams wailed from down the pitch-black tunnel, followed by pounding footsteps.

"Light 'em up!" Kekoa yelled and dropped to the ground, pulling Hayward with him.

The flamethrower gushed to life, shooting thick sheets of blazing liquid down the tunnel. That should have stopped the Japanese in their tracks, but they kept coming despite the inferno. Four men rushed through the wall of fire as if it were nothing more than a light breeze and launched themselves at the soldier handling the flamethrower and his partner. Before his partner could get a shot off, they viciously stabbed both Americans with bayonets even as they burned.

Seeing that there was no way to save his flamethrower team, Kekoa shouted, "Open fire!"

Bullets poured down the tunnel from every available man. Even Hayward was firing.

Yet the Japanese still kept coming. Kekoa could see the rounds hitting them, but incredibly they wouldn't go down, like they were straight out of a Superman comic.

Kekoa got onto his knees and fired at the head of the closest one coming at them. His body went down in a heap, still on fire. At least they weren't indestructible.

He turned to the next one, who pounced on Kekoa before he could bring his weapon to bear. Kekoa blocked the bayonet with his rifle and kneed him with a savage hit to the midsection. It didn't seem to do a thing.

In the dim light, Kekoa could make out a few details. These Marines weren't like the nearly starving soldiers who were charging at his fellow troops on the rest of the island. This man was muscled like a bodybuilder, and the single glimpse of his eyes that Kekoa saw flashed a feral lust for blood.

Kekoa could feel the bayonet getting closer to his throat. He was unable to push the enemy back, despite the terrible wounds the man had already suffered.

Then the Japanese soldier's head flew sideways as a shot rang out from Kekoa's right. Hayward still had his carbine at the ready as the enemy fell.

Before Kekoa could say his thanks, the last Japanese soldier rushed at Hayward, slashing at him with a machete. Hayward screamed and dropped to the ground. Kekoa unloaded the rest of his Thompson submachine gun's magazine at the attacker, who finally lay silent. They prepared for more attackers but none came.

The remnants of the flamethrower's output provided enough light to see. Kekoa knelt down beside Hayward, who was holding his side. Blood oozed from between his fingers.

Kekoa lifted him up. "We need to get you to a medic." He started walking to the exit, but Hayward stopped him.

He grimaced in pain as he spoke. "Not before . . . I see what's in this tunnel." When Kekoa hesitated, he added, "That's an order, Sergeant."

Grudgingly, Kekoa supported Hayward as they walked farther down the tunnel. Two of his soldiers led the way, one of them now holding his dead squadmate's flamethrower.

A hundred feet in, they reached a laboratory, with equipment that must have made sense to Hayward. There were also several file cabinets and a desk littered with papers. A faint hiss came from the tunnel.

"My camera," Hayward said. "It's in my pack."

Kekoa reached in and found the camera, with a flashbulb attached. He handed Hayward off to another soldier while he snapped a photo of the equipment. When the flash went off, Kekoa noticed something on the ceiling down the tunnel.

"What is that?" he said to one of the men, who took a flashlight to investigate. When he lit up the spot, Kekoa realized in horror what he'd been hearing. On a set of dull gray bars strapped to the ceiling he could make out the Kanji characters for *Explosive*. The hiss was burning detonation cord.

"It's rigged to blow!" he yelled. "Everyone out of here!"

"No!" Hayward protested. "We need the intel!" He lunged for a file on top of the desk and grabbed it before Kekoa could yank him away.

With the help of another soldier, Kekoa carried Hayward by the shoulders as they sprinted for daylight. Kekoa's lungs burned from the exertion, but the thought of being trapped under thousands of tons of rubble kept him going. They were the last ones through the tunnel entrance when the underground fortress erupted like a volcano. The concussive force flung them to the ground.

The explosives must have been linked to bundles in other tunnels because the entire hill shook from multiple aftershocks. Trees were uprooted and rocks tumbled down the slopes, raising a cloak of dust so thick that Kekoa couldn't see more than fifty feet in any direction.

He found Hayward lying prone next to him, not moving. Kekoa flipped him over and saw that he was still breathing. His hand continued to clutch the file from the tunnel.

"Medic!" cried Kekoa. "I need a medic!" He looked down at Hayward, who opened his eyes. "Stay with me, Captain."

"I'm not going anywhere."

"That file almost got us killed."

"Had to take it," Hayward said. His finger tapped a picture on the front next to Japanese characters. It looked like the leaf of some kind of plant. "Tell me what the cover says."

"That can wait until . . ."

"No, it can't," he said between ragged breaths. "That's why I asked for you. You know Japanese. Tell me. Please."

Kekoa saw a medic running toward them, so he indulged the captain.

"It says Project Typhoon. Morale Division, Unit 731." At the mention of Unit 731, Hayward's face went even whiter than it already was. Kekoa didn't know what that meant, but it obviously terrified the military scientist.

The medic began tending to his wound and injected Hayward with morphine. As the drug began to take effect, Hayward mumbled, "Where . . . is it located?"

"You mean this Morale Division?"

Hayward nodded, his eyes barely open.

"It doesn't list the name of a base, if that's what you're hoping for," Kekoa said, "but it does mention a city."

"Tokyo?"

Kekoa shook his head. "Hiroshima."

Eddie Seng stood at the curb of Da Nang International Airport's arrivals area, just as he'd been instructed. The awning of the modern facility shaded him from the midafternoon sun, but it made the muggy July day only marginally more comfortable in his light wool suit. An elegant black limousine showed up as expected and glided to a stop next to him. Eddie was familiar with executive vehicles and immediately recognized it as a Mercedes Maybach V12, the crème de la crème of exotic automobiles.

The uniformed chauffeur walked around the front of the car and opened a wide door. Eddie entered a resplendent interior and settled into a soft cream leather seat, wondering if he would get out alive.

A man in a black suit, sitting in the middle rear-facing row of seats, waved a metal detector over Eddie to check him for weapons, but he had followed instructions and was unarmed. In the rear seat next to Eddie, Zhong Lin, field agent for China's Ministry of State Security, stared at him as the car pulled away. Instead of a suit, he wore a black T-shirt and pants, and his thin lips were creased with lines, the sign of a longtime smoker. For a moment, Zhong said nothing, merely appraising the person he thought was a Taiwanese traitor known as David Yao.

Eddie had, in fact, grown up in New York City's Chinatown, learning Mandarin and English simultaneously from his parents. Because his normal accent was bland in both languages, he'd spent the past two weeks in Taiwan's capital, Taipei, getting accustomed to the local dialect.

Most of his career with the CIA had been as a deep-cover operative on the Chinese mainland, so playing a part was nothing new to him. However, he hadn't been this close to an agent from the MSS, China's intelligence organization, since his CIA cover had been blown and he was forced to escape back to the United States. As a wanted fugitive, he'd been sentenced to death *in absentia*, with his face well known to China's authorities. If Zhong Lin even suspected who he was, he would be whisked out of Vietnam in shackles to Beijing for a swift execution.

His current disguise was meant to prevent that from happening. The real David Yao was a member of the Ghost Dragon triad, one of Taiwan's most notorious gangs. Yao was suspected of being responsible for numerous extortion, racketeering, and murder plots, but his mutilated body had been found floating on the ocean by a U.S. Navy ship two weeks ago. When the CIA realized that his corpse provided the opportunity for Eddie's current operation, they asked the Navy to delay notifying the Taiwanese authorities of the discovery.

Like Eddie, Yao had been in his mid-thirties, lithe and athletic, but they never would have been confused for brothers. Completing the disguise required a radical transformation of his face—widened nose, bulked-up chin, reshaped eyes, and an added mustache and beard, as well as fake tattoos on his arms and neck.

After a few moments, Zhong said, in Mandarin, "You have the information we need?"

Eddie didn't betray his relief at not being recognized. "It's confirmed. They're making the exchange on a train. All of the seats have been reserved, so there won't be any other passengers, and the crew are all Vietnamese recruited and paid off by the triad."

"Where?"

"Somewhere between Da Nang and Hue. They'll text me which train it is so I can meet it at the station to pick them up when they arrive."

"And the Ghost Dragons have the memory stick with them?"

Eddie nodded. He'd originally opened the dialogue with the Chinese Secret Service by telling them what kind of data was stored on the USB flash drive, a piece of information very few people on the outside knew. The Taiwanese Ghost Dragons, who were enemies of the communist regime on the mainland, had carried out a daring heist to steal the memory stick from an MSS courier. Eddie was playing Yao as if he were a traitor not only to his home country of Taiwan but to his brethren in the triad as well.

"Why are you doing this?" Zhong asked him.

"You know why," Eddie replied. "Five million U.S. dollars."

"You won't be able to return to Taiwan. Not after this. The triad will know who betrayed them."

"I don't want to. It's been clear for some time that I will never rise to my proper rank in the Ghost Dragons. I plan to find a woman in Melbourne, Australia, and settle there."

Zhong shrugged. "If you're willing to sell out your country, I'm happy to pay." He tapped on his phone. When he was done, he said, "Two-point-five million has been transferred to your account."

Eddie checked and confirmed that the transfer had been made. "And the rest?"

"When we recover the memory stick."

Instead of turning onto the freeway, the Mercedes headed toward a private section of the airport.

"Where are we going?" Eddie asked. "You're supposed to drop me off at the train station."

Zhong smiled. "You didn't think we'd leave you to warn your brothers that we'd be ambushing their exchange?"

"I told you, I'm through with them."

"That's what you *told* me. But why should I believe someone who has already lied to his comrades?"

The car stopped next to a Eurostar AS350 helicopter, its rotors spinning to life. Next to it was a second chopper full of black-clad men armed with assault rifles and carrying coils of rope.

"I know you have experience with the Taiwan Army," Zhong said, "so you're coming with us to make sure we get that memory stick." The agent plucked Eddie's phone from his hand and waved a detection wand over his body, checking for communication devices. The absence of telltale chirps satisfied him that Eddie wasn't bugged.

The helicopter took off as soon as they were on board, with Eddie stuck between two Chinese agents in the back and Zhong next to the pilot in front.

"What are we doing?" Eddie asked over his headset.

"You'll understand when we get there," Zhong said. "How much are the Americans paying for the flash drive?"

"The Ghost Dragons wanted a hundred million, but the Americans negotiated down to half that."

"Fifty million? Not bad, since there are only two potential buyers, us and the Americans. And, of course, the triad didn't make us a similar offer. You better hope the data on that drive doesn't fall into the hands of the Americans."

Eddie feigned fear at the threat. "But what if the Ghost Dragons have copied the flash drive and are able to sell the data to the Americans later?"

Zhong shook his head. "Not possible. That drive has special encryption. It can only be read by mainframe computers kept at secure locations in China. If they try to read the files on the memory stick, it will automatically erase itself, rewriting the memory so the data can never be recovered. In fact, I hope the Ghost Dragons have tried to read it. My problem would be solved."

"Then why do the Americans want it?"

"Because they have the only other computer system in the world that might be able to read it. But it's currently located at the National Security Agency headquarters in Fort Meade. As long as we obtain the memory stick before it gets back to the United States, we can be assured that it hasn't been compromised." Zhong turned and looked at him. "That's why you're coming along on this raid. If the memory stick isn't where you say it will be, there is no limit to the pain you will experience until I find out where it is."

Eddie gulped, his eyes wide with feigned fear.

"Do you wish to change your story?" Zhong asked. "I'll be forgiving if you do so now instead of after a failed mission."

Eddie shook his head vigorously. "I swear that the exchange is taking place where I said it would."

Zhong held up Eddie's phone. "You'd better hope the text comes through."

The helicopters sped low across the mountainous jungle, paralleling the train tracks winding along the coast. A few minutes later, they both set down in a valley clearing.

As soon as the eight men exited, including Zhong and Eddie, the helicopters took off again.

Eddie looked around in confusion. It seemed like they were in the middle of nowhere.

"This way," Zhong said.

They hiked through the tropical forest for ten minutes until they reached a slope, where Eddie could see the ocean. The train tracks far below disappeared into a tunnel.

"That's our destination." Zhong pointed at the mouth of the tunnel.

Now the coils of rope made sense. Trying to get on board the train by helicopter would have telegraphed their approach from miles away. Dropping down quietly onto the roof of the train when it exited the tunnel would be much stealthier.

"Do I at least get a gun?" Eddie asked as they marched toward the tunnel opening.

Zhong gave him a grim laugh. So did the other men. They kept walking.

If Zhong returned to Beijing empty-handed, Eddie was sure Zhong and the rest of his men would face a firing squad for their failure. The memory stick they were trying to recover and keep out of American hands held the names of every Chinese spy currently operating in the United States.

 **THE PHILIPPINES**

The squall arrived earlier than Luis Navarro expected. The forecast had said it wouldn't hit until after sundown. Wind buffeted the front window of their 90-foot-long vessel, lashing it with sheets of rain. Visibility was limited. He looked behind him toward Negros Island, but he could no longer see the city of Dumaguete. The GPS unit said their destination of Dapitan City on Mindanao was still thirty miles away.

Captain Garcia ordered the first mate to cut back on the throttle. The smaller escort boats on either side slowed to match their speed. The officers manning the deck machine guns on both boats looked miserable in the downpour.

"What are you doing?" Navarro demanded. "Don't slow down."

The first mate looked to Garcia, an old salt who obviously wasn't used to his orders being countermanded. "Inspector, if we stay at full speed in these conditions, we could be swamped."

Despite being younger and more compact than the captain, Navarro wasn't intimidated. "The chief of the Philippine National Police has put me in charge of this mission and I order you back to full speed."

"You may be in command of the mission, but this is my boat. Do you want to make it to Mindanao or not? If the chief of the PNP were here, I think he'd want to live."

"You know who we're carrying," Navarro said.

Garcia nodded. "And I want him off my boat more than you do. So let me do my job."

Navarro grumbled but didn't push it further. His country's reputation for sunken vessels was well known. With a population of over one hundred million scattered across the seven thousand islands comprising the Philippines, a vast amount of commerce and transportation was done by water. Dozens of boats and ships went down every year, many of them in storms just like this one.

He couldn't afford to alter the plan for this operation. Their prisoner, Salvador Locsin, was the most wanted man in the country, the leader of a splinter cell of the New People's Army, a communist insurgent group dedicated to overthrowing the democratic government of the Philippines. Talks between the government and the rebels had dragged on for years, and Locsin had grown tired of the stalemate. His terror campaign had targeted important officials and government facilities, causing dozens of deaths and destroying several buildings. How he was funding his efforts was still a mystery, but Navarro intended to find out as soon as they got him to a secure interrogation room.

Thanks to an anonymous tip, he'd been captured in a raid in Kabankalan City. However, with thousands of rebels on Negros Island loyal to him, getting him off the island had proven perilous. The first attempt to transport Locsin back to the capital of Manila was by air, but the rebels mounted a failed attack at the airport, damaging the plane and killing three officers in the process.

The decision, then, had been to fake another attempt at flying him out from a different airport on the island. At the same time, Locsin was taken by road to Dumaguete, where three boats were waiting. There were fewer rebels on Mindanao, so flying him off that island was thought to be much less hazardous.

The walkie-talkie on his belt squawked. The voice was panicked. "Senior Inspector Navarro, you need to come down here right now!"

"What is it?" Navarro replied.

"Officer Torres is dead."

When he heard the news, Captain Garcia, who had seemed wary but calm about the storm, looked at Navarro with fear. He stepped next to the first mate and inched the throttle forward.

"I'm on my way," Navarro said.

Navarro took the stairs two at a time down to the hold. The fishing vessel had been modified by the police force as a prisoner transport. In place of the freezer where mackerel or tuna might have been stored, tiny barred cells had been installed with only enough room for a prisoner to sit on the steel bench.

When he reached the hold, he saw Torres sprawled on the floor in front of one of the cells. His head was cocked at an unnatural angle, his eyes wide and staring. Two other officers stood behind him.

Navarro stalked forward, enraged at losing another man. "What happened?"

The older officer glanced nervously at the cell, then looked at Navarro. "Torres was going to use the head. I guess we weren't paying attention because, the next thing we knew, he was on the floor with a broken neck."

Navarro looked at the sole prisoner on board. Salvador Locsin sat on the bench with his eyes closed, smiling beatifically. Ropey biceps strained at the sleeves of his shirt, the veins in his forearms looking as if they were about to explode from under the skin. His black hair draped across his forehead, where it mingled with the beads of sweat trickling down his face.

Navarro, furious, stared at his men and jabbed a finger in Locsin's direction. "Didn't I warn you not to get too close to his cell?"

"But he looked like he was asleep when Torres got up," the younger officer protested. "How could he break someone's neck through the bars?"

Navarro walked over to the cell, stepping between Torres's legs. Both of the officers brought their weapons up to cover him.

"You're going to answer for that, Locsin," Navarro said.

Locsin replied in an unfamiliar dialect of one of the over one hundred and seventy languages native to the Philippines. Navarro knew only the country's two official languages, English and Tagalog.

"Come on, Locsin," Navarro continued in English. "I know you understand me."

Locsin opened his eyes. His irises were so dark that they seemed to merge with the black of his pupils. Navarro nearly stumbled backward from the force of his gaze, an evil that seemed to stab at his very soul.

"I said, I am dead already, aren't I?"

Navarro composed himself enough to respond without faltering. "I don't know what your punishment will be, but you'll have to pay for your crimes."

"I have, Inspector Navarro, and with a price more costly than you'll ever understand." Locsin closed his eyes again.

Navarro stepped back, and the two officers moved in as if they were going to pick up Torres.

"Leave him there," Navarro said. "We'll take care of him after we get the prisoner off the boat."

The two officers looked at him in shock but didn't challenge his command.

"What should we do about him?" the older one said, motioning with his rifle at the prisoner.

"Keep watch on him at all times. I want him alive for questioning. Wound him, if you have to, but don't kill him."

"Yes, sir," they both said.

The engine suddenly wound down to idle, and the boat slowed to a crawl.

"Now what?" Navarro muttered as he charged back up to the bridge.

When he got there, Captain Garcia was on the radio, peering out the window, while the first mate spun the wheel away from their destination.

"It looks like the ferry is on fire," Garcia said into the handset. "We've got survivors in the water, and more still on the boat. How long until you arrive?"

Navarro followed Garcia's gaze to the foundering vessel, more than a mile off the port bow. The stubby car ferry's stern was already awash, and smoke poured from the superstructure. Navarro counted more than two dozen people in the water, some wearing life jackets, others flailing as they tried to stay afloat in the waves.

"The nearest patrol vessel is at least an hour away," said a voice on the radio that had to be with the Coast Guard. "We'll notify any vessels in the vicinity to provide assistance."

"Thanks. We'll pick up as many as we can." Garcia put the handset down and ordered the first mate to bring them alongside the survivors.

Aghast, Navarro said, "What do you think you're doing?"

Garcia looked at him in astonishment. "I'm rendering aid to a stricken vessel and its passengers and crew, as we are bound to do under maritime law."

The smaller, more maneuverable escort vessels had already

arrived at the scene of the accident and were pulling survivors aboard.

"You're not stopping," Navarro commanded. "You will continue on and complete this mission as ordered."

"Are you insane? We can't leave these people to die!"

"I already have a dead officer down there. Locsin is as cunning as he is vicious. What do you think will happen if we start crowding civilians onto this boat with him?"

"We'll keep them up on deck."

"No. They'll interfere with the assignments of my officers. I won't allow it."

"And I will not violate my duty as master of this vessel. I won't leave people to drown!" Garcia turned back to the first mate and waved for him to move toward the wreck.

Navarro's hand went to his sidearm pistol. He didn't want to use force, but the captain was leaving him no choice. He didn't understand the threat that Locsin posed.

But Navarro didn't have time to draw his weapon before a shrill voice shrieked over the radio.

"Transport One, this is Escort One! It's a trap! They're not ferry passengers! They've overpowered my men, but I sabotaged—" The officer was interrupted by the sound of a gunshot, and then the radio went dead.

Navarro looked back at the ferry and now saw that Escort 1 had turned and was heading back toward the prison transport. It was only two hundred yards away, and Navarro could see a man in civilian clothes on deck. He was swinging the mounted machine gun in their direction.

"Get down!" Navarro yelled as he threw himself at Garcia and tackled him to the deck. Thirty-caliber bullets riddled the bridge, shattering the glass and killing the first mate, who crumpled into the captain's chair.

"Get us out of here!" Navarro shouted.

He peered out and saw Escort 1 start to weave back and forth, then it exploded. That must have been the sabotage the officer on Escort 1 had mentioned before he died.

Garcia scrambled to his feet and slammed the throttle to its stops.

"The navigation computer was damaged by the gunfire. I'll have to guide us by compass."

Navarro snatched up a pair of binoculars and saw that Escort 2 was now headed in their direction, its machine gun manned and ready to use when they were in range. "How long until we reach Dapitan City?"

"At least an hour, in these seas. We might be able to make better headway than that smaller boat. Depends on how long the squall lasts."

Navarro recalled the captain's conversation with the Coast Guard. "We should find out which direction the cutter is coming from and go toward it. Give me the radio."

Garcia picked up the radio handset, chuckled ruefully, and tossed it to him. It had a bullet hole through it.

Navarro smacked his hand against the bulkhead in frustration at getting ambushed like a rookie cadet.

He got on his walkie-talkie and addressed his officers on the prison transport.

"This is Inspector Navarro. To every one of my men who is still alive, shoot to kill."

 VIETNAM

The massive diesel locomotive approached from the north, slowing as it neared the railroad crossing on the outskirts of Hue. Juan Cabrillo counted nine passenger cars plus the engine. The Ghost Dragons' instruction was for Juan and Eric Stone to jump on as it passed since stopping the train would draw unwanted attention.

While Eric scanned the houses around them for spectators, Juan looked at the burner phone again, a prepaid model he'd bought in Hue. No message from Eddie. That either meant his cell phone was taken from him or he was in a situation that didn't allow him to make contact.

"We still haven't heard from our friendly neighborhood mole," Juan said. "Has he gone underground?"

Like Juan and every other operative in the Corporation, Eddie Seng had a subdermal tracking chip implanted in his thigh. Using the body's own energy for power, it sent out a pulse beacon each minute that wasn't detectable by standard bug-scanning devices.

With GPS technology, his location could be pinpointed to within a few dozen yards.

Eric checked his tablet computer. "I've got him, Chairman. The most recent broadcast from his chip was near the railroad tracks ten miles south of us."

"That must be where the Chinese are planning to intercept us. We'll need to make the exchange by then."

Juan had to assume the Chinese Ministry of State Security agents were monitoring their communications. He texted Eddie the train information.

Engine #9736. Leaving Huong Thuy in 2 minutes.

He dropped the phone on the asphalt and ground it to pieces with his foot. Eric watched him but said nothing. He understood that Juan didn't want the MSS agents to know Eddie's supposed contact wasn't already on the train with the rest of the Ghost Dragons.

Like all missions that the Corporation undertook, this was one their client couldn't handle themselves. After leaving his field agent position at the CIA, Juan had created the mercenary organization to carry out operations that his old employer wasn't able to, because either it didn't have the capabilities required for the job or have plausible deniability in case of failure. The Corporation also took on other clients as long as the operation was never in conflict with the interests of the United States.

Today's mission came straight from the top.

When the Ghost Dragons had approached the American government through Taiwanese back channels with their sales proposal, the CIA was dubious that the memory stick they were offering actually contained the names of the undercover MSS agents operating in the U.S. The problem was finding out what was on the flash drive while they were in the field. The National Security Agency had long known about the self-erasing technology China used for its sensitive information transfers, but the only way to crack the code was with gigantic supercomputers the NSA had designed specifically for the task. Since Juan couldn't check out the flash drive contents on a laptop without inadvertently deleting it, he wouldn't be able tell if he was handing over fifty million taxpayer dollars for sensitive Chinese state secrets or the Premier's grocery list.

Eddie had needed to make contact with the MSS himself to confirm what was on the memory stick. Based on the information Eddie had fed to them, the Chinese security agency was undertaking a risky plan to intercept the exchange and retrieve the flash drive. That's when Juan knew the Ghost Dragons were selling the real thing.

The rules for the handoff itself were relatively simple. When the train slowed at the railroad crossing, Juan and Eric would jump onto the platform of the train's rear car as it passed. They would then make their way to the center dining car, likely being monitored by the triad on hidden cameras as they walked through each car. They could bring no weapons with them. Once it was confirmed they were alone and unarmed, the exchange would take place. They would take possession of the flash drive while fifty million dollars of U.S. government money was wired to an account of the triad's choosing. Then the train would slow again to let them off at another road crossing.

"Chairman," Eric said, looking at his phone, "I just got acknowledgment from Linc and Murph. They're ready."

"Then let's get this party started."

Their appearance was designed to put the triad at ease. Eric was one of the youngest members of the Corporation, a Navy vet who had been in technology development during his short stint in the service. He looked like the shy computer geek he was, down to his neatly combed hair, black glasses, blue button-down shirt, and creased khaki chinos. Eric was there to confirm that it really was an MSS secure flash drive, and he didn't look like much of a threat.

On the other hand, Juan, with blond hair, blue eyes, a tan dating from his days surfing in his native California, and a swimmer's lean physique, looked like a man able to take care of himself. The Ghost Dragons would anticipate a trained operative making the buy, but instead of wearing the expected suit, Juan went casual, wearing a short-sleeved shirt, jeans, and boots.

As the locomotive chugged slowly past, the Vietnamese engineer scowled at them. Juan was impressed by the luxurious appointments in the passenger cars as he scanned for signs of the triad members. Not only did the triad have some pull to get this train at all, they apparently wanted to make the exchange in style. Nobody was visible in the first two cars, but the third window's curtains were drawn. The fifth car, where the exchange was to take place, was a dining car.

The remaining cars were similarly empty. When the last car reached them, Eric hopped on, followed by Juan.

"Time to meet our hosts," Juan said.

He and Eric walked forward as the train began to accelerate back to its cruising speed. Juan spotted the cameras tucked into the lighting fixtures but gave no indication that he knew they were there. They'd be feeding a wireless signal to the Ghost Dragons, who had to be wary of a double cross. Eric didn't pay attention to them, either, busily tapping on his tablet as they walked.

When they reached the seventh car, they were met by two armed triad soldiers who were young, sinewy, and dressed in tailored black suits. Both carried Brügger & Thomet MP9 machine pistols that weren't much bigger than regular semiautomatics but could be fired on full auto. Not very accurate, but in the confines of a train car they could be deadly. Juan and Eric raised their hands.

"I'm Thomas Cates," Juan said, giving them the name he'd used to set up the meet. "Let's get this over with."

While one of the men covered them with his machine pistol, the other carefully came toward them and patted down Eric, inspecting the tablet in his hand and the satchel slung over his shoulder that carried his laptop. Satisfied that Eric was unarmed, he frisked Juan.

When he checked Juan's right ankle, he looked up in surprise and motioned for Juan to lift his pant leg, revealing a prosthetic limb attached just below the knee.

"Courtesy of the communists," Juan said, which was the truth. His missing leg was the result of a shell fired from a Chinese destroyer. "See? We have a common enemy."

The man said nothing. He just shrugged and nodded at his companion. They had passed inspection.

The second man gestured for Juan and Eric to wait while the one who had frisked them left.

Juan noticed that the train had now reached the rugged coastal portion of their route. As it snaked around the region's mountains, the view out one side showed nothing but dense jungle while the opposite side was a scenic panorama of the ocean. Neither of the Ghost Dragons seemed to care about the vistas, which was just fine with Juan.

The Ghost Dragons were keeping watch toward the front of the train's exterior in case of an ambush, but their range would be limited to a few hundred yards on either side. It was doubtful they'd pay any attention to the decrepit tramp steamer a mile out to sea, just another of the hundreds that plied Vietnamese waters. At this distance, it wouldn't seem odd that such a creaky old cargo ship could keep pace with the speed of a modern train.

Despite its seemingly dilapidated state, Juan was proud to be captain of that ship. The *Oregon* was doing exactly what she was designed to do.

Hide in plain sight.

Marion MacDougal "MacD" Lawless was only five feet away from Franklin Lincoln, but he was completely invisible. His ghillie suit, typically worn by snipers as camouflage, was custom-designed to blend into the Vietnamese jungle foliage. The color, density, and arrangement of artificial plant life on his outfit perfectly mimicked the bushes and ground cover where they lay only a dozen feet from the railroad tracks. Linc wore one just like it and could hardly make out his own arms stretched in front of him.

A snake slithered across the barrel of Linc's assault rifle, oblivious to the person only inches away. Linc had no idea if it was venomous, but he wasn't about to rile it and find out.

"I hate the jungle," the former Navy SEAL muttered in his basso voice. The snake slinked past his hiding spot and into the trees.

"At least we're not lying on top of a fire ant nest," MacD replied in his syrupy New Orleans drawl. "Ah did that once in Louisiana during a camping trip and Ah went to my junior prom looking like Ah had the measles."

Linc seriously doubted that bothered his date too much. If MacD hadn't become an Army Ranger before joining the Corporation, his good-looking features could have earned him a great living in Hollywood.

"The most dangerous animals we had in Detroit were rottweilers and pit bulls," Linc said. He still had a scar on his right thigh where a guard dog had sunk its teeth into him while he was taking a short-cut home as a kid.

MacD shifted slightly, just enough to rustle the suit and make himself visible for a fraction of a second. "Just between you and me, Ah would have taken Eddie's spot in a heartbeat if Ah thought Ah wouldn't be as out of place as the Pope at Mardi Gras."

"Stupid genetics," Linc said. "Always messing things up for us."

Not only did neither of them speak Mandarin, Linc was an African-American who spent so much time in the *Oregon*'s weight room that he could have been a competitive bodybuilder, and MacD was a tall blond who couldn't pass for a Taiwanese triad member no matter how much makeup and latex prosthetics were applied to his face.

As the Corporation's director of shore operations, Eddie Seng would normally be with Linc and MacD right now. But the two "gundogs," as the *Oregon*'s former Special Forces operators were known, were on their own today.

Linc felt a slight tremor in the ground. But unlike the suddenness of an earthquake, this shaking grew slowly and steadily stronger.

"That's got to be them," MacD said.

"Right on schedule."

Soon, the quaking was accompanied by the squeal of steel wheels grinding on the rails. In the distance Linc could see the engine swing around one bend in the track before disappearing again behind an outcropping. At the same time, the *Oregon* came into view, parallel-ing the train's course. Whitecaps curled from its bow as it raced to keep up.

"Did Eric take care of the cameras on the train?"

Linc checked his satellite phone and smiled. "Stoney just sent me confirmation that he was able to intercept the wireless feeds. They're now on a loop."

When Eric got on the train with Juan, his job was to record the cameras' view of each of the unoccupied cars and rebroadcast that using a specially built transmitter embedded in his tablet. Now, no matter what was happening in the cars he'd already passed through, the triad would think they were still empty.

When the engine reappeared, the ground's vibration was matched by the throb of the diesel motor's five thousand horsepower. Linc and MacD remained absolutely still as it went by. Linc had a good view of the engineer, who was focused on the track ahead. He gave no indication that he'd noticed anything unusual. Within a few more seconds, the dense jungle would be blocking his view rearward because of the curved section of track.

"Get ready," Linc said as the seventh passenger car passed. "It's slowed just as expected because of the winding track. We'll have less than twenty seconds once you fire."

"No sweat." MacD adjusted his position and brought his cross-bow to bear. Linc was the best sniper in the Corporation, but that was with a rifle. MacD was an expert with the crossbow from his days hunting deer in the Louisiana swamps.

The final car passed them, and MacD fired. Amid the clacking of the train's wheels, the bolt whizzed away in utter silence, trailing a fishing line designed to haul in thousand-pound marlins. The bolt cracked through the window of the car's rear door, activating the spring-loaded grappling claws that secured it to the frame.

"Nice shootin', pardner," Linc said as he leapt up from his hiding spot.

They threw off the camouflage that covered a device that looked like a toboggan, with Teflon guide sleeves on each side of a shallow carbon-fiber tub. A thousand feet of fishing line continued to unravel as the train pulled it out of its reel. The other end was tied to the front of the sled.

They lifted the lightweight but sturdy sled onto the tracks and placed the guides on the rails. With only a hundred feet of line left, they dived into the rigid tub. Just as they got their feet anchored against the back of the tub, the line went taut, yanking them backward as it matched the train's speed.

After the initial shock wore off, Linc activated the motorized reel. The Teflon guides thunked every time they hit a joint in the rail. The sled was working as expected.

"It'd be nice if the marlins did this once in a while when I went fishing," MacD said, watching the motor pull them toward the train.

"Reeling themselves in?" Linc replied with a smile. "Where's the fun in that?"

When they reached the rear passenger car, Linc hauled himself up, perching on the ledge while MacD joined him. Linc cut the line with his Ka-Bar knife. The sled skidded to a stop and receded behind them.

"After you," he said.

MacD grinned. "Why, thank you, sir."

He opened the door and picked up his spent grappling claw bolt as he went through.

Confident that Eric had successfully rigged the camera feed to show an empty car, they put down the backpacks and doffed their ghillie suits, revealing black tactical gear, including ballistic vests. Linc unzipped his bag and removed the weapons inside: four Glock semiautomatic pistols and four FN P90 submachine guns.

"How long do you think we have?" MacD asked as he removed two extra ballistic vests from his bag. He also took out the components of a handheld grenade launcher that had been dismantled for transport.

Linc checked his watch. "Given Eddie's last position, I'd say we've only got five minutes before our visitors arrive."

 THE PHILIPPINES

For fifteen minutes, the squall's choppy waves had kept the more stable prison transport out of range of the machine gun on the hijacked escort boat, which was getting pounded by the whitecaps. But now the storm was easing, flattening the rough seas.

Inspector Luis Navarro looked back nervously and saw the sleek boat beginning to gain on them. The machine gun wildly sprayed .30 caliber bullets in their direction. Some of them were connecting. His own men were conserving ammunition, holding fire until the escort boat got closer.

He prodded Captain Garcia. "Can't you go faster?"

"What do you want me to do?" Garcia said. "This is our top speed."

Navarro squinted at the horizon in the dwindling glow of dusk. He thought he could make out some lights in the distance. "Is that Dapitan City?"

"For what it's worth. We're still at least twenty miles out, and I don't see any help on the way."

"Locsin's men on the escort boat must have radioed that we didn't need any assistance."

Garcia ducked instinctively as another round pinged off a metal fitting. "Those idiots! They could just as easily kill Locsin as any one of us."

"I doubt it. With the amount of planning they've obviously done, they'd know the freezers in the hold that were converted into cells are lined with insulation thick enough to absorb the bullets' impact. More likely, they're trying to disable the engine."

"Well, you better come up with an idea," Garcia said, "because at this rate they're going to catch up to us in another few minutes, whether or not they take out our engine."

Navarro racked his brain for options. He was down to five men, plus himself and Garcia. He counted at least ten men on the other boat, and they had the heavier firepower of the machine gun. His men were equipped only with assault rifles.

"You know what we have to do, Inspector," Garcia said. "Throw him overboard."

"What?"

"Locsin. If they want him so bad, give him to them."

"No."

"But they're going to—"

Navarro slammed his fist on the console. "I said no! We are not dishonoring ourselves and the National Police by giving up our prisoner. I'd rather die fighting."

Garcia glared at him. "Unless you can think of something, you'll get your wish."

More bullets ricocheted off the wheelhouse. Navarro grimaced. Garcia was right. They weren't going to last long under that kind of withering fire. As soon as the escort boat caught up and disabled the prison transport, they'd be boarded and wiped out.

He patted Garcia on his shoulder. "No matter what happens, keep going."

"What are you going to do?"

"I'm going to see how badly they want us to stop."

Navarro left Garcia looking confused and went out on deck, crouching as much as he could to avoid the hail of bullets. He spotted a length of heavy chain hanging next to an old fishing net hoist and took it with him.

He went down to the hold. Torres was still lying on the floor, and the two guards cringed every time more bullets hit the hull. Sweat poured off their brows. Their lips were set tight in fear.

Locsin looked at Navarro with a vicious gleam in his eyes.

"Having some trouble up there?" he asked, grinning as he relished their predicament.

"You two cover him," Navarro ordered his men. They raised their rifles and pointed them at the prisoner.

Navarro pulled out his cuffs. "Locsin, turn around and give me your hands behind your back. Put them both between the same bars."

"I don't think so. I'll wait right here for now." He closed his eyes. "Let me know when we reach Dapitan City. That is, of course, if we do."

Navarro drew his pistol. "The captain suggested that I dump you over the side. We all have a duty to uphold, but if you don't follow my commands precisely, I will shoot you myself and accommodate the captain's request. Now, what's it going to be?"

Locsin sighed and opened his eyes. Without a word, he stood, stepped up to the front of the cell, and turned, inserting his hands between the bars.

Navarro turned to his men. "If he tries anything, don't hesitate. Kill us both, if you have to. Understand?"

The two officers were stunned into silence by the command.

"Do you understand?" Navarro yelled.

They nodded.

Navarro carefully snapped the handcuffs around Locsin's wrists. The prisoner didn't resist.

"Now step back."

Locsin complied. After putting aside his sidearm and knife, Navarro took the handcuffs on Torres's belt, unlocked the cell, and went inside with the chain.

He held it up to Locsin. "I'm going to wrap this around your waist. Don't move."

Locsin regarded the chain with amusement and shrugged. Navarro wound it six times around his midsection and cinched it tight so that Locsin wouldn't be able to squirm out of it. Then he snapped Torres's cuffs on the chain to secure them.

Navarro stepped out of the cell and took back his weapons. "We're going up on deck. If you try to escape or attack any of my men, I will push you overboard and you'll go straight to the bottom, thanks to that chain."

"Oh, I wouldn't miss this for anything," Locsin said. "I can't wait to see what you're going to do."

"Come on, then," Navarro said. Locsin sauntered out of the cell. Navarro grabbed Locsin's meaty arm and put the pistol's barrel against his head. "Lead the way. Slowly."

They went up the stairs together, one step at a time, with one officer in front of them and the other trailing.

When they were up on deck, Navarro walked him to a point where he could see the escort boat, making sure to put Locsin between him and them. Just one officer remained alive up top. The other two were sprawled on the deck, rivulets of blood draining into the scuppers. The hijacked police vessel was less than a hundred yards away now, so he was confident they would realize his prisoner was no longer in the cell. If they tried to shoot Navarro, they'd have to go through their leader to get him.

The chattering of the machine gun stopped, but the boat kept coming.

Navarro pulled Locsin with him so that his back was against the hoist, Navarro peeking past Locsin's ear. The prisoner reeked of body odor and a putrid smell akin to garlic oozing from his pores, but enduring the stink was preferable to dying. Not even the best marksman in the world would be confident of hitting him instead of his hostage.

When the men on the escort boat saw that they didn't have a shot, they came up behind the prison transport until they were only fifty feet away. Navarro made it clear that he had a gun against Locsin's skull. The remaining three officers either had their rifles pointing at the escort boat or at Locsin. An opening in the railing was conveniently close by in case Navarro got the impulse to shove Locsin into the ocean.

Navarro didn't need to shout for the pursuers to back off. His threat was clear. If they attempted to board, Locsin would die before a single one of them could set a foot on the deck.

"What are you going to do now?" Locsin asked. "Hold me here until we get into the harbor at Dapitan City?"

"That's the idea. Two squads of Special Action Force officers are waiting for your arrival."

"And you think my men won't follow us all the way there?"

Navarro chuckled drily. "It would be suicidal on their part, but I'd be happy for them to try."

"You're right," Locsin said. "They should probably just shoot you now."

"Shoot me?" Navarro said in disbelief at Locsin's audacity. Even though the storm had passed, the boats were still heaving up and down on the lingering swells. "Without hitting you, too? Nobody is that good."

"Right again, Inspector. Nobody is that good."

Then, to Navarro's complete shock, Locsin yelled at the top of his lungs.

"Fire!"

As one, his men blasted away, cutting down the three officers in a storm of bullets. At the same time, multiple shots tore into Locsin. He fell to the deck, stripping away Navarro's protection. Navarro tried to dive for cover, but two bullets slammed into his midsection.

Navarro could do nothing but lie there as the escort boat charged forward and bumped against the hull of the transport. As Locsin's men leapt out, Navarro knew Garcia was already dead and that he would soon join him. His mind began to fog as he felt the life seeping out of his body.

Locsin's soldiers, like their leader, were muscled beyond even the fittest officers on the Special Action Force. Two of them lifted the slain communist leader up as easily as if he were a doll.

Navarro got some small measure of satisfaction at seeing the dead man in his soldiers' arms. Despite the colossal failure of the mission to bring Locsin to justice, at least he had prevented the rescue of his government's greatest public enemy.

Despite the grievous wounds, Navarro felt no pain, an indication of how far gone he was. He watched as the soldiers dragged Locsin's corpse toward the escort boats, then suddenly stopped.

Navarro thought his eyes were playing tricks on him when he saw Locsin's feet deliberately plant themselves on the deck. It was as if he were seeing a zombie reanimate after death.

The soldier to either side stepped away. Locsin stood for a moment before turning slowly to face Navarro.

Navarro couldn't believe it. Locsin had ragged wound holes in his thigh, stomach, and shoulder. He shouldn't be alive, let alone standing.

Inhumanly, Locsin seemed to ignore the pain. He leaned down until he was eye to eye with Navarro, that sour garlic smell radiating off of him in waves.

"Nice try, Inspector Navarro," Locsin said with wicked glee. "But, you see, I have things to do. Big plans."

He stood up again and waved for his men to help him. They each put one of Locsin's arms over a shoulder.

"Scuttle the boat," Locsin ordered in a strong voice. "Let them wonder whether I'm dead."

"Yes, sir," they said in unison.

"Oh," Locsin said, nodding toward Navarro, "and finish him off."

Without hesitation, one of the men raised a pistol and aimed between Navarro's eyes. The last thing he saw was its barrel spitting fire.

6 VIETNAM

Eddie steadied himself on the concrete lip at the top of the train tunnel opening. He had ditched the suit jacket and wore a harness around his legs and waist. The rope lashed to his harness was connected to a nylon line. One end of the weighted line dangled below them, just above the tunnel, while the other end was threaded through a winch anchored farther up the forested slope. Zhong Lin and the six other operatives with him made last checks of their harnesses and QBZ-95 assault rifles as the sound of the approaching engine echoed through the tunnel.

Zhong kept his eye on Eddie for any sign of betrayal or that he would chicken out of the assault. He made it clear that Eddie would be among the first four to drop onto the train, and if he didn't do it, Zhong would shoot him on the spot.

Eddie had no intention of backing out, despite the challenge of getting onto the roof of a train moving at thirty miles an hour. He'd rappelled down cliffs and jumped out of helicopters many times, but this operation was something new. Although he could feel the surge of adrenaline that marked the beginning of any operation, he had no fear. Of course, he didn't want Zhong to know that, so he maintained a mask of abject terror.

"Remember," Zhong said to his men, "we drop the lines just as the engine passes beneath us, not before."

They all returned a crisp "Yes, sir."

He looked at Eddie. "Last chance to tell me the truth."

"This is the train," Eddie said in a deliberately shaky voice. "I'm sure of it."

Zhong nodded. "It had better be." Via a camera that had been set up at the tunnel's opposite end, they had already confirmed the engine's number was the same as the one Juan had texted to him.

They all lowered goggles over their eyes. Eddie gripped the rope tighter when the diesel motor reached a thundering crescendo below them. Just as it burst out of the tunnel, Zhong's men took their cue.

They dropped two lines straight down onto the diesel engine. The weights at the ends were powerful neodymium magnets that attached themselves to the top of the steel chassis. The lines were yanked tight as they spooled out from the winch above.

"Now!" Zhong yelled.

The first two men jumped from the ledge and sailed down the temporary zip line. As soon as they were away, Zhong and Eddie followed.

Eddie sat into his harness, the straps digging into his thighs. His full weight was supported by the dual-bearing trolley that hung on the line like a miniature monorail.

Gripping the braking mechanism, he shoved off and accelerated down the line, quickly matching the train's speed as he approached the top of the engine. The wind buffeted him, but the goggles kept his eyes from watering. When his feet were nearing contact, he hit the brake and came to rest on top of the train as if he were alighting from a street tram.

He detached the quick release and dropped to his knees as the other men came to rest on the roof within seconds of each other. When all eight of them were aboard, two men cut the lines, which snapped back toward the winch leaving nothing but the magnets still clinging to the metal. They all slipped out of their harnesses.

Zhong sent one man to take control of the engineer and the train, and he sent three men along the top toward the very back of the train to cut off any possible escape. For the rest of them, the next task was getting inside the first passenger car to begin the attack.

Eddie stole a look toward the ocean and saw the *Oregon* out there pacing the train. And in the jungle behind them, he barely glimpsed the flash of a black object brushing the treetops, something he would have thought was a bird if he didn't know it was actually a quadcopter drone.

He hoped Juan was getting an update on where he was because it wouldn't be long before the train was even more crowded.

FLANKED BY his most faithful bodyguards, Jimmy Su, the head of the Ghost Dragons triad, sat at a table in the train's dining car and told his men to bring in the Americans. Six more triad soldiers lounged at the tables around them, relaxed but alert. Like him, they were all dressed in black suits and white shirts unbuttoned far enough to expose the tattoos on their chests.

Su had built up the organization to be one of the most powerful in Taipei. His most daring exploits had occurred in the last month. First, he had David Yao, his main rival in the triad, killed and thrown into the ocean. Then he orchestrated the theft of the USB drive carrying the names of the Chinese undercover agents operating in the U.S.

His real target had been a drive listing the Chinese moles on the island of Taiwan. If he had gotten hold of that information, he could have used it to his own advantage in infiltrating the Taiwanese security forces for his personal gain. But when the courier they'd kidnapped had revealed what the drive actually held, he'd had to change his plans. The data was worthless to Su but extremely valuable to the right buyer.

There was no way he would sell the drive back to the Chinese, no matter what price they were willing to offer. He wanted them to suffer the loss badly. Although he hated the communists, Su didn't plan on simply handing over the drive to the Americans. They had to pay, and pay dearly, for the intelligence coup of the decade. The revelations would set Chinese intelligence gathering back years.

The thought brought a smile to his face as the two Americans were led in. One was tall and athletic, obviously the man in charge. He had to be the one who called himself Thomas Cates, although that certainly wouldn't be his real name. The other was the thin, nerdy sort, and held a tablet in his hand.

"Mr. Cates," Su said without standing or offering his hand, "please sit down."

"Oh, good," Cates said. "You speak English."

"Six years at the American School in Taipei."

Cates and the other man took a seat opposite him. The two men who had led them in stood behind them in the aisle.

"It's much better than my Mandarin," Cates said.

"Interesting. I thought they would have sent someone who knew my language to make the transaction."

Cates shrugged and grinned, showing off bright white teeth. "I was the lucky guy available. So, can we take a look at the merchandise?"

"You know that attempting to open or copy the file will erase the whole drive?"

The other man, apparently the technical analyst, nodded. "But I need to verify that the flash drive actually originates from the MSS. I won't be able to see the data, but I can check the code on top of it without triggering an erasure. MSS code has a very distinctive signature."

"You understand that we can't hand over fifty million dollars for an empty drive," Cates said coolly. "We need confirmation."

"Are you accusing me of trying to swindle you?" The triad soldiers and bodyguards tensed at Su's sharp tone.

Cates smiled again and put his hands up to calm the situation. "Not at all. But I'm sure you understand that we have to inspect the drive."

Su looked at his men, indicating they should ease up. He withdrew the USB drive from his jacket pocket, brushing the holstered machine pistol under his armpit.

Before handing it over, he said, "If you erase this, you will still owe us fifty million dollars."

Cates nodded. "And if we don't get off this train with the flash drive, you won't make it off, either."

Su sat up straighter. "What do you mean?"

"I mean that a Predator drone is circling over us at fifteen thousand feet armed with a Hellfire missile. It will blow this train to splinters if we don't get off at our rendezvous point."

Cates's poker face was good. Su couldn't tell whether he was bluffing or not.

He stared at the American for a moment, expressionless, then turned to his men and smiled, speaking in Mandarin. "This guy has a set on him, doesn't he?"

That brought a chorus of laughter from them.

"All right, Mr. Cates," Su said. "We have mutually assured destruction on the table if this doesn't work out. I hope you're willing to die, because I am."

"Willing," Cates said, "but not eager."

Su held out the flash drive. "Do what you need to do."

Cates took it and gave it to his analyst, who removed the laptop from his satchel and plugged in the flash drive. He peered intently at the screen as he typed.

While he waited for his analyst to confirm that the USB drive was the real thing, Cates nonchalantly watched the passing scenery as the train wound along the curving mountain track. Su had no idea what the analyst was doing to verify its provenance, but he didn't care as long as he got his fifty million.

Behind Su, the door to the passenger car banged open. He turned to see one of his men charge through, breathless and pointing back toward the way he came.

"They're here!" he shouted in Mandarin. "The MSS found us!"

Su felt the blood drain from his face. He'd been so careful in his planning that he couldn't believe they'd figured out where he was selling the drive. "What are you talking about?"

"While we were rounding the curve, I was looking out the window at the front of the train and saw them climbing into the first passenger car from on top. They'll be here any second."

The panicked face of his soldier made Su a believer, and his men drew their weapons. He swung around to get the flash drive from the Americans and ready his men to repel the attackers. But he hesitated when he saw the Americans' bizarre reaction to the commotion.

Both of them were hunched over and had the heels of their palms against their eyes with their mouths hanging open.

In quick succession two of the dining car's windows shattered as small objects broke through and bounced onto the floor at either end. The other men were as surprised as he was and whirled around in confusion.

In horror Su realized what the objects were. He yelled, "Get down!"

But none of the men had even begun to drop when the flashbang grenades went off.

The searing bright light and concussion of the dual blasts incapacitated Su instantly. He toppled over in his seat, disoriented and pawing at his eyes, his eardrums traumatized by the sudden change in pressure.

He couldn't even hear his own screams.

Despite shielding his eyes and opening his mouth to equalize the overpressure in his ears, Juan was still partially dazed from the effects of the flashbang grenades. With the USB drive gripped firmly in his hand, he staggered to his feet, then collapsed back into the seat.

His vision cleared quickly enough to see Jimmy Su and his men crawling around as if they were drunks trying to stand up after a bender. Next to him, Eric looked as out of it as Juan felt.

Juan attempted to get up again, and this time he flew out of his seat as a huge hand grasped his arm and yanked him up. Franklin Lincoln's grinning face met his.

"Let's get you two out of here before they recover," Linc said, picking up Eric, too. He virtually dragged Juan and Eric with him to the sixth car, where they had waited to enter the dining car.

Once Linc closed the door behind them, they both leaned against the wall and got their bearings.

"You guys okay?" Linc asked as he covered the door with his P90 submachine gun.

"I feel like someone smacked me in the head with a frying pan," Juan said, although he was quickly regaining his senses.

"Let's not ever do that again," Eric said.

"Just be glad we had some warning. A few of those guys probably won't be able to hear for weeks."

"I brought you some presents," Linc said, handing them a couple of ballistic vests. "Your guns are on the seats back there."

Juan and Eric strapped on the vests and picked up their weapons.

MacD came jogging in with the grenade launcher hanging from his shoulder.

"Y'all don't look too bad," he said. "My aim must have been pretty good."

"Right on target," Juan said, yawning to clear his ears.

Using precise maps of the train's route, this section of track had been selected for launching the stun grenades because of the extreme curve of the track. MacD could open a window three cars away, lean out, and have a perfect view of the dining car. Juan and Eric had used a peculiarly shaped rock outcropping that they passed to cue them when to cover their eyes.

"Did you get the Chinese agents, too?" Juan asked.

"Harder shot because they were farther away," MacD said proudly, "but I planted two in the third car where they were."

"Good, that should give us some extra time. Eric, set up the trip mines while they cover you. I've got a delivery to make."

Eric, who seemed to be back to normal, nodded and took a bag from Linc. He opened it and removed the first of a dozen laser-activated flashbang grenades. They'd place them at random intervals to cover their retreat. When either the MSS or the Ghost Dragons tried to come through, they'd trip the invisible sensors, setting off the grenades.

Juan got on his phone and called the *Oregon*. Hali Kasim, the ship's communications officer, answered.

"Are you all right, Chairman?" he asked. "We saw the explosions but couldn't see much inside the train."

"No casualties," Juan replied. "The first phase is complete. I'm heading to the window now. Have Gomez get the drone over here for pickup."

Gomez Adams, the *Oregon*'s helicopter pilot, was also the resident expert in flying its complement of drones.

"He says it'll be there in a few seconds."

Juan opened the window and watched the quadcopter, no more than a foot across, coming in to match the train's speed. Gomez's placement of the drone was perfect, lining it up with the opening. It darted inside, corrected instantly for the sudden change in wind speed, and came to rest on the floor. The propellers shut down and went silent.

Juan picked up the drone and clicked open a tiny compartment on its underside. He stuck the flash drive into the padded slot and locked it shut, then put the drone back down.

"It's all yours, Hali," Juan said.

"Roger that," Hali said. The drone's propellers whirred to life. It lifted up and buzzed toward the window like an angry hornet. Gomez guided it back out through the window, and once it was outside, it shot up as if yanked by a string. The drone was out of sight in the blink of an eye.

"What's our position?"

"You're ten minutes from the river."

Juan checked his watch. "We'll hold them off for that long. Let me know when the package is secured."

"Roger that. By the way, three of the Chinese agents were walking along the roof of the train when MacD fired the grenades. They just climbed down inside the rear car."

"Did they see the drone?"

"No chance."

"Good."

A barrage of gunfire broke out in the forward cars. Juan rejoined Linc, MacD, and Eric.

"Sounds like our two groups of friends have met each other," he said. "We've got another group flanking us from the rear. They're probably there to make sure no one gets off the train."

"Should we hole up here?" Linc asked.

Shots continued to ring out from up ahead. "No, let's go back to car seven. I don't think the Ghost Dragons will be much of a match for the MSS agents. When they're done with the triad, they'll be coming after us next."

"Ah hope Eddie is keeping his head down," MacD said.

"Let me ask him." Juan inserted a tiny earpiece that was wirelessly connected to his phone's transmitter. The Wi-Fi signal was linked directly to Eddie's phone. As long as his phone was within thirty feet of him, Eddie would be able to hear the communication and reply through his bone conduction microphone subvocally, which would be masked by the surrounding gunfire.

"Eddie, do you read me?"

"Here," came a guttural whisper in response.

"We're going to passenger car seven. ETA to river is nine minutes thirty seconds."

"Agents are in the fourth car and heading your way," Eddie replied. "And they're not happy."

There was one more Ghost Dragon gang member at the end of the fourth car making a valiant effort to stall the MSS agents from entering the dining car, but he soon went down in a hail of bullets. Zhong hadn't lost any men to this point, and the numbers on the other side were dwindling fast. The Ghost Dragons were putting up a good resistance, but the MSS agents were better trained and had more effective firepower. Eddie, who was still unarmed next to Zhong, could see that it was just a matter of time before the triad soldiers were wiped out.

Zhong had assumed the triad launched the flashbang grenades that had temporarily stunned his assault team and he took pleasure in exacting revenge for it. The doors between cars created a bottleneck that made it easier for the defenders than the assault team. Progress slowed down at each of these junctures, which is exactly what Eddie was hoping for.

The Ghost Dragons were apparently making their last stand in the dining car, which was the fifth passenger car on the train. Zhong ordered his two operatives to move forward until they were on either side of the door leading to the dining car. Unlike Juan, the agents were equipped with fragmentation grenades, two of which they tossed through the opening.

As soon as they went off, the MSS agents charged through, blazing away with their assault rifles and taking down anything that moved. The firefight continued for a few moments, and then the dining car went silent.

"Clear!" one of the men yelled.

"Dining car," Eddie said quietly for Juan's benefit. His earpiece had been stowed in a tiny pocket sewn into his belt line. He had inserted it into his ear when he was sure no one was looking.

Zhong motioned for Eddie to follow him in. Dead triad soldiers littered the car.

"Find Jimmy Su," Zhong said. "If they weren't able to make the exchange already, he'll have the flash drive."

Eddie looked around and said, "Where are the Americans?"

"They must have fled to another car. The agents who went to the rear car are making a sweep forward. If the Americans try to jump off the train, my men are ordered to shoot them. They'll be found."

While Eddie waited at the front of the car, Zhong's men searched the corpses for the drive. Zhong kept watch at the far end for a counterassault.

A hand grasped Eddie's arm from behind. Someone must have been hanging from the undercarriage, was his thought when he felt a pistol barrel against his temple.

"Put your guns down," Jimmy Su barked. His breath was hot on Eddie's neck.

Zhong whipped around and raised his assault rifle. "Or what? You'll kill him?"

"No. I'm just using him as a shield. If you don't put your guns down, you'll never see that flash drive again."

"You picked a bad choice for a shield. I don't really care if you kill your own man."

Su whirled Eddie to the side and his mouth gaped when he saw what appeared to be a phantom standing in front of him. Before Su could say anything, Eddie took advantage of the surprise and lashed out with his elbow, pushing the gun away from his face. With the immediate danger gone, he chopped Su in the throat. While the Ghost Dragon leader went down clutching his neck, Eddie kneed him in the side of the head, knocking him cold.

Eddie was about to pick up the gun when Zhong told him to freeze. He sensed the three guns trained on him and went like a statue.

"Back away," Zhong ordered. Eddie did as he was told.

Eddie smirked at Su's unconscious form. "Did you see the look on his face? He thought he had me killed and yet here I am. I think this proves I'm on your side."

"Do you think I'm an idiot? You're on your own side." He nodded to one of his men. "Search him."

"Which one?"

"Both of them."

The MSS agent did a thorough pat-down on Eddie, then frisked Su's inert form.

"Nothing, sir."

"Then the Americans must have the flash drive," Zhong said. "If we don't find it on them after they're dead, we'll tear this train apart until we do."

"What about Su? Should I kill him now?"

"No. We may need him later to help us find the drive. Bind him."

The agent took out some zip ties and cuffed Su's hands and feet and tethered him to a metal grab bar so he couldn't crawl away.

When Su was secure, they moved toward the sixth car. Seeing that it was empty, the first agent walked in and promptly set off the flashbang trip bomb that was waiting.

While the agent writhed on the floor, Eddie said, "We must not have finished off Su's men." He knew full well that bombs were set by Juan.

Zhong leaned over and checked out the cylindrical grenade, still intact because this type of flashbang didn't destroy its casing.

He held it up and said, "Have you ever used anything this sophisticated in the Ghost Dragons?"

Eddie shook his head.

"This is made by the United States," Zhong said. "Military-grade. Laser trip sensor. The Americans must have put it here."

"Then there might be more of them ahead," Eddie said.

Zhong stood up and rolled the spent grenade down the center aisle of the car. It didn't set any more trip bombs off, but that didn't mean there weren't any there.

"We'll have to proceed slowly, which will give them an opportunity to escape." Zhong looked at Eddie. "If they do, you die."

Eddie nodded hastily. "Have your men coming from the other direction made contact with the Americans yet?"

Zhong radioed his men and asked the question.

"No, sir," came the reply. "We're in the eighth car."

"They're in the eighth car?" Eddie repeated for the benefit of Juan. He knew he had to buy time not only for the Chairman but also for the team out on the *Oregon*. "Then I have an idea how to attack the Americans."

On the deck of the *Oregon*, near the tramp freighter's superstructure, Mark Murphy paced, impatiently waiting for the drone carrying the flash drive to arrive. He squinted into the sun as he watched the locomotive enter another tunnel and wished he'd brought some sunglasses with him. He hated not being able to see what was going on in the train. Before coming outside, he'd been down in the ship's darkened operations center listening to both Juan's and Eddie's conversations. He'd heard the threat that the Chairman had given the Ghost Dragon leader about the Predator drone and its Hellfire missile ready to blow up the train. While there was no attack drone circling above, his threat wasn't a bluff. The *Oregon* had more than enough firepower to destroy the entire train from its position a mile offshore.

Murph would be the best one to know since he served as the ship's weapons officer. As the only crew member without a military or intelligence background, he had joined the Corporation after getting his first Ph.D. by the time he was twenty and then working in the defense industry as a weapons designer. One of the reasons he loved his current job was because the crew accepted him for who he was. The Chairman didn't make him change his punk rock style, even letting Murph convert the deck of the *Oregon* into a skateboard park during R & R and putting him in a cabin far away from the others so he could blast his music at full volume and play video games with Eric Stone late into the night.

Like on most days, Murph was dressed all in black, a pair of torn jeans and a T-shirt bearing the name of the band Screeching Weasel. His hair was dark and shaggy, with matching scruff on his chin that he passed off as a beard, and the caffeine in the energy drinks he constantly consumed made it tough to put weight on his tall, gangly frame. Not only did he like the nonconformist look, any more effort thinking about his clothes and appearance just wasn't worth the time.

When Eric, his best friend, was on board the *Oregon*, he and Murph were usually inseparable. They were the youngest crew members and shared an appreciation for complex software coding, gaming, and Internet dating, the last of which didn't work nearly as well or as often as they hoped. They had been working together on a still-classified weapons system for the Arleigh Burke class destroyers when Eric convinced him to join the Corporation.

That was why Murph was so anxious to retrieve the drone. He knew that every minute Eric and the others were on the train, they were at risk. The *Oregon* was more than a workplace. The crew was family. Murph took pride in his job, but helping his crewmates get through dangerous situations was what really drove him.

It was also a very lucrative workplace, although he had earned an even higher salary as one of the world's top weapons designers. The Corporation was formed as a partnership and all the crew members shared in the profits. The riskier and more difficult the job, the greater the payday. All of them anticipated retiring as multimillion-aires.

The current job was one of the trickiest they'd ever undertaken. In this case, the most important part of the operation was out of their hands, which made Murph itchy to get the mission over with.

"Drone One coming in," Gomez said over the headset Murph was wearing. "Starboard side, four o'clock."

Murph turned and put his hand up to shield his eyes from the setting sun. The view across the *Oregon*'s deck would have concerned anyone not familiar with the ship. From far away she looked like she was ready for the breaker's yard. Up close, her exterior looked even worse.

The 560-foot *Oregon* had been built to haul lumber from the Pacific Northwest to Japan, but it'd been years since the 11,600-ton freighter was in her prime. Rust seemed to coat everything, from the leaking barrels and broken machinery scattered randomly about the deck to the chains connecting the sections of railing that were missing. The flaking paint was slathered on haphazardly in several different shades of a sickly green, and the fraying cables of the ship's five cranes looked as if they were in danger of snapping just from their sagging.

From her blade-like bow to her graceful champagne-glass-shaped stern, steel plates were welded to the *Oregon*'s hull as if to conceal cracks that threatened to rip it in two. The dingy white superstructure separated the five cargo holds, three forward and two aft. The bridge was barely visible through the mold-covered windows, one of which was covered in plywood. It was topped with bent antennas held together by duct tape.

Murph was so used to the ship's rickety appearance that it didn't even register, as he watched the small quadcopter zoom toward him. It came to rest on the barrel next to him and shut down. He scooped it up and ran toward the nearest door.

"Got it," Murph said as he went inside. "Let them know I'm on my way down."

The chipped linoleum of the interior corridor was stained brown every few feet from some unknown substance, the peeling walls bowed out as if they were about to collapse, and the few fluorescent lights that did work flickered and buzzed. A bathroom Murph passed was coated with a layer of grime and emitted a stench so powerful that any harbormaster coming aboard for an inspection would spend the least time possible before fleeing in disgust.

Murph opened a broom closet, which was stacked with mops and cleaning supplies that had never been used. At the slop sink, he twisted the hot and cold handles in a specific order as if he were a safecracker. With a distinct click, the back wall swished open noiselessly. Murph raced through and tapped a button on the other side to close it again as he passed.

It was like stepping from a sewer into a luxury hotel. Instantly, the stink was gone. Paintings by masters like Monet and Renoir adorned mahogany-paneled walls, and recessed lighting cast a warm glow in the halls. Plush carpeting softened Murph's footfalls.

All of the apparent decay and shabbiness was merely a meticulously designed façade. Though she still outwardly appeared to be a tramp steamer, the *Oregon* had been refitted from the keel up at a naval base in Vladivostok after a generous payment to a friendly commandant. He told his workers that they were constructing the Russian Navy's latest secret weapon. Everything on the outside of the *Oregon* was meant to repel and disgust so that it would go by unnoticed or unsuspected, but the interior was designed for her true mission as a spy ship and as a home for her crew.

Each cabin was uniquely decorated according to its occupant's specifications. Murph's wouldn't have looked out of place as a rich college student's dorm room. Other than a functional bed and a huge desk with the latest ergonomic chair for work, the key furnishings of his cabin were centered on the leather sofa and gigantic television connected to all of the latest consoles.

When he was out of his cabin, Murph spent much of his time with the *Oregon*'s vast array of hidden weaponry. The welded plates on the side of the hull could drop away to reveal 20mm Gatling guns modeled on the ones aircraft carriers used for antimissile defense, and clamshell doors in the bow opened for a 120mm cannon like those mounted on Abrams tanks. A Metal Storm hundred-barrel gun could rise out of the stern to fire tungsten projectiles at the fantastic rate of a million rounds a minute. Six of the leaky oil drums on deck held .30 caliber machine guns that would pop up to fend off boarders and were remotely manned from the operations center. A closed-circuit camera system gave expansive views of the ship itself and anything around it out to the horizon.

Defensive capabilities also included surface-to-air antiaircraft missiles, Exocet antiship missiles, and the latest Russian torpedoes, all purchased on the black market so they couldn't be traced back to the U.S. Someday Murph hoped to add antimissile lasers and electromagnetic railguns to the arsenal after a previous mission had shown him up close how powerful they could be in battle.

In addition to the Magic Shop, which contained racks of clothing, various props, and a makeup department that would make a movie studio envious, the ship had a waterline boat garage for handling all types of small vessels, including wet bikes, Zodiacs, and her RHIB—short for "rigid-hulled inflatable boat," the same kind Navy SEALs took into combat. The center of the *Oregon* contained the moon pool, the largest single space on the ship. The pool in the cavernous room had a water level equalized with the sea level outside and was used to launch underwater missions through massive keel doors—anything from scuba divers to its pair of submarines.

Of the five deep cargo holds in the *Oregon*, two of the forward holds had been modified to house the crew quarters, and one of the rear holds housed a hangar with the ship's MD 520N helicopter that rose up on a platform for takeoff. Those three had been cleverly covered by false roofs of crates and containers to fool anyone looking down on them from the deck into thinking that the holds were full of cargo.

The other two holds, which could be serviced by the two working cranes on deck, often carried actual freight to throw off inspectors. But today the forward hold carried a secret cargo, which was Murph's destination.

He opened the hatch to the hold, and instead of timber or containers, he was met by row upon row of server racks surrounding a massive computer that took up fully half the space. A giant refrigeration unit cooled the hold so that the electronics didn't overheat in the sweltering tropical environment.

Three workstations were occupied by two men and a woman, all on loan from the National Security Agency. When the offer to sell the flash drive was made by the Ghost Dragons, Langston Overholt IV, Juan Cabrillo's venerable CIA mentor who had been instrumental in encouraging Juan to build the *Oregon* and had assigned most of the Corporation's missions from the government agency, had seen the potential for an opportunity that might never present itself again.

He knew that the *Oregon* had been operating in Southeast Asia hunting down pirates targeting American containerships and quickly got agreement from the NSA chief to provide the equipment they'd need for a special mission. Fort Meade's newest cryptographic supercomputer, one of the few in the world that could break the Chinese code, was loaded onto a C-5 Galaxy cargo jet and flown to Guam, where it was transferred to the *Oregon*.

Not only did the *Oregon* have enough space to hold the computer, she had a revolutionary engine that could supply its huge power requirements. Instead of the original diesels, the *Oregon* was powered by a pair of magnetohydrodynamic engines that used magnets cooled by liquid helium to strip free electrons from the seawater. Four pulse jets forced water through Venturi tubes to propel her to speeds that shouldn't have been possible on a ship her size, and the vector nozzles on the jets made her as agile as a jackrabbit.

"Here it is," Murph said to Abby Yamada, a slender woman in her forties who was the NSA's chief cryptanalyst on the mission. He removed the flash drive from the drone and handed it to her. He looked at his watch and added, "You've got six minutes fifteen seconds."

"Thanks," she said, inserting it into the USB port. "Let's get this done."

Since Murph had a top secret clearance, they allowed him to stay while they worked. English was the universal coding language, so he could understand most of what they were doing. He watched in curiosity as they attempted to hack into the drive without erasing it, but he would have much rather been doing it himself. He wasn't used to being a bystander on his own ship.

A minute into the job, one of her colleagues said, "I've got a serious problem here."

"What is it?" Yamada asked as she continued to type.

"When I was hacking into the code, I somehow activated a timer."

All heads turned toward him. He looked ashen.

Murph went over to his terminal and saw that the drive was asking for a password. If the correct one wasn't input within three minutes, the drive would erase itself and the entire mission would be for nothing.

10

Memories churned to the surface for Max Hanley as Vietnam's coast passed by on the huge screen in front of him. He had served two tours of duty during the Vietnam War on Swift Boats patrolling the coastline and the Mekong Delta, sweating through every square inch of his uniform and swatting at the incessant mosquitoes as he and his fellow sailors waited for the ambushes they knew would come. His crewmates were some of the best men he'd ever known. Many of them had been killed or gone missing. He almost joined them when his boat was destroyed and he was captured. He spent six months in a POW camp before escaping.

Now, more than forty years later—with twenty extra pounds at his belly and a ring of ginger circling his chrome dome where a full head of hair used to be—it was hard to believe he was sitting in air-conditioned comfort as he watched another battle unfold on the same soil. The operations center was the heart of the *Oregon*. Located directly below the window-dressing bridge in the superstructure, virtually every function of the ship could be handled from this one room through a new Cray supercomputer. Max noted with pride that the *Oregon*'s computer nearly matched the sophistication of the NSA's, if not its raw computing power.

With its banks of touch screen workstations and a massive high-definition screen that dominated the front of the room, the op center resembled a futuristic bridge straight out of *Star Trek*, so much so that the large seat at the center of the room where Max sat had been dubbed the "Kirk Chair" by Mark Murphy and Eric Stone. The *Oregon* could even be operated from controls in the chair's arms, if the need arose. As chief engineer, Max would normally be at his engineering station at the back, but with Juan away on the mission, the Corporation's vice president was in command of the ship.

Linda Ross, a Navy vet and the Corporation's vice president of operations, sat at the helm, which was usually Eric's station. Except for Juan, Eric was the *Oregon*'s best ship handler, but Linda wasn't far behind them.

"I've got a fishing boat right in our path a mile ahead," she said, pointing at the screen. Her pixie-high voice matched her petite figure, elfin features, and upturned nose, but having served as an officer aboard an Aegis cruiser, she spoke with authority. Known for updating her hair color and style regularly, she had recently grown out her dark tresses and tinged them with eggplant highlights. "Shall I adjust course toward the coast?"

"Yes," Max said. "I don't want to get any farther away from the train than we have to. Give the fishing boat a wide berth, but once we're past them, get us back to our original distance."

"Changing course," she said, and deftly moved the *Oregon* to its new heading.

"Max, I just got a call from Murph," said Hali Kasim, the ship's Lebanese-American communications specialist. He lowered the old-fashioned headset he preferred, but his mop of crushed hair didn't move. "He says they've got a problem down in the hold. He's on his way back up here."

"Did he say what kind of problem?"

"No. He sounded out of breath, like he was running."

"What's going on with Juan?"

"They've run into resistance from the back of the train, but they're taking care of that. He said they've moved on to Plan C."

"Already? I didn't even know we'd tried Plan B. Did he say what Plan C *was*?"

Hali shrugged. "Sorry."

Max peered up at the screen and saw someone hanging from the door at the rear of the train's seventh car on the side away from the *Oregon*. From the size of the man, he guessed it was Linc doing something with the train coupling.

"I can't tell what he's doing. Gomez, can you zoom in any closer on the train?"

Seated next to Hali was George "Gomez" Adams, their resident drone and helicopter pilot. Dressed in a flight suit in case his services were needed in the air, his matinee idol looks rivaled MacD's. The main difference was that Gomez sported the handlebar mustache of a Wild West gunfighter. The nickname stuck after he had an illicit liaison with a drug lord's wife who was a dead ringer for Morticia Addams, the matriarch on the sixties television show *The Addams Family*.

"It's already zoomed in as far as it'll go," Gomez said, "but I can fly Drone Two closer."

"Not too close. We don't want to take the chance that it will be seen from the train."

"No problem. I'll keep it between the train and the sun."

As Gomez flew the observation drone in for a closer look, Murph burst into the op center, panting from the run. He took his seat at the weapons control station next to the helm and began to furiously type on his keyboard.

"What's going on?" Max asked.

"One of the NSA guys triggered a password entry screen on the flash drive," Murph said breathlessly while his fingers continued to fly. "If we don't get the right one, the flash drive will erase itself. Even with that monstrosity in the hold, they'll never crack it in time."

"How long do they have?"

"Two minutes."

"You mean we're going to lose the data?"

"Not if I can help it. Hali, get the NSA team on the line."

Hali tapped on his workstation. "On speaker."

Max had the urge to ask what Murph was doing, but he didn't want to be a distraction. If Murph thought he had a solution, Max trusted him.

With a flourish, Murph finished typing. "Done! Abby, the link is established."

From the hold, Abby Yamada said, "Thanks. We've nearly doubled the processing speed. It's cranking through the possibilities now."

"Okay," Murph said. "Let me know if it works."

"What did you do?" Max asked.

Murph swiveled in his chair to face him. "When we installed their supercomputer in the hold, we added some compatibility software to our Cray so we could test the linkage to our power system. With the connection already made, I just had to hand over control of our computer to theirs so they could draw on its power to crack the password."

"Will that affect our systems?" Linda asked.

"Nothing vital," he said with a grin, "but the Internet may be slow if you're looking to download any videos."

Max leaned forward. "How will this affect the time to decipher the data?"

"Hard to say. But the minutes we've spent cracking the password are delaying the data decryption."

"Then we might not have as much time as we thought." Max looked at Linda. "We'll have to chance them seeing us. Take us within three-quarters of a mile of the coast."

"Aye, aye," she said, an old Navy habit, and the *Oregon* edged closer to the coast.

The plan for the mission wasn't to steal the flash drive. The goal was to download the data on it and get it back to the Chinese without them knowing it had been read. Learning the identities of the undercover MSS agents operating in the U.S. would be a major intelligence coup, but if the Chinese knew their agents were compromised, they'd pull them out or shut them down. The few that were captured and interrogated might reveal some useful information, but the real value would be lost. The Chinese would send in new agents, and the cat-and-mouse game would start all over.

But if they could return the flash drive without them knowing it had been read, the Chinese would think the identities of their agents were secure. Then the NSA, FBI, and CIA could not only track their movements and conversations but could feed false information to the Chinese for years. It was a dream scenario for U.S. intelligence, which was the reason for the highly risky, off-the-books operation.

While they waited for news from the NSA people, Gomez was able to get the observation drone close enough to see Linc's distinctive form clamping something onto a hose linking the seventh car to the one behind it. Max could see flashes of gunfire coming from the eighth car. The train was approaching yet another tunnel.

"Put Juan on speaker," Max said.

"You've got him," Hali said.

The sound of gunshots came through the speakers.

"Everybody okay?" Max asked.

"No casualties," Juan replied, "but we're trying to even the odds a little."

"I can see Linc working on Plan C."

"We're about to say good-bye to three of the MSS agents."

"Anything we can do to help?"

"Let us know if there's anyone hanging out a window."

"You got it."

On-screen, MacD leaned out and handed a gray block to Linc, who stretched his long arms and mashed it against the coupling. He pulled himself back in and gave a thumbs-up before he disappeared from view.

"Fire in the hole!" Juan shouted.

The coupling disintegrated in a ball of flame. As the train entered the tunnel, the accordion windscreens between the two cars ripped apart as they pulled away from each other. Then they were gone into the darkness.

Static came on the line.

"The tunnel's blocking their signal," Hali said.

Gomez gunned the drone and flew it to the other end of the tunnel.

Max kept his eyes on the screen. When the train emerged, it was missing two cars.

"They'll be stuck in there," Juan said when the static disappeared. "The air brakes kicked in as soon as Linc severed the line. And if we're lucky, their radio won't work in the tunnel, so their comrades up front won't notice they're gone."

"Nice work for a Plan C."

"It's not over yet. How's the decryption coming?"

"We've hit a snag there," Max said. "Long story, but we're working on it."

"That doesn't sound hopeful."

Murph, who had gone over to Hali's station and picked up a spare headset, looked at Max and said, "Got some good news on that score."

"They cracked the password?"

Murph nodded. "With about twenty seconds to spare. Now do you want the bad news?"

Max frowned. "What?"

"The data is going to take longer than they thought to decrypt, even with the *Oregon*'s computer helping."

"How long?"

"They estimate that it won't be done until two minutes before Juan and the others reach the extraction point at the river."

"And it needs to arrive at the train a minute before that. Can you fly it back that fast, Gomez?"

Gomez stroked his mustache and grimaced. "From this distance? It'll be really close."

Murph took the cue and left the op center so he'd be ready to put the USB drive back in the drone the moment it was available.

Max turned to Linda. "Get us within a half mile of the coast, and let's hope Juan keeps the Chinese too distracted to notice us."

THAILAND

Beth Anders traveled around the world for her job and she knew all the scams. When a young Bangkok street urchin approached her to beg for money, she politely but firmly declined, knowing he would just take her charity straight back to some scuzzball who took advantage of these poor kids. As she walked down the busy road in the Patpong District, she kept her bag in front of her and her hand on the clasp.

At night, the shops would be lit up in flashy neon, and girls would be standing outside of the clubs enthusiastically advertising their wares. But in the late afternoon, the scene just seemed sad. In addition to many umbrella-topped food carts, street vendors hawked all kinds of magazines and items that Beth didn't even want to look at. Pharmacies sold nearly any prescription drug you could ask for at a fraction of the cost in other countries. Valium and psychedelic mushrooms were particular favorites. For those who preferred liquid anesthetics, there were bars everywhere. Drunken tourists were getting a head start on their nightlife, weaving their way among the motor-cycles and three-wheeled tuk-tuks that crowded the road.

Although Beth knew she was probably safe at this time of day, she was glad she wasn't alone. Raven Malloy walked next to her, constantly scanning her surroundings. Unlike Beth, she carried no purse, keeping her hands free at her sides.

"Of course, they had to pick one of the sleaziest parts of Bang-kok for the meeting," Beth said.

"They're drug dealers," Raven replied in a clipped contralto. "What did you expect?"

"Originally, they wanted this meeting at two in the morning, but I told them that wasn't going to happen."

"Smart, but this is still a big risk. If they figure out what you're doing, they'll kill us both."

"That's why I brought an Army Ranger with me. You're there to watch my back."

Raven kept scanning. "I was a military police investigator. I only *applied* to Ranger School. They didn't start allowing women in until after I had left the Army."

"I'm sure you would have passed."

Raven shrugged. "We'll never know. Maybe they did me a favor. This job pays a lot more."

"Your fee is definitely worth it if we're successful."

A white man in his thirties, dressed in shorts and a T-shirt, stag-gering in their direction, caught sight of Raven and made a beeline for her. Raven didn't stop walking, so Beth didn't, either. The man, who was at least six inches taller and forty pounds heavier than ei-ther of them, lurched around to walk next to Raven, matching her pace despite his condition. Beth could smell the gin on his breath from three feet away.

"Hey, baby," he said to Raven, completely ignoring Beth. "I've been looking for a girl like you all my life."

"To kick you in the crotch?" Raven asked without missing a beat.

The guy's eyes went wide. "Hey, you're American like me! I'm from Florida. Name's Fred. What's yours?"

"I guess you were too plastered to hear the crotch-kicking part. You think you're too drunk to feel it?"

"Now, is that any way to talk to a fellow countryman? I just think you're pretty, that's all. What's wrong with telling a pretty girl that?"

"For one, I don't care what you think. And, two, that's how I always talk to idiots."

He finally noticed Beth next to Raven and said, "Wow, you're smoking hot, too. If she's not in the mood, maybe you and I can have some fun."

"Listen, Fred," Raven said. "I'm giving you one more chance. If you don't leave us alone, my knee and your privates are going to become mortal enemies."

"Stop being such a buzzkill," he said. "You know you want to party, otherwise you wouldn't be here."

And then Fred made the mistake of putting his hand on Raven's shoulder.

With lightning speed, she grabbed his hand and bent it backward. He let out a yelp as he tried to keep her from breaking his wrist. True to her word, Raven launched her knee into his crotch in a vicious strike.

The breath whooshed out of Fred in an audible gasp, and he collapsed to his knees before keeling over into the fetal position and cradling his groin with a whimper.

Raven continued on, barely breaking stride, as if she had just plucked an annoying pebble from her shoe.

Beth would be surprised if that was her guardian's first unsolicited proposition. With long jet-black hair tied in a ponytail, high cheekbones, and smooth caramel skin that Beth would have killed for, Raven was a stunner, even without makeup. Her snug T-shirt showed off her buff biceps and shoulders but was loose-fitting around the waist, and her jeans followed the curves of her perfectly shaped legs. Just listening to a recitation of her grueling training regimen made Beth break out in a sweat.

Looking at her again, Beth could understand why Fred had assumed Raven was Thai. She had a look that was hard to pin down. Depending on the angle, she could be Arab, Indian, Hispanic, or Polynesian, but she was actually Native American, a mix of Cherokee and Sioux. Her Irish surname came from her adoptive parents, who had both been in the military. Her features meant she could blend in with dozens of different cultures around the world.

Beth, on the other hand, was so Caucasian she could have appeared in a commercial for Scottish tourism. She was tall like Raven but had a flaming red mane of wavy hair, and her skin was alabaster white. She was in good shape, jogging whenever she could, but she was envious of Raven's athletic physique. She resolved to hit the hotel gym more often.

Beth could still hear Fred groaning behind them when they reached a club called Nightcrawlers. She stopped and looked up at the sign, which was outlined in neon light beside the image of an impossibly thin woman.

"Remember," Raven said, "if this goes bad, stick close to me." She had explained the layout of the building to Beth, including all of the exits, after scouting the club the night before. Raven said she always liked to know how to get out of a building if she had to.

"I've dealt with guys like this before," Beth said. "All they care about is the money." She didn't add that these guys were tougher than most, but it apparently came out in her voice.

"We can still call it off," Raven said. "We could head back to the car and give Interpol a call."

Beth may have been apprehensive, but she was also determined.

"And give up a chance for a five-million-dollar payday, not to mention solving the greatest art heist in history?" she said. "No way."

They entered the club and were met by a huge bouncer.

"Club is closed until nine," he said in English.

"I'm Beth Anders," she said. "Udom is expecting us."

The bouncer nodded and pointed to a flight of stairs at the back.

Udom was the first name of the Thai drug dealer that had set up the meeting. He didn't give a last name, not that Beth had asked. Surnames had been required in Thailand after a law was passed in 1913, but many Thai still preferred to use just their first names when they could.

They went upstairs and were met by another guard, this one even bigger than the one at the front door. She gave her name again and was allowed in.

A spindly man in his forties, Udom was leaning against a desk. She hadn't thought a drug pusher would use the crystal meth and ecstasy that he dealt to the tourists on their hedonistic holidays, but now, seeing his rail-thin frame and sunken eyes, she wasn't so sure.

There were a dozen men in the expansive office. Half of them looked Thai, but the other half, who all looked jacked on steroids, were from some other South Asian country she couldn't put her finger on.

"Come in, Dr. Anders," Udom said with a smile. "Who is this lovely lady with you?"

"This is my assistant, Raven."

"All right. Then let's get down to business."

Beth's heart pounded when she saw what he was casually twirling in his hands. It was a ten-inch-high bronze eagle finial that fit on the top of a flagpole.

The finial she was looking at had been sought after for over twenty-five years, and this drug dealer was playing with it like it was a cheap paperweight.

Beth's expertise was art history. She'd earned a Ph.D. in the subject from Cornell before attempting to secure a position in academia. But that plan was derailed when she was hired by an insurance firm to appraise a Picasso in a billionaire's penthouse in New York City. She discovered that it had been replaced with an excellent forgery, and her help in the investigation led to the recovery of the ten-million-dollar painting.

When she found she had a talent for investigation, her unique skill set put her in high demand in the art world. Not only did she save insurance companies millions by recovering artwork, her knack for identifying suspected forgeries allowed her to supplement her income by authenticating art for prospective buyers and auction houses.

Beth had built up a reputation in the art black market as well. After being recommended to Udom by someone else she'd worked with, he had asked her to authenticate and appraise a very valuable painting, one she would immediately recognize. She didn't work with just anyone, so to prove his seriousness, he had sent her a photo of the eagle finial next to a recent newspaper as a calling card.

"May I," she said, reverently moving toward him with her hands outstretched.

He held it out for her. "That's what you're here for."

She took it and suppressed a shiver of excitement at holding what was an almost mythical object in the art world.

In 1990, the Isabella Stewart Gardner Museum in Boston was robbed in the largest private property theft in history. Thirteen works of art were stolen, including paintings by the masters Vermeer, Rembrandt, Degas, and Manet. All told, the paintings were valued at five hundred million dollars, and a five-million-dollar reward for their return remained unclaimed. The eagle finial alone, which had topped a pole carrying a Napoleonic flag, would fetch a reward of a hundred thousand dollars.

For decades, it was feared that the artwork had been destroyed by the thieves, and many had given up hope of ever recovering the paintings, which still had their spots waiting for them in the museum. But the finial was proof that at least some of the art still existed.

It was breathtaking to hold the eagle Beth had memorized from photographs. The detail in person was even more striking, but she had to remember she had larger goals than this one object.

She opened her purse to take out a jeweler's loupe to examine the finial up close, but she already had no doubt it was authentic. Her real goal was to attach the microtransmitter in her palm so they could track it back to the paintings.

It had been rumored for years that drug smugglers used valuable paintings as collateral in their trades. A painting was much easier to roll up and transport on an international flight than millions of dollars in cash, so the art supposedly made its way back and forth between the gangs as a sort of currency. The only problem was verifying that the art was real so that they wouldn't be left holding a worthless counterfeit. The bronze finial was obviously being used to verify the provenance of the paintings to be used in the trade.

Beth had considered bringing Interpol in to carry out a raid, but she was afraid they'd lose their one shot at finding the paintings. So she'd come up with the plan to find the whole lot at once.

The transmitter was smaller than the tiny SIM card in her phone. It was flexible, almost transparent, and had a strong adhesive backing on it. All she had to do was place it inside the finial's flagpole sleeve without anyone noticing, and then they could be on their way. Once the finial went back with its owner to its original storage location, she'd bring in Interpol for a raid to recover the paintings and her reward.

"Well?" Udom asked.

With her thumb, Beth pressed the transmitter into the sleeve of the finial, when she saw the men's attention trained on Raven. It would go undetected unless someone were looking for it.

She looked up at Udom. "I can verify conclusively that this is the object stolen from the Gardner Museum."

Udom looked at one of the non-Thais and smiled. "It looks like we're in business, then, Tagaan."

Tagaan, who must have been the leader of the other group, nodded and stepped forward holding a plastic tube. He removed a rolled-up canvas from it and unfurled it on the desk.

"Tell us how much this is worth," he demanded.

Beth couldn't keep her jaw from dropping at the sight of it. Tagaan had casually spread out a ten-by-thirteen-inch masterpiece called *Chez Tortoni* by the impressionist Édouard Manet.

"Yes, tell us," Udom said, and, with a nod to his men, they all drew pistols and aimed them at the visitors. "You said you had a test to verify it's real. Prove to me that we aren't being cheated with a counterfeit."

Beth looked to Raven, who seemed as calm as ever, but it was clear the mental gears were working furiously behind her eyes. She gave Beth a reassuring glance, which helped ease her back from the edge of panic to mere terror.

As Beth walked over to the Manet, she understood how much was riding on her appraisal. If the small painting lying on the drug dealer's desk was a genuine Manet, it was valued at twenty million dollars. If it wasn't, they were all dead.

12

VIETNAM

While Linc, MacD, and Eric kept their guns trained on the entrance from the dining car, Juan had his eyes on the *Oregon*.

"Where's that drone, guys? We're approaching the last tunnel before the river."

"We see you, Chairman," Hali said. "The NSA analysts finally got the data from the flash drive downloaded. Murph just launched it from the deck."

"Eddie, what can you tell me?"

Eddie's low whisper responded, "They bought my idea. We're in place."

Juan could see the drone flying in only because he was looking for it. Instead of heading for one of the windows, Gomez brought it in directly behind the train so that it wouldn't be seen by the Chinese, who were no longer distracted by an ongoing firefight.

The drone flew in the open door and neatly settled on the seat nearest Juan. He opened it and removed the flash drive. The drone whirred to life again and disappeared the way it had come just as the train went into the tunnel.

Juan gathered with his team and got confirmation everything was ready. This would be the most dangerous part of the mission. If they didn't play their parts exactly right, they wouldn't live to see another day.

Juan opened the door to the dining car and peered in over the sight on his P90 submachine gun.

The MSS agents were gone. Only the dead bodies of the triad soldiers remained, some on the floor, others draped over the seats.

Juan crept in a few feet, scanning for agents who might be concealing themselves farther down the car. As he crabbed forward, he balanced himself by placing a hand on each seat cushion as he passed.

When he reached the place where he'd been sitting with Jimmy Su, he yelled, "Clear!" That was the signal.

Eddie, who was pretending to be one of the dead Ghost Dragons, leapt up and grabbed Juan around the neck, pressing a machine pistol against his temple. Juan dropped the P90, and Eddie kicked it backward.

Eddie shouted something in Chinese, and three MSS agents jumped up from their hiding places. Zhong was in front, and all three had assault rifles pointed at him and Eddie.

"Where's the flash drive?" Zhong demanded in English.

"If you kill me, you'll never find it," Juan said.

"It's obviously still in the dining car somewhere," Eddie said, "or he wouldn't have come back in here."

"Can you be sure about that? How do you know I didn't toss it out the window somewhere along the way?" Juan made it sound like a bluff.

"What if we don't kill you?" Eddie said. "What if we just hurt you?"

Then, with lightning speed, he jerked the gun down and shot Juan in the foot.

ZHONG WAS ASTONISHED when David Yao shot the American in the foot, primarily because he thought the machine pistol wasn't loaded.

Blood erupted from the American's foot and he went down howling in agony. Yao pulled him back up and pointed the gun at his head.

"Tell us!" he shouted.

"All right, I'll tell you," the American gasped. "But how do I know you won't kill me?"

"I'll kill you if you *don't* tell us," Zhong said. "You can be sure of that."

"Then *my* men will kill *you*."

"They can try."

A strange look came over Yao's face, and he began dragging the American backward toward the rear of the train.

"Come with me if you want to live," Yao said.

Zhong moved forward. "Yao, what are you doing?"

"I think you're going to kill both of us when you get the flash drive. I'll make him give it to you, but then I'm going to take my chances with asylum in the United States."

Zhong laughed. "You think they'll give you asylum after what you've done?"

"If I save an American agent, they might." He withdrew into the space connecting the dining car with the one behind it and stopped. He pressed the gun harder into the American's temple. "Now tell them where the flash drive is or we all die together."

The American gritted his teeth, but his eyes flicked over to one of the seats near where Zhong and his men had found a Lenovo laptop during the search of the dining car.

Zhong smiled. With his assault rifle still pointing at the two of them, he edged forward and knelt beside the seat. He pushed his hand deep into the seat cushion and ran his fingers along the back until they brushed against hard plastic. He removed it and saw that it was the flash drive. The serial number on it matched the one that had been stolen.

He grinned and was about to give the order to fire when the American surged backward, pushing Yao with him. With Yao's balance thrown off, the machine pistol fired into the air, and they both tumbled to the floor in the next car.

Then the section between the cars exploded.

The coupling must have been the target because the brakes squealed on the car behind them and it began to fall back. That was the Americans' exit strategy all along, and it was the reason they had the explosives to sever the link to the cars carrying Zhong's other agents. The car with the Americans would come to a stop near the beginning of the bridge they were now crossing.

Gunfire came from Americans in the receding train car, but Zhong didn't care about a fight with them anymore. They could do what they wanted with Yao. It didn't matter now that he had the flash drive.

He plugged it into the adapter on his phone and initiated the memory wipe just in case the Americans had more surprises in store up ahead and tried to recapture the flash drive. In thirty seconds, the app responded that the flash drive had been completely overwritten seventy-five times. Now no computer on earth could recover the data it had carried.

Zhong smiled and pocketed the flash drive to show to his superiors. He also had Jimmy Su still alive to interrogate and find out how the Ghost Dragons had stolen the drive in the first place.

He notified the pilots to have the helicopters meet them at the rendezvous point. But he'd teach a lesson to the agents who'd let themselves be cut off from the rest of the train. They could hike out of the jungle and hitch a ride home.

AS HE WATCHED the train disappear, Juan said, "Is everyone all right?"

He got four affirmatives.

Eric knelt down by the blood-soaked bullet wound in Juan's foot. "That's cool. It looks so real."

"When I told Kevin Nixon what we were planning, he didn't think it was so cool knowing he'd have to patch up my prosthetic foot yet again." To complete the illusion, the blood was his own, drawn by the *Oregon*'s doctor, Julia Huxley, the day before and sealed in a packet inside his boot.

He leapt to his feet, none the worse for the experience, and clapped Eddie on the shoulder. "That was some nice acting back there. You almost had me convinced you were a Ghost Dragon."

"I'm just glad I was able to get my hands on one of the spare magazines."

"I did like the expression on Zhong's face when he realized the gun he gave you was no longer empty."

"You should have seen the look on Jimmy Su's face when he saw David Yao alive and kicking, literally," Eddie said. "He must have thought his own men betrayed him and didn't kill Yao as ordered."

"Well, you can go back to being yourself, and Yao's remains will be 'discovered' in about a week when the Navy gets rid of the body. If anything, Zhong will think the triad got back at him for his betrayal."

"You know, I think you should keep some of those tattoos," MacD said, pointing at Eddie's neck. "The dragon looks pretty awesome."

"No, thanks. I'm washing them off as soon as we get back to the *Oregon*."

"Speaking of which," Linc said, "we should get going. I don't want to be here when the Vietnamese find out what we've done to their train system."

"Good point," Juan said. He called Hali. "Is the RHIB still where we left it?" They had pre-positioned the rigid-hulled inflatable boat before the mission started, prepped for a quick getaway should one have been required.

After a moment, Hali replied, "Thanks to Gomez's drone, we've got eyes on it. It's still hidden in the bushes by the river's edge."

"Then tell Max to lay in a course to Guam."

"He says we're ready to go when you are."

"Thanks." Juan hung up and said, "Let's get moving. I'm starving."

They got out of the train car, which had traveled twenty yards onto the trestle. He saw Eddie peering over the side at the water far below.

Juan stopped next to him and smiled. "Aren't you glad we didn't have to go to Plan D?"

Eddie nodded and grinned back at him. "I think a nice hike down the slope is going to be much more relaxing than jumping from a moving train."

 **THAILAND**

"What are you doing?" Udom demanded.

Trying to keep my hands from shaking, Beth Anders thought about saying as she hunched over the painting with armed men surrounding her. Instead, she said, "I'm checking the edges of the Manet."

"Why?" asked Tagaan, who she'd learned was Filipino. He was holding the bronze eagle finial, which was apparently his. She tried to stay far away from him since he smelled of rancid garlic.

"The paintings stolen from the Gardner were cut out of their frames, which are still hanging in the museum. High-quality scans were made of the remaining canvas borders so that they could be matched up with the paintings to verify that they were the originals. It's as unique as a fingerprint. I have a contact at the Gardner who gave me a copy of the scans." She held up her phone and showed them the image. The magnified edge was clearly visible. "Although the painting itself could be forged, it would be virtually impossible to duplicate the color pattern and weave of the sliced canvas edges."

After she examined all four sides of the painting in various spots, she had no doubt the painting was the one that had been stolen. In any other scenario, she would be shaking from excitement at holding such a rare and valuable piece of lost art instead of trembling with fear.

She must have gone on too long because after a few more minutes Udom growled, "That's enough time. Tell us your conclusions."

She stood up and looked at Raven, who nodded almost imperceptibly for her to go ahead. Udom looked at her expectantly, while Tagaan seemed to have no concerns about what she'd say.

"After carefully inspecting the painting, I must conclude that it's the original."

"You are certain?" Udom asked.

"No doubt." She showed him when the scans matched up with the painting's edges. "See? They line up exactly. This is definitely *Chez Tortoni* by Édouard Manet."

At his instruction, Udom's men lowered their guns, and Beth had to prop herself on the desk to keep from keeling over in relief. He handed her a wad of hundred-dollar bills, which she put in her purse without counting.

"As we agreed, five thousand dollars," Udom said. "We may ask you to perform this service again in the future, so I expect you to keep quiet about this."

Tagaan stepped forward. "What is your estimate of its value?"

"If it came on the open market, it would fetch anywhere from fifteen to twenty-five million U.S. dollars at auction."

"We can't use a range," Udom said. "We need a number for future transactions."

"Then I would put the value at twenty million." She looked at Tagaan. "May I roll it back up for you? It's very delicate." As an art historian, she would have preferred the painting remain flat for transport, but she knew that would be asking too much.

He furrowed his eyebrows at her, then nodded and handed her the tube.

Beth tried not to wince at the damage she might be doing to the painting as she carefully rolled it on the desk. She slid it into the plastic tube and capped it. She hated to give back such a masterpiece to a dirtbag like Tagaan.

Udom reached out and said, "I'll take that."

Tagaan glared at him. "What are you doing? We agreed to this meeting so that we could set the value of the painting for future trades."

"You forget, Tagaan, that you owe us for the shipment that was lost in transit to Singapore. An entire shipload of product destroyed. This painting is our rightful payment."

Tagaan was fuming and seemed to forget he had spectators. "That wasn't our fault, you *hudas*. Our informant at Interpol told us they would be inspecting that freighter. You should have had it unloaded faster."

"We paid for delivery and the shipment didn't get delivered. Consider this a refund."

For a tense moment, every person in the room was frozen. Beth didn't know what to do with the tube, but handing it to either one of them seemed like suicide. In the end, she didn't have to decide.

Beth had never been in a car accident, but she now understood what people who'd gone through one meant when they said it appeared to happen in slow motion.

She perceived both groups of men drawing their weapons as if they were moving through molasses. She was aware of every acute detail, from the jackets being flung aside to get at pistol holsters to the shouts in two different languages.

She caught a glimpse of Raven slamming into her and flinging her to the floor as guns fired in all directions, chewing into wood, drywall, and bodies. Beth wanted to put her hands over her ears to shut out the deafening gun blasts and the shouting men, but her arm was against her side, pinning the tube to her body.

The door swung open, and the bouncer stationed outside ran in, gun blazing.

"Come on!" Raven shouted in her ear as she dragged Beth to her feet and pushed her into the hallway.

She involuntarily turned to witness the carnage and saw one of Udom's men pointing his pistol at her. Before he could fire, a bloody hole appeared in his forehead and he went down like a sack of cement.

It was only then that she registered the shot had come from behind her. She turned in astonishment to see that Raven had fired the pistol she had shown to Beth when she slipped it into her rear waistband back at the hotel room.

"Move!" Raven yelled and yanked the door closed behind her as they ran into the hall. Shots poured through the door, but they tore harmlessly into the wall.

As they scrambled downstairs, the huge bouncer at the front door was coming up, his gun drawn.

"Oh, my God!" Raven cried out to him, sounding hysterical. "They're killing each other up there!"

That spurred the bouncer to run faster. He tore right by them without giving them another glance.

When they reached the ground floor, Beth heard the door above slam open and more gunshots in the hall. There was a huge thump, which sounded like the bouncer collapsing. It was followed by heavy footsteps heading their way.

"Outside!" Raven shouted and took Beth by the arm.

They sprinted for the exit. As the evening approached, the street scene had gotten livelier and more crowded. As they ran onto the road, Beth crashed into a woman, who went sprawling and cursed at her in Thai.

"Sorry!" Beth yelled instinctively before Raven pulled her away.

As they rounded the corner, screaming erupted behind them, probably from the emergence of menacing killers from the club brandishing pistols.

"We're not going to make it to the car," Raven said. She wasn't even breathing hard, while Beth's lungs ached from the adrenaline, shock, and exertion.

"What do we do?"

Raven steered her over to an idling motorcycle, whose owner was buying some food from a street vendor. She threw her leg over the seat and shouted, "Get on!"

Beth shoved the tube through her purse strap, hopped on behind Raven, and grabbed her waist.

Raven revved the throttle and laid down a skid mark as they accelerated away, leaving the owner shouting as he ran after them with a skewer of pork in his hand. Beth had a death grip, as she hung on.

She turned to see Tagaan sprinting toward them at full speed. It was obvious he wasn't going to catch them, so he stopped abruptly and raised his pistol. Beth ducked as they swung around a corner. Two bullets ricocheted off a wall, and then Tagaan was out of sight.

Raven took three more quick turns and merged with traffic on a busy boulevard. They were now one of a hundred motorcycles cruising down the road.

"Nice work back there," Raven said over her shoulder. "For a civilian, that is. I'm impressed you didn't panic."

"I didn't?" The vibration of the motorcycle must have masked her shaking.

"You have your passport with you, right?"

"Always," Beth replied. "Why?"

"Because we can't go back to the hotel. We need to get out of Thailand as soon as we can."

"That's okay. Everything in my room is replaceable. But we'll have to figure out what to do about the painting."

"You want to turn that over to Interpol now? We just heard Tagaan say they had a mole."

Raven had a point. If his gang still had the other Gardner paintings, a report to Interpol might make them too hot to handle. They could all be destroyed to wipe out the evidence.

There was still the microtransmitter Beth had attached to the finial. "Tagaan was holding the bronze eagle when we left. We can track it."

"If they really have an informant at Interpol, they'll know as soon as we start following it and deactivate the transmitter."

"That's why we're not going to Interpol," Beth said.

"Then how are we going to recover the other paintings? We can't do it on our own."

"The guy who gave me the transmitter can help us. I consult with him on art that he acquires for his firm. His name is Juan Cabrillo."

 **THE PHILIPPINES**

In his spartan private quarters, Salvador Locsin wolfed down a huge traditional Filipino breakfast as if he were an athlete training for the Olympics. Heaping plates of corned beef, garlic-fried rice, salted milkfish, and chocolate rice pudding took up nearly the entire teak table. In the week since he was shot by his own men escaping from the prison transport, every one of his meals was a feast. It was the fuel his body needed to recover from his bullet wounds, injuries that would normally have confined someone to a hospital for weeks. Not only did Locsin feel better than ever, his scars were barely visible and would be completely gone in a day or two.

Locsin had grown up the son of a local politician and a teacher. As avowed socialists, his parents had been at the forefront of the island's agitation for better services for the people. Then an attempt by the police to break up a socialist rally went bad.

The police claimed they were there to arrest radical elements of the communist insurgency when someone in the crowd started firing. The police fired back, and Locsin's parents were supposedly caught in the cross fire and killed. The subsequent investigation concluded that the radicals were at fault, but Locsin knew better. Witnesses told Locsin that his parents were deliberately shot by the police, but the final official report covered it up.

Locsin could see that there'd be no justice for his parents, so he didn't return to his university. Fighting corruption by working through a rigged system was obviously a useless gesture. Joining the communist insurgency was his best chance to take down a government designed for the benefit of the rich and then rebuild it from scratch.

As he demonstrated his tactical abilities for inflicting maximum damage on government targets, he quickly gained a following in the insurgency. His methods became increasingly brutal because he adhered to Machiavelli's maxim *The ends justify the means*. When financial support from the communist governments of China and North Korea wasn't enough to fund his rebellion, he turned to smuggling drugs. The main consumers of his heroin and methamphetamine products were the rich capitalist countries, and he took satisfaction in knowing that the narcotic epidemic helped weaken those supposedly robust economies.

But, until now, nothing he had accomplished was revolutionary enough to make a real difference. It was another drug that would soon let him transform the world.

As he shoveled another spoonful of pudding into his mouth, Locsin glanced down at the round white pill sitting in a small dish next to his plate. It was etched with the symbol of a swirling cyclone and symbolized the wholesale destruction he was about to unleash.

Nikho Tagaan, a trusted comrade who had been with Locsin since the beginning, opened the door to his quarters and brought in a fresh pot of coffee. He poured mugs for both of them and took a seat on the opposite side of the table.

"Any progress from our laboratory on Luzon?" Locsin said, between bites of pudding.

"Nothing yet. Dr. Ocampo hasn't been able to isolate the formula and he doesn't have an estimate for when he will."

"Does he understand the urgency of the situation?"

"I made that very clear when I was there yesterday. He's as motivated as we are, but he says that without the original list of the drug's components, it's virtually impossible to re-create."

Locsin picked up the white pill and twirled it between his fingers like a worry bead.

"Why is this so hard to duplicate?"

Tagaan slurped his coffee and shrugged. "I don't understand the chemistry. Ocampo says he doesn't know what plant makes up the key ingredient and he can't produce a replacement for it. It would be like trying to make cocaine without coca leaves or heroin without opium poppies."

"What about a synthetic substitute?"

"If that was even possible, he said it would take years of research to create."

Locsin's uncontrollable rage that emerged on an ever more frequent basis threatened to bubble to the surface, and it took all his will to suppress it.

"We don't have years," he growled, popping the tablet in his mouth and washing it down with the coffee. He knew it would take several minutes for the drug to take effect, but a rush of invincibility surged through him. He'd been smart enough to sew an emergency supply of pills into the waistband of his pants, which was why he'd still been able to take his daily dose while in police custody.

When several of his men had been in retreat from police forces through the jungle, they had stumbled upon a cache of twenty thousand pills. The tablets had been stored in a secret underground bunker built by the Japanese in the middle of Negros Island during World War II, but the base must have been abandoned during the American assault. The entire supply of pills had been vacuum-sealed and stored in a steel drum with no papers to explain the contents. A code name was stenciled on the drum: *Typhoon.*

There were many guesses as to the drug's purpose. Was it a narcotic? A stimulant? The Japanese were notorious for providing their kamikaze pilots with crystal meth. Or perhaps it was a poison for their soldiers to commit suicide with instead of surrendering. An antidote? An antibiotic? There was no way to tell.

Locsin could have sent the pills for analysis to a scientist sympathetic to their cause, but that would have taken too long. He used a more expedient method: he made one of his government prisoners take the pill.

It didn't take long to observe the effects on the obese bureaucrat, an Interior Ministry functionary named Stanley Alonzo. Every day, Alonzo's physical transformation was noticeable. He complained of constant hunger, and each time he was fed, his muscles grew rapidly and he shed fat as if he were exercising ten hours day. Torturing him for information became less fruitful as he fiercely resisted the beatings, seemingly oblivious to the pain being inflicted. Bruises healed in hours instead of days. Then when the drug was withheld, Alonzo's muscles withered, and torture again became intolerable. His drug doses were restored, and within another week, his metamorphosis was so total and dependent on Typhoon that Locsin thought he could be effectively controlled and become an agent for their side. Alonzo was sent back to his post to spy for the insurgency.

In his research, Locsin discovered that steroids had been developed by the Germans in the lead-up to World War II to treat dysfunctional growth syndromes. The scientists even received the 1939 Nobel Prize for their work. Then, during the war, anabolic steroids were used to help malnourished German soldiers gain muscle mass long before they were distributed to athletes in the Soviet Union and East Germany so they could dominate the Olympics.

But Typhoon did more than improve strength and stamina far beyond anything possible with anabolic steroids. The Japanese had apparently developed a drug that enabled the user to tolerate an inhuman level of pain, rapidly healed wounds normally considered fatal, and allowed users to recover from grievous injuries within days instead of weeks or months. Typhoon was like steroids on steroids. Users weren't invincible—broken bones and bullet holes didn't mend themselves in seconds like they did for superheroes in movies—but quick blood clotting and accelerated tissue regeneration meant that almost nothing less than a headshot or a knife to the heart would be lethal. All the user needed was time and food to fuel the repair process.

It didn't take long for Locsin and his revolutionary comrades to see the profound benefits of Typhoon, so they started taking the drug themselves. They'd enjoyed the effects for the past six months, and his victories over the Filipino government had grown exponentially. Now he had the most fearsome soldiers in the world.

The problem was that their supply was swiftly dwindling. Within two months, it would be exhausted.

"I'm going to the lab tomorrow," he said to Tagaan. "I want Ocampo to explain to my face why he can't figure out the type of plant we need to find." He had a project under way to get more Typhoon, but Ocampo and the lab were his backup.

"Yes, comrade. I'll prepare your helicopter." Tagaan nodded at the aluminum briefcase holding the eagle finial from the Gardner Museum. "The Manet we lost in Thailand has not surfaced yet. What should we do about the other artwork?"

Locsin felt his fury building anew at the setback, but he tamped it down. He'd been counting on Udom to be his conduit to Southeast

Asia for Typhoon, but Tagaan had wiped out his men after the deal went sour. Not only would he have to build a new network in Thailand, he'd have to delay using the paintings as collateral. For now, they would have to go back to transporting money the old-fashioned way, in five-hundred-euro notes and hundred-dollar bills.

"We'll keep the rest of the paintings for the future," Locsin said. "Once production ramps up, we'll be dealing in huge sums of money, and we'll need them for our transactions. Any word about Beth Anders?" She was the only loose thread tying his men to the paintings.

Tagaan shook his head. "She disappeared, along with her companion. Our informant at Interpol says they haven't contacted the authorities." The spy within Interpol was another beneficiary of Typhoon.

"Did you find out who the other woman is?" Locsin asked.

"Our contact is working on that, but he hasn't been able to identify her."

"If you find them, try to get the painting back, although that's not our highest priority."

Tagaan nodded, but the white knuckles on his fist showed that he was on the brink of crushing his mug at the thought of his failure, another effect of the Typhoon. Like testosterone, it amplified aggressiveness in users.

"I will kill them both," Tagaan said. Locsin didn't share his desire to avenge being embarrassed for letting the two women escape. Their deaths were simply necessities.

Finally sated, Locsin left the empty plates and exited his quarters with Tagaan. They emerged into the center of a soaring cavern fifty stories high. It was one of the largest caves in the world but remained unknown to the outside world. Like the massive caverns discovered in Vietnam only a few years ago, this cave system was hidden in the jungle, and only a select group of his comrades knew the location. All others brought to it were blindfolded before making the journey.

Men carrying out their duties shuttled across the main square centrally located among the buildings that had been constructed to house the soldiers and their equipment. Power was provided by large diesel generators lowered through a massive sinkhole that allowed sunlight to illuminate the interior. It also made it possible for the insurgency's helicopters to descend directly into the cavern. The only other access point was a truck-sized opening in the hillside where the original discovery of the cave had been made by a loyal communist. Now it was well concealed.

As he and Tagaan made their way toward the armory, Locsin stopped in the middle of the square where a huge stalagmite had formed. Steel rings had been drilled into the limestone, and a limp man was shackled to them.

The man looked up at Locsin with false hope. It was Stanley Alonzo. The bureaucrat had grown a conscience and betrayed Locsin to the police.

Just a week ago, Alonzo had looked like a bodybuilder, the epitome of health. Now he was little more than skin and bones.

Alonzo had made the mistake of thinking that when his supply of Typhoon ran out, he would simply revert to his previous tubby form. But as with many other drugs, Typhoon's addictive properties meant that the lows were even worse than the highs. A week after taking the first pill, the user was addicted for life. Locsin had found that out when one of his men was arrested and couldn't get his supply of Typhoon in jail. Racked by the agony and severe muscle deterioration caused by withdrawal, he died within a week. The perplexed medical examiner, noting that the man's body literally consumed itself, chalked his death up to a non-contagious autoimmune disease. Locsin himself had avoided a similar fate when his men made the bold rescue from the prison ship.

He leaned down to Alonzo. "I told you that traitors would be dealt with severely. I lost six men in my prison escape because of you."

Alonzo grabbed his pant leg. "Please," he rasped, tears streaming down his cheeks. "I'm begging you. I need Typhoon. Just one pill. I'll do anything you want."

Locsin yanked his leg away. "You're already doing it."

As he and Tagaan walked away from Alonzo's pitiful cries, Locsin vowed that he would not go out that way if they couldn't regenerate their supply of Typhoon. He'd rather eat a bullet.

 GUAM

With the NSA supercomputer removed from the *Oregon* and loaded back onto the C-5 for its return trip to Fort Meade, Juan finally had time to meet with Beth Anders and Raven Malloy. He chose one of his favorite bars on the island, a dim little pub called Abandon Ship. Most of the evening's patrons were American sailors and airmen from the military bases that dominated the U.S. territory's economy. A live band pounded out covers of classic rock songs by Lynyrd Skynyrd and The Eagles, so their conversation would stay private.

As they waited for the two women to arrive, Max Hanley dug into a plate of nachos while Juan nursed a tumbler of scotch.

"Do *not* tell Doc Huxley that I am eating this," Max said as he crammed a chip laden with guacamole and cheese into his mouth. He chased it with a bottle of Budweiser. "You wouldn't believe how few calories I'm allowed to have on the diet she put me on. She's even got Chef in on it. This is the only chance I've had for some real food in two weeks."

"I don't think Julia will believe the bar sells wheatgrass smoothies and low-salt quinoa."

"If she asks, tell her I had a glass of club soda and some carrot sticks."

"It's the scale you better be worried about tattling, not me."

Max patted his stomach, which strained against his belt. "Hey, this isn't bad for a guy my age. I'd like to see what *you* look like in another thirty years." Max may have put on ten or fifteen pounds since his days in the Navy and wasn't going to qualify for a 5K run anytime soon, but he could still handle himself in a fight and was reasonably fit for a guy in his sixties. Though Hux hounded Max about his nutrition, Juan figured his friend deserved a pipe and a bowl of ice cream when he felt like it.

"Julia just wants to make sure you're around when you're eighty," Juan said.

Max snorted. "Maybe my ex is paying her off, so she can keep those alimony payments coming."

On several occasions, Mark Murphy had accused Max and Juan of bantering like an old married couple. The two of them had been together since the Corporation was formed, even before the *Oregon* was purchased and refitted to its current state. Juan not only counted on his number two to keep the company and ship running smoothly but also confided in him more than anyone else.

Both of them were single and considered the *Oregon* their permanent home, and they shared an easy friendship because of it. Most of the crew knew about Max's ex-wife, primarily because of his frequent comments about her, but few besides Max had heard about how Juan had become a widower, that his alcoholic wife had died in a single-car crash while intoxicated, despite his repeated attempts to get her help. The guilt for not being able to save her from herself ached more than the phantom pain where his right leg ended.

The stinging memory brought to mind the thought of another more recent loss to the *Oregon* family.

"Mike Trono sure would have enjoyed that operation in Vietnam, don't you think?"

Max nodded with a melancholy smile at the mention of the shore operations gundog and former Air Force pararescue jumper who'd died on a mission not long ago. "He was always a sucker for the adrenaline rush. I miss the guy."

"Me too."

They were both quiet for a moment as they remembered their lost crewmate and friend.

"I know it's tough to move on," Max said, "but have you thought any more about bringing in a new crew member? I can send out feelers to the special forces community whenever we're ready."

Juan took another sip of his scotch. He always hated the process of replacing a lost crew member, but he supposed it was time.

"Sure," he sighed. "Why don't you get started. And I'll see if there are any candidates coming out of the CIA."

The bar door opened, and Beth's scarlet hair glowed from the setting sun behind it. She spotted Juan immediately and came over to the table, giving Juan and Max hugs before she took a seat.

"Your friend decided not to come?" Juan asked with a wink at Max.

Beth gave them an embarrassed grin. "Ever since our experience in Thailand, she's been leery of bars. I told her you guys were beyond reproach, but she thought it was better to get here early and scope out the situation."

"Oh, I know," Juan said, and turned to look at a woman sitting with a sailor at the end of the bar. She wore her hair pulled up underneath a USS *Nimitz* baseball cap and was nodding along to the band's music as she flirted with him. "You can ask her to come over now."

Beth gaped at him, then nodded at Raven to join them. The disappointed sailor tried to talk her out of leaving, but her flirtatiousness was suddenly gone and she was all business, gently but firmly telling him the fun was over.

"How did you know?" Beth asked as Raven walked toward them.

"Like you, we do our research."

Raven sat down and shook their hands with a strong grip. "Raven Malloy."

"I'm Juan Cabrillo, and this hale and hearty fellow is Max Hanley."

"Dig in, if you're hungry," Max said, pointing at the plate of nachos that was three-quarters gone. They declined but ordered beers from the waitress.

"You were very good," Juan said to Raven. "I almost overlooked you because I thought you were with that guy."

"So did he." She lifted her hat and her long black hair spilled out. "Then you've seen my photo?"

Juan nodded. "You have impressive credentials. Top ten percent in your class at West Point where you double-majored in psychology and Middle Eastern studies. Fluent in Farsi and Arabic. Earned a Bronze Star and a Purple Heart in Afghanistan as a military investigator before leaving the Army with an honorable discharge as captain. No wonder Beth trusts you as her bodyguard."

Raven's expression didn't change during the recitation of her accomplishments. "Are you trying to see how I'll react or are you just showing off?"

Juan smiled. "Maybe a little bit of both."

"Then let me return the favor. Information about you was tougher to get hold of, but I have my own resources. Full name Juan Rodríguez Cabrillo. Grew up in Orange County, California, where you spent a good amount of your time surfing. Double-majored in political science and mechanical engineering at Caltech. Fluent in

Arabic, Spanish, and Russian. Recruited out of your college ROTC program to become a foreign operative with the CIA, though I could find no record of postings or missions. Left to form the Corporation, which provides a variety of services ranging from protective details for Emirate sheiks to rescues of kidnapped corporate executives and everything in between. Spent six weeks in the hospital after losing a leg in some unknown op. For what it's worth, you conceal it well. I couldn't detect a limp when you walked in."

"It's amazing what they can do with bionic limbs these days." Although there were many gaps in Raven's information, it was all accurate. "I'm impressed. That information's hard to come by. You must have some good connections."

Raven shrugged like it was no big deal. "When you're on the run from murderous drug dealers, it's good to know who you're meeting with."

"And since you're here, I'm guessing we passed the test. So why don't you tell us how we can help."

Beth told them the whole story, from being hired to authenticate the painting to the gunfight at the Bangkok nightclub.

"Where's the Manet now?" Juan asked.

"In a safe-deposit box in a Bangkok bank," Beth replied. "I've given instructions to my attorney to turn the contents over to the Gardner Museum if I die or go missing for more than a month."

"We didn't trust handing it over to Interpol," Raven said. "Not after Tagaan said they had someone on the inside."

"And trying to smuggle it out of the country would've been risky."

"So you want us to help you find the rest of the paintings?" Max said. "Since I'm head of the Corporation's finances, I have to ask. What's the reward?"

"Five million dollars, split fifty-fifty between you and us."

"A tidy sum," Juan said.

"All together, the paintings are worth a hundred times that. Not to mention their value to the art world in general. The Vermeer is one of only thirty-four known works of his, and *The Storm on the Sea of Galilee* by Rembrandt is a masterpiece of the Dutch Golden Age. They truly are priceless."

Beth had never been aboard the *Oregon*, but Juan had gotten to know her during their many consultations on artwork purchases. He knew full well that the money was only part of what drove her and saw in her a passion for recovering stolen art that mirrored his own dedication to his work. She really cared about the artwork itself and would be heartbroken if the paintings remained lost to the world.

"I hope the tracker we gave you worked as intended," Juan said.

"Yes, thanks to you we actually have something to go on." She pulled an electronic tablet from her purse and pulled up a map of Southeast Asia. Three red dots were highlighted: one in Bangkok, one in Manila, and a third farther up the island of Luzon in the Philippines.

Juan pointed at the dots. "Those are the only transmissions you received?"

Beth nodded. "We figured they were carrying it in a shielded case, but they had to open it at the airport security lines in Bangkok and Manila."

"What's at the third location?" Max asked.

"We don't know," Raven said, zooming in on a satellite view of that location, showing a set of low-slung buildings in the middle of the jungle. "The ownership of those buildings is routed through a holding corporation, and I couldn't find any information about what goes on there."

"Either the finial is still there," Beth said, "or they've packed it back up and haven't opened the case again in a place where the signal is readable."

"Then it looks like this is a place we need to check out," Juan said.

"You're taking the job?"

"We don't have a mission in the works right now, and we're always happy to help a friend in need."

"A potential two-and-a-half-million-dollar payday doesn't hurt, either," Max added.

"Give us a couple of days to get our ship from here to Manila," Juan said. "We'll meet you at the port there."

He could see the gears working in Raven's head.

"Just two days?" she said, confused. "The distance between here and Manila is sixteen hundred miles. Don't you mean four days?"

He shared an amused glance with Max.

"You may be well connected," Juan said with a sly grin, "but apparently you haven't heard about the *Oregon*."

 **THE UNITED STATES**

Jet engines screamed in the distance as the two A-10 Warthog pilots circled their target above Dugway Proving Ground eighty miles west of Salt Lake City. On the main screen inside the mobile command post, Greg Polten watched twelve pigs shuffle around in a pen five miles away, spooked by the din made by the lurking attack planes. Despite the air-conditioning unit pumping out a chilling draft, he continually wiped his sweaty palms on his pants. The future of his career rode on the success of this test. If his serum worked, the pigs would remain spooked but healthy. If it didn't, the animals would be dead in minutes.

As large as the state of Rhode Island, Dugway was the main testing site for American chemical and biological defensive systems. Like most of the employees at the top secret facility, Polten was a civilian contractor instead of a military service member. But today, in addition to Polten's small staff, the command post was filled with Army officers observing the classified test.

Syrian chemical weapons were a major threat to U.S. soldiers fighting in the Middle East against ISIS and other terrorist organizations. Donning bulky chemical protective suits significantly hampered soldiers' fighting ability, so efforts had been made in recent years to develop a serum that would ward off the effects of chemical weapons like sarin and VX nerve gas if soldiers were caught in the field without their gear.

A trim man in his forties, with graying hair at his temples and frameless glasses perched on his nose, Polten had staked his career on developing the Panaxim serum, but years of experiments and tens of millions of tax dollars had yielded nothing usable. His classified program was in danger of being cancelled if he didn't produce results soon, and this demo was his best chance to show what the serum could do. Lab tests had shown some promise, but the field trial was the ultimate chance to show whether soldiers in battle would be protected.

The air outside was calm, which would not only concentrate the effects of the gas near the pigpen but would also mean that the gas would dissipate before it could reach the edge of the range. In 1968, a test of VX nerve gas had released a cloud much larger than anticipated on a windy day and it had drifted over huge flocks of sheep on surrounding ranches. The Army never admitted liability but paid the ranchers for the loss of more than six thousand sheep. Since then, airburst releases of chemical weapons at Dugway had been carefully controlled and monitored.

General Amos Jefferson, who had been conferring with his aide, startled Polten when his gruff voice boomed out, "Mr. Polten, how long until we see the effects of the gas on the pigs?"

Jefferson, a stout veteran of both the Iraq and Afghanistan wars, was in charge of Polten's funding. If he wasn't satisfied with the results of the test, the money would dry up. Polten hated the fact that he had to suck up to the military. He thought it should be the other way around.

"General," he said, crossing his arms to mask his nervousness, "you shouldn't see any effects of the gas. That's the point of this test."

Jefferson turned and narrowed his eyes, as if that was supposed to intimidate Polten. "I know that, Mr. Polten. That's why you've been draining huge amounts of money out of my budget for years now. My soldiers are depending on your success. So let me rephrase the question. When will we know if this Panaxim serum works?"

Polten returned the stare with equal force. "A single pig, marked by a large red A on its side, will be our control. Since it won't be injected with the serum, it should die within two minutes of exposure. If the other pigs haven't shown any effects by that time, we can assume they'll be fine."

"How are you injecting the Panaxim?" the general asked as he peered at the screen. "I don't see anyone out there."

Polten rolled his eyes. Obviously, Jefferson hadn't read his briefing kit thoroughly.

"If you look closely, you can see that each pig is wearing a collar. When the gas cloud reaches them, I will activate a remote injector embedded in the collar, which will deliver a dose of the serum. It's similar to the auto-injectors we supply to soldiers in the field."

"Will they show any effects at all? If this doesn't work better than atropine, it won't be any good to us."

So the general had done at least some of the homework. Atropine was the most effective antidote for nerve gas exposure on the battlefield. It prevented death and minimized the degradation of essential bodily functions, but it didn't counteract the loss of muscle control brought on by the chemical weapon, which could leave the soldiers vulnerable to attack for a significant length of time.

"Of course, we'll analyze the pigs by necropsy after exposure to determine the full effects," Polten said, "but we shouldn't see any overt symptoms on camera."

A Humvee approached from the direction of the target and pulled up next to the command post. Charles Davis, Polten's chief chemist on the project, jumped out of the driver's seat and ran inside. A heavyset, balding man with a messy beard, Davis was panting as he launched himself through the door.

"Everything is set," he said and plopped himself into a chair. "I double-checked all the injectors on the pigs and they're ready to go." Davis tapped on his laptop keyboard, and Polten could see that the status of each injector had a nominal reading. With one press of a button, the Panaxim would be injected into all eleven pigs simultaneously.

Polten looked at Jefferson. "General, you can tell the pilots to begin their attack run."

The general nodded to his aide, who told the communications officer to radio the pilots. "Tango One and Two, this is Sierra Base. You have a green light. Cleared to start the attack sequence."

"Acknowledged, Sierra Base. Tango One and Two beginning our run."

Polten picked up a pair of binoculars and focused them on the Warthogs wheeling over the mountains. They plunged down to a thousand feet and rocketed over the desert floor. When they were within a thousand yards of the pigpen, the jets released two bombs each. Then the pilots yanked their sticks up, and the A-10s shot skyward.

The bombs detonated on the ground without the usual fireball, which would have consumed the gas encased inside the shells. Instead, they blew apart in a cloud of smoke and mist that immediately began drifting toward the pigs, now climbing over each other in a frenzy because of the explosions.

The chemical warheads had been seeded with red powder so that the cloud could be tracked more easily. The scarlet mist lazily drifted toward the pen. When it reached the first pig, Polten instructed Davis to activate the injectors.

Davis tapped a key. "Injectors firing." After a pause, he said, "All eleven injections have succeeded."

Now all they could do was wait. Polten felt a bead of perspiration trickle down his brow as he watched the screen while keeping an eye on the clock. He had Davis turn up the audio feed, and the squeals of the pigs filled the room.

The pig marked with the A collapsed within seconds. It shuddered on the ground before going still. None of the other pigs exhibited any signs of distress beyond their fright from the jets and bombs. They shuffled around the pen as they normally did, futilely rooting in the dirt for food.

The timer seemed to move agonizingly slow. When it reached two minutes, Polten exchanged a triumphant glance with Davis. He looked at General Jefferson, who nodded at the screen in appreciation before turning to Polten.

"Looks like you've made some real progress here, Mr. Polten. I suppose the next step is deploying Panaxim in the field. When can you—"

He was interrupted by a high-pitched squeal from one of the pigs. They all looked at the monitor, and Polten froze in horror when he saw what was happening.

One of the pigs was lurching around, trying to stay on its feet. It was clearly having trouble breathing. It keeled over and slumped in the dirt. Soon, two more pigs were staggering, then all of them were. It didn't take long after that. Within a minute, nothing but silence from the speakers.

The general let out a heavy sigh and shook his head. "It seems your timing was a little off."

Polten tried to salvage the situation. "General, we just need to adjust the dosage. I'm sure with a few more tests we can—"

"Mr. Polten, I told you to give me your best effort on *this* test."

Polten, wrung out, couldn't restrain his annoyance. "That's not how science works, General. You don't always get it right the first time."

"Then when are you going to get it right? Five more years and another truckload of funding?"

"If that's what it takes."

"Sorry, Mr. Polten," Jefferson said, putting on his hat. "I'm going to recommend that we stop throwing money away on this project. We've got other more promising avenues to investigate."

"Nothing is more promising than this! I've seen the reports from your other projects and they're no closer than we are to developing an effective serum."

"And you're no closer than they are, even though your project has cost three times as much . . . Gentlemen."

With that, he headed out with his retinue of officers, leaving Polten and Davis alone with the rest of the development team. They all looked at Polten in pity mixed with fear about their own jobs.

"I'll talk to him," he muttered. "Get out to the hazmat truck and collect the pigs for dissection."

They shuffled outside, but Davis didn't follow them.

"What?" Polten said to him. "I don't need a pep talk."

"How much do we have left in our budget?" Davis asked.

"Enough to keep the lights on for a few more months. Why?"

"And you have wide latitude for how to use it, right?"

"It's my budget. I can use it however I see fit. What are you getting at?"

"I've got something to show you."

Davis pulled up a video on his laptop. "This was shot a week ago in Bangkok, Thailand. It came from a police report about a drug deal gone wrong. Just found it this morning, so this is the first chance I've had to show it to you."

He started the video, and it showed a room littered with bloody bodies. It was clear they'd been in some kind of gunfight, with bullet holes everywhere. Police officers and crime scene investigators picked their way over the corpses as they collected evidence.

"These are members of two drug gangs, one from Thailand and one from the Philippines. It seems the Filipinos came out of it better since most of the bodies are Thai."

Polten could feel his blood boiling. "We've just had a major setback, possibly losing our jobs because of it, and you're showing me the aftermath of a battle between rival drug gangs? What does this have to do with anything?"

"Remember when we were doing our literature review of World War Two drugs in the classified archives?"

Polten shrugged. "And?"

"We noticed one called Typhoon, a relative of steroids that we thought might help us in our work."

"Yes, I remember that one. Typhoon would be revolutionary if it did everything it was reported to do, which is frankly hard to believe. But we didn't have a formula or any idea how it was made. All we had was a photo of a pill, white with a typhoon cyclone symbol on it. Everything else about it was lost in the war."

"Maybe," Davis replied with a sly grin. "You know, I have a constant search going on the Internet for any mentions of unidentified drugs just to make sure we don't miss anything that might be useful. Well, I think we've found something useful."

He fast-forwarded the video to the point where one of the investigators was emptying the pockets of a victim.

"That's one of the Filipinos," Davis said.

The investigator stood up while looking at something in the palm of his hand. Someone asked him a question and he shook his head. He held a white pill up to the camera, and Davis paused the image.

The pill had the same symbol as the tablet of Typhoon they'd seen in the archives.

Polten looked at Davis in amazement. "Is it the same?"

Davis nodded. "Exactly the same. I checked. Someone found a cache of Typhoon pills somewhere."

"Still intact after seventy years?"

"If they were vacuum-sealed, there's no reason they wouldn't be just as potent today as they were back then."

Polten suddenly saw the opportunity to do something even bigger than Panaxim. If he was able to develop a contemporary analog of Typhoon, he could write his ticket in the chemical warfare community.

"We need to do this very quietly," Polten said.

"I know. That's why I waited until we were alone. And I expect to be a full partner in this."

Polten smiled, though he had no intention of sharing the limelight once the project was a success. "Of course, I couldn't do it without you. But first we need to know where these drug dealers got their supply."

"I already dug into the Thai report. Since they don't know what it is, the pill is locked up tight until they can get some answers. But the police didn't capture any of the Filipinos who survived."

"Then we need to send someone in to get the answers. Do the police know who they are?"

"Based on the identity of one of the men, they think it's a radical member of a communist insurgency based in the Philippines."

"Communists? They're still around?"

"Apparently. With the rise of radical jihadists in the southern part of the country, they've been out of the limelight for a few years, but it seems like they're starting to make a comeback."

"That's the Philippines's problem. All we need is someone to tell us where they got the Typhoon. And I know just the man. Gerhard Brekker, a South African who owns a small private military contracting firm. He's done some work for us before, off the books, and he isn't afraid to get his hands dirty if the price is right. Brekker's told me that he can have contractors anywhere in the world within twenty-four hours."

"If General Jefferson finds out were doing this, he'll shut us down immediately," Davis said.

"Then we won't tell him," Polten replied. But it was actually worse than that. Polten wasn't supposed to have access to the classified files where he'd found out about Typhoon. Those files were supposed to be dead and buried. If the general discovered the Pandora's box the two chemists were opening, Polten wouldn't be surprised if both of them ended up in prison.

 **THE PHILIPPINES**

Beth wrinkled her nose in disgust at the rickety ship tied up at the Manila dock where she and Raven had been told to meet Juan. The bright morning sun didn't do the vessel any favors, throwing a harsh light on the rust spots, mismatched green paint, and cracks in the hull. It looked like it was in danger of sinking right there in the harbor.

"Are you sure this is the place?" she asked Raven, who regarded the ship with nothing more than an arched eyebrow.

"That's what the text message said," Raven replied.

"But this ship is called the *Norego*." Beth pointed at the name painted in black on the fantail. The jackstaff flew a flag she didn't recognize, and it certainly wasn't American. "Maybe the *Oregon* couldn't make it here so fast from Guam after all."

Raven frowned at the corroded hulk. "Maybe not."

She and Raven had holed up in a Manila hotel for the last two days, and Beth had been bored out of her mind waiting for a chance to retrieve the stolen Gardner paintings. Raven, on the other hand, had spent her time going out into the city to acquire new equipment that she thought they'd need, including a pistol and knife, neither of which she could have gotten through customs.

Beth was about to suggest that they text back to make sure they'd understood the message correctly when a uniformed Filipino man appeared at the top of the gangway accompanied by a weather-beaten old man in dirty khakis and a sweat-stained denim shirt unbuttoned down to his round belly.

The Filipino waved his hand like he was hastily refusing some kind of offer and hustled down the wobbly gangway. As he passed them, his face was ashen, and he mopped his brow with a handkerchief. He looked as if he'd lose his breakfast at any moment.

The old man lurched down the plank as if he'd drunk his breakfast. He stopped at the bottom and leaned against the railing.

"What do you want?" he rasped in a voice as rough as sandpaper. Deep lines etched his leathery face like a geological formation around his bulbous nose. His head was hairless except for gray muttonchop sideburns and bushy eyebrows that could have served as birds' nests.

"We're looking for Juan Cabrillo," Beth said.

He scowled at them. "If you want a burrito, go find a restaurant. I'm a captain, not a cook."

Raven choked down a laugh.

Beth gave him her best smile and raised her voice so he could hear her. "Sir, we're supposed to meet a man named Juan Cabrillo here."

"All right, all right. You don't need to shout. So you're Beth Anders and Raven Malloy?"

"That's right."

He pursed his lips as if he was considering whether they were legit, then nodded. "I'm Herb Munson. Juan's this way. Come on."

He staggered up the gangway. Beth and Raven looked at each other and shrugged before going after him.

The deck was a mess, and they had to step over trash and broken chains as they made their way toward the superstructure. Munson weaved his way ahead of them, and Beth expected him to take a spill on the cluttered deck with every step.

She leaned over and whispered to Raven, "Do you think this is a good idea?"

"He knew who we are, so obviously we are expected."

"How could this guy be a part of Juan's organization? He looks old enough to have been a stowaway on Noah's ark."

Over his shoulder, Munson suddenly said, "Of course I know how to park. We're docked, aren't we?"

Beth looked in amazement from Munson to Raven. "How could he hear that?"

"I don't know. But something's not right here." Beth noticed that Raven's hand hovered near her holstered weapon.

Munson waved for them to enter the ship's interior, and once they were inside, Beth could understand why the Filipino had been so sick. A foul smell greeted them, and it only got worse as they entered a small office that reeked like an overflowing dumpster. The major source of the rancid odor seemed to be a connected bathroom. Before Munson closed the lavatory door, Beth got a glimpse of a level of filth that would give her nightmares.

A familiar voice behind them surprised Beth. "Hey there. Looks like you found us."

She whipped around to see Max Hanley in the doorway.

"Juan," he said, looking at the wizened captain, "we're unloading the Powered Investigator Ground now."

Beth turned and stared in astonishment at the man calling himself Munson. But when he replied, Juan's strong baritone came out.

"Good. Send Eddie up. I'll get changed while you ready the PIG."

"Do you have to call it that?" Max said.

"You designed it, so you got to pick the name. You should have realized what was going to happen."

"Acronyms. Everyone around here has to use acronyms." Max continued to grumble as he walked away.

"Sorry about deceiving you ladies," Juan said as he pulled off his bald cap and glued-on sideburns, "but I couldn't reveal myself out on the wharf where prying eyes might have seen me."

"Then this is the *Oregon*?" Raven asked matter-of-factly.

Juan grinned as he removed his prosthetic nose and fake belly. "You don't seem very surprised."

"*Norego. Oregon.* It adds up now. But that's a good disguise. I'm not fooled easily."

"I noticed. We do it to get in and out of ports without much attention. None of the harbormasters like to spend more time on board than they have to, and I get to remain incognito. Well, Beth, are you ready for a little road trip?"

Beth shut her mouth, which had been gaping open at Juan's transformation. "I'm just a bit confused right now. What's the PIG?"

"That's our transportation for today. Here's Eddie now. He'll show it to you while I get out of these brown contacts and change clothes."

A lean Chinese man appeared where Max had been. Juan introduced him as Eddie Seng, chief of shore operations.

"What does that mean?" Beth asked.

"I'm in charge of any excursions we take off the ship," Eddie said.

"But I'm coming along, too," Juan said. "I'll meet you down there."

As he ducked out of the office, Eddie said, "Why don't we get some fresh air."

"Yes, please," Beth said.

When they got outside, Beth couldn't believe how good the oily seawater of the dock area smelled. She inhaled in relief like she'd just been released from prison.

One of the ship's deck cranes was hauling a boxy-looking truck from the hold. With oversized tires and a stout cab on the front, it must have been formidable in its day, but now it looked as decrepit as the ship it had emerged from. The crane's motor whined in protest at the load, but the truck swung smoothly over the pier and settled onto the dock as lightly as a feather.

"We're going in that?" Beth said, pointing at the truck as they walked down the gangway. "Why don't we just rent an SUV?"

"The PIG may not look pretty, but I think you'll be comfortable." He noticed another Filipino man walking around the truck. "Just a moment. I need to take care of the inspector."

When the PIG was unlatched from the crane, Eddie opened the back doors, which, like the sides, featured the faded logo of an oil exploration company. The cargo area was full of metal drums. "Spare fuel," Beth heard Eddie say to the inspector, who nodded. He made a few notes on a clipboard, and Eddie signed it. Beth caught him slipping a few American hundred-dollar bills under the paper.

When the inspector left, Eddie said, "Sometimes we have to grease a few palms to avoid questions."

Beth nodded but said nothing. She'd done the same in a few seedy locales when she needed answers to awkward questions.

They stood by while Eddie made preparations in the PIG. A few minutes later, Juan strode down the gangway in a black T-shirt and light cargo pants.

"I like this version much better," Beth said.

"Me too," Juan said. "I'm done with Herb Munson for the day. How's it looking, Eddie?"

Eddie poked his head from the cab. "Everything checks out, Chairman. We're ready when you are."

"Then let's load up. Beth and Raven, I'll ride shotgun, if you don't mind."

Beth got in back with Raven and was happy to find that it had already been cooled down by a powerful air conditioner. Though the seats were torn and faded, the leather was surprisingly supple and the cushions provided good support.

When all the doors were closed, Eddie flipped a switch, and the ancient dashboard retracted and flipped around. It was replaced with a state-of-the-art computer display and high-tech switches.

Eddie engaged the powerful diesel and drove away from the *Oregon*. The ride was limousine smooth.

Juan turned in his seat. "The PIG's got a few more hidden features that might come in handy, since we don't know what we'll find up in the mountains. GPS says it's a four-hour drive. There are drinks and sandwiches in the cooler between you, if you want some."

Beth shook her head and laughed. "What hidden features? Am I sitting in an ejector seat? Does it have machine guns in the headlights?"

Juan gave her a mysterious smile. "No, not in the headlights."

He didn't say anything about the ejector seat.

MEL OCAMPO nervously watched Salvador Locsin's helicopter land inside the compound in remote central Luzon. He'd been stalling as long as he could to avoid this visit, but he could no longer disguise his lack of progress in replicating the Typhoon drug.

He pined for his days as a research scientist at a pharmaceutical conglomerate in Manila. It had been solid if unexciting work that paid well, but when this new job offer had come along—with three times the pay—he'd jumped at the chance. At the time, it seemed like the opportunity of a lifetime. With the money he'd been advanced, he sent his wife and two children to the United States to live with a cousin until he could join them. Now he wished he'd never answered that phone call.

For four months, he'd been trapped in this remote compound in charge of five other chemists who were given the impossible task of divining the formula for a pill none of them had seen before. Now he wasn't sure any of them would ever leave this place alive.

Locsin and his right-hand man, Tagaan, got out of the helicopter and marched toward him.

"Dr. Ocampo," Locsin said, his annoyance obvious, "why am I here?"

Ocampo stammered, "To . . . to see the headway we've made on your project—"

"Wrong. I'm here because you aren't doing the work you said you could do."

Locsin brushed by him and walked toward the main lab facility with Tagaan. They pushed open the doors and walked in without caring about sterilization procedures. Ocampo scurried after them.

Five scientists were hard at work, hunched over high-powered microscopes, operating gas chromatographs, and poring over computer data. Although Locsin kept them captive, at least he provided them with the latest equipment. All of the chemists looked up for a moment but turned back to their jobs when they saw who had entered not because they were ignoring him but because they wanted to appear busy.

Ocampo knew it was a sham. Their work was futile without more information about what they were attempting to produce.

"Why aren't you able to create more of the pills?" Locsin demanded.

"Mr. Locsin, you've given us only ten of the pills to work with," Ocampo said. "We need at least fifty more to effectively analyze its chemical makeup."

"I thought you only needed a small sample to identify a chemical."

"If we were comparing it to something else that already exists, then yes. For example, if we were trying to match a chemical residue from an arson investigation, there's a known database to compare with the sample. But what we're trying to do is much more difficult. You want us to figure out the exact chemical formula for this drug from scratch."

Without warning, Locsin picked up a heavy metal desk with one hand and flung it at the wall as if it were as light as balsa wood. The loud crash stopped all work, and the scientists looked at him in fear.

Locsin, his face scarlet with rage, got nose to nose with Ocampo and screamed, "I don't care about the details! What I want to know is if you can do it!"

Ocampo's mouth was suddenly bone dry from terror. Finding a way to replicate the drug was a long shot at best, but there was no way he was going to say that. "With time and resources, yes. But I must have more of the drug."

"And if there is no more to give you?"

"Then it will take even longer."

"How long?"

"It's hard to estimate."

"And if you have more pills?"

Ocampo swallowed reflexively. "Three months. I feel like we are close to a breakthrough." He caught one of his chemists, a woman named Maria Santos, eyeing him when he made that proclamation.

Locsin's face instantly transformed. The furious expression was gone and a beatific smile took its place. He put his arm around Ocampo's shoulder like he was an old friend.

"A breakthrough," he said. "That's what I like to hear. I knew I could count on you, Dr. Ocampo. However, I need the formula in two months, not three. I'm sure you can do it. We have a limited supply of pills, so I can't give you any more, but I can bring in more people if you need them. Just say the word."

The thought of dragging more innocent souls into this nightmare nearly made Ocampo shudder. He couldn't bear the responsibility for that.

"Perhaps if you told us more about the drug's effects, we could narrow our focus."

"Your expertise is in the development of steroids," Locsin said. "That's why you're here. You don't need to know what Typhoon is for, you only need to make more of it." He turned Ocampo toward him and looked him in the eye. "Now, if you can't do it, tell me and we'll shut down the project right now."

Shut down the project. What a nice way of saying that he'd have them all killed and buried in a shallow grave.

"We can do it, Mr. Locsin," Ocampo said reassuringly. "As I said, the breakthrough could come at any time."

Locsin patted him on the back. "I hope my presence here has provided the needed motivation."

"Of course it has."

"Good. Now I'm going to get my breakfast. When I come back, I want a detailed report on how you plan to accomplish your task."

Ocampo felt the blood drain from his face. "Yes, sir."

Locsin and Tagaan left. Maria Santos jumped up from her desk and raced over to Ocampo.

"Are you crazy?" she said. "We're nowhere close to a breakthrough."

"But he doesn't know that."

"We might be able to come up with some kind of bogus plan today, but he's going to find out sooner or later that we have no idea how to do what he wants. My guess is sooner."

"I agree. That's why we're all going to escape from this place."

"Escape? You really *are* crazy."

Ocampo put his hands on her shoulders. "I already have an idea for how to do it. The only thing left is to come up with the proper distraction."

The Halsema Highway, a mountainous route north of Manila, was considered one of the ten most dangerous roads in the world. Juan didn't have to share that ranking with Beth and Raven. They could see for themselves how hazardous it was.

The winding route through the mountains of central Luzon often narrowed to one lane, which meant they'd had to back up hundreds of yards several times during the five-hour trip to let a bus pass in the other direction. The poorly maintained road was little more than a dirt path in some places, but the asphalt wasn't much better because it could become as slick as ice in the frequent tropical downpours. Sheer, unprotected drops, landslides, and accidents in fog-shrouded conditions claimed dozens of lives every year. The PIG's wide, self-sealing tires sometimes skirted the edge of five-hundred-foot drops, but Juan trusted Eddie's assured driving skills, which were apparent when he had steered them around a pile of rocks from a previous slide and then accelerated to avoid a bus barreling toward them out of the mist.

Juan had just as much confidence in the PIG. Based on a Mercedes Unimog chassis, Max's from the ground up modifications included an armored cab that could withstand rifle fire and an eight-hundred-horsepower turbodiesel that could push past one thousand with a nitro boost. Although the PIG didn't have ejector seats, Beth's guess that there were guns in the headlights was wrong only in location. A .30 caliber machine gun was tucked behind the front bumper, mortars could be fired from a retractable hatch in the roof, and guided rocket launchers were hidden in drop-away side panels. A smoke generator was capable of pumping out a thick cloud behind it. The fifty-five-gallon drums in the back did contain extra fuel, but they also served as a concealment for a cargo area that could be configured as a mobile surgical suite, radio listening post, or personnel carrier for up to ten fully outfitted commandos.

For today's mission, the PIG was set up as a reconnaissance vehicle, with observation drones that could take off through the roof hatch. Juan wasn't as adept as Gomez at flying them, but he'd get to test his recent training.

Guided by the satellite GPS navigation, Juan told Eddie to turn when they reached a dirt road near their destination, the last location of the homing beacon broadcast by the transmitter attached to the bronze eagle finial. The trail was well worn by truck treads, but the dense jungle foliage threatened to overgrow it, and branches scraped against the sides of the PIG.

A mile into the dirt road without passing a single vehicle, they arrived at a turnoff fronted by a heavy steel gate topped with razor wire. A ten-foot-high chain-link fence disappeared into the jungle on either side. Eddie slowed the PIG as they passed.

"That kind of security seems a tad excessive," he said, "since we're about an hour from nowhere."

"They're either very intent on keeping people out," Juan said, "or they really want to keep someone from leaving."

Raven peered at the sturdy gate. "It's definitely the type of precaution I'd take to safeguard half a billion dollars of artwork."

Beth shook her head. "But why keep it way out here in the middle of the jungle? Wouldn't they want to have it more accessible if they're planning to use it for trading purposes?"

"Only one way to find out," Juan said. "Why don't we see what our eye in the sky can tell us?"

Eddie drove another three hundred yards, out of sight of the gate, and stopped. The vegetation was so dense that he couldn't pull off the road, but it didn't seem like they'd be blocking traffic anytime soon.

Juan hit the switch to retract the rooftop hatch, and humid mountain air flooded the cabin. Using his smartphone as a controller and watching the camera's feed on the dashboard screen, Juan launched the gull-sized unmanned aerial vehicle.

The UAV shot up above the treetops, then whizzed toward its target. Although a quadcopter would have been more maneuverable, the buzzing of four rotors would draw unwanted attention in a quiet location like this. Instead, the drone had wings and a tail, with a compact gimbaled camera in the nose and a variable-speed propeller at the rear. Its top speed was sixty knots, but the prop could be slowed to stealth mode for silent reconnaissance. Painted to resemble a hawk, the drone looked like a bird of prey soaring on an updraft.

Flying at a thousand feet, the drone followed the road for a half mile until it reached a clearing with a large central prefab-style building, surrounded by several smaller ones, and a helicopter pad where a chopper idled, its rotors slowly churning. The gravel driveway continued on past the compound and into the jungle beyond.

Nobody seemed to notice the circling drone. A half-dozen guards in green fatigues armed with assault rifles patrolled the compound, and five Humvees were parked at the edge, two of them with mounted .50 caliber machine guns.

"That's some heavy firepower for an art storage facility," Eddie said.

"With that many guards, we'll have to wait until nightfall to get a closer look," Juan said. "Raven and Beth, you'll wait here and watch us with the drone while Eddie and I go through the fence and see if we can find out what's going on here."

"I'll go with you on the infiltration," Raven said.

Juan shook his head. "We'll move faster if it's just the two of us. Besides, your file said you've operated small drones before, and I'm guessing that's not Beth's forte."

"If you wanted me to crash one," Beth said, "I'm your woman."

"Then it's settled . . . Raven, I'll show you the controls for this—"

Juan was interrupted when a door on the large building opened and six men walked out. The two in the lead were talking as they headed toward the waiting helicopter.

"Looks like someone's getting ready to leave," Juan said.

Raven leaned forward to get a closer look at the screen. "Can you zoom in on them?"

Juan focused on the two men in front, both powerfully built Filipinos.

"That's him," Beth said. "The guy in the Bangkok club."

"He was called Tagaan," Raven added.

"Do you know who the man next to him is?" Eddie asked.

Beth and Raven shook their heads.

"Maybe we can get an ID," Juan said. He took a freeze-frame of the image and uploaded it by satellite to the *Oregon*'s computer. He texted Murph to run it through the CIA facial recognition database to see if they could get a match.

Tagaan and the other man stopped and talked animatedly, pointing several times at the building they'd just left.

"Something inside sure has them worked up," Eddie said.

"I just hope they aren't arguing about whether to destroy the paintings," Beth said.

"If Eddie and I determine that the artwork is inside," Juan said, "we'll decide if we can get it out ourselves. If not, we'll return with a bigger team. But remember, that transient signal from the homing beacon doesn't mean this is the storage facility. It could have been taken somewhere else while it was shielded in its case."

"I know," Beth said. "I'm just nervous about coming up empty after getting so close."

"We got an ID on our mystery man," Eddie said. On the screen was a photo of the man with Tagaan, but in this photo he looked much skinnier.

Juan read the name aloud. "Salvador Locsin. It seems your drug dealers are also communist revolutionaries looking to overthrow the Philippine government, and this guy is the leader."

Eddie leaned toward the screen. "His men wiped out a dozen policemen during an attempted prison escape at sea last week. The Philippine National Police are still unsure whether he was actually rescued or went down with the ship."

Juan nodded at the drone feed. "He's the healthiest-looking dead person I've ever seen."

Eddie scrolled through the list of charges against Locsin. "Murder, political assassinations, extortion, corruption, racketeering. There are pages of this stuff. It would take less time to name the crimes he hasn't committed. And he has a price on his head. Two million dollars."

"Our first priority is the paintings," Beth said.

"Agreed," Juan said. "But if we can get a two-for-one deal on this job, we might as well help the Filipino police get their man."

Locsin and Tagaan finished their discussion and both boarded the helicopter.

"This might be good for us," Eddie said. "Security could loosen up once he's gone."

"When the boss is away, the mice will play?" Juan said with a smile.

Eddie chuckled. "Present company excluded, Chairman."

The chopper took off and pivoted over the compound before accelerating away.

Right toward them.

The sound of the throbbing rotors grew quickly.

"Juan," Beth said, craning her neck to the window, "isn't he going to fly right over us?"

Of all the directions he could have flown, the pilot happened to pick the one that would do exactly that.

"Too late to leave now," Juan said. "They'd notice our dust trail for sure. We'll just have to hope they don't spot us through the foliage." The drab green paint provided some camouflage, but the squat outline of the truck wasn't designed to blend into a jungle background.

They all held their breaths as the helicopter approached. It didn't fly directly over, which was actually worse because it meant that one side of the chopper had a decent view. That is, if anyone was actually looking in their direction. The sun glinting off the canopy made it impossible for Juan to tell if anyone was facing them.

The helicopter passed without slowing.

They all sat back in relief, but it was short-lived. The feed from the drone, which was still circling the compound, showed a frenzy of activity as gunmen poured out of the buildings fully armed and piled into four of the five Humvees, including the ones equipped with machine guns.

Two of them sped off on down the driveway leading into the jungle while the other two raced toward the front gate.

"Smart," Eddie said appreciatively. "The chopper pilot kept going so we wouldn't know they had spotted us. Good thing they didn't realize we're watching them." He started the PIG and threw it into reverse.

"There must be another exit from the compound onto this road," Juan said. "They're trying to catch us in a pincer move. I'll recall the drone. Eddie, get us out of here."

Eddie punched the gas, and they shot backward.

Before he could set the drone to return to the PIG, its camera showed six people in white lab coats being roughly removed from the main building by the two remaining guards. They looked around in bewilderment at the suddenly empty compound.

"Who are they?" Beth asked.

"I don't know," Juan said. "But they don't look like they're there willingly."

One of the guards shouted at the lead man, who turned and threw something at him. It exploded in a gush of flame, and the guard dropped his weapon as he ran amok trying to extinguish the white-hot fire.

Two more of the people in lab coats tossed objects at the second captor. Both of the makeshift grenades exploded. The guard rolled to the ground in an attempt to put out the flames, but he still held on to his assault rifle. Despite being ablaze, he picked off one of the captives. The man who had thrown the first grenade snatched up the dropped gun and killed the armed guard with a sustained barrage. The remaining guard, still on fire, ran at him like a madman before being taken down.

Beth gasped at the carnage and said, "Are they trying to escape because of us?"

"They must be desperate," Juan said and glanced at Eddie, who nodded, knowing what Juan already had in mind.

The man who'd instigated the jailbreak sprinted to one of the smaller buildings and emerged seconds later triumphantly holding an item in his hand. It had to be the keys to the last Humvee because the four other captives ran for it and got in. Soon, the Humvee was driving at high speed toward the main gate.

"We might get away," Raven said, "but if those people run into the other Humvees, they're going to be wiped out."

"I know," Juan said as he heard the rotors of the helicopter returning to direct the coming ambush. "That's why we're going to help them."

Ocampo's hands were shaking as they gripped the wheel of the speeding Humvee. He couldn't see the compound entrance through the trees, but he knew it wasn't far.

"Where did they all go?" said Maria Santos from the passenger seat, her voice trembling. The three other scientists in the back were silent with fear.

"I don't know," Ocampo replied, "but it looked like they were in a hurry."

Maria choked down a sob. "Paul's dead."

Ocampo couldn't shake the sight of the chemist's lifeless body riddled with bullets. "But we're alive."

"For how long? If they catch us, they'll kill us."

"They would have killed us eventually anyway."

"How do you know they're not waiting for us up ahead?"

"I don't. But this is the fastest way out."

When they rounded the next bend, Ocampo stood on the brakes, and their vehicle skidded to a stop. Two Humvees, one with a mounted machine gun, were positioned ahead of them just outside the gate as if they were waiting for something farther up the road. Guards were crouched behind the doors, their weapons at the ready.

"What are they doing?" Maria said.

"It looks like an ambush," Ocampo replied.

"But there should be two more Humvees. I counted five this morning."

"We'll have to take the chance that they're not farther ahead."

None of the guards seemed alarmed by their presence. One of them even waved for their Humvee to come closer.

Ocampo gunned the engine.

"What are you doing?"

"They don't realize it's us. They think we're the other guards from the compound."

"They won't for long."

"Right. Which is why you should all get down. We're going to try to get by them before they recognize us."

He jammed his foot on the accelerator, and the Humvee shot down the road.

"You don't have enough room to get by!" Maria cried out.

Ocampo's heart raced as they rocketed forward. "We'll make room. Hang on!"

He heard seat belts click while he drew his own across his chest.

The guard who had waved at them was now motioning for Ocampo to slow down. Only too late did he recognize the face looking back at him.

Ocampo tried to thread his vehicle between the compound gate and the Humvee without the machine gun, but there wasn't enough room. The left side of the Humvee scraped along the gate while the right side smashed into the back of the other Humvee.

Two of the guards went flying when their Humvee was tossed

into the other one. The rest of the guards dived for cover at the unexpected impact.

The wheel was torn from Ocampo's hands as it spun. The Humvee plunged into a ditch and then back out as it bounced onto the dirt road.

No vehicles were in front of them.

Ocampo regained his senses and took off down the road, but something was wrong. The steering wheel was trying to yank itself to the right, and he couldn't build any speed.

Either the impact with the other Humvee or the drop into the ditch had damaged the suspension. There was no way they could outrun the other Humvees now.

Assault rifles cracked behind them, and bullets splattered the rear of the vehicle.

"Get down!" he yelled, then screamed when one of the rounds pierced his right arm on its way through the windshield.

With just one good arm, he couldn't hold the wheel straight any longer. The Humvee veered right and crashed into a tree.

For a moment, Ocampo was dazed by the impact. He came around only when Maria shook his shoulder, sending a fresh jolt of agony down his arm.

"The trees!" she yelled. "Our only chance is to try to lose them in the jungle."

The dense foliage seemed impenetrable, but Ocampo wasn't giving up if she wasn't. He unbuckled himself and threw the door open. Holding his injured arm, he got out as quickly as he could.

They never had a chance to run. The guards' damaged Humvee roared toward them, assault rifles pointing out the windows.

The other scientists all stopped and put up their hands. Ocampo didn't even bother.

The Humvee swerved as it came to a halt. The guards jumped

out, but they didn't fire. They must have known how important the scientists were to Locsin's goal of finding the formula for Typhoon.

"Down on the ground!" one of the guards yelled.

The other chemists complied, but Ocampo remained standing. He knew this was the end. He'd either die now or when Locsin realized he'd caused the others to mutiny. But he wouldn't go back to work for Locsin.

"I said get down!"

Ocampo simply stared at him.

A moment's hesitation crossed the guard's face, but his anger at Ocampo not following his orders overcame any fear of what his boss might do later. He raised his rifle and pointed it at Ocampo's head.

Ocampo closed his eyes, waiting for death.

He was shocked to hear an explosion. He thought everything would simply go dark, that he'd be dead long before he could hear a shot.

Then he realized it wasn't the rifle that fired. It was an explosion down the road.

He opened his eyes to see smoke billowing up where the other Humvee had been.

All of the guards were facing the direction of the explosion, as confused as he was about what had happened.

Then a truck barreled through the smoke. It seemed like an ordinary cargo vehicle, but the flash of machine gun fire unexpectedly erupted from the front bumper.

Rounds tore into the guards' Humvee and the guards themselves. This time, Ocampo voluntarily threw himself to the ground as high-velocity rounds whistled through the air.

The two guards who were still standing returned fire, but their bullets just seemed to bounce off the truck. Oily smoke belched from the hood of the shot-up Humvee.

Ocampo lost sight of the truck's cab when it stopped behind the guards' Humvee. A few more shots rang out and then the air fell silent.

He heard the crunch of footsteps in the dirt as someone rounded the front of the Humvee. A blond man holding a compact submachine gun emerged from the smoke like an apparition.

He strode over to Ocampo and knelt down beside the scientist, a slight smile playing across his face.

"Hi, I'm Juan. Did someone call for a taxi?"

20

For a moment, the injured man in the lab coat looked at Juan slack-jawed. Juan wondered if it was because the man didn't speak English or that he didn't like the joke.

"I'm Mel Ocampo," he finally said. "Where did you come from?"

"Good question. Let me answer it in our truck."

Juan reached out a hand to help Ocampo up, while Beth and Raven ushered the rest of the shaken passengers to the PIG. Eddie sat in the driver's seat, ready to take off as soon as they were all inside. The two Humvees that had circled around to cut them off would be there any second.

The moment Ocampo was on his feet, a weight like a cement mixer slammed into Juan from behind, hammering his MP5 submachine gun from his hand and pounding him into the dirt.

The force of the impact nearly knocked the wind out of him, but Juan was able to use the momentum to roll forward and crouch on his knees so he could see the attacker who had come out of nowhere. The sight that greeted him made him blink in confusion.

It was the guard Juan had shot just moments ago. He thought the guard could have survived because he was wearing body armor, except Juan could see the torn flesh under the guard's shirt. Only a small amount blood oozed from the two bullet holes in his torso, wounds that should have killed him. The heavily muscled guard looked at Juan with a crazed expression as if he were energized by what should have been agonizing and fatal wounds.

Both Juan and the guard lunged for the gun. Juan reached it first and raised it to fire, but the guard dived behind the hood of the burning Humvee and out of Juan's line of sight.

Juan left Ocampo frozen in place and raced around the Humvee's front end, ready to take down the seemingly indestructible guard, but by the time he got there, the guard had already found a hostage.

He held a wicked-looking serrated knife at Beth's throat. A dead guard lay by his feet, the likely source of the weapon.

Beth looked at Juan with pleading, terrified eyes. The guard crouched behind her, preventing Juan from taking a clean shot. It was clear he was just biding his time until his comrades in the other Humvees caught up with them.

The sound of their revving engines was growing stronger, joined now by the throbbing rotors of the returning helicopter. If Beth wasn't freed soon, they'd be sitting ducks.

Juan kept his eye on the MP5's red-dot-targeting scope, ready for any slight opening the guard might give him for a headshot. But the guard was too smart to expose himself.

Movement noticeable through the windows of the burning Humvee caught Juan's eye. It was Raven, holding a SIG Sauer pistol. She motioned to Juan that she didn't have a shot, either.

Juan had to take a chance that the guard wanted to keep Beth alive as a hostage. He changed his grip on the submachine gun so that he was holding it by its stock, the barrel pointed straight down at the ground. Then he slowly circled left, his eyes locking with the guard's one visible eye. The guard turned Beth to keep her between him and Juan.

Juan had moved five feet when a single shot rang out. A bullet went through the guard's head. His suddenly lifeless corpse collapsed to the ground, the knife slashing Beth's shirt, just missing flesh.

Juan rushed to Beth and grabbed her trembling arm. "You're okay. Come on." He guided her toward the PIG. "We need to leave now."

They got to the truck at the same time Raven reached it with Ocampo in tow.

"Nice shot," Juan said to her as they got in.

She shrugged like it was no big deal. "I'm just glad you realized that he was dumb enough to keep his eye on you."

As soon as he got in the PIG, Juan intended to find out from Ocampo just what kind of supermen they were up against. With such a severe injury, that guard shouldn't have been on his feet, let alone strong enough to take Juan down.

As he was about to close the door and tell Eddie to floor it, Juan saw that his questions would have to wait.

The rooftop of the first of the two Humvees bearing down on them was no longer equipped with a machine gun. They must have switched it out when they realized the firepower they were facing.

Now the Humvee was mounted with an RPG.

"FIRE NOW!" Locsin yelled into the radio. "Before they get away!"

Using binoculars from the helicopter's front seat, he could see that the last man had gotten into the heavily armed truck that had surprised the first two Humvees and taken out half his men with barely a shot being fired in return.

Locsin couldn't let these rescuers get away with his scientists even if he had to kill them all.

His guard in the lead Humvee followed the order and launched the rocket-propelled grenade at the truck, which lurched forward with incredible acceleration just as he fired.

The RPG round missed the truck by less than a foot, tearing past its rear and blowing a tree in half.

Locsin cursed his man's sluggishness. If these people got away, death would be too light a punishment for his failure to stop them here.

He turned to Tagaan, who was in the chopper's rear seat. "You're sure those are the two women from Bangkok?" He'd given Tagaan a look through the binoculars when the rescuers were outside their truck.

Tagaan nodded. "The redhead is Beth Anders, and her companion is the one with the dark hair. I don't know how they located our base, but I will find out."

"You'd better. We have to get rid of them."

Tagaan nodded again and began unpacking the stored six-barreled minigun and its floor mount. Like the rest of the weapons Locsin had acquired for his rebellion, the rotary, belt-fed gun was supplied by Chinese sources sympathetic to his communist cause.

The Humvees were having trouble keeping up with the enemy truck on the dirt road because of its surprising power. As the truck reached the main road, the Halsema Highway, the trailing Humvee fired another RPG, which exploded on the road behind the truck as it turned toward Manila.

But then for some reason the truck began to slow down. Locsin raised the binoculars and saw that one of its right rear tires had been shredded by the latest blast. The damage didn't stop the truck, but the flapping rubber kept it from pulling away on the twisting mountain road.

"You've crippled it," Locsin radioed to his guard. "Catch up with them and finish them off."

"Yes, sir" came the instant reply. The Humvee screeched around the hairpin turn in an attempt to get a clear shot. The second one followed close behind.

Around the next tight corner, a sudden fog that these mountains were known for seemed to spring from nowhere, obscuring the truck where the road disappeared into the trees.

Then Locsin realized what had happened. The truck had released a smoke screen. He could see the dense vapor pouring from the back of the truck the few times it popped into view.

Because the truck driver had waited until he was around the curve to churn out the smoke, there was no way for the pursuing guards to see it coming.

"Watch out ahead! He's laid down smoke!"

But his warning came too late for the lead Humvee. It raced around the corner and into the thick smoke. The next time Locsin saw the Humvee, it had missed the turn and was plunging off the side of the mountain. Screams erupted from the radio, then went silent when the Humvee finally hit the ground in a fiery explosion a thousand feet below.

"We lost number three," the guard in the fourth and last Humvee called.

Locsin's grip on the binoculars nearly shattered them in his fury. "Don't worry about them," he growled. "Keep going."

"We've had to slow down to get through this smoke."

"I know! Keep going!" Locsin shouted. He would find out who these people were, but not before he wiped them from the earth.

Like an answer to his unspoken wish, Tagaan said from the back of the chopper, "Ready." He flipped the switch on the minigun and rotated the barrel to arm it. From its mount in the center of the rear cargo area, he would now be able to fire it out of either door.

"Get us closer," Locsin said to the pilot with a smile. He loved having air superiority. All they had to do was wait for the truck to emerge from the jungle foliage and they could leisurely cut it to ribbons.

While Raven and Beth tended to the injured and frightened passengers in the back, Juan operated the PIG's defensive systems, leaving Eddie to keep his eyes glued to the road. All Juan had overheard from the discussion behind him was that the people they'd rescued weren't in the art field. They were scientists. Ph.D.s.

"The shimmy is getting worse," Eddie said, straining to control the PIG. "I think we may be close to losing the other right rear tire if we keep up this speed." The self-sealing tires were designed to withstand rifle fire, but the RPG explosion had caused far more extensive damage.

"This might not be the best time to install the spare," Juan replied.

"Maybe they'll let us call a tow truck."

Juan heard the helicopter approaching and said, "No need. That must be the auto club arriving now."

He looked up to see Salvador Locsin clearly visible in the front seat next to the pilot. He was focused on Juan with a nasty grin. He waved jauntily and mouthed the word *Good-bye.*

Then the rear door behind him slid open, revealing the spinning barrel of a minigun aimed directly at him.

"Stop!" Juan yelled.

Without hesitation, Eddie stood on the brake just as the minigun spat fire. Tracer rounds chewed into the road directly in front of the cab. The forward momentum of the chopper kept the gun's operator from compensating fast enough to hit them. The PIG's armor was stout, but it would be no match for the high-powered rounds.

In the side mirror, Juan saw that the smoke was lingering in the calm air.

"Back into the smoke!"

Eddie threw the gear into reverse and launched the PIG backward as the helicopter came around for a killing pass, but their view of it blurred as they were enveloped by the smoke.

"What now?" Eddie asked once they were concealed yet still moving backward slowly. "They may not be able to see us, but they could still hit us with a lucky shot."

"And their friends won't be far behind in that Humvee."

"Too bad we don't have any antiaircraft capabilities."

At this point, Juan couldn't see more than ten feet in front of him. "Believe me, I will be having a talk with Max about upgrades." They did, however, have the mortars and guided rockets.

Juan looked at the steep mountainside that rose out of the smoke. The loose earth had to be soaked from the rain of the last few days.

"How about we give ourselves a little breathing space between us and that Humvee?"

He opened the roof hatch and used the targeting screen on the dashboard to aim the mortar at the steep hillside along the road between them and the pursuing Humvees.

Over his shoulder, he called out to the passengers, "Fire in the hole!" They looked at him in confusion until he mimed covering his ears. They followed his example, and he launched three mortar shells in quick succession, the thump of each reverberating through the PIG.

Juan couldn't see the blasts as the rounds landed, but soon the ground shook as an avalanche of mud and rock tumbled down the hill in the distance.

"That sounds like it was plenty to cover the road."

"And keep that Humvee and its RPGs off our back. Now to deal with this Locsin guy."

The rockets that could be fired from drop-away panels on the side of the PIG were meant to be antivehicle weapons, and their guidance systems were minimal. They certainly couldn't home in on a moving aircraft.

Juan could hear the helicopter out there waiting for them to emerge from the smoke. It was perpendicular to the road, hovering in place, providing a stable platform for its gunner. He wouldn't miss a second time.

"Eddie, turn us to face the sound of the helicopter."

Eddie raised his eyebrows but turned the wheel, and the truck began turning. "The road's not much wider than the PIG's length. There won't be much room to maneuver and make an escape if things don't go well."

"Then I'd better not miss, but I think having another set of eyes out there will help."

Juan launched one of their quadcopter drones. He maneuvered it until it was just above the smoke.

On the screen transmitting the drone's camera feed he saw the helicopter exactly where he was expecting to see it.

They must have seen the drone because the minigun began spitting shells directly at the camera. The tiny quadcopter danced around in the air, gracefully evading the rounds.

Although the image of the helicopter bobbed and weaved on the screen, the drone had done its job, giving Juan enough information to target the chopper.

He fired two rockets.

At the same instant, the helicopter banked hard, before the rockets had come out of the smoke screen. Either Locsin or the pilot must have suddenly realized the drone was a prelude to an attack.

The first rocket flew harmlessly past the chopper, missing the fuselage by inches. The second rocket, however, hit the tail rotor, blasting it to pieces.

The helicopter banked crazily to the side as the pilot struggled to keep it from spinning out of control. It flew over them and looked as if it was going to crash into the mountainside, but at the last second it angled over the road and the dissipating smoke screen. It crossed over the landslide that straddled the road two hundred yards behind the PIG and dived out of sight. A moment later, a ball of fire rose above the road, contributing its own black smoke to the haze.

"Looks like you got them," Eddie said. "Although it might be hard to collect that two million if he's a crispy critter."

Juan thought back to the mutant guard who'd attacked him after suffering injuries that should have brought down a rhino.

"Let's make sure," Juan said and maneuvered the drone so that he could see past the landslide.

There was the chopper lying on its side, burning. It had just missed obliterating the Humvee that idled nearby. Two men lay in the road. They must have jumped out of the helicopter just before it landed.

Juan got the drone closer and saw that one of the men was Locsin. He was on his back, one pant leg on fire. But, to Juan's amazement, he wasn't dead. As Juan watched, Locsin sat up as if he'd simply been taking a nap and patted out the flames with his hand.

The other man, who Juan could now see was Tagaan, also rose.

Neither of them seemed particularly concerned about surviving a helicopter crash and explosion. Locsin stood up and shouted orders to the guards in the Humvee, pointing back the way they'd come.

"What do we need to kill these guys?" Eddie asked, incredulous. "Silver bullets?"

"I hope it's not kryptonite," Juan said. "Because the last time I checked, we were fresh out."

Before Locsin got into the Humvee to leave, he turned to face the quadcopter hovering above them. He said something and held out his hand. One of the guards gave him a pistol.

Without pausing, Locsin aimed it at the drone and fired. His aim was better than the guy on the minigun, because he hit it with his fourth shot. The camera feed winked out.

"Lucky shot," Eddie said.

"Sometimes it's better to be lucky than good," Juan said. "But he might be both."

The last remnants of smoke cleared, and it was obvious that the landslide would keep them from pursuing Locsin.

"I suppose it's time to alert the authorities to seize Locsin's compound," Juan said.

Eddie pointed to the dashboard. "Since we didn't have time to recall the observation drone before our little road trip, it's still circling the buildings." Sure enough, the video feed was still coming in sharp. "It should be able to remain on station for at least a few more hours in low-power mode. If we're the lucky ones this time, we'll see Locsin returning to the base, and we can call in the Philippine Special Action Force to take him down."

It was as if Locsin had heard them. The main building on-screen erupted in a massive explosion, followed in quick succession by all the other buildings in the compound. Within seconds, there was nothing left except the burning hulks of the structures. Locsin must have preset the explosives for just such an eventuality.

Juan cocked an eye at Eddie. "You were saying about us being lucky?"

"I did say *if.*"

A bus was approaching them, slowing as the driver saw the landslide blocking the road and smoke curling up from the helicopter wreckage.

Juan nodded at the bus, which began disgorging curious onlookers, and said, "Let's get out of here before we have to answer awkward questions."

Eddie eased the PIG around and moved off at a leisurely pace to avoid further damage to the remaining rear tires. Once they put some distance between them and the helicopter wreck, they'd check the extent of the tire damage.

Juan turned in his seat and saw that Raven was bandaging up Mel Ocampo's arm. Beth and the rest of the passengers looked dazed from the action.

"How's his injury?" Juan asked.

"Painful but not serious," Raven replied. "He'll need stitches at a hospital, but it can wait until we get back to Manila."

"I'm fine," Ocampo said, his voice thin from fatigue. "I'm just glad the rest of my people are uninjured. Thank you for saving us."

"Glad we could help, Dr. Ocampo," Juan said. "Now, we've got a long ride back to Manila and plenty of time on our hands. When Raven finishes dressing your wound, I think it's time you told us a story."

THAILAND

Call me now!

Alastair Lynch, who was on his way home from work at Interpol's Bangkok duty station, glanced at the text message in confusion as he steered his Mercedes S-Class through the dense traffic. The phone number prefix was familiar, but the texter wasn't on his contact list. Then his stomach went ice cold when he realized why the number wasn't stored in his phone. It was coming from his mole at Bangkok police headquarters.

Normally, they communicated through an untraceable Internet email app. Lynch told the mole his phone number was only to be used in case of an emergency.

Lynch hated emergencies. He liked boring routine. After studying statistics at a university in London, the Brit had joined Interpol and was sent to the Bangkok office to analyze the routes and organization of drug smuggling networks. Usually, he spent most of his time in air-conditioned offices, poring over data related to the drug trade and generally leading an existence as straitlaced as a single man could in Southeast Asia. It was only in the last few months that his life had taken a turn toward the darkness that he'd joined Interpol to thwart.

He clicked the number to call back and it was answered on the first ring.

The mole, a staff member at the police headquarters evidence locker, spoke in a low voice, his English mangled by urgency. "Why you send someone to take the pill?"

"What are you talking about?" Lynch responded.

"Interpol came and took it. You not warn me."

Lynch's heart raced, and he sat up straighter in his seat. The Typhoon pill that had been confiscated after the firefight at the Nightcrawlers club was supposed to remain in the evidence locker. Lynch was planning to remove it the next day when he was already scheduled to visit police headquarters so that he had a reason for being there. That way he would not be a suspect when the pill disappeared.

Now his mole was telling him that the pill was already gone. If it got away, there would be no telling what Salvador Locsin would do to him.

"I didn't authorize any Interpol officials to take custody of it!" Lynch yelled. Since he'd started taking Typhoon, his mood could transform from calm and logical to uncontrollable rage in an instant. Even some of his colleagues had commented on it recently.

"They had correct papers," the mole said in broken English. "What else can I do?"

"Who took it?"

"He said he from Interpol headquarters in France, but he not French. Baxter is the name. Big white guy with dark brown hair, mustache, and expensive gray suit."

Lynch racked his brain for anyone in the organization named

Baxter, but he was drawing a blank. He certainly wasn't informed about anyone coming from France to consult on the case.

"When was this?"

"He finish signing for it just now."

"You mean he's still there?"

"He leaving the building any minute."

That was a stroke of luck for Lynch. For obvious reasons, the Interpol duty station was located only a few blocks from Bangkok police headquarters. He wrenched the wheel around in the middle of the street and headed back the way he'd come, causing even more honking horns to be added to the city din.

A minute later, he reached the massive compound housing the huge headquarters building of the Royal Thai Police. It was likely that the unknown Interpol official had gone through the main entrance, so Lynch flashed his credentials at the guard at the gate.

He pulled in just in time to see a dark-haired man emerge from the building. It had to be Baxter. He walked with the purpose and alertness of a soldier, not like the bureaucrats and analysts that made up most of Interpol's employment. Baxter strode over to a waiting Jaguar XJR sedan and got in. It took off as soon as the door was closed.

Lynch couldn't let them out of his sight. He was certain Baxter wasn't with Interpol. Lynch had been the one consulting on the case, and if someone was coming halfway across the world to assist him or even take over the case, he would have known about it.

Which meant this guy was an impostor. An impostor with the capability to pass himself off convincingly as an Interpol official. But why did Baxter want to get his hands on a single Typhoon pill?

For a nanosecond, Lynch considered calling Locsin for help before he realized how idiotic that would be. Announcing his incompetence in securing the pill to the man who now controlled his life would be the stupidest thing he could do.

A year ago, Lynch had injured his back when the tuk-tuk he'd been riding in collided with a taxi. The surgery on his spine staved off paralysis, but the pain had been excruciating. His doctors tried to wean him off the painkillers, but the pain wasn't going away. Soon, even the narcotics he could get at the local pharmacies weren't strong enough. Luckily, he knew how to find drug dealers.

At first, he stuck to opiates like OxyContin, but the painkillers were making it difficult to focus at work. And caffeine wasn't doing the job, so he started taking amphetamines to give him a boost.

That's when Salvador Locsin came along. His gang had been the one supplying Lynch with his meds. Locsin claimed that he had a brand-new drug, a pill that would take care of all of Lynch's problems. He called it Typhoon and gave Lynch two weeks' worth of samples free of charge.

Lynch was dubious, but he knew the path he was currently on would end in ruin, so he took the pills.

Lynch didn't believe in miracles, but if he did, Typhoon would have qualified. Within two days, his back pain was completely gone. In fact, Lynch felt better than at any other time in his life. Not only that, in just a few more days he noticed that his scrawny frame was putting on muscle. All he had to do was eat, ravenously consuming more noodles than a sumo wrestler could choke down.

When the two weeks' supply was up, he looked and felt like an Olympic athlete and begged Locsin for more. He'd pay anything. He was already concocting plans for how he might be able to find the cash.

But Locsin didn't want money. He wanted Lynch's allegiance. Lynch would be his inside man at Interpol.

Lynch balked at first. Locsin shrugged and said, "Fine." No threats. No coercion of any kind.

But Lynch wouldn't be getting any more Typhoon pills. If he changed his mind, he was told how to contact Locsin.

It took only two days for Lynch to realize that Locsin owned him. If he thought the pain from the back injury was agonizing, it was nothing compared to the withdrawal he experienced without Typhoon. He suffered debilitating nausea and could barely hold down any food. He sweated profusely, and the headaches were beyond anything he'd ever imagined. But the worst was the agony he endured as his newly developed muscles began to wither. They cramped so badly that it felt like they were being torn apart by razor-sharp tiger's claws.

When he called Locsin, Lynch was so far gone that he was sobbing as he pleaded for more Typhoon.

After that, he did anything that Locsin asked without hesitation. And his latest task had been to make sure that the Typhoon pill recovered from the drug gang fight was never taken in for scientific analysis. Lynch had been counting on the backlog of cases to keep that from happening before he could get it back himself.

Now someone had beat him to it. And if Locsin found out, Lynch might never see another Typhoon pill again. He was due for another week's supply tomorrow. He couldn't show up at the exchange empty-handed.

He kept the Jaguar in view yet tried to stay back as far as he could. He wasn't a trained agent, but he had begun taking classes in the Muay Thai kickboxing discipline, in addition to lifting weights. But he didn't think he'd need any of that. He had a Glock pistol under the front seat.

His plan was simple. When the Jaguar stopped in a good location, Lynch would shoot the driver and the so-called Interpol official, Baxter, and retrieve the pill. He'd like to wait for a remote location, but that might not be possible in a city as crowded as Bangkok. However, he was even willing to risk witnesses if it meant staving off another round of Typhoon withdrawal.

When the Jaguar made the next turn, at a sign indicating that road would take them to the airport, Lynch thought he might have to reassess his plan. Shooting them at the airport would be suicidal.

But, a mile later, Lynch breathed a sigh of relief. The Jag turned off the main road and made its way toward the parking lot for Rama IX Park, the biggest green space in Bangkok. If his targets had a rendezvous in the park with someone else, he could easily wait until they reached an isolated section and take them out there without anyone seeing him.

He pulled into the lot a hundred feet behind them and into a space. Baxter and his driver got out of the Jaguar and began walking toward the park. They never glanced in Lynch's direction.

Lynch reached under the seat and withdrew the semiautomatic pistol and its holster. He snapped it to his belt and got out of the car.

Before he could walk ten feet, a windowless white van screeched to a stop next to him. The side door flew open and four men in black masks jumped out brandishing automatic weapons.

One of them clubbed Lynch over the head with his gun, the Typhoon making it feel like little more than a love tap. He kicked the man in the solar plexus and he went sprawling. He tried to draw the pistol, but that was something he'd never practiced in a high-stress situation. The other three men tackled him before he could get it fully out, knocking it from his hand.

Lynch fought back ferociously, taking down another man with a powerful punch to the head, but they were expert fighters and he was not. They managed to pin him to the ground and cuff his hands behind his back. They tossed him into the van just as Baxter and the Jag driver got in and closed the door behind them.

The van's tires squealed as it took off.

The man with the mustache reached into Lynch's coat pocket and took out his wallet as well as a thin metal case.

"Let's see who our mixed martial arts fighter is," the man said with a slight Dutch accent. He opened the wallet and raised an eyebrow at the ID. "It says he's Alastair Lynch. Looks like we've got ourselves a member of Interpol here, boys."

Then the man popped open the metal container. This time, both eyebrows went up when he saw what was inside.

In a mindless panic, Lynch leapt up and shouted, "That's mine!"

Two of the masked men shoved him back down. Lynch continued to struggle, but he couldn't move.

With a bemused expression, the dark-haired man reached into his own coat pocket and took out a small Thai police evidence envelope. He said, "My name is Gerhard Brekker, Mr. Lynch. Not only are you going to tell us why you were following us, I'd also like you to explain why you have one of these in your pocket."

Brekker emptied the envelope and showed him the Typhoon pill he'd taken from the police station. Then he upended the metal container from Lynch's pocket and held up the pill that had been inside it next to the one from the envelope.

Both tablets were etched with identical symbols of a cyclone.

 **THE PHILIPPINES**

With a fresh tire on the PIG, Juan climbed back in with Eddie, and they continued toward Manila at a fast clip. Juan swiveled in his seat and saw Mel Ocampo looking at him with a mixture of weariness and curiosity, the torn sleeve of his lab coat replaced by a white gauze bandage expertly wrapped by Raven. The other four scientists, looking shell-shocked after the escape, sipped from water bottles and ate sandwiches Beth had given them. They chewed in silence.

"Thank you for saving us," Ocampo said.

"We just happened to be there at the right time," Juan replied.

"Actually, if you hadn't been there, we might never have been able to make an escape attempt in the first place."

Juan nodded in understanding. "When the Humvees took off after us, you took the opportunity to make a run for it."

"I had been hoping for a distraction, and you and your people provided it for us."

"And the grenades?" Eddie asked from the driver's seat.

"Made from chemicals in our lab," said Maria Santos, one of the other chemists. "Mel had us make them over a week ago. I'm just glad they worked. We didn't have a chance to test them."

"Why were you there in the first place?" Raven asked.

"Locsin brought us there," Ocampo said. "We thought it was to do top secret research for a pharmaceutical company. When we weren't allowed to leave, we soon realized that his goal was more sinister."

Maria nodded. "He is an evil man."

"What was the real purpose of your research?" Juan asked.

"He wanted us to replicate a drug," Ocampo said. "It was a small white pill he called Typhoon. The image of a cyclone is embedded on its face."

Juan imagined the buildings they just saw as a high-tech meth lab. "I've never heard of Typhoon. Is that a street name for a narcotic?"

Ocampo shook his head. "Nothing like that. After we were gathered together, it became clear that we all are experts in the development of steroids."

Juan thought back to the guard who'd shrugged off two gunshot wounds to the chest. "Are Locsin's men users of Typhoon?"

Ocampo nodded. "They showed many of the effects of prolonged steroid use: massive muscle growth, hair loss and severe acne in some of them, and wild mood swings. Locsin would be charming one moment, then lash out in rage the next. A Jekyll and Hyde."

"They also had some side effects I've never seen before," Maria said. "All of them smelled terrible. The rancid odor like garlic oozed out of their pores. I could barely stand being next to one of them."

"The drug also seemed to have remarkable benefits besides muscle growth. Maria, tell them about the guard who cut himself."

A look of profound confusion crossed Maria's face as she recalled the memory. "It was the strangest thing. One of the guards was moving a crate of equipment into the lab and slashed himself on a nail sticking out of it. He didn't even seem to notice until I pointed to the blood. He looked at the gash on his arm, shook his head, and wiped the blood on a towel like it was just a scratch. But the cut looked so deep that I thought he'd need stitches."

"But it stopped bleeding almost instantly," Juan said.

Maria gaped at him. "How did you know that?"

"Because the guy who was holding the knife to Beth's throat should have been bleeding profusely from the shots I put into him. Instead, he had barely any blood on his uniform."

"You're right," Ocampo said. "But that's not all. I saw the wound myself. It was at least three inches long. The next day, I saw it again. Except for a thin scar, it had completely healed. Two days later, I couldn't even tell that he'd been injured."

"So these guys heal in less time than it takes to talk about it?" Eddie said.

"Nothing so fast," Ocampo said. "The cut didn't close itself instantly. But it does seem as if Typhoon speeds up the body's natural healing process dramatically."

"How is that possible?" Juan asked.

"That's something I wish I knew. This kind of advanced healing isn't unheard of in vertebrates. Dolphins can survive gaping wounds from shark attacks with little pain and no infection, and the missing flesh is completely replaced in a matter of weeks. We don't know if the rapid healing process is stimulated by stem cells or proteins, but the Typhoon drug could be activating a similar mechanism in humans."

"The problem is that the other side effects could be worse than the benefits," Maria said. "I've noticed that the guards' angry outbursts have become more frequent and violent during the last few weeks. There have even been fights between some of them. If they weren't under orders by Locsin himself to leave us untouched, I have no doubt that we would have been attacked as well."

"It may also be addictive," Ocampo added. "Such profound effects may produce strong withdrawal symptoms if the user suddenly stops taking the drug."

"If Locsin already had this drug," Raven said, "why did he want you to figure out how to make more of it?"

"I got the impression that he only had a limited supply and was desperate to make more. When I told him that it would take at least three months to decipher the formula, he went crazy and demanded that we find it in two months."

"Even the three-month time line was insane," Maria said.

"Why?" Juan asked.

"Because we couldn't figure out the key component without the formula itself. The main ingredient of the drug seems to be an organic compound, most likely from a plant. If we knew which plant the compound was from—which we don't—it would likely take mere weeks to get production up and running."

"So where did he get the drug in the first place?"

"We don't know. We did a radiometric analysis on one of the samples to see if we could determine its age. There was no evidence of radioactive decay, which means they had to be created before the use of atomic weapons, which have left a radioactive signature on all organic compounds since they were first detonated."

Raven leaned forward. For the first time in the short span that Juan had known her, she seemed genuinely surprised. "Are you saying these pills date from before 1945?"

"Yes. It means the pills were developed just before or during World War Two," Ocampo said. "They had to be well preserved to survive intact for over seventy years, probably vacuum-sealed. And I know he's looking for more of them. He threatened us by saying he had a backup plan if we failed."

"I don't suppose he told you exactly where he was looking," Juan said.

"If you have a map with a nice big X on it," Eddie said, "that would be even better."

Ocampo smiled. "Why? Are you going after him?"

Juan nodded. "It seems like that would be in the interest of my biggest client." As soon as he could, Juan planned to call Langston Overholt at the CIA and brief him on the situation. He had no doubt that Overholt would want him to go after Locsin.

"Your client? Who is that?"

"I'm afraid that the less you know about that, the better."

Ocampo narrowed his eyes at Juan. "I don't mean to sound ungrateful, but just who are you people?"

Up to this point, Juan had only used their first names. Revealing who they really were would just raise a lot of inconvenient questions when Ocampo and his people talked to the Philippine authorities.

"Let's just say we're on the side that doesn't want a supersoldier drug in the hands of a communist madman."

Ocampo stared at Juan for a moment, then looked at each person in his group. They all returned his look with a silent nod.

"All right," he said, turning back to Juan. "We owe you our trust after you put your lives on the line for us. I have some other information that might help you."

"About where Locsin is looking for the drug?"

"Not really. All I know about that is he's got a dig going on somewhere on a small island in the Philippines. Since there are well over a hundred languages spoken in our country, the guards thought I didn't know what they were saying. But apparently my mother was from the same area they were from, so I could understand snippets of their conversation. They said they're expecting a shipment to arrive tomorrow night from China."

"A shipment of what?" Eddie asked.

"They didn't say. But it's coming in on a cargo ship called the *Magellan Sun*, the same ship they used to deliver equipment for the dig. The guards were expecting to rendezvous with it off the west coast of Negros Island. Maybe you can have the Philippine Coast Guard intercept it."

"That's one possibility," Juan said. He wouldn't reveal that he had the *Oregon*, a better solution than trying to convince a foreign nation's coast guard to stop a ship at sea.

Beth, who'd been silently watching up until now, said, "This might seem like a strange question, but did you see any artwork while you were held captive?"

Ocampo gave her a confused look. "What kind of artwork?"

"Paintings."

Ocampo shook his head slowly. She looked hopefully at the other chemists, but none of them had seen any, either.

"What are you going to do with us?" Maria asked. "Locsin will kill us if he finds us."

Juan had been considering that question during the discussion. If they simply dropped Ocampo and his people at a hospital, it was possible that Locsin and his men might track them down to keep them from talking to the authorities.

In return for the information Ocampo had given them, Juan thought he could convince Overholt to put them up in a CIA safe house until Locsin was captured or killed. They might also be able to think of additional info that would help them further.

"I think I have somewhere you can stay safely until we can find out what Locsin is up to. And I have a friend who can sew up that arm." He'd have Julia Huxley, the *Oregon*'s doctor, meet them and tend to Ocampo's wound before they were taken to the safe house.

It was still a few hours before they would get back to Manila, and Juan wanted to be ready to go as soon as they arrived. He texted Max to prepare the *Oregon* for sailing and had him tell Murph and Eric to search for anything they could find out about the *Magellan Sun*.

 **THAILAND**

Gerhard Brekker was fascinated by the behavior of Alastair Lynch, who was handcuffed to a metal chair bolted to the floor. During the entire night of "enhanced interrogation techniques," as the Americans liked to call them, Lynch had barely uttered a whimper no matter how much water was poured on his face or how many electrical shocks he endured. But now, as dawn broke through the remote shack's grimy window and Lynch watched Brekker wave a small white pill in front of his face, the compromised British Interpol agent howled and screamed as if the mere sight of the withheld Typhoon tablet was the worst torture imaginable.

"Please!" Lynch cried to Brekker, his lips flecked with spittle. "I need my morning dose!"

Brekker looked at the other men in his employ with an amused smile. He'd seen a lot of violent and strange behavior in his days with South Africa's National Defence Force, as had the five men who'd left it to join his private military contracting firm. All of the native Afrikaners around him—compatriots who remembered the glory days of Apartheid from their youth—had participated in police actions and fought against rebellions throughout Africa, but they'd never seen someone blubber uncontrollably at the prospect of not getting his drug fix.

Brekker leaned over until he was only inches from Lynch's face.

"Why do you need it so badly?" he calmly asked in a soft Afrikaner lilt. Shouting was not his way. He found he was more likely to get the results he wanted when he was rigorously in control, both of his captive and himself.

"It's my medicine!" Lynch yelled. "You have no right to keep it from me!"

"I don't care about what you think I have a right to do. Besides, you still haven't given me the information I asked you for."

"I told you! I don't know where the pills come from!"

Brekker stood up, wiped his face with a handkerchief, and took a seat on a beat-up wooden bench opposite Lynch. He ran his hand over his mustache and shut his eyes for a moment. Though the yelling wouldn't attract any attention because they had chosen this crummy hovel for its isolation, it was getting tiresome. Brekker hadn't slept all night, and Lynch's screeching was giving him a headache.

"I've had enough with the shouting," he said, fixing Lynch with a glare. "The longer you shout, the longer it will take for me to give this to you."

Lynch's desperation was still evident, but he managed to lower his voice. "I'm sorry. I'm sorry. Just give me the pill and I'll tell you what you want to know."

"I don't think you will. I think you'll just shut up again."

"I won't!" Lynch yelled, before calming down again. "I won't. I promise."

"You got this from somewhere," Brekker said. "We know it's

from some Filipino gang, but we haven't the slightest clue where to start looking for them. Now, it's obvious you know something or you wouldn't have been tailing us in the first place. So, tell me what you know."

Lynch's eyes flicked back and forth between Brekker and the pill. Something was still holding him back. Brekker had seen it before. Lynch was scared of someone who he thought would do far worse to him than anything Brekker could do.

A little push was needed.

Brekker took out the second pill and put both of them on the floor. He adjusted the position of his boot so that the heel was poised over them. He slowly lowered the heel, making it clear he was close to crushing them to powder.

"No!" Lynch wailed.

"I'm waiting for the information I know you have." His heel kept moving down.

Lynch watched in wild-eyed horror until the boot's rubber sole was almost on top of the pills. "All right! All right! I'll tell you."

Brekker stopped but didn't move his boot away from tablets. Lynch was convinced that Brekker would destroy these precious commodities, even though the South African had no intention of harming what was a potential gold mine for him.

"I'm listening," he said.

"His name is Locsin. Salvador Locsin."

Brekker glanced at Altus Van Der Waal, his second-in-command. The short but powerfully built former commando thought for a moment, then said, "Communist insurgent from one of the southern islands. Not much known about his financial dealings." It was Van Der Waal's job to keep up on all the hot spots around the world so they'd know where their services would most likely be needed.

"How do they deliver the pills?"

"It's a dead drop somewhere in Bangkok. The location changes every week."

"Is this your last pill? Does that mean you have a drop tomorrow?"

Lynch nodded quickly.

"Why did Locsin want this pill back so badly?"

"I don't know. He doesn't tell me everything."

"But you're with Interpol," Brekker said. "Surely you know much more than one of his average clients."

"I suppose he didn't want anybody else to get their hands on it," Lynch said.

"I think I can see why." Brekker pulled out Lynch's ID. He looked at the picture, which seemed to be less than three months old. In it, Lynch had a pencil-thin neck and narrow shoulders. Brekker looked up, and the sunken cheeks and cleft chin were the same, but Lynch's bulging neck and muscular trapeziuses now seemed to belong to a professional bodybuilder.

"Have you been working out a lot lately?" Brekker said.

Lynch shrugged. "I suppose so."

"Or has this Typhoon given you a little boost?"

Lynch averted his eyes for a moment before going back to the pills on the floor. "It helps."

"I bet it does. What do you do for Salvador Locsin? I bet someone in your position would be perfectly placed to give him warnings about any potential interceptions of his drug shipments."

Brekker's boot still hadn't moved.

"Yes, you're right," Lynch said, his lips trembling. "He needed someone on the inside, and I have access to police databases and major operations throughout Southeast Asia."

"And I'm guessing the person who makes the dead drop knows even less than you do. So even if we were able to capture him, it wouldn't do us much good."

Tears were streaming down Lynch's face. "What do you want me to say?"

"Until you give me something useful," Brekker said, picking up the pills, "I'm afraid I'm going to have to keep these myself."

"Okay! Okay!" he screamed. "I do know about Locsin's shipments. I know where they come from."

"Where?"

"Manila."

"Manila's a big city. You'll have to do better than that."

"It's a warehouse near the docks. That's where they store the product before they load it onto their ship."

"What ship?"

"The *Magellan Sun*. Locsin thought it was better to buy his own ship after one he'd chartered was confiscated."

"Do you know where I can find this ship?"

Lynch shook his head, then blurted out, "But I know where the warehouse is. I can give you the address." He recited an address, which Van Der Waal entered into his phone. "Now, please. Please, can I have my dose?"

Brekker studied Lynch, but he couldn't detect any deceit. "Let me make a phone call first. Just to check your story."

He pocketed the pills and stepped outside while, behind him, Lynch cried for him not to go.

The hut sat in the middle of a vast grid of flooded rice paddies, and the rising sun reflected off the still water. Mist rose around Brekker, obscuring the nearest building, another shack a mile away in the distance. He took out his phone and called his current employer.

Greg Polten answered on the second ring. "I'm in L.A. about to get on a flight to Bangkok. Did you get any info?"

"You might want to change your flight plans. Lynch cracked when I held back the Typhoon pill that was on him when we took him, just as you predicted. Perhaps it's time you told me what this drug does."

"That's not important for you to know," Polten said, the air of superiority in the American chemist's voice oozing through the phone. "I'm paying you to retrieve that pill for me and find more of it if you can. That's it."

The tone convinced Brekker that he was holding something far more valuable than the contract he'd taken.

"All right" was all he said.

"So *can* you find more of it?"

"Yes, I think we can. We're going to Manila next."

"Good. I'll meet you there."

"You will?"

"Yes," Polten said. "I need to test the pill you have before we go any further, just to make sure you have the real thing."

After seeing Lynch's behavior, Brekker had no doubt that it was.

"And Lynch?" he asked. "What should I do with him? Eliminate him?"

"No. Bring him with you."

"With us? Why?" Transporting him would bring extra security risks, though he thought Lynch would do anything he asked as long as he dangled the prospect of his dose in front of him.

"I want to see the effects of his withdrawal in person. It will give me a lot of useful data for my analysis of the drug."

"It'll be expensive to move him."

"I can cover the expense," Polten said.

"Very well," Brekker said. "When can you be there?"

"I'll get the next flight out to Manila. My colleague and I will be there by tonight."

"You're paying the bills, so whatever you say. We'll see you there."

Brekker hung up and went back inside the shack.

"No commercial flight for us this time, boys," he announced. "We're going to hire a charter so we can take Mr. Lynch with us."

"Can I have my Typhoon now?" Lynch pleaded.

"Not until we get to Manila and verify your story about the warehouse. If the product is there, you'll get as many pills as you want for helping us."

Although Lynch was still agitated, the thought of a huge supply of Typhoon pills soothed him. If he knew that he'd already taken his last dose, Brekker had no doubt Lynch would go wild with panic.

But that's why Brekker was so good at his job. His unflappable attitude not only got him results like it had just now, it also made him an expert liar.

THE PHILIPPINES

Baylon Fire, one of the largest suppliers of fire trucks and firefighting equipment in Asia, sold its products to over a dozen countries, from India to South Korea. The privately owned company's monstrous shipping warehouse by the Manila docks sat beside its main manufacturing plant and testing facility, where its fire engines were put through their paces on a proving ground that could simulate anything from a structure fire to a plane crash.

Dozens of trucks of all types stretched to every corner of the building, from pumpers and ladder trucks to gigantic eight-wheeled airport firefighting vehicles, colored bright red or yellow, depending on the specifications of the country that had ordered them.

When Locsin traveled through Manila, he wore a cap and sunglasses to disguise himself, since he was a wanted man. But inside the warehouse, which was now empty of people on his orders, he had nothing to worry about. For months, he had cultivated the loyalty of Baylon Fire's fitness-conscious owner by getting him hooked on Typhoon. Getting him to clear out the warehouse for an hour this early in the morning was a simple matter.

While he watched, Tagaan supervised a group of his men passing brick-sized white packets from a series of crates to the top of a scarlet red fire truck. The man on top of the truck systematically dropped each packet into the opening where water would normally fill the three-thousand-gallon tank.

"How much longer will this take?" Locsin asked Tagaan. He was impatient to get back to the dig.

Tagaan regarded the pallet holding the crates. "It looks like we've got about three hundred packets to go."

The setback at the chemical lab compound made this shipment even more important, which was why Locsin felt the need to oversee the loading himself. The extensive search for more Typhoon was burning through their cash hoard. In all, the packets of methamphetamine going into the fire truck had a street value of over fifty million dollars.

"Good," Locsin said. "When we're done here, inform Lynch that we'll be loading the truck onto the *Magellan Sun* tomorrow night. I want the money transferred to us as soon as it reaches Jakarta."

"Yes, comrade."

It was Tagaan, a marine engineer by training, who had come up with this smuggling method. The packets were designed so that not only were they watertight, but they would also float. No customs inspector would think to examine the interior of a sealed water tank inside a fire truck. When the truck reached its destination and received its clearance, it would be prepped for delivery to the customer at a secure facility where the tank would be filled. The packets would float to the top, and they would be removed by a large, four-pronged retriever snake like those used to pull cables from inside walls.

That kind of ingenuity was the only reason Tagaan was still alive. The drive back to Manila had been a long and miserable trip, with Locsin browbeating his most trusted comrade the whole way for somehow leading Beth Anders and her friends to them. There was no other explanation for how they happened to show up at one of his most secret facilities.

Negros Island hadn't been raided, but he'd put his men there on high alert just in case.

In fact, all of their operations from now on had to be strictly controlled and protected until they knew how they'd been compromised. The cargo being transferred from the *Magellan Sun* this evening was critical to their plans. Locsin couldn't be there because he was focused on the important dig they had going on, but he could make Tagaan available.

"I want you to fly down to Negros today," Locsin said. "You'll take charge of the unloading of the *Magellan Sun*."

"But the dig—"

"Is going as planned. I'll send for you if I need you."

Tagaan hesitated before nodding. He was just as anxious as Locsin was about their dwindling supply of Typhoon.

"What's the status of the *Magellan Sun*?" Locsin asked. "Is it on schedule?"

Tagaan checked his phone. "The GPS tracker says that it will arrive at the rendezvous as expected tonight at midnight." He handed the phone to Locsin. The dot on the map display indicated that the *Magellan Sun* had already entered the Sulu Sea west of Negros.

"All right. You'll have plenty of time to get down there." Locsin liked being able to know where his specially modified cargo ship was at all times. With the kind of payload it was carrying, they couldn't take any chances that it was being diverted, and the GPS tracker confirmed that the captain was staying the course.

Locsin was about to give the phone back when he stopped, transfixed on the map showing where his ship was.

An electronic tracker. That had to be the explanation for how the lab compound had been found.

"What did you bring back from Thailand with you?" Locsin asked Tagaan.

Tagaan cocked his head at Locsin, confused by the question, then shrugged. "It was a short trip. Just the briefcase holding the eagle finial. Beth Anders made off with the painting."

"Did she touch the finial?"

"Yes. She inspected it before I brought out the painting."

"How long did she have it?"

"Just a minute, while she examined it."

"And the other woman? Did she touch it?"

"No. When I lost them after the gunfight, I went back to the club, put the finial inside the case, and got out of there with my surviving men."

Locsin knew the metal case was lined with a thin layer of lead, which meant it had to be opened at customs. But it would also shield any electronics inside as well.

"Did you open the case when you stopped at the chemical lab on the way back?"

Tagaan thought for a moment, then said, "Yes, I did. I gave the two pills to Ocampo as you instructed." Those had been the last pills Ocampo had received for his research, and he got them only because the two men who'd died in Bangkok wouldn't need them anymore.

It also meant that the finial was exposed for a short time while the case was open. It had remained closed ever since it arrived back at their headquarters.

A look of recognition dawned on Tagaan's face. "That redhead placed a tracking device on the finial?"

"A very small one."

As the enormity of his mistake became apparent, Tagaan reared back and kicked an empty crate so hard that it shattered.

Locsin called one of his men at the headquarters and told him to retrieve the case from his room. He told the man to go to the most remote part of the cavern and open the case far from the opening in the roof so it wouldn't be in the direct line of sight to any satellites overhead. He was to inspect the finial and replace it in the case before reporting back.

Ten minutes later, as the last packets were being loaded into the fire truck's tank, Locsin's phone rang.

"Yes," Locsin said as Tagaan listened intently to the speaker-phone.

"There was a small electronic chip inside the finial's base," the man replied breathlessly.

"You didn't remove it, did you?"

"No, comrade leader."

"Good. Have the finial brought to me in Manila at once. Do not open the case again. Do you understand?"

"Yes, comrade leader. It will be there by this afternoon."

"Good. And send another ten men with it." He hung up.

Tagaan fumed as Locsin put the phone away. "I'm a disgrace."

"Spycraft isn't your strength," Locsin said, surprising himself about how calm he was about the setback. "Your other abilities are more valuable."

"You're not going to destroy the tracking device?"

Locsin shook his head. "It's much more useful intact."

Tagaan looked at him, puzzled, until he realized what Locsin meant.

"Do you still want me to supervise the unloading of the *Magellan Sun*?"

"Yes, I can handle things here." Locsin understood why he was so serene. It was because he was back to being on the offensive. When he was in control of the situation, it kept the anger at bay. "I want to find out who was helping Beth Anders. And now that we know there is a tracker on the finial, we have the perfect lure."

After arriving in Manila and loading the PIG back onto the *Oregon*, Juan had the ship cast off and race down to its current anchorage five miles off the west coast of Negros Island in the central Philippines. The crew had spent the day planning and prepping for the midnight mission to intercept the *Magellan Sun* when it was scheduled to off-load its mysterious cargo. With only three hours until the anticipated arrival of their target, Mark Murphy was monitoring the radar in the op center and would inform Juan as soon as the ship appeared on the scope.

He and Julia Huxley were in his quarters finishing a pre-mission dinner loaded with carbs. Although the cabin was situated in the center of the ship, what looked like a huge window dominated the far wall. Only close inspection revealed that it was actually a 4K display screen feed of the view from a high-definition camera up on deck. The sun had set long ago, but the reflection of the brilliant half-moon shimmered off the calm sea.

The state-of-the-art TV was the only item to remain from Juan's recent cabin renovation. He had grown tired of the modern design, so using his share of the generous budget all crew members received to decorate their homes at sea, he had it converted back to its previous style: retro classic forties based on Rick's Café Américain from the movie *Casablanca*. The antique desk, dining table, chairs, and even the black handset telephone wouldn't have been out of place in Bogie's smoky office. Though he didn't have room for Sam's upright piano, the bedroom held a massive safe where he stored the ship's working cash and his personal weapons. Other than the old-fashioned electronics, the only object that would have seemed unusual sat on his desk, a detailed model of Robert Fulton's nineteenth-century hand-powered submarine that had been given to him as a gift by the French government after the successful completion of a past mission.

"How did Beth take it when you told her and Raven that they couldn't come with us?" Julia asked as she nibbled on the remainder of her pasta. She had met the women briefly when she stitched up Mel Ocampo's wound. Instead of the scrubs the Navy-trained physician favored while on board, Julia was still wearing the peach blouse and black pants from her shore excursion. As usual, her hair was tied back in a ponytail, and her soft, dark eyes conveyed both the intense focus and caring empathy of a first-rate doctor.

"They weren't happy about it," Juan replied, taking a drink from his coffee mug. He would have preferred to savor a glass of "Sori Ginestra" Barolo, but because of tonight's upcoming mission, he restricted himself to caffeine instead of alcohol.

"She's never been on the *Oregon*, has she?"

Juan shook his head. "And I didn't think participating in this operation was the proper introduction since we don't know what we'll face. I'll show her around when we get back to Manila."

"I think she'll like what we've done with the art she's consulted on."

"I don't know about that. She probably thinks we've got it displayed in some corporate headquarters in New York, not on a ship loaded with weaponry."

"After yesterday's excitement, I think she might be more understanding."

Juan still couldn't get the image of the gravely injured guard holding the knife to Beth's throat out of his mind. That was one reason he'd asked Julia to join him for dinner, as she also served as the ship's counselor. But his main reason was to pick her brain to see what she thought of Ocampo's assessment of the Typhoon drug, and, so far, she hadn't been able to poke any significant holes in his story.

"I should have made sure that guard was dead," he said. He often confided in her about things he couldn't talk about with anyone else, like the fact that he continued to endure pain from phantom leg syndrome.

"You couldn't have known," she said matter-of-factly. "I mean, it's possible I might not have noticed. You said the guy wasn't bleeding?"

She knew Juan was no stranger to witnessing gunshot wounds. "There was blood, but it wasn't flowing out like I've seen in the past."

"From where you said the shots were placed, I'd have expected him to be incapacitated at the very least, if not dead instantly. You know, Ocampo wasn't wrong about dolphins surviving massive shark bites. I looked it up before dinner."

"So you think Typhoon really is this miracle drug?"

"I wouldn't say 'miracle.' Steroids are powerful drugs based on hormones produced naturally by the human body. When we use the term, most people think of anabolic steroids taken by athletes to increase muscle mass, but I use them all the time in treatments for allergic reactions and to reduce severe inflammation. On the other hand, they can have serious harmful health effects if they're used over a long period or in high doses."

"He said the pills are stamped with the image of a cyclone. Can steroids be taken in pill form?"

"Corticosteroids are typically taken orally, while anabolic steroids are usually injected. But steroids can also be inhaled or applied topically as a cream or gel. But, there must be more to Typhoon than just steroids. It sounds like it's a combination drug. I've never heard of anything like it. Ocampo really said the pills date from the 1940s?"

"That's what he claimed. Is it possible?"

Julia shook her head in amazement at the thought. "I guess. Steroids were first discovered in the thirties in Germany, and the Japanese, who occupied the Philippines for the majority of World War Two, were notorious for conducting obscene medical experiments during those years."

"You mean their biological and chemical warfare group called Unit 731."

Julia nodded solemnly. "I could go into their wartime atrocities, but you wouldn't be able to keep your meal down. They might've been trying to perfect a drug to make their soldiers stronger and more aggressive. In fact, a Japanese chemist was the first to synthesize methamphetamines, which were supplied to kamikaze pilots to make them fearless. They had such a huge stockpile left over after the war that it caused an addiction crisis in Japan until the use of it was outlawed in the fifties and the remaining supplies destroyed."

"It sounds like there is another stockpile still left over of this Typhoon drug."

Julia put her fork down and pushed her plate away. "If there is, you might run into more of these guys. And given what you told me, I have advice for you that goes against my nature as a doctor."

"What's that?"

She leaned toward Juan to emphasize her point. "I'm telling you this as a friend and colleague. If you have another battle against someone taking Typhoon, aim for the heart or head. It may be the only way to make sure he goes down for good."

A gentle knock at the door broke the sobering spell of her words.

"Come in, Maurice," Juan said.

The *Oregon*'s chief steward had a knack for knowing within seconds when to make an entrance. As the only member of the crew older than Max, he carried himself with a regal sophistication from his days in Britain's Royal Navy. Dressed in black tie and white jacket, with a spotless napkin draped over the arm and carrying a silver tray, Maurice was in his element in the luxurious surroundings of the *Oregon*'s hidden interior.

"May I clear those away, Captain?" Unlike the rest of the crew, Maurice adhered to naval tradition instead of addressing Juan as "Chairman."

"Yes. Thanks, Maurice."

"I will indeed, sir. Would you care for anything else?"

"Nothing for me right now. Maybe later. Hux?"

"No, thanks. I've got to get back to work." Julia had a ritual of preparing the med bay before a mission in case it was needed. When she stood, her voluptuous five-foot-three figure provided a stark contrast with Maurice's tall, thin frame.

"Remember what I said, Juan," she said before excusing herself.

As Maurice cleared the dishes, he said, "I understand you are currently working with Ms. Anders. Will you please convey my gratitude for the magnificent art she has brought to our lives?"

Juan suppressed an amused chuckle. He was always amazed at how well connected the steward was with shipboard scuttlebutt.

"Happy to. I plan to invite her on board in the near future. If you'd like, you could give her a guided tour."

Little could scratch Maurice's stoic demeanor, but Juan thought he could detect a slight curl of a smile. "I'd be delighted, Captain." With the tray full, he glided to the door and turned before exiting. "I shall have your favorite Cuban from your private humidor and a vintage port awaiting your return from the mission. A 1985 Fonseca, if that will suit you."

On the *Oregon* it was considered bad luck to wish someone "good luck" before an operation, but Maurice had his subtle way of expressing his wish for a safe return.

"Thank you, Maurice. Looking forward to it."

Maurice nodded and eased the door closed behind him. A few seconds later, the phone rang. It was Hali Kasim.

"Chairman, Murph spotted a cargo ship matching the *Magellan Sun*'s profile approaching on long-range radar thirty miles to the west."

"ETA?"

"At their present speed, they'll reach the coast in two hours. And I've got Langston Overholt on the vid line."

"Okay, put him through to my cabin screen. And tell Linc and Eddie that I'll meet them in the moon pool for mission prep as soon as I'm off the call."

"Aye, Chairman."

Juan hung up, and the moonlit waters of the Sulu Sea on the wall monitor were replaced by the giant face of Juan's octogenarian mentor. Dressed in a tailored three-piece suit, the patrician career intelligence official with the shock of white hair sat behind a spartan but elegant desk. A copse of trees dappled by the morning sun was visible out the background windows, reminding Juan that his old mentor was twelve hours behind him.

Overholt looked just the same as he did the day he brought Juan into his group as a Foreign Service officer, and he seemed just as imposing up on the big screen.

"How's it going out there, Juan?"

"Just about to go down and prep for the mission. Do you have any new info for us?"

"Well, we've got Dr. Ocampo and his friends squared away in a safe house outside Manila, where CIA officers are debriefing them. And through anonymous sources we've informed the Philippine National Police about the incident at the chemical lab. They're scouring the crime scene as we speak."

"I doubt they'll find anything useful," Juan said.

"That's our assessment as well. Which is why we are giving you our support to go after Salvador Locsin. If Typhoon is as dangerous as Dr. Ocampo says it is, it could pose a clear and present danger to U.S. national security. In recent years, the Philippines remains one of our most important allies in the region to push back against Chinese expansion in the South China Sea. They're even allowing us to base naval vessels there again. If Locsin were to threaten government stability, it might give China a blank check for taking over Taiwan and the rest of Southeast Asia."

"Understood. Were you able to find any information about the *Magellan Sun*? Murph and Eric could only trace ownership to a Hong Kong shell corporation called Tai Fong Shipping and that it sails under the flag of the Marshall Islands." Registering a cargo ship under a flag of convenience was common, and the *Oregon* herself often hoisted a Liberian, Panamanian, or Iranian flag on her jackstaff to maintain her anonymity.

Overholt shook his head. "Sorry. The only thing we can add to what you already know is that it was owned by the Chinese government before it was sold to Tai Fong."

"Then we'll have to assume everyone on board is a member of Locsin's insurgency."

"I think that would be wise."

"In Ocampo's debriefing, did he mention recalling anything about what they're off-loading?"

Overholt picked up a piece of paper and scanned it. "He did remember a few words about parts for something they are manufacturing, and one word in particular stood out. *Weapon*."

"It makes sense that the Chinese would be shipping weapons to them."

"Or they're building one."

"You mentioned the U.S. naval base. They could be planning to attack it."

"All the more reason to find out what Locsin is up to."

"Then I'd better get moving."

"One final thing before you go. Our meteorologists report that a tropical storm has formed to the east of the Philippines. They're calling it Hidalgo. It's headed your way, but it'll be a few days before it arrives. However, they're estimating that it'll pick up strength by the time it makes landfall."

Juan shook his head and gave Overholt a wry smile. "Typhoon Hidalgo?"

"Looks like it, my friend."

 MANILA

"This is a bad idea," said Raven, who was at the wheel of a tiny rental car. Even at nine-thirty at night, traffic was chaotic, though not as thick as the daytime mess.

Beth didn't look up from her phone. She was glued to the dot that intermittently appeared on the screen. "You said that already. Turn here."

Since the bayside U.S. embassy was on the left, the only way to turn was right. "I wasn't sure the 'bad' part had registered."

Ten minutes ago, the tracking signal from the transmitter hidden on the eagle finial had suddenly come alive again right there in Manila. With Juan and the *Oregon* gone, they had no backup. After Beth's brush with death the day before, Raven thought she might be hesitant to take more risks, but Beth was so intent on finding the paintings that she brushed off the risk. Raven had reluctantly given in, with Beth's agreement that they would pull back at the slightest hint of danger.

"We're not assaulting a fortress," Beth said. "We're just going to take a look. If it seems like a good chance that the paintings are at the location where we're headed, we'll wait and call in the cavalry. Consider this a first look. What do you call that in the military?"

"A reconnaissance mission."

"Right. This is just one of those."

"That's what we were doing when we went to check out Ocampo's chemical lab. I'd like to remind you it's now a smoldering pile of ash."

Beth flashed her a smile and gave her a thumbs-up. "You've done a great job so far. Keep up the good work."

Raven just sighed in response. She could take care of herself. It was protecting someone else that was the tricky part, especially if they were intensely focused on another goal like Beth was. The pistol digging into her hip gave her some comfort, but the men they were facing weren't like anything she'd come across before. She'd keep her head on a swivel in case this was a trap.

They drove another few blocks until Beth said, "The building on the left. We're here."

Raven stopped the car at an open space by the curb and stared up at a set of three luxury towers next to a brightly lit multistory structure, fronted by a semicircular drive with palm trees and manicured topiary. The sign on the front of the building read "Robinsons Place Manila."

"This is a shopping mall."

Beth looked up from her phone at the multiple advertisements for stores and restaurants inside. "Oh, yeah. That's weird."

"You sure this is it?" Raven had been expecting to be directed to some run-down industrial area where an ambush would be easy to execute.

Beth checked the phone again and nodded. "The signal keeps popping up every minute or so inside this building."

"Not in one of the towers?" An apartment would have been a more likely place for it to be but impossible to check without careful planning.

Beth, exasperated, shoved the screen toward her. Raven pursed her lips when she saw the dot in the center of the mall.

"Let's go," she said, putting the car in park. "Stay close to me." She opened the door and stood, scanning the street around them. Couples going to the movies, groups of teens out on the town, and families coming home from a late dinner crowded the streets. No one seemed to be paying particular attention to them, so Raven motioned for Beth to come with her.

Beth joined Raven as she crossed the street. "I think you meant to say, 'You're right, Beth. How could I have doubted you?'" Raven scowled at her. "Because this doesn't seem right."

"Why not?"

"Why would the signal be dead for days and then suddenly reappear in the middle of a Manila shopping mall?"

"I don't know. That's what we're here to find out."

The unknown was the worst enemy for someone on a protective detail. Raven didn't know the layout of the mall, and there was no explanation for the abrupt renewal of the signal. She would have called this off if she didn't think Beth would have gone in anyway. At least they were in a public location full of witnesses.

Once they were inside, Raven was happy to see that the upscale mall wasn't quite as packed as it would have been during the day. It would be easier to spot anyone who looked out of place.

The four-story-tall central atrium was awash in light, its pristine white walls complementing the stone floor's colorful rectangular pattern. Raven guided them to a bank of escalators. She wanted the advantage of height.

When they reached the top level, they had an expansive view of the atrium, and they also had multiple escape options if it came to that, Raven having already identified several emergency stairways.

"Where exactly was the signal?"

"Juan told me it's only accurate to fifty feet," Beth said, "but the last time it was activated, it was coming from somewhere in this atrium."

They looked down at the many clusters of chairs that had been placed there for the convenience of weary shoppers. In one cluster, a couple of dazed parents watched their toddlers running around in circles. In another, college-age kids were laughing and fiddling with their phones. Some isolated patrons were even napping on the seats.

In all the groups, one man stood out. He sat alone in a corner cluster of chairs, alert, and watching each passing customer as if he were a leopard sizing up which prey was worth taking down. His suit couldn't hide the muscular build that Raven had noticed in the rest of Locsin's men, and his bald head reflected the lights like a shiny Christmas ornament.

She nudged Beth and nodded to the man.

"Is that him?" Beth wondered.

"Does he look like he's shopping for bath towels?"

"It looks like he's waiting for someone. You think he's expecting us to show up?"

"I don't know," Raven said. "We'll keep an eye on him, but let's get some cover by that pillar in case he glances up this way."

They sidled over to the pillar and leaned against it so that only a small portion of them was visible from the main floor below. While Beth was focused on the man downstairs, Raven kept checking the people approaching them from either side. She felt so exposed that the back of her neck itched.

Beth patted her on the shoulder and urgently pointed at the man. He had shifted in his seat, and now a metal case was exposed behind his legs.

"He's got the same case Tagaan had in Bangkok," Beth said, barely able to contain her excitement. "The eagle finial from the Gardner Museum must be inside. That explains why we're not getting a signal right now."

"Maybe" was all Raven said.

A minute later, the man picked up the case and opened it for a brief moment. Beth checked her phone and said, "I've got the signal. The finial is still in there. What do we do now?"

"We wait to see what he does."

"If he leaves, we have to follow him. He might not open the case again, once he goes, and then we'll lose our lead."

Beth was right about that, but Raven knew following him was a big risk. If they were spotted, Raven would have to work fast to get away. And Beth would just slow her down. Not to mention Beth's scarlet hair, which would make tailing the man undetected even more difficult.

"If he leaves, I'll follow him on my own," Raven said.

"Oh no you're not," Beth protested. "I'm not letting him out of my sight."

"You're not trained for this. I am. No offense, but you'll be a liability."

"Offense taken."

Raven gestured at the people passing them. "You might have noticed there aren't a lot of tall redheads in this country. He'd make you about ten seconds after we started after him. Then they could set an ambush without us even realizing it."

"But I—"

"Let me do my job. Like you said, it's just reconnaissance."

Beth opened her mouth, then closed it again in a huff.

"I think you meant to say, 'You're right, Raven.'"

"Whatever," Beth said with a smirk. "Hey, who's that?"

A second man, this one dressed in a casual shirt and jeans, approached the man in the suit, who stood and shook hands with him. They both sat down, and the man who'd been waiting opened the case.

He withdrew the finial that Raven had seen in Bangkok, its gilt finish flashing in the lights. Beth held her breath when the second man took it and began an examination, turning it over in his hands and checking every surface.

He turned it over and looked intently into the base, where Beth had placed the tracker chip. Beth grabbed Raven's arm.

"He's going to find it!"

Beth's fear came true when the man reached his fingers into the hole and drew something out that he held between his thumb and forefinger. It was too small to see from this distance, but it had to be the tracker.

The man stood and raged at the other man, jabbing the tiny object toward his face. The two of them argued so loudly that some of the other patrons began staring at the scene. After a few moments, the two of them suddenly stopped fighting and looked around the atrium as if they were about to be surrounded by unseen forces.

The man in the casual shirt flicked the tracker away like a used cigarette, jammed the finial into the suited man's gut, and took off, sprinting for the main entrance. The man in the suit put the finial back in the case and walked quickly in the opposite direction.

"Stay by your phone," Raven said, getting ready to make a break for the stairs, when Beth pulled on her arm.

"Oh, no," Beth said. "He's throwing it away!"

Sure enough, the man in the suit strode right to a trash can and stuffed the case inside as if he feared that there was another tracker somewhere in the case and didn't want to risk being followed. He walked away without looking back.

Before Raven could stop her, Beth ran for the escalators. Raven called behind her to wait, but Beth had a head start, and with a runner's physique and long legs, she was able to maintain a distance between them. Nobody else seemed to be running after them.

When they reached the main floor, Beth got to the trash receptacle a few steps before Raven.

"No, don't!" Raven yelled. She couldn't shake the feeling that all of this was wrong.

Despite her plea, Beth opened the case anyway, eager to make sure the finial was still intact. Raven couldn't see what was inside, but when she saw the horrified expression on Beth's face, she knew the whole thing had been a setup.

Beth turned the open case toward her, and Raven could now see a display that read ARMED and a small block of C-4 explosive next to the finial. There was also a small radio inside.

It crackled to life, and a voice said, "Do exactly what I say or the case will explode. If either of you tries to run away, you'll die before you get two steps from it. Look toward the entrance."

Beth looked past Raven's shoulder, and her face went so white that Raven was afraid she might pass out, holding a bomb in her hands. Raven turned slowly, angry with herself about being duped but already running through ideas about how they were going to get out of this situation.

She already knew who she'd see, but she still felt a deep chill when she spotted him standing by the main entrance with a wicked grin on his face. Flanked by four of his imposing soldiers, and crooking a finger for them to come toward him, was Salvador Locsin.

28 MANILA

Finding an isolated location in the bustle of the city would have been difficult, so Gerhard Brekker rented a yacht big enough for his team and docked it away from the main marina so that Alastair Lynch's periodic screams for more Typhoon would go unheard. The 60-foot power cruiser with sleeping quarters for ten passengers reminded Brekker of the fishing charter his father owned in his home city of Cape Town.

After getting Lynch squared away on the boat, he and Van Der Waal had spent the day casing the Baylon Fire factory and warehouse, where Lynch claimed the smuggling operation was based. Lynch had divulged how the drugs were packed into fire trucks for shipment, and he knew one was supposed to be loaded by this evening and shipped out the next day. Brekker's target was Locsin himself. It was easy enough to find the rebel leader's photo on websites advertising the bounty put on his head by the Filipino government.

The facility was surrounded by a chain-link fence topped by

razor wire, and access was controlled by a gate with two guards, posted twenty-four hours a day. Getting in unseen wouldn't pose much of a problem. Brekker had planted minuscule cameras on light poles, with views of the plant from six different angles, including the guard gate, to allow remote observation. They relayed the images via a phone hidden under what looked like a discarded box on the side of the road. The setup would give them twenty-four hours of surveillance before the batteries died.

The plan was to sneak into the warehouse in the middle of the night and steal the fire truck filled with the smuggled methamphetamine. Then he would have a powerful bargaining chip for reeling in Locsin.

While he waited for Greg Polten and his colleague, Charles Davis, to arrive, Brekker munched on a sandwich and watched feed from the cameras on three monitors set up in the cruiser's luxurious main dining area. Van Der Waal sat on the other side and drew the curtains before cleaning and oiling his trusty Vektor SP1 pistol, the standard sidearm for South Africa's Defence Force. Lynch was in a cabin below with one of Brekker's men watching him while the others got some shut-eye in the bedrooms. Equipment bags were piled on the marble floor along with several fifty-pound kettlebell weights to keep the mercenaries fit during extended ops, though they often proved handy for other purposes as well.

Ten minutes later, just as Van Der Waal finished snapping his weapon back together, Polten and Davis climbed aboard the boat. Brekker had not met either of them in person before, but he knew the Dugway Proving Ground chemical weapons experts by sight, having carefully studied what info he could find on them before agreeing to the job.

Davis, whose sweaty, flowered shirt clung to his oversized belly, dropped his carry-on in the middle of the room and said, "Finally, some decent AC. Hey, nice digs!"

Polten didn't seem bothered by the heat and humidity. He calmly set his bag down and took off his frameless glasses to clean them with a pocket wipe.

"You didn't have any trouble getting here with Lynch?" he asked before putting his glasses back on. With his graying temples and jogger's form, he looked to Brekker like the kind of college professor the coeds all had a crush on.

"He's downstairs," Brekker said.

"I'd like to see him while Davis tests the Typhoon pill."

He moved toward the stairs, but Brekker put up a hand to stop him. "This operation has gotten much more complicated. Now that we know the type of man we're up against, I'm afraid I'm going to have to double our fee. Consider it 'danger pay.'"

Polten furrowed his brow and said, "I can't get that kind of money to you now, but I'll triple your fee when I get the Typhoon formula."

Brekker was surprised at how quickly Polten responded. No blustering objection, no negotiating. That was exactly what he wanted to know.

"And this operation is off the books? I don't want it to come back to us if something goes wrong."

Polten shook his head. "We routed your payment through a dummy corporation, as you requested. No one but me and Davis knows you're involved."

Brekker nodded, satisfied with the answer. He took the tin container from his pocket and dumped one of the pills into Davis's hand. Davis eagerly examined the pill, then unzipped his bag and removed portable chemical testing equipment.

"It's amazing what you can get through customs if you've got the right government permits," he said as he pulled out tubes and small vials of liquid.

"This way," Brekker said to Polten. They walked down the stairs and entered the room where Lynch was lashed to the bed with nylon rope.

The guard, who was watching a movie on his phone, glanced up and said, "He's been whimpering nonstop. And he reeks like moldy garlic."

Lynch looked much worse than he had just that morning. His cheeks were sunken, and his muscles were already withering. Perspiration soaked the bedcover, and the stench of his foul body odor was overpowering.

"It's been twelve hours since he missed his dose?" Polten asked.

"More like twenty-four. He was supposed to take it last night, but we caught him before he could."

"Interesting." Polten walked over and took out a small penlight. He flashed it in Lynch's eyes as if he'd examined patients in the past. Lynch, who'd seemed dazed, lunged at Polten and snapped at him with his teeth. Polten pulled back just in time to avoid losing a chunk of his hand.

"Give me my pill now!" Lynch yelled.

Polten stood back and appraised him with a cold eye. "This is happening even faster than our records indicated it would."

"What records?"

Polten nodded for them to go back to the main cabin. When they got there, he said, "We have some files on the use of this drug. Its beneficial effects are potent, as you've seen. Its withdrawal symptoms are even worse. It's the price you pay for becoming an addict."

"And you think there's more of this Typhoon somewhere?"

Polten nodded. "The drug was developed in the early forties. We had thought the last remnants of it were wiped out when Hiroshima was nuked. The Japanese had built a large plant to put the manufacture of the pill into large-scale production, enough to supply every man, woman, and child in the country in anticipation of the coming invasion of the home islands. The drug's effects combined with fanatical loyalty to the Emperor could have cost us millions of soldiers before Japan was conquered. No one knows if Hiroshima became the target for that reason or if the destruction of the factory was merely a side benefit of the atomic explosion, but no Typhoon pills survived there, and the formula was lost."

"Then how did the Filipinos find it?"

"We suspect some of the pills had been shipped to kamikaze pilots here during the Battle of Leyte Gulf. But that's only speculation. Although a supply of it was supposedly carried out by a destroyer called the USS *Pearsall* at the end of the war, the ship never made it back to the U.S. and was thought to have been sunk by a Japanese sub."

Brekker narrowed his eyes at Polten, whose lip twitched ever so slightly. A liar knew a liar, and Polten certainly wasn't sharing the whole truth about the shipment of the Typhoon pills.

"The ship was never found?"

"Not until recently," Polten said. "Some recreational divers found the wreck buried in sand, so the U.S. agency named NUMA— the National Underwater and Marine Agency—is sending a vessel to secure any live munitions that might still be on board."

"Does NUMA know about the cargo?"

"I doubt it. It was top secret at the time. We only knew about it from the classified archives at Dugway. That must be why the NUMA ship isn't scheduled to arrive for another three weeks." Polten showed Brekker a map of the sunken *Pearsall*'s position at an uninhabited atoll near Samar Island. "But Locsin may have already found it and removed the cargo. We have to find him if we're to have any chance of getting that formula."

"Why is this formula so important?" Brekker asked, nodding at Davis, who was analyzing the tablet. "You already have the pill sample."

"It's complicated," Polten said, "but the critical ingredient is a plant that grows only in the Philippines. The problem is, we don't know which plant it is. It may be something that grows on only one island. With seven thousand islands in the chain, each with its own endemic species, the plant we need would be virtually impossible to find without that formula."

"And with that formula, you could make as much Typhoon as you wanted?"

"Sure," Davis piped in as he continued his analysis. "As long as you had the formula and a good supply of the plant, anybody with a chemistry degree could make it."

Polten's eyes blazed with anger at Davis's interjection and he hastily added, "But to reduce the extreme side effects, it might take years of testing and reformulation."

"I see," Brekker said. He glanced at Van Der Waal, who responded with the barest nod.

"Got confirmation," Davis said triumphantly. He looked at Polten with a big smile. "This is definitely the original Typhoon formulation."

"You're sure?" Brekker said.

"No doubt."

"Now," Polten said, "I want to know how you plan to find—"

A rapid double report from Van Der Waal's Vektor pistol interrupted Polten, who coughed twice before slumping to the floor. Davis pitched over onto the table, a surprised look in his open eyes. Van Der Waal had hit each of them in the center of the chest. Blood soaked Polten's shirt and pooled on the marble floor.

"At least it'll be easy to clean up," Van Der Waal said, holstering his pistol. "Moron. He agreed to the increased price too fast."

Brekker nodded in agreement. "You could practically see the dollar signs in his eyes. If he was willing to pay that price, imagine how much the formula would be worth to Locsin."

"We could always sell it ourselves on the open market."

"*If* it's still on that destroyer, *if* the formula still exists, and *if* we can successfully manufacture it. That's a lot of ifs. I'd rather get paid now. Let Locsin take the risk of being a drug dealer."

The men who'd been asleep had been waiting for the gunshots. They came up and began tying the feet of Polten and Davis to the heavy kettlebells. They'd take the bodies to the middle of Manila Bay later for an unceremonious burial at sea.

Van Der Waal pointed to the computer screens and said, "Looks like we've got some activity."

Brekker looked at the feed from the remote cameras stationed outside the Baylon Fire factory and saw two SUVs enter the gate. They were waved through by the guards without even stopping. When they reached the warehouse, a half-dozen men got out, including one that looked like Locsin, though it was impossible to be sure at this distance. Two women got out with them, one a redhead, the other raven-haired. Both were shoved roughly toward the warehouse and taken inside.

"You think they're going to have a party?" Van Der Waal asked in amusement.

"I don't know," Brekker said, unzipping one of the equipment bags and taking out his assault rifle. "Let's go find out."

 **OFF NEGROS ISLAND**

From the catwalk at the top of the chamber housing the moon pool, Juan looked down at the unusual vessel that hovered above the water, making sure it was positioned correctly as it was lowered by the gantry crane. The distinct smell of ocean brine and machine oil filled the cavernous room, the largest on the *Oregon*. It was in the center of the ship and contained an Olympic-pool-sized opening that was equalized with the sea level outside the ship so that subs and divers could leave unnoticed through huge double doors that swung down from the keel. Eddie, Linc, MacD, and Murph, clad in black night camo, were down below getting ready to load their tactical gear on board.

The Gator was the newest addition to the ship's complement of watercraft. The test dives they'd put it through over the last few months had gone off without a hitch, but this was the first time it would be used on an operation. Modeled after the U.S. Navy Sealion and other semi-submersibles employed by countries like Singapore and North Korea, the 40-foot-long Gator was a craft specifically designed for infiltration of targets both at sea and onshore. The *Oregon*'s Discovery 1000 had been used for similar missions in the past, but its replacement boasted significant advantages.

Shaped like an angular cigarette boat, the stealthy Gator's surfaces were shaped to reduce its radar signature to that of a bathtub toy, and the mottled black and charcoal paint made it difficult to see at night when surfaced. Like the Discovery, the Gator could carry up to eight passengers, dive to one hundred feet, and maneuver with electric thrusters, but the newer vessel's sound-insulated diesel engine allowed it to reach over forty knots on the surface while simultaneously recharging the batteries. The Gator's most unusual and useful capability was its ability to semi-submerge so that the small viewing cupola for the single pilot was the only part of it above the water, just like an alligator cruising through a swamp with nothing but its eyes visible. Since the Gator ran on its powerful diesel engine in this state, it could sneak up on a moving ship, match its speed, and deliver a boarding party through a portal in the roof while still in motion.

The Gator complemented the larger Nomad, which hung from a sling above the moon pool. The 65-foot-long deep-water submersible was built to descend to one thousand feet with six passengers and had an air lock for swimmers to exit while submerged. Though the Nomad could remain underwater for long periods before the batteries needed to be recharged, its bulky pressure hull and electric motors meant it moved much more slowly than the sleek Gator.

As the Gator settled into the water, and the mission team climbed aboard with their equipment, Linda Ross joined Juan on the catwalk and leaned on the railing, her head barely even with Juan's shoulder. Like him and the rest of the team, she was dressed all in black.

"I'll miss the Discovery," she said, "but, I have to say, her replacement is extremely sexy."

"Don't let Nomad hear you or she'll get jealous."

"Oh, I love all my children equally." She mouthed *Not really*, then pointed at the Gator and gave Juan the thumb-and-fingers *OK* sign.

"Well, now we get to prove to Max that it was a wise investment."

Linda chuckled and said, "I think his hand was shaking when he signed the purchase order," referring to their notoriously stingy VP.

Knowing that Linda's arrival meant the *Magellan Sun* was nearing its destination, Juan asked, "What's the good news?" Gomez was observing the 400-foot-long ship with a drone equipped with a night vision camera.

"Seems like she's preparing to hold station a mile off Campomanes Bay, just like we thought she would." They had surveyed the coastline of Negros, and the bay was the least populated spot on the west side of the island. Satellite imaging showed a small dock in the bay that was normally used for scuba diving boats and sightseeing tours. At this time of night, the entire place would be deserted, the ideal spot for illicit activity. The dock was too small for a large cargo ship, so they knew the *Magellan Sun* wouldn't be entering the bay. The *Oregon* was positioned five miles to the north, far enough away so that it wouldn't seem to be any kind of threat.

"How is she getting her cargo off-loaded?" Juan asked.

"There's an old offshore supply ship, the kind used for oil rigs, heading out from the island, and the crane on the *Magellan Sun* is getting set to lower cargo from her deck."

"Then we should get going," Juan said and nodded at the Gator. "Ready to take her for a spin?"

Linda rubbed her hands together with glee. She was going to be driving the Gator during the mission. "I thought you'd never ask."

They took the stairs down to the well deck. Juan picked up his own gear bag that he'd packed earlier, and they went aboard. Linda sat in the pilot's seat and went through her pre-dive check, while Juan secured the top hatch and joined the rest of the team in the passenger area at the rear. Because of the Gator's low profile, the accommodations were cramped but still comfortable, with cushioned benches along both sides of the cabin and seat belts if the seas got choppy. The interior was solely lit by red illumination so that their eyes would quickly become dark-adapted.

"What's the weather report?" Juan asked Murph, whose tablet was connected to the *Oregon* via satellite linkup.

"Cloudy and dark right now," he said, "but the moon could put in an appearance."

"Have you got the feed from Gomez's drone?"

"As if you were there," Murph said and turned the tablet toward Juan.

The *Magellan Sun* was clearly visible against the flat black sea. Although she was only two-thirds the length of the *Oregon*, she had a similar outline, with a superstructure rear of amidships, four cranes for loading and off-loading cargo at smaller ports, and a deck stacked with pallets and containers. Judging from the diminishing wake behind her, she seemed to be coming to a stop.

One part of the two-pronged mission would put Murph, Eddie, and MacD on board the *Magellan Sun*. Since she was a standard Chinese design, Langston Overholt was able to send them CIA archived blueprints of the ship, which they studied to plan their infiltration.

"Where's the equipment room that you three are sticking your noses into?" Juan asked.

Since Ocampo reported that the ship had been used to deliver supplies for Locsin's dig, the goal was to download the ship's computerized navigational logs in the hope of narrowing down which island Locsin was searching for more Typhoon. The computers were located on the bridge, which would be manned at all times. The CIA blueprints indicated that there was a junction box in an equipment room nearby, where Murph thought he could access the network.

"It's right about there," MacD drawled, pointing at a spot directly below the bridge. "That kind of room should be unattended, but Ah've got good ole Diana here in case we're wrong." He patted his crossbow like it was a faithful dog.

Eddie tapped the port side away from the crane. "That looks like the best place to climb up. Our guests should be busy with their cargo on the other side, but Gomez will let us know if anyone is getting too close while we're boarding."

Juan nodded. "How long will you need?"

"Once I'm in there," Murph said, rubbing his scraggly beard, "no more than five minutes to crack the system and download the data. They shouldn't even know I was there."

While they were on the *Magellan Sun*, Juan and Linc would be conducting the second part of the mission.

Juan inserted his encrypted communications earpiece and checked it before calling Gomez, who was in the op center, where Hali was on radar, in Linda's absence, Stoney was at the helm, and Max was in command of the *Oregon*.

"Gomez, show us the supply ship."

In an instant, the camera slewed around and focused on the supply ship heading toward the *Magellan Sun*. The design of the much smaller vessel looked at least forty years old and had a two-story superstructure at the front and a flat cargo area taking up the rear half of the ship.

"That's a lot of open deck space, Chairman," Linc said. "I don't think we'll get a friendly welcome if they spot us hanging around their precious cargo."

Juan and Linc's objective was to tag some of the cargo that was being off-loaded from the *Magellan Sun* so they could track it to where it was being delivered. And if they had the opportunity, they would open it to find out just what was being transported.

But Linc was right. Trying to do that on the unprotected deck of the supply ship would be a death wish. They might as well put neon bull's-eyes on their chests.

"You up for a shore excursion?" Juan said.

"As long as it's the package tour," Linc replied, "a mai tai would hit the spot."

"Sorry, refreshing beverages not included. They've got to have trucks for transporting whatever they're bring ashore. I think we'll have a better shot at getting close to the cargo on land."

"I wouldn't mind getting on dry land."

Juan leaned toward Linda and said, "Linc and I are getting out on our way to the ship." He checked the satellite map of the bay. "There's a nice beach about half a klick from the dock. Linc and I will hoof it the rest of the way."

"Aye, Chairman," Linda said. "My checklist is done and we're ready to rock and roll."

"Then let's get moving."

She radioed that they were departing, and the crane released the Gator. It sank below the keel doors and motored away from the *Oregon* with a barely perceptible whirr of the electric motors. When it was out from under the ship, Linda brought the Gator to the surface. She cranked up the diesel, which reverberated through the interior but would be inaudible outside except when they were cruising at high speed.

She pushed the throttle forward until they were rocketing toward the shore without any worry that the *Magellan Sun*'s radar would pick them up.

Just five minutes later, Linda eased the throttle back, which meant they were within two miles of the ship. Any closer and the sound of the engine might be heard. She activated the ballast tanks, and the Gator sank until the water's surface lapped at the bottom of the cupola. Linda's face glowed red in the soft light, but it wouldn't be visible through the tinted windows. They continued forward at fifteen knots, reaching the beach a short time later, where they stopped, with the Gator's bow resting on the sandy bottom.

Linc popped the hatch and climbed out. Juan handed their gear up, then turned to Linda and said, "We'll meet back here for extraction when you're done. See you soon." Then he looked at Eddie, MacD, and Murph. "Don't get into too much trouble."

"Don't worry about these jokers," Murph said with a grin. "I'll keep an eye on them."

"You're the real problem. I bet you're planning to plant a virus that'll back up their toilet system or something."

Murph raised his hand in mock salute. "Guilty."

"Linda, you're in charge of this motley crew," Juan said with a laugh. "Just get in and out and back here quick."

She shook her head at the banter. "Aye, Chairman. I'll make sure they behave."

Juan had no doubt about that. He knew as soon as they were away, they'd all get their game faces on and become supremely focused on the upcoming operation.

He climbed out and buttoned up the hatch before walking along the sunken bow as if he were walking on water. Holding his equipment bag over his head, he followed Linc into the gentle surf and was submerged up to his chest. His prosthetic combat leg was designed to withstand immersion in water, but it always felt strange having only one soaked foot.

As soon as Juan was off the Gator, Linda revved the motor and backed away from the beach. In the distance, he could see that the supply ship had reached the *Magellan Sun* and was pulling alongside. The crane was already in motion off-loading pallets.

After he kitted himself out with his tactical gear and body armor,

Juan slung an MP5 submachine gun over his shoulder and lowered night vision goggles over his face. Even with the enhanced imaging, the noiseless Gator had already disappeared from view.

Without a word, he and Linc put on their own serious game faces and began the trek through coastal jungle. Their footsteps were so soft that the only sound was the constant chirp of insects and the shouts of a dozen men at the dock ahead of them.

 MANILA

Having seen Locsin's men in action before, Raven knew they were a ruthless group and wouldn't hesitate to kill her and Beth if they resisted, so she simply did what they told her to do. Beth followed her lead. Still, she was constantly watching for their best opportunity to either escape or call for help. Beth seemed frightened, but her initial panic was gone, and Raven knew she could depend on her when they attempted to make a break for it.

The briefcase bomb had been deactivated as soon as the two of them had climbed into the SUV and were under Locsin's control. Now they were sitting in a glass-walled warehouse office, unshackled, apparently no threat to the six men around them, including Locsin, who seemed to be studying them. The smell of sour garlic wafted off the guards like a putrid perfume. Raven, not wanting to give them any satisfaction at their capture, yawned and stretched as if she were bored by the whole thing. She looked out the third-story window at an enormous warehouse filled with more fire trucks than she had ever seen in one place.

Two of Locsin's men were standing guard next to a particular pumper engine with Vietnamese writing on the side that sat on the edge of the warehouse, right between a heavy rescue vehicle destined for the Manila Fire Department and a gigantic yellow airport crash tender with nozzles jutting from its front. Hoses coiled up next to the eight-wheeled truck were still wet, as if its water tank had just been filled.

Locsin, who had been pacing around the room like he had more energy than he could contain, must have noticed Raven looking at the crash tender because he strode to the window and boasted, "They were testing that this afternoon on the proving grounds outside. I saw it myself. Very impressive. The nozzle is so powerful that its water can reach a burning plane from over one hundred yards away." He spoke English like an educated man, not the brutal thug that he was.

"Skip the ridiculous lecture," Raven said. "What do you want?"

She got the response she was expecting. Locsin was obviously not used to being sneered at by a woman. He stalked over to her, his face twisted in anger, and smacked her cheek with a vicious open-handed slap. Beth gasped, but Raven merely winced and worked her jaw to get through the pain, which was nothing compared to what she'd gone through when she was caught in the explosion of an IED in Afghanistan. She had endured two abdominal surgeries, and received the Purple Heart and a Bronze Star, for two minutes of what the Army deemed a heroic act, even though she just thought of it as her job. The scars on her torso were a daily reminder that she could live through anything, including this.

But she could tell Locsin had held back. He could easily have broken her jaw if he'd wanted to.

"By the time we're done with you, you'll give us anything we want," he said, letting that sit for a moment to stir their imaginations. However, Raven felt sure that any assault would be limited to torture. She knew heavy steroid use often left men performance-challenged.

Locsin reared back to strike Raven again, but Beth shouted, "Wait! I'll tell you what you want to know."

Locsin lowered his hand. "Which is what?"

"I was the one who planted the tracker on the finial. Don't take that out on her."

"You wanted the other paintings, didn't you?" He sat on the edge of the desk, suddenly calm again.

Beth nodded. "I thought I might be able to follow you to them. Do you have them?"

Locsin grinned. "That would be something, wouldn't it? Maybe I'll keep you alive just in case I do. Your services as an art historian might be useful. But I'm still confused about the man with the weaponized truck. Who is he?"

"He's a friend."

"Name?"

She looked at Raven, who nodded for her to tell them. Withholding his name wasn't worth getting tortured.

"Juan Cabrillo."

"Is he American like you?"

Beth nodded.

"Government?"

"Not anymore," Raven said. "Former CIA. Now he's a private contractor."

Locsin's grin disappeared. "And what does he want with me?"

"He was working with us to find you."

"And he just happened to be there to kidnap my scientists?"

Raven shrugged. "We can't help that you run a shoddy operation."

Locsin bristled, and his tone got menacing. "Where is Ocampo now?"

"Some safe house somewhere, blabbing his guts out. Anybody who wants to kill or capture you now knows whatever Ocampo and his people know. You really should consider a new occupation."

Locsin ground his jaw, never taking his eyes off Raven. She seemed to have struck a nerve.

"I think everything you've said is a lie," Locsin said. "I've got a helicopter coming to pick you up and take you somewhere you won't ever be found, but I can't join you for a few days and I'm not very patient. You remember that airport truck out there? I think a few minutes being blasted by eight hundred gallons of water per minute will change your story."

Raven smirked at him. "I need a shower anyway. I feel pretty nasty being around you. In fact, I might need two showers to get your stink off me."

Locsin shook his head slowly. "Not you." He tilted his head at Beth, then stared at Raven. "You get to watch."

Two men pulled Beth and Raven to their feet and manhandled them down the stairs. When they reached the main floor of the warehouse, Beth was shoved in front of the airport crash tender while Raven was made to stand next to it, a gun pointed at her knee by Locsin.

The rest of his men fanned out beside them, except for one who climbed into the tender's cab. All the trucks in the building must have had the keys in them for easy movement around the warehouse because the engine rumbled to life immediately. The nozzle rose from its slumber and angled around until it was pointing directly at Beth.

"If you move," Locsin shouted at Raven over the din of the monstrous diesel next to their ears, "you will never walk the same again.

Now, I'm going to show you what this water pump can do, and then you will tell me the truth about what you and your friend know about us."

Raven tensed every muscle in her body as the water pump whined, preparing to fire. She was severely overmatched, but she wasn't going to let them torture Beth, even if that meant getting killed in a futile escape attempt.

She readied herself for Locsin's signal, but it never came. A single shot rang out from somewhere in the rafters of the warehouse, drilling a hole through the center of the crash tender's windscreen. Judging by the placement of the headshot, the shooter was an excellent marksman. The operator inside slumped over dead.

Raven didn't waste the moment. Locsin and his men were formidable, but they lacked high-quality military training, and she took advantage of that. She sidestepped out of Locsin's aim and rammed him in the gut with her elbow. He pitched backward, firing as he fell. The round missed her by inches.

"Beth, run!" she yelled and dashed behind the heavy rescue truck. Locsin's men, who had dived for cover, had been so distracted by the gunshot from above that they began shooting at her too late. The bullets pinged off the metal body of the fire engine behind her.

In the side mirror of the truck, she could see Beth, whose face showed a mixture of fear and confusion, running crouched toward her position. She had almost reached Raven when Locsin came out of nowhere and tackled her. In one fluid motion, he hopped back to his feet and pointed the gun at Beth's head.

Raven cursed under her breath. Trying to get to Beth now would be suicidal. Expecting Locsin's men to chase her, Raven retreated to consider options for how to help her unknown rescuer. She stealthily began winding her way through the maze of trucks.

"Don't shoot again, Cabrillo," she heard Locsin yell, "or your friend dies." Raven knew it couldn't be Juan but Locsin didn't.

She stopped when a disembodied voice boomed over the warehouse intercom system.

"I don't know who Cabrillo is, Mr. Locsin, and I don't know or care about the redhead. My name is Gerhard Brekker. I know you're a devout communist, but I have a business proposition for you."

The Gator pulled alongside the rear quarter of the *Magellan Sun* with just a whisper of its electric motors, so silent that even someone standing on deck thirty feet directly above the submarine wouldn't have heard it. Eddie opened the hatch and climbed out, hefting his MP5 submachine gun, equipped with a noise and flash suppressor. MacD and Murph followed, closing the hatch behind them. In their black clothing, they were nearly invisible. MacD notched the bolt with the rubberized grappling claw into his crossbow and nodded at Eddie.

"We're ready, Gomez," Eddie said quietly.

"Hold on," replied Gomez, who was watching the ship on his monitor back on the *Oregon*. "I've got one guard coming toward you. Man, he's a big boy. I can practically see the veins popping out of his muscles from here."

Eddie looked up, prepared to take the guard out if he peered over the side. If that happened, they might still be able to salvage the mission by getting up top fast enough to hide the body, but it would definitely make for a riskier operation.

After a minute, Gomez said, "Okay, he's passed you and turned the corner around a container. The supply ship has just left with a load, and the rest of the crew seems to be getting the next batch of crates ready for another transfer. No one else is close to you."

"How many guards in all?"

"I count ten Schwarzenegger types on deck. The rest of the crew look like they're not Typhoon users."

"Ten-to-three," MacD said with a raised eyebrow. "I say we keep out of their hair."

Murph nodded his agreement with that sentiment. "I love having our eye in the sky."

"They don't mess with us, we don't mess with them," Eddie said and turned to MacD. "Our elevator cable, please."

MacD aimed the crossbow and fired. The bolt went between the tubular steel railings and hit the container behind it with a dull clang. The prongs snapped out, and MacD reeled in the nylon line until the claw was snug against the railing tubes.

He handed the rope to Eddie, who clamped on a miniature motorized winch, then attached it to his climbing harness and pressed the switch. The tiny gears inside pulled him up with a soft whine until he was able to grab the bottom railing. He checked for hostiles, pulled himself over, unhitched the winch, and put it in his pack before shouldering his MP5.

Gomez would be able to see anyone already on deck, but there was still the danger that someone inside could make a sudden appearance through a door. They'd specifically chosen this spot fifty feet from the superstructure because the nearest door was far away.

Satisfied that they were alone, Eddie motioned for MacD to join him, then Murph, both of them using their own winches. When the three of them were on deck, MacD retrieved the rope and claw so it wouldn't be seen by a patrolling guard.

"We're on deck," Eddie said to Linda.

"Roger that," Linda said. "Submerging. Let me know when you want a pickup." Although the Gator was virtually undetectable on the surface, her orders were to take no chances. She would take the Gator down ten feet so that only the radio antenna jutted out of the water and wait for Eddie's signal.

"Let's go," he said.

While the portion of the deck where they were standing was relatively dark, the area around the crane was awash in floodlights, reflecting off the top of the white superstructure.

The three of them crept along the deck in the opposite direction, guided by Gomez. The equipment room was located two decks up, right under the bridge and next to the captain's quarters. Once they were indoors they'd be on their own, out of Gomez's view. The door closest to the stairway they needed was right beside the ship's orange free-fall lifeboat, a bullet-shaped craft locked into a downward-facing cradle for quick escapes in an emergency.

The door had a thick glass window inset into it. Eddie poked a tiny camera above the sill and watched the wireless feed on a handheld screen. The hallway was empty.

He went inside and listened for footsteps or voices. Hearing nothing, he waved for Murph and MacD to follow him. They moved to the stairs quickly, knowing the longer they were out in the open, the likelier it was that they'd be discovered.

They went up two flights of stairs and found the equipment room underneath the bridge. They would have walked right in except for one small problem—the sturdy metal door was padlocked.

"Looks like someone ain't too trusting," MacD said, examining the brand-new combination lock.

"It's just supposed to be electrical and fiber-optic trunk lines and some control equipment," Murph said. "Why would they lock it?"

"Only one way to find out," Eddie said. He dug into his pack and removed a collapsible bolt cutter. He extended the titanium-reinforced handles.

"Guys," Gomez said, "two guards just walked into the super-structure. They didn't look like they were in a hurry, but they could be headed your way."

To punctuate Gomez's warning, the sound of two guards talking rose from the stairwell and was getting closer.

As Eddie clamped the bolt cutters around the hasp of the padlock, MacD said quietly, "If they notice the lock is gone, we're gonna have some party crashers."

The voices got louder. Eddie knew they were committed, and he pressed the strong bolt cutter's handles together. The hasp of the combination lock snipped in half as if it were made of plastic. Eddie removed it and pocketed the pieces.

They hustled inside the dark room, and Eddie shut the door behind him.

Using a flashlight to guide him, Murph stuck a thick, square panel with a screen the size of a small tablet computer against the inside of the door, held in place by magnets at the corners. He pressed a button, and the screen on the panel came to life. The door was thick, so the voices outside were muffled as they approached, and the footsteps were impossible to hear.

The two guards didn't slow down. They ambled by, still talking. Soon, even the muted voices were no longer audible.

"Turn on the lights," Eddie said.

Murph found the switch and flicked it on.

The ten-foot-by-ten-foot room was unassuming, just a collection of conduits and LCD control panels on the walls around them. No stacks of dollars or euros, no poor souls being trafficked, no piles of smuggled Uzis and AK-47s. Just the equipment room they were expecting.

At least that's what Eddie thought until Murph said, "Some things are different here."

"What things?" Eddie asked while MacD kept an eye on the door.

"There are more conduits than the CIA schematics showed."

"Conduits for what?"

"I don't know."

Eddie was curious about what was locked in there, but it wasn't important to their mission. "It doesn't matter. Let's get the navigational data and leave."

"In a jiffy," Murph said. He cut into one of the conduits and exposed the cables inside. He attached clips to the wires and connected the leads to his tablet computer, immersing himself in the task as his fingers danced across the screen.

"Someone else just walked inside," Gomez said over the radio.

"More guards?" Eddie asked.

"No, this guy looks like one of the crew."

"All right, we'll keep an eye out for him." Eddie turned and saw Murph peering at his screen in confusion. "What's wrong? You can't find the data?"

"No, that's not it. I'm sure it's here somewhere."

"Then what?"

"It's just strange," Murph said and looked up at Eddie, his brows knitted together like he was about to deliver bad news. "I think this ship has a fire control system."

At first, Eddie thought he was talking about a fire suppression system, but then he realized Murph would never confuse the terms *control* and *suppression*.

He meant the *Magellan Sun* was armed.

As Brekker had expected, getting into the warehouse had been a simple task once his men had taken out the guards at the front gate. Locsin hadn't posted any of his soldiers outside, the mistake of someone who was overconfident in the security of his position. Now Brekker had the high ground in the warehouse office, which still bore the distinct smell of garlic body odor. Locsin and his men had taken up defensive positions next to the fire trucks. Van Der Waal, acting as the sniper, was up in the rafters of the warehouse while the rest of his men were spread out around the perimeter, ready to open fire at his command.

At first, the only response Brekker had received from Locsin about discussing his business proposal was a few potshots at his men and some choice curse words about their predicament, but, with several well-placed sniper rounds, Brekker made it clear that any attempt to fight back would come at a high price. He keyed the microphone for the warehouse PA system.

"Right now, you're wondering who I am and how I found you

here," he said. "Alastair Lynch sends his best wishes. He couldn't be here, however, because he's feeling under the weather. Apparently, a couple of days without a dose of Typhoon will do that to a man." He paused to let the information sink in.

"All right," Locsin finally yelled back. "You have my attention. You're obviously not with the authorities or we wouldn't be talking like this. What do you want?"

"I have a business transaction that you might be interested in. Specifically, the Typhoon business. I think it could be lucrative for both of us."

"Why should I trust you? You killed one of my men."

"You and I both understand the need for force to make a point. Obviously, my point was that I could have killed you and all your men before you even knew I was here, but where would that have gotten me?"

Brekker knew Locsin's type. Capturing him at gunpoint wouldn't work. He may have been nabbed by the police once, but he wouldn't let that happen again. Locsin would go down fighting rather than be taken alive. He'd never submit to the kind of torture that Lynch was going through.

Brekker continued, "If I hadn't made my demonstration, would you have listened to me?"

"I'm listening now."

"Good. Then I think we can help each other. I know you have found a supply of Typhoon secretly stored since World War Two."

"I won't tell you where it is."

"I'm not expecting you to. But I may know where more of it is."

"Then why are you talking to me?"

"Because I think you know where more of it is, too. It would be a shame for it to be destroyed before either of us could find it."

Another pause. Brekker had hit a nerve.

"How do I know you're telling the truth?"

"There's a shipwreck somewhere in the Philippines that carried a large supply of Typhoon in its hold. It was sunk by a submarine during the Second World War. I know its location."

"What is your proposal? You're going to tell me where it is?"

So Locsin didn't know about it. He must have another potential source of the drug. Interesting.

"It depends how much that knowledge is worth to you," Brekker said.

"Why don't you keep it for yourself?"

"I'm a pragmatic man, Mr. Locsin. The Typhoon may still be inside the ship or it may not. There's no guarantee that the cargo was actually on board. And even if it had been, it might have been destroyed either in the sinking or by deterioration during the last seventy years on the ocean floor. I'd rather go for the sure thing than risk coming away with nothing."

"How much is a sure thing worth?"

"Fifty million dollars."

Brekker heard laughter coming from the warehouse floor.

"What makes you think I even have that kind of money?"

"Because Alastair Lynch told us about the meth shipment in that fire truck down there. Fifty million dollars' worth headed to Indonesia." Brekker neglected to mention the fact that he didn't know which fire truck it was.

"And if I refuse your offer?"

"Then the National Police Force will be making a raid on this facility in the very near future, and you'll be out fifty million dollars anyway."

"Then *you* won't have Typhoon."

"I'll just have to take my chances that I can find the cargo on my own."

"All right. When do you want the money?"

"According to Lynch, the meth is scheduled to be delivered in a

week. I expect the money to be wired to my account the same day
you receive payment."

"How do I know you'll tell me the location of the shipwreck once
you have the money?"

"I'm going to tell you *before* you wire the money."

Silence.

"What's the catch?" Locsin asked.

"The catch is that if you don't wire the money once I tell you the
location, I'll blow up the entire shipwreck and everything in it. You'll
get nothing."

"I'll have to verify the ship is there first before I pay you."

"Of course," Brekker said. "That won't be hard to do before the
meth arrives in Indonesia. And when I get the money, I'll tell you
how to disable the explosives. They'll obviously be booby-trapped,
so don't try to disarm them without my instructions. Do we have a
deal?"

"We have one other problem," Locsin said. "There's someone
else after the Typhoon drug. His name is Juan Cabrillo."

"Yes, you mentioned him. That sounds like it falls under the category of 'not my problem.'"

"It's your problem if he finds the ship before you do."

"He won't. I'm the only one who knows it's there and what's inside."

"The woman who got away from me. She's heard everything you
just said. She works with Cabrillo."

"Then I suggest you find her and get rid of her. Again, not my
problem. I repeat, do we have a deal?"

While he waited for Locsin's answer, Brekker heard Van Der
Waal speaking in his earpiece. "We've got movement at the airport
crash tender."

Brekker released the microphone button and replied, "One of
Locsin's men?"

"No, we've got them all accounted for. I think it's the woman."

"Take her out. We'll do it as a favor to Locsin."

"I don't have a clean shot. Now I can see the cab door opening. The dead guy in the driver's seat just fell over."

Brekker looked down at the airport crash tender, but he didn't have any better view inside the cab. What he did see was the nozzle on the front slewing around.

It was pointing directly at Van Der Waal's sniper position on the catwalk.

"Get out of there!" was all he could yell before a jet of water rocketed from the nozzle all the way across the warehouse and hit Van Der Waal just as he rose to run away. The powerful stream lifted him off his feet and tossed him over the railing like a rag doll, his rifle tumbling in the air next to him. As Brekker watched in horror, his closest friend plummeted fifty feet to the concrete floor, lethally smacking his head into a ladder truck on the way down.

The détente was gone. "Kill them all!" Locsin shouted. As gunfire erupted throughout the warehouse, he shoved the redheaded woman into the nearest fire truck and started it up.

"Don't let anyone leave the building!" Brekker yelled into his comm unit.

But it was too late. Despite the furious barrage of rounds pouring into it, Locsin's truck smashed into the closest garage door and tore through the thin aluminum. That had to be the one carrying the load of meth.

"We can't let him get away!" Brekker shouted to his team. "Forget the other men and meet me outside. I want Locsin's head on a pike."

Apparently, he wasn't the only one who wanted to hunt Locsin down. The woman in the airport crash tender revved up the enormous engine and jolted forward, tearing an even bigger hole in the building as she took off in pursuit.

33

Beth held on to the console in front of the fire truck's passenger seat as it smashed through the front gate and careened onto the road. The terror that had gripped her before was now numbed, replaced by a resolve to get out of her predicament. Locsin, incandescent with anger, was driving so wildly that she had the urge to buckle her seat belt, but she decided she'd rather risk dying in a fiery wreck than go any farther with this madman. At her first opportunity, she'd open the door and jump out no matter how fast the fire truck was going.

Locsin seemed to read her mind.

"Don't try to escape," he said, brandishing the pistol in his right hand. "I never miss."

Beth had no doubt that, even if he did miss, he'd turn the truck around just to run her down. Still, she had to try.

Locsin flicked on the emergency lights but left the siren off. The early-morning streets of Manila were nearly deserted, and the few cars that remained pulled aside for the approaching fire truck. When the cars were going too slowly, Locsin smashed them out of the way.

He thumbed the fingerprint reader on his phone and tossed it to Beth. Then he trained the pistol on her.

"Call the first number in the contact list and put it on speaker." When she hesitated, he yelled, "Now!"

She did as he demanded.

"Tagaan here."

"We were ambushed," Locsin said through gritted teeth. The words almost seemed to pain him. "I'll try to lose them, but I may not be able to."

"Cabrillo?"

"Not him. New player. I need to meet the helicopter somewhere else."

Another helicopter? Beth thought. The last thing she wanted to do was get in a helicopter with this guy, especially after he crashed his last one.

"Where?" Tagaan asked.

"We're headed toward the Navotas Fish Port Complex. Tell the pilot to track my phone. I'm in the fire truck. He won't be able to miss me."

"And the meth?"

Locsin paused, then said, "We'll make more."

"But that's fifty million—"

"I know how much it is!" Locsin screamed, before calming his voice. "Just get the *Magellan Sun* unloaded, and let me know how the Kuyog test goes. And get that helicopter here now!"

Locsin nodded for Beth to give the phone back to him and she did. He turned on the siren, emitting an ear-piercing wail.

They turned onto a wide road separated by a median. Beth recognized it from their drive to the mall earlier that evening and knew they were near the harbor. There wasn't much time until they reached the fish complex, where the helicopter was supposed to rendezvous with them.

A siren behind them began to blare. Beth thought—hoped—the police were after them, but when she looked in the side rearview, she saw that it was the huge airport crash tender that had almost been used to blast her with water.

Streetlights lit up the driver's face. It was Raven, her eyes laser-focused on her quarry.

Beth felt a sudden pang of guilt at getting Raven stuck with this mess. If she hadn't rushed to get the eagle finial, which she realized now that they'd left back in the warehouse office, the two of them wouldn't have gotten captured.

But Raven wasn't giving up on her. And that made Beth even more determined not to give up, either, but the truck was going at least sixty on the four-lane road. Jumping out now would kill her for sure.

Two black SUVs came up fast and tried to pass the crash tender. Those had to be Brekker and his men. The smaller vehicles were more nimble than the crash tender, but one of them made the mistake of lagging behind to try to shoot out the massive tires. Raven wrenched the wheel sideways and crushed the SUV against a concrete wall abutting the street. Cinder blocks went flying as the SUV plowed into it.

The other SUV, however, managed to sneak by the crash tender and was approaching fast.

Locsin wasn't about to let it get close. He weaved back and forth across the road in an attempt to smash it into a wall like Raven had. But the driver of this SUV had learned his lesson. He jumped the median and drove on the other side the wrong way.

Now Locsin couldn't stop them from pulling up even with him.

Gunshots rang out from the SUV. Beth screamed and covered her face as bullets shattered the side windows. Several of them ricocheted around the interior and put holes in the windshield safety glass. Locsin returned fire with his pistol while he swerved all over the road.

Beth tried to hang on with both hands, but her right arm wouldn't work. At first, there was no feeling in it, but then there was a stab of agony as her shoulder rammed into the door.

She looked down and got light-headed when saw blood soaking her shirt.

She'd been shot.

WITH THE FIRE TRUCK slowing down ahead of Raven as it weaved back and forth across the road, she caught up until she was right behind it. She saw Brekker reloading his weapon in the passenger seat of the SUV and knew it was only a matter of moments before he aimed a kill shot at Locsin. If it had been only Locsin in the pumper truck, she would have gladly let him, but Beth was in there, too. Raven had to do something to keep her from being badly injured or, worse, dying.

The eight-wheeled airport crash tender wasn't much different from the trucks she'd learned to drive in the Army during convoy escort duty. The biggest distinction was the dashboard's firefighting control system. From her seat, she could reach the joystick controlling the nose-mounted water nozzle, the one she'd used to take out Brekker's sniper.

She aimed it at the open window of the SUV and pressed the trigger, unleashing a combination of water and foam.

Her aim was off, and the jet of liquid arced up high over the front of her target, spraying the road with the slick white foam. Brekker, who had finished reloading, saw the stream of water and turned to fire at her, but the SUV was having trouble maintaining traction.

She adjusted her aim down, and the foamy water hit Brekker square in the face, knocking him out of view and flooding the SUV. It spun as the driver lost control and plunged into a concrete wall. Probably not a deadly crash but enough to take the SUV out of the action.

Raven shifted her aim to the fire truck. The foam poured onto the top of the cab. She was hoping it obscured Locsin's vision, and it seemed like it worked. The fire truck slowed enough for her to pull along the passenger side.

She eased closer, hoping to let Beth escape the truck and jump onto the airport tender. But when she saw Beth looking back at her, a grimace of pain on her face, she knew that wouldn't be possible. Her shirt was covered with blood.

Locsin leaned forward and raised a pistol to fire at Raven. She ducked, but, to her surprise, only one bullet lodged in the cab door. She looked up and saw him disgustedly throw his empty pistol out the window.

Raven's only hope was to run them off the road, disable Locsin somehow, and get Beth to a hospital.

She rammed them twice, but the fire truck was resilient and absorbed the blows without much damage. She was about to make a third attempt when the fire truck veered left.

The airport crash tender was less maneuverable, and she struggled to follow the fire truck into the Navotas Fish Port Complex, smashing through part of a run-down building as she heaved the steering wheel left to make the turn.

She saw where Locsin was heading. A helicopter was coming down up ahead. That was her new target. If she could take out the chopper, his only avenue of escape would be gone.

The fire truck turned into a narrow alleyway with stacked shipping containers on either side. Raven followed, but she soon realized that had been exactly what Locsin had been hoping she'd do.

The crash tender was far wider than the fire truck, and the sides impacted the containers, causing them to begin a cascade of falling steel.

Raven screeched to a stop and threw the crash tender into reverse just before it could be buried by the containers. They eventually settled into a jumble, blocking the alley. She backed out and turned to find a wider street that would let her through.

By the time she reached the complex's boat storage facility, the only spot with space large enough for a helicopter to land, it was already taking off again. Locsin looked down at her with an expression of pure hatred before the chopper banked and took him out of view.

Raven pulled to a stop next to the abandoned fire truck, jumped out, and ran over to the passenger side. She pulled open the door, and her heart sank when she saw the interior.

Beth was gone. Only then did Raven notice the trail of blood leading toward the helicopter's landing zone.

To get a good view of the dock where the cargo from the *Magellan Sun* was being unloaded, Juan and Linc had crept uphill through the jungle and crouched behind a tree where Juan could watch through a pair of binoculars. There was so much activity around the bustling dock area that they were in no danger of being heard, but the cloud of buzzing mosquitoes around their heads was almost as loud as the men below.

"I'm glad we're wearing this greasepaint repellent," Linc whispered as he swatted one of the flying menaces away from his face. "I swear, I've seen smaller vampire bats."

Juan nodded in agreement. "They're big enough to be registered as private aircraft. I think I saw a tail number on one of them."

"At least it's probably worse for those guys. The ones that are just standing around look miserable."

Juan counted more than two dozen men in the group, and the

ones standing guard were constantly smacking their arms and necks. The oil platform supply ship loomed over the tiny dock, its crane working nonstop lowering cargo over the side, where three forklifts took turns hauling the palletized cargo toward fifteen waiting trucks idling on the road, which dead-ended at a small turnabout just past the dock. Instead of eighteen-wheeled trailers, the trucks were the three-axle types, which were better for navigating narrow mountain roads. Powerful portable lamps had been set up on the dock, but the only other illumination was provided by the headlights on the trucks and forklifts.

They had already filled six trucks with crates big enough to hold dishwashers. Two men armed with assault rifles circulated amongst the trucks, but the main cluster of guards was positioned on the road leading up to the dock. They didn't seem too worried about an attack from the jungle.

"See anyone familiar?"

Juan had been hoping Locsin was supervising this operation personally, but, so far, he was nowhere to be seen. Juan adjusted his binoculars and focused on a man bossing the others around, gesticulating wildly and shouting orders. He recognized the man immediately.

"That's Tagaan," he said, handing the binoculars to Linc. "The one waving his arms around like an orchestra conductor having a seizure."

"Got him," Linc said. "He looks like his head is going to explode every time he yells. That's the one who tried to turn the PIG into Swiss cheese, right?"

"Before I shot him out of the sky and he walked away from the crash without even a limp."

"I guess we should assume everyone down there has the same mutant powers."

"Hux says that since they're all probably taking this Typhoon drug, wounding these guys won't do much. Seeing the effects first-hand, I have to agree."

Linc grinned. "So don't try to shoot the gun out of their hand?"

"Only if you want them to shoot back with the other hand. But I'd prefer to get in and out without being seen at all."

"It looks like they're not paying much attention to the first couple of trucks they loaded. I say we take a look inside one of them."

"Great minds think alike," Juan said. He keyed his radio. "Gomez, you there?"

"Read you loud and clear," Gomez said over the comm link.

"We're ready for our sortie. We're going to be in the headlights of one of the trucks while we break into the cargo area of the truck in front of it. We'll need you on overwatch to let us know when we're in the clear."

"All my attention is on you, since Eddie and his team are out of sight right now. You're good to go."

Juan led the way, creeping through the foliage as silently as a leopard on the prowl. Despite his bulk, Linc was equally quiet, making no sound, as he followed behind.

When they reached the first truck, they ducked behind the cab. The engine was still running so that the bright headlights wouldn't drain the battery. Linc stuck a magnetized GPS tracker to the underside of the fender. Now they'd be able to follow the course of the convoy to where the cargo was being delivered.

"You've got a bogey approaching on the opposite side of the third truck," Gomez said in their ears. "If he keeps to the same pattern, he'll head around the front of the first truck and back down the row. Then you'll have about three minutes before he returns."

Juan sent a burst of static to acknowledge that they'd heard. He and Linc crawled under the truck, their weapons at the ready in case the guard took a look underneath.

The clomp of boots on gravel and the occasional smack of a hand against skin announced the arrival of the guard. Juan watched his feet as the man ambled around the truck, likely bored with the duty.

When he was out of earshot, Gomez said, "You're clear."

Juan and Linc scrambled out and examined the roller door of the truck's cargo bed. It wasn't locked, so Linc didn't need to extract his set of bolt cutters. Since they were at the truck farthest along the road, they were shielded from the view of the dock by the truck behind them.

Juan eased the door up far enough for Linc to crawl inside. Juan followed him in and pulled the door down behind them. They both turned on the flashlights mounted on their weapons. There was only about two feet of space between the door and the cargo.

"It's good I'm not claustrophobic," said Linc, who could barely turn his massive frame.

"Let's try to get a look at the cargo without leaving any trace we were here," Juan said. He climbed up to the top of the crates, which were stacked to within a yard of the roof. According to the photo translator on Juan's phone, the crate in the middle was marked with Chinese characters that read *Machine Parts*.

He took a small crowbar from his pack and jammed it under the top. After pulling it off, he rummaged through the packing material until he'd pushed enough of it aside to see what was inside.

"What is it?" Linc asked. "Drugs?"

Juan ran his hand over the gleaming stainless steel propeller mounted inside a cylindrical housing. "It's an impeller."

"Like for an oil pump?"

"I don't think so. This one looks like the high-speed kind that powers a Jet Ski."

Linc snorted at that. "They're building Jet Skis? That might be the dumbest thing I've ever heard of someone smuggling."

"It definitely raises some interesting questions about what they're up to. They've gone to a lot of trouble to keep this cargo from going through a commercial port."

He looked at the crates on either side of him. One was labeled *Machine Parts*, just like the first one, but the other had characters that read *Fragile* and *Handle With Care*. There was no mention about what might be inside.

Juan opened the crate and dug into it until he felt a brick wrapped in plastic. He took it out and saw what was printed on the side. With a sinking feeling, he looked around him and saw that at least half a dozen of the crates that stretched toward the front of the truck were also labeled *Fragile*.

"I think I know why they couldn't go through customs with this cargo," Juan said, holding up the brick for Linc to see.

"Oh, wonderful," Linc said, shaking his head. "Is that what I think it is?"

Juan nodded, sharing Linc's uneasiness about what he was sitting on. "It's Semtex. Given that they have fourteen more trucks being loaded, it looks like they have enough plastic explosives to put the *Oregon* on the moon."

35

So far, none of the *Magellan Sun* crewmen had noticed the missing lock on the equipment room door when they passed, but Eddie assumed their luck wouldn't last much longer.

"Time until you finish?" he asked Murph.

"Got it," Murph said, closing up his tablet and putting it in his bag.

"Where has the ship been?" MacD asked.

"Don't know yet. It'll take some time to analyze the data."

Eddie kept an eye on the radar image of the door. No one was outside. "What about the ship's armaments?"

"All I could see was that there were three linked fire control systems. They looked like guns, not missiles, but I've got no clue on caliber or location on the ship. I could keep looking if you want more details."

"We don't have time. They must have installed them to protect the cargo from pirates."

"Or the Coast Guard," MacD added.

"Another reason to get out of here quietly," Eddie said. "Gomez, anyone come inside lately?"

"Not that I've seen," Gomez replied. "You're clear on drone view."

Eddie nodded to MacD and Murph. "Okay, let's go."

MacD put up a hand. "Hold up. We've got movement out in the corridor."

The white outline of a man sauntered past on the screen of the radar imager. When he passed, Eddie said, "Give him a minute to get out of the hall."

Instead, the figure returned and faced the door, cocking his head at where the missing lock should have been.

"We've been made," MacD whispered.

"We can't let him warn the others," Eddie said. He put his hand on the door handle. Murph moved back, and MacD raised his crossbow. "Ready?"

MacD nodded.

Eddie yanked the door open and was greeted by the shocked face of a ship's crewman, identifiable because he didn't have the muscled build of a guard.

The man instantly threw his hands in the air when he saw the crossbow. MacD grabbed him by the shirt and pulled him inside. Murph closed the door.

Eddie frisked the man. He held a radio in his hand, but he had no weapons. Eddie took the radio and gave it to Murph, who clipped it to his belt.

"Is anyone else with you?" Eddie asked.

The man shook his head. The surprise on his face was now gone. He eyed them warily.

"Why are you on my ship?"

"*Your* ship?" Eddie said. "Are you the captain?"

The man's lip curled into a vicious smile. "I guarantee you'll never get off this ship alive."

MacD chuckled at the man's bravado. "That sounds like something a captain would say."

"What is your cargo's destination?" Eddie asked.

"Somewhere on this island."

"That narrows it down," Murph said. "Any more details on the location?"

"Why should I tell you anything?"

MacD shook his head in disbelief. "In case you didn't notice, buddy, we're the ones with the weapons."

"And that's supposed to scare me? You have no idea what my employer would do to me if I told you anything."

"You mean Salvador Locsin?" Eddie said.

The captain's expression of defiance faltered, but he said nothing.

"Yes, we know who your boss is," Murph said. "Surprise!"

"And we know you've delivered cargo to a dig on a small island," Eddie said. "What island?"

The captain hesitated, then his resolve completely evaporated. "I'll tell you," he said with a quavering voice. "But take me with you. Locsin tricked me into this job. You can make it look like a kidnapping. It's the only way I'll get away from him. His men are animals."

Eddie had heard a similar story from Dr. Ocampo and the scientists from the lab, but the captain's transition to trembling captive seemed too abrupt. He looked at MacD and Murph. "What do you think?"

"He might have some useful intel," Murph said with a shrug.

MacD peered at the captain with a furrowed brow. "Ah don't trust him any further than Ah can throw a moose."

"Neither do I," Eddie said, "but leaving him here to rat us out isn't a much better option. He goes with us."

Without another word, MacD pulled out a zip tie and clasped

the captain's hands behind his back while Eddie improvised a gag from a portable tourniquet and gauze in his med kit.

With the captain trussed up, Murph held on to him while Eddie opened the door. MacD leaned out and swept the corridor with his crossbow. When he had checked both directions, he nodded that it was clear.

The four of them crept down the corridor single file, with MacD in the lead and Eddie taking the rear. MacD had reached the stairwell just as the radio on Murph's belt crackled to life.

"I hear them coming," an accented voice said over the handheld unit.

Someone else rasped, "I said radio silence, you idiot."

Eddie and the others froze. The captain grinned wickedly at him. He must have alerted while he was offscreen in the corridor before being captured.

MacD backed into the captain just as one of the guards charged up the stairs, firing blindly with his automatic weapon.

MacD and Murph dived out of the way. The captain caught a round in his leg and went down, howling into his gag.

Eddie fired back, taking out the guard with a well-placed trio of shots, but others were running up the stairs. More footsteps were pounding toward them from the direction of the equipment room.

"This way!" Eddie yelled. Murph tried to drag the captain with him, but Eddie shouted, "Leave him!"

They reached the end of the passageway, which had no exit door since they were two stories above the deck. Eddie pushed into the room at the end of the hall, and Murph and MacD followed him in, as bullets plunked into the wall behind them.

It was one of the crew quarters, with three bunk beds, lockers, and a metal desk. Eddie wrenched the desk from its spot and propped it upright against the door.

The guards outside didn't waste any time. They began pouring rounds into the door, but the bullets were stopped by the desktop. Then the gunfire abruptly ceased.

Eddie could hear the captain say, "I want them alive. Get a tank of acetylene. We'll smoke them out."

A single, rectangular window, only two feet wide, overlooked the deck below. If the captain and his men funneled smoke into the room, it wouldn't be able to ventilate enough air to keep them from suffocating.

Still, the window was the reason Eddie had chosen the room. The free-fall lifeboat was cantilevered in its cradle outside, just twenty feet away and one story down.

"Linda," he called on his radio, "Eddie here. Extraction is about to get more complicated." He bashed the glass with the butt of his assault rifle, shattering it. "And tell the Chairman that the 'stealth' part of our plan is literally out the window."

36

"Sounds like our cue to leave," Juan said to Linc when he heard Linda's warning. "I think we've seen enough."

Juan had opened a few other crates and found more explosives and impellers, but he also discovered several sophisticated radar imaging units like those installed on self-driving cars. They were small enough that Juan took one and put it in his pack, protecting it with a dry bag in case they had to swim out to the Gator.

Someone had used a marker to scrawl one word on the outside of the box. *Kuyog.* Juan's translator app told him it was a Tagalog word meaning *swarm*.

Juan closed up that last crate and climbed down. He patted his pack and said, "This might tell us something about what they're building. We'll have Stoney and Murph take a look at it when we get back."

"Think Locsin will miss it?" Linc asked.

"Probably. Let's hope they blame it on the Chinese shorting them. Ready to go?"

Linc nodded. His hand was on the door handle.

"Gomez," Juan said. "How's it looking?"

"Hali here, Chairman. Gomez is busy with Eddie's team, so he asked me to look out for you. You need to get out of there right now. Guards are coming your way, and it looks like they're searching inside every truck."

"Got it, Hali." Juan looked at Linc and said, "Let's move."

Linc silently nudged the door up just enough for them to slip out. They each rolled onto the ground, and Linc pulled the door shut behind him.

He was about to crawl under the truck again when Juan grabbed his shoulder. He pointed at the approaching flashlights on either side of the third truck behind them.

While some of the guards were noisily opening all the doors and climbing in the trucks to check for intruders, others were sweeping their lights underneath.

That made hiding below no longer an option. And if they made a run for it now, they'd have ten angry guards hot on their trail.

Juan looked up and pointed at the top of the truck. Linc nodded that he understood.

Juan gave the hulking former SEAL a boost so he could reach the lip of the truck's roof. Linc slithered up and over, then leaned down to give Juan a hand. With a yank, Juan was on the roof. They flattened themselves as they heard the voices approaching.

Both of them kept their submachine guns at the ready. If one of Tagaan's men got the bright idea to look up above, it was going to get very messy.

IT'S THE VIETNAM MISSION all over again, Eddie thought, while MacD loaded a barbed bolt into his crossbow. Except, this time, he'd be using the zip line to escape instead of sneaking aboard a moving train.

Eddie unspooled the other end of the line so that he and Murph could tie it to the bunk frame as soon as it played out. If the *Magellan Sun*'s captain figured out what they were doing, they'd have very little time to get down to the free-fall lifeboat before the guards opened fire.

A drill whined outside the door, and Eddie could see the bit bore through the bottom. A tube was inserted through the hole, and he could hear an acetylene torch fired up.

Smoke began to belch into the room.

"Time to go," MacD said, shouldering the crossbow. He aimed at the bright orange hull of the lifeboat and fired.

The bolt whizzed away, tethered to the nylon line. It embedded in the roof of the lifeboat, and Eddie and Murph pulled the line taut and quickly wrapped it around the bunk frame, while billowing smoke poured into the room.

MacD was the first out. He crawled through the window and threw a nylon strap over the line. He zipped over to the lifeboat and landed on the roof.

While Murph did the same, MacD opened the rear door of the lifeboat and went inside. Eddie knew that simply jumping overboard into the water to climb back in the waiting Gator would have exposed them to murderous fire from the deck of the *Magellan Sun*. The lifeboat would allow them to put some distance between them and the ship before they boarded the sub.

By the time Murph made it to the lifeboat's roof, the smoke inside the crewmen's room was nearly suffocating. Eddie held his breath and squeezed through the window just as the door was bashed open, pushing the desk back. Voices shouted for them to put down their weapons, but Eddie was already gone.

He landed on the lifeboat, cut the zip line, and ducked inside, slamming the door behind him. MacD and Murph were already strapped in.

Now that the smoke inside the crew quarters had dissipated enough for the guards to see that they'd escaped, bullets peppered the lifeboat. Though they couldn't penetrate the thick plexiglass windows, an alarming number of shots were making it through the fiberglass hull.

Eddie took the nearest seat and yelled, "Go! Go!" before he even had his four-point seat belt buckled.

MacD pulled the lever to launch the lifeboat, and gravity did the rest, the boat sliding down the rails. Eddie got his belt snapped together just as the boat hit the water, hurling him against the straps.

The lifeboat plunged into the water, then bounced back up above the surface. MacD started the motor, and the boat surged forward. No more bullets hit them, but Eddie wouldn't rest easy until they were back aboard the Gator.

"Linda, we're on our way to you," he said. "We'll rendezvous five hundred yards off the port bow."

"Meet you—" Linda replied, abruptly pausing. "Hold on. I've got some strange movement on board the *Magellan Sun*."

"What do you mean?"

"It looks like three of the containers are opening up."

Eddie unstrapped his belts and went to the small window by the captain's seat, where MacD was driving the boat.

He peered at the cargo ship they'd just escaped from. Men were taking potshots from the railing with assault rifles while others pointed at the fleeing lifeboat.

But what had him most worried was the three gun barrels jutting out from where false containers had covered them.

It was the fire control system Murph had discovered. These

weren't small-caliber machine guns meant to repel boarders. They looked like four-inch cannons big enough to sink a Coast Guard cutter, and they were slewing around to aim right at the lifeboat.

WHILE HIS MEN finished searching the area around the truck convoy, Tagaan watched the *Magellan Sun* from the dock, irate that infiltrators had made it aboard unseen. He'd learned his lesson after the debacle at the chemistry lab compound and had acquired a drone to watch over the cargo ship as it unloaded, supplementing the radar watching for any boats or ships. The only vessel to pass anywhere near was an old tramp steamer five miles to the north.

He looked at the screen from the drone feed and saw the ship in the distance silhouetted by the moonlight glinting off the calm sea.

"Keep an eye on that ship," he told the drone operator. "If it comes any closer, I want to know." Then he called on the radio to the *Magellan Sun*.

"Captain, do you have the intruders on board your ship in custody?" he demanded.

There was a hesitation before a strained voice responded, "No, sir. They got away, using our lifeboat."

"What! How?"

"They went out the window, using a rope, and landed on top of the boat. I'm readying our guns now. Or do you still want them alive?"

"It's too late for that. Blow them out of the water. Then get ready to load the rest of the shipment onto the supply ship."

"Yes, sir."

The line went dead. Tagaan turned to one of the guards.

"Get the two Kuyogs ready to deploy. I don't trust that captain to finish the job."

"Aren't we using them on the supply ship?"

"It will be a useful test, one way or the other."

"Yes, comrade."

Then something the captain said made Tagaan stop the guard.

"Did you check the roofs of the trucks?" he asked

"The roofs?" the guard repeated, confused.

"So you didn't. You idiot, recheck all the trucks again. Now! This time, from top to bottom. And expand your search to the jungle."

The guard nodded and ran off, shouting to the rest of the men.

A flash lit up the *Magellan Sun*. Seconds later, the first shot from its guns echoed across the bay.

In the *Oregon*'s op center, Max leaned forward in the Kirk Chair as he watched the dual drone feeds on the big screen at the front of the room. On the left, he saw Juan and Linc lying flat on top of the truck as Tagaan's men continued searching the area, with some of them venturing into the jungle. On the right was the bright orange lifeboat, dodging and weaving as the first shot from the four-inch gun splashed into the water only fifty feet off its port stern. One or two more shots and they'd have the targeting solution for a kill shot.

There wasn't much he could do to help Juan and Linc, but he wasn't going to let the *Magellan Sun* blast Eddie, MacD, and Murph from the water right in front of him.

Using the helm controls embedded in the arm of the chair, Max pushed the *Oregon* to full speed on an intercept course.

"What's our range to that ship?" he asked Eric, who sat at Murph's weapons station.

"Five miles and closing fast," he replied.

At this distance, their own bow-mounted 120mm cannon with its two-mile range was useless, and a torpedo wouldn't reach the ship before it got off a dozen more shots.

"Ready an Exocet," he said. Guided by its own active radar, the powerful French-made antiship missile was designed to skim only six feet above the water at seven hundred miles per hour.

"Aye, sir," Eric said, falling back on his Navy training as he smoothly activated the weapons system. "Missile armed and ready."

"Fire."

The *Oregon*'s hull reverberated with the thump of the Exocet blasting from its launch tube.

"Missile away," Eric said. "Twenty-five seconds to target."

Too long, Max thought as he saw another round splash into the water, this one much closer to the lifeboat. He turned to Hali at the comm station. "Tell Eddie that the cavalry is coming, but it may not arrive in time."

"ACKNOWLEDGED," Eddie said in response to Hali. "We're not sticking around."

The lifeboat was far enough from the *Magellan Sun* that it was out of reach of the cargo ship's lights, and cloud cover momentarily obscured the half-moon, cloaking them in darkness. The gun had to be aimed by radar.

He looked at MacD and Murph. "Time to go, gentlemen." He opened the rear hatch.

MacD tied off the steering wheel so that it was locked in place, and he shoved the throttle to its stops. He and Murph went to the back of the lifeboat, and they all put on life vests.

"After you," Eddie said to Murph, who jumped through the door. MacD followed. Eddie was the last into the water.

The lifeboat continued motoring forward, quickly leaving them behind.

Eddie saw another flash of light from the *Magellan Sun.*

"Incoming!" he yelled.

They covered their heads, but the gesture wouldn't do much if the gunner's aim was off. A hit in the water anywhere near them would crush their bodies to pulp.

A second after it fired, the shell whistled overhead and landed right on the lifeboat. It blew apart in a hail of fiberglass. Pieces of it peppered the water around them, but none of them were big enough to cause injury.

Eddie thought that would be the end of it, but, a moment later, yet another round fired from the deck gun.

"Another incoming!"

"What the . . . !" MacD shouted.

"They should think we're dead," Murph said at the same time.

The round landed halfway between them and the lifeboat, rattling Eddie's teeth, and showering them with water. The next one would blow them away.

At that moment, Eddie saw a red flame shooting toward them, from the direction of the *Oregon,* just feet above the surface of the ocean. The roar of the rocket engine reached them just before it screamed by at nearly supersonic speed.

The three of them pumped their fists and shouted as the Exocet slammed into the center of the *Magellan Sun* directly under the gun that had been firing at them.

The explosion rose in a fiery plume over the midship deck, surrounded by a cloud of black smoke. It was almost immediately followed by a secondary explosion. The missile must have hit the cannon's ammunition magazine.

The gun mount was tossed into the sky and overboard, landing with a huge splash. Containers on the deck were crushed like alumi-num cans and somersaulted across the deck.

But that wasn't the end of the explosions.

Juan had mentioned over the radio that a large part of the ship-ment on the trucks was plastic explosives. The blast of the shipboard ammo must have been enough to set off the Semtex remaining on board because a huge explosion lit up the night sky.

Eddie could feel the heat on his face as the *Magellan Sun* was ripped in half as if it were made of cardboard. The entire topside was engulfed in fire.

Simultaneously, the bow and stern sections rose out of the ocean as water gushed into the exposed holds of the ship. They pointed skyward for a few seconds and then slipped beneath the surface, leaving only a burning oil slick to mark the cargo ship's passing.

The Gator's cupola rose out of the water next to Eddie. Linda waved from the cockpit for them to come aboard.

"Get inside, you guys," she said. "The Chairman is in trouble."

38

The guards checking the roofs of the trucks behind Juan and Linc were making quick work of it. They had only a minute left before a flashlight would catch them lying atop the cargo section of the lead truck.

Linc nudged Juan. "Our escape route is blocked," he whispered.

Juan followed his gaze to the flashlights of a dozen guards scouring the jungle. And stealing the truck was out of the question since they'd have to take time to turn around and run the gauntlet of the guards behind them, all of whom were armed with automatic rifles.

Since the road ended at a rocky hill that would be impossible to climb without being exposed to gunfire, that left only one option.

"Looks like we're going for a swim," Juan replied, looking at the bay. He spoke quietly into his mic. "We need evac, Linda. What's your ETA to the dock?"

"Three minutes submerged," she said, "but we can be there in a minute if we surface."

"No, stay under. I don't want to tip our hand. We'll meet you two hundred yards offshore and two hundred yards west of the supply ship."

"Acknowledged. See you there."

"Got your Spare Air?" Juan asked Linc as he removed a tiny air tank and goggles from his pack and stuffed them into his front pocket for quick access. The disposable tank had a mouthpiece and enough air for fifteen breaths.

Linc nodded and readied his own tank and goggles.

They edged closer to the truck's cab, ready to climb down and make a dash for the sea, when the clouds parted. The uncovered half-moon bathed them in light.

They froze in place, but it was too late. One of the men in the jungle spotted their silhouettes through the trees and yelled to the others.

Juan and Linc tumbled onto the hood and to the ground as bullets raked the truck, smashing windows and tearing up the side of the hood. One of the rounds hit the still-hot radiator, and steam shot out of the grille. Another must have hit the fuel tank because Juan could smell gasoline, gushing onto the gravel road.

"So much for a stealthy escape," Juan said, crouching by the hood.

"It's a long way to the water," Linc said. They were thirty feet from the seawall that had been built to buttress the road.

Juan took aim at the flashlights in the jungle. "I'll cover you. You can return the favor from behind the seawall. Go!"

Juan opened up on the foliage, knowing he'd have to be incredibly lucky to hit anyone. Linc ran as Juan emptied his magazine. When he was out, he reloaded and stole a look behind him in time to see the huge former Navy SEAL dive over the seawall. Water erupted onto the rocks like he'd done a cannonball.

Then he saw Linc pop up, his submachine gun at the ready.

As Juan got into a sprinter's stance to make his run across the open stretch of road, he looked to the dock and saw Tagaan level a scoped assault rifle in his direction.

Juan jumped back, narrowly avoiding the rounds that whizzed past. No way was he going to cross that distance without getting hit.

Then he heard Gomez's voice in his ear.

"I got you, Chairman," he said. "Get ready to run. Linc, start firing."

Linc didn't bother asking what their eye in the sky had in mind. He began hosing down the jungle with bullets.

"Now, Chairman," Gomez said calmly.

Juan took off, his eyes on Tagaan as he ran. The communist no longer had his rifle aimed at Juan. Instead, he was swatting at the air with the weapon, vainly trying to smack the quadcopter drone that buzzed around him, but Gomez was too skilled a pilot to let it get hit.

It provided just the distraction Juan needed. He raced across the road, rolled over the seawall, and slipped into the water. He didn't surface, instead taking the Spare Air tank from his vest and clamping his teeth around the mouthpiece attached directly to the small tank.

He breathed in and put his goggles on. The water was so clear that he could see Linc join him underwater with his own tank.

Juan checked the compass on his wrist and pointed in the direction where he told Linda they'd meet.

They descended to six feet to avoid the bullets hitting the water around them and began swimming.

"KEEP SHOOTING!" Tagaan yelled to his guards. "They'll have to come up eventually."

Twenty men lined the water, firing at any shape that looked vaguely human, but no bodies bobbed to the surface.

Tagaan had recognized the man who'd been in the missile-armed truck that had taken down the helicopter. Mel Ocampo or one of his chemists must have told him about this cargo drop. But the burning remains of the *Magellan Sun* meant they weren't attempting to hijack the shipment. They were after something else.

He didn't know how the two men remained underwater, but he knew that someone was going to have to pick them up. For that, he had a solution.

"Get the Kuyogs ready to launch," he said to his lead mechanic.

The mechanic nodded and removed the tarps covering two objects floating in the water next to the dock. Painted a glossy black, each of the sleek watercraft was the size and shape of a Jet Ski, with the seats and handles removed. The only protrusion that interrupted the streamlined hull was a state-of-the-art imaging sensor that could detect anything bigger than a scuba diver's marker buoy. Once the target was tagged by a laser, the internal sensor would lock on. The Kuyog would then doggedly continue its pursuit until it came within three feet of the target and detonated the hundred pounds of Semtex inside.

An accomplished marine engineer before joining Locsin's cause, Tagaan had designed the Kuyogs himself. Though he had only two of them tonight, an unlimited number of Kuyogs could be unleashed on a single target, which was why he'd given them the Tagalog name for *swarm*.

Locsin had known that to control an island nation like the Philippines would require taking out its Navy, and the Kuyogs were specifically designed for the task. *Asymmetric warfare* was the term. Tagaan had learned the lesson from the bombing of the USS *Cole*, an American destroyer crippled by suicide bombers in a fiberglass boat that had come alongside and detonated four hundred pounds of explosives. But with Tagaan's expertise, they now had a much more sophisticated attack plan. Hundreds more Kuyogs were already in various stages of construction, and this shipment from China was the final load that would allow a communist takeover of the country with the help of foot soldiers fueled by Typhoon.

Tonight was supposed to have been the test run for the Kuyogs. Tagaan had been planning to launch them at the oil supply ship once the cargo was unloaded from the *Magellan Sun*, but now he had a real challenge. If no boat showed up to pick up the two men who'd dived into the water, he'd send them after the disguised cargo ship that had fired the missile against the *Magellan Sun*.

The mechanic checked the diagnostics on each Kuyog, then said, "Ready, comrade."

Tagaan held the powerful targeting laser as he scanned the sea. His drone showed the mystery cargo ship continuing toward them at high speed. It would be in range of his laser as soon as it came around the northern point of the bay.

Then Tagaan's eye was drawn to movement two hundred yards away. He wouldn't have seen the small submarine conning tower surfacing if it hadn't been for the two men climbing out of the water onto it.

"Launch now!" he shouted.

The mechanic flipped a switch, and the two Kuyogs raced away from the dock. In seconds, they reached such a high rate of speed that they rose up out of the water to ride atop drag-reducing hydrofoils jutting from the hull.

Tagaan focused the laser on the sub's conning tower. He heard the two-tone beep from the control pad indicating that the Kuyogs had locked onto the target.

Tagaan felt a surge of pride at how well the system was working, and soon he'd see the results of thousands of hours of effort. Given how close the sub was, there was no way the two men would be able to get inside and submerge before the Kuyogs blew it out of the water.

Juan heard them coming before he saw them. The two bullet-shaped watercraft were backlit by the lights at the dock. Their engines sounded like the sinister growls of attacking predators.

Once Linc was on the deck of the Gator, Juan pounded on the hull.

"Linda, purge the ballast tanks and get out of here!"

"Aye, Chairman," she replied over the radio. "I see them."

The Gator's big diesel engines rumbled to life as the pumps emptied the tanks. The submarine-boat hybrid rose out of the water and shot forward. Salty spray washed over them as Linda weaved back and forth in evasive maneuvers, but she couldn't shake the pursuing craft.

Juan gripped tight to one of the deck handholds so he wouldn't be thrown off the slick deck and into the water. "Those must be a couple of the Kuyogs that the parts in the truck were for."

"Which means they're loaded with a good chunk of Semtex," Linc said. "And they're gaining on us."

"I'm assuming those things aren't friendly," Linda said as she turned the Gator toward the open sea. "The *Oregon* is on its way to take them out with her Gatling guns."

Juan looked forward but couldn't see the *Oregon*. The distance between them and the Kuyogs chasing them was closing too fast.

"We won't make it in time. Turn around."

"Turn around?" Linda asked. "Did I hear that right?"

Juan eyed the supply ship still tied to the dock. "Yes. We're going to give these things another target."

Linda sounded dubious, but she said, "Aye, Chairman." The Gator swung around in a wide turn and headed back the way they'd come. The Kuyogs nimbly banked with them, their hydrofoils knifing through the water.

"Refill the ballast tanks, but keep the Gator trimmed with the bow up."

"Got it," Linda said with obvious understanding of what he had planned. "Filling tanks. I'll straighten out so you can come below."

"Not yet. Come in on a parallel course to the supply ship. Stick with the evasive maneuvers until we're within five hundred yards of her."

"That's cutting it close."

Juan glanced at Linc, who gave him a thumbs-up. "I know. We'll make it work. Tell Eddie to open the hatch as soon as you are level."

"Will do," she said.

"You really think this will work?" Linc asked. "As far as I know, this tactic wasn't one we simulated during the Gator's testing phase."

Juan smiled and shrugged. "We never tested it because it was too risky. I'd say it's worth the risk now."

"Have to agree with you there," Linc said over the menacing snarl of the gaining Kuyogs.

"Get ready, Chairman," Linda said.

Juan watched the Gator's hatch. "We're ready. You first," he said to Linc. "Just don't get stuck."

They tossed their guns away, but Juan kept his pack with the Kuyog imaging sensor inside.

The supply ship loomed ahead and the Gator suddenly straightened out. The hatch flew up, and Linc lunged for the opening. He neatly slid inside, and Juan quickly followed, tumbling down as his feet slipped on the metal hull. He tucked and landed in the cabin.

Eddie sprang up and slammed the hatch down, whirling the wheel to seal it. When it was tight, he said, "Buttoned-up."

Linc pulled Juan to his feet. Juan went forward to the cockpit and said to Linda, "Now turn us toward the supply ship."

She yanked the wheel to port, aiming the Gator in the direction of the supply ship's stern while continuing her evasive maneuvers.

Juan stuck his head into the cupola and looked back. The Kuyogs were no more than twenty yards behind them.

"When should I dive?" Linda asked, her hands tight on the wheel.

Juan turned and pointed at the supply ship. "Get as close to her as you can."

TAGAAN WATCHED with a grin as the strange vessel aimed straight for the supply ship on what seemed to be a suicide mission. He didn't really care if they wanted to kill themselves, since the supply ship was no longer of any use to him with the *Magellan Sun* on the ocean floor. He was more excited to see the performance of the Kuyogs. So far, they had outdone even his lofty expectations.

Then his grin vanished when he saw the fleeing boat plunge beneath the surface like a diving dolphin. With a surge of white water, it disappeared, leaving the pursuing Kuyogs with no target.

No, they did have a target. The sensors were programmed to reacquire the target as quickly as possible if they lost their lock.

So the supply ship directly ahead of them became the target.

They reached the stern of the supply ship simultaneously, detonating just as Tagaan had designed them to do.

He flattened himself on the dock as a hail of debris fell around him. The stern of the supply ship erupted in a geyser of flames, its fuel tank ruptured and burning. The crew fled the bow superstructure as the ship began to sink.

Tagaan blinked and stood up. He searched the water for signs that the submarine-boat had been damaged or destroyed by the explosions, but he saw no telltale slick or debris, though he didn't know if they'd be distinguishable from the remains of the supply ship. He had to assume that the daring maneuver had worked and they had got away.

But even if the sub hadn't escaped disaster in the sudden dive, the mystery cargo ship speeding toward them was still a threat. If it had more missiles or other weaponry on board, it might use them on the trucks loaded with half the shipment he'd come to collect.

Only now he noticed his mechanic still cowering on the dock with his hands over his head.

"Get up, you imbecile," he said.

The mechanic gingerly got to his feet and surveyed the supply ship that was now partially underwater. He smiled timidly at Tagaan. "At least the Kuyogs worked."

Tagaan gave him a withering look and barked at him through clenched teeth, "We're leaving. Now! Get the drivers to their trucks."

"Yes, comrade."

While his orders were being carried out, Tagaan checked the approaching cargo ship on the feed from his airborne drone, which was following her on autopilot. Now that she was closer to coming around the point of the bay, he could see how dilapidated the ship was. If she was equipped with a missile battery and carried a submarine, he wondered what other secrets she held. If only he had more Kuyogs with him, he'd test out her defensive capabilities.

The mechanic came running back to him.

"Comrade Tagaan, the lead truck's radiator is damaged, and the fuel tank is punctured. It will take an hour to fix them enough to drive."

"We don't have time for that."

"Should I move its cargo to another truck?"

Tagaan grabbed the mechanic's shirt and screamed in his face, "I told you we're leaving this minute!" Then he shoved the man away. He hated to leave so much of their precious cargo behind, but he couldn't risk losing the entire shipment instead of just half. He'd also have to abandon the drone.

Tagaan took one last look at the unassuming cargo ship racing toward them and said, "Now, get me a lighter."

TEN MINUTES LATER, the *Oregon* stopped just long enough for the Gator to surface inside the moon pool and to pluck Eddie, MacD, and Murph from the water. Juan was the first out and he made a beeline for the op center, with Murph tagging along behind, still turning the Kuyog imaging sensor over in his hands. He reclaimed his chair from Max, who returned to his customary position at the engineering station. Murph handed the sensor to Eric and sat at the weapons console, tapping away at the tablet holding the data from the *Magellan Sun*'s navigation system.

"What's this?" Eric said, inspecting the object.

"That's one of the items in the shipment," Juan said.

"Imaging tech," Murph added absently without looking up from his handheld computer. "Chinese-made. Can't wait to take it apart and check out what they came up with."

"Anything salvageable from the *Magellan Sun*?" Juan asked Max.

Max shook his head. "Went up like a Roman candle. Linda said you found Semtex on the truck. That must have been what cut it in half. Straight to Davy Jones's locker."

"Then that's our only insight into the Kuyog's design," Juan said, first pointing at the sensor, then nodding at the big screen.

The feed from the deck camera showed the dock and road where he and Linc had infiltrated the truck. The supply ship was gone, and so were all but one of the trucks. The remaining truck, still parked near the end of the road, was ablaze. The Semtex wouldn't be detonated by the fire, but it would probably burn brightly all through the night, reducing the truck and its contents to molten slag.

Max raised an eyebrow at Juan. "Please don't tell me that's the truck you planted the tracker on."

"Okay, I won't," Juan said with a resigned look.

"But it is."

Juan nodded. "So we have no way to follow where those trucks are going."

"That's a bigger problem than you think," Max said.

"What do you mean?"

"Raven called a few minutes ago. She said Locsin kidnapped Beth Anders."

While Max summed up what happened to Beth and Raven, Juan rubbed his temples, sick at the thought of what she must be going through.

"And now we have no way to find him," Juan said.

Murph cleared his throat. "Actually, we might."

"I like your timing," Juan said, glad to get some good news.

"I was able to extract the GPS logs from the *Magellan Sun* and create a map of her shipping courses over the last month. We're looking for an islet, right?"

Juan nodded. "Dr. Ocampo told us Locsin had a dig going on somewhere in the Philippines, but he didn't know the exact location, just that it was a small island. There are thousands in the country that could fit that description."

"Well, most of the *Magellan Sun*'s stops were either in Chinese or Filipino ports. Or right here, of course, when she was off-loading her illicit cargo. But there was one small island where she made multiple visits."

"Put it up on the screen so we can see where we have to go," Juan said.

"No need," Murph said. "We saw the island just yesterday when we sailed out of Manila Bay. Locsin's dig is on Corregidor."

 **MANILA BAY**

The morning sun lit up the forested island of Corregidor like a glittering emerald set against the brilliant sapphire expanse of the Pacific behind it. Salvador Locsin sat in the bow of a pump boat, a large outrigger canoe fitted with an automobile engine at the back, a vessel common in the Philippines. He watched the tail end of the tadpole-shaped island pass by their port side, but he couldn't see the abandoned dirt airfield that was hidden by the trees. A mile behind them to the north was the Bataan Peninsula, infamous for the merciless Death March that the Japanese forced the surrendering Americans and Filipinos to endure in 1942.

Corregidor, the former fortress and current historic monument, sat at the entrance to the bay thirty miles from the city of Manila. The tiny pump boat was the most inconspicuous way for Locsin and his seven communist soldiers to get to the island, which would be teeming with curious, photo-happy tourists.

For the past three weeks, Locsin's men had been digging on the island under the pretense of a restoration project to excavate one of the tunnels that the Japanese had collapsed during the American invasion in 1945. The cache of Typhoon pills that his men had discovered also contained information that indicated the main research lab had been housed in one particular tunnel on Corregidor and gave its exact location. Locsin's best hope for maintaining his supply was to dig out this tunnel and find either more Typhoon pills or the formula itself.

Their progress had been slower than Locsin wanted because they could only dig during the day, otherwise they would draw unwanted attention to the project. His diggers told him that they were close to breaking through, so he'd come out himself today to oversee the final push.

Locsin's phone beeped with the call he'd been waiting for.

"Are you back at the cavern?" he asked Tagaan.

"Yes, comrade," Tagaan replied. Even though their headquarters on Negros Island was situated far from any cell phone towers, he was able to call through the cavern's Wi-Fi and illicit satellite Internet connection.

"Has Beth Anders arrived?"

"Yes, comrade. She's currently unconscious, but we've already begun the experiment on her."

"Good," Locsin said. "Let me know when you have any results. The information could prove useful to future operations. And if she recovers enough to work, have her examine the paintings and give us an appraisal. With our meth shipment now in the custody of the police, we'll need another source of revenue soon. How did the Kuyogs perform?"

In a brief conversation earlier, Tagaan had told him only the bare minimum about the sinking of the *Magellan Sun* and the attack on the truck convoy.

There was a moment of silence from the other end of the phone. "The Kuyogs performed as intended" was Tagaan's terse reply.

"Then how did the attackers get away?"

"I designed them to attack surface targets, not submarines. Our goal is to destroy the Philippine Navy, which has no subs."

Locsin fumed. "Are you making excuses?"

"No, comrade. Just explaining the situation."

Locsin felt himself going ballistic, so he paused until he was able to calm himself. "How many Kuyogs do you have ready now?"

"We have forty-five operational, and another ninety-five in various stages of production."

"Would they be effective against the ship that sank the *Magellan Sun*?"

No hesitation this time. "Absolutely. But the ship does seem to have some defensive capabilities."

"I don't care. If we have a chance to sink her, I would use every one of the Kuyogs we have now to put her at the bottom of the ocean. This Juan Cabrillo has caused extensive damage to our cause. He needs to pay."

"If the opportunity arises, I will make it happen. But we don't know where he or his ship is."

"You said earlier that the captain of the *Magellan Sun* called you before she was sunk and told you that the reason he knew about the intruders was because he happened to be reviewing his computerized navigation charts at the time they were being downloaded."

"That's correct. He said if he hadn't been looking at them at that exact moment, he never would have known they were hacked, let alone that intruders were on board."

"Then I know where Cabrillo is headed next," Locsin said. "The *Magellan Sun* stopped at Corregidor multiple times over the last few weeks to drop off equipment. The navigation logs had to be what they were looking for when they boarded the ship. They're coming here."

The pump boat was now passing Malinta Hill in the middle of the island's tail, an area called Bottomside, where the stronghold's extensive tunnel system had been turned into one of the Philippines's most popular tourist attractions.

"You don't have much time before they arrive," Tagaan said.

"You said the ship had to be bigger than the *Magellan Sun*."

"I think so, though there was no frame of reference in the dark for me to be sure."

"Then it can't make more than fifteen knots. That gives us at least fourteen hours."

"It seemed to be going very fast for a ship its size."

"Twenty knots, then," Locsin said with a shrug. "That still won't put them here until nightfall. By then, we should have broken through and made off with whatever is inside the tunnel."

Locsin couldn't take anything sizable with him on the small pump boat, which was why he had an alternative way off the island ready to go at a moment's notice.

"What about this Brekker who came after you last night?" Tagaan asked. "Do you think he's dead?"

"I doubt it," Locsin said. "His wreck didn't look bad enough to kill him."

"Do you think he was right about the World War Two ship carrying more Typhoon pills?"

"If he was, then he has a head start on us, and we don't know where he's going. Unless we find out the name of the ship, it will be impossible to find Brekker. Be ready with the Kuyogs, just in case we run into Juan Cabrillo again. Get them loaded into the trucks for quick transport. I will contact you when we are successful here."

"Yes, comrade."

Locsin hung up as they pulled up to Corregidor's north side and tied up at the pier beside the Lorcha Dock, where Douglas Mac-Arthur had made his departure in 1942, abandoning the Philippines to the vicious Japanese invaders. A high-speed catamaran from Manila was unloading a mix of Filipino, Asian, and American tourists next to them, where they were being herded into *tranvías*, open-sided trams that were the main form of transportation on the island.

He made his way through the throngs of eager tourists and joined his men at the van that had been unloaded earlier in the week at the *Magellan Sun*, along with two Bobcats and other digging equipment, as well as any weapons they might need in the event the police caught on to their scheme.

He donned his yellow work vest and helmet and climbed into the passenger seat of the van. They set off for the south side of Malinta Hill, where the tunnel dig was located, passing a souvenir shop and a bronze statue of MacArthur, smiling and waving, upon his return three years after his escape to Australia. When Locsin got control of the nation, one of his first acts would be to tear down that smug symbol of American colonization.

The thought made him smile, and, for the first time, his rage was at bay. He felt even better when he imagined his swarm of attack drones sinking Juan Cabrillo's precious ship.

 MANILA

When one of the *Oregon*'s two lifeboats reached the Manila dock at noon, Juan met Raven at the gangway. With bloodshot eyes and rumpled clothes, she looked like she'd gotten even less sleep than he had. As soon as she was aboard, the lifeboat cast off and headed back to the *Oregon*, anchored south of Corregidor in Manila Bay.

"Has there been any ransom demand?" she asked without preamble, her ebony hair blowing in the breeze.

Juan shook his head. "Locsin's group hasn't even publicly acknowledged that they have Beth, and they have no way to contact us directly. We found out that Gerhard Brekker is a South African mercenary, but we don't know how or why he's involved in all this. It sounds like he thinks that this unnamed shipwreck he mentioned might contain more Typhoon, although if it's been under the ocean for seventy years, the cargo is likely to have been destroyed long ago. And the fire truck with the meth on board is in police custody, so you hurt Locsin's smuggling operation badly."

"What about the helicopter he used to escape with Beth?"

"There's no way to track it."

"It's my fault that she was taken," Raven said, her hands tightly balled into fists. "I have to get her back."

"It's Locsin's fault, not yours. And we'll all work together to get her back."

"How?"

"We have a lead in the search for Locsin." He told her about the previous night's operation and the discovery that the *Magellan Sun* had visited Corregidor several times.

"You think that's where he's digging to find more of the Typhoon drug?"

"It makes sense, given Ocampo's claim that the pills date back to World War Two. Corregidor was the most heavily defended island in the Philippines during the war. If the Japanese wanted a place to develop the drug, they couldn't have picked a more isolated location."

Raven nodded. "If I remember my West Point history lessons correctly, many of the tunnels on Corregidor collapsed during the final American assault to retake the island."

"Corregidor is riddled with tunnels and caves," Juan said. "Gomez Adams, our helicopter and drone pilot, is getting ready to do an aerial survey of the island and look for any unusual recent activity."

"I want to be there when you get Locsin. If you try to stop me, I'll—"

Juan put up his hands in surrender. "I thought you might, so I'm having Eddie prepare some gear and weapons for you. As far as I'm concerned, you're part of this operation now. "

When they got to the *Oregon*, where it was anchored south of Corregidor, Juan went straight to the unused cleaning supply closet and led her into the secret bowels of the ship. Even someone as seemingly jaded as Raven had to stop for a moment when she saw the plush carpet, soft lighting, and stunning paintings inside the outwardly decrepit cargo hauler.

"It gets better," Juan said with a smile. "Come on."

A full tour of the ship would have to wait. He took her directly to the op center, where Gomez was at his usual spot, piloting the drone that was circumnavigating Corregidor. Juan took his seat while Raven wandered around the high-tech command center with her mouth agape. Max, Linda, and the rest of the bridge crew each nodded to her as she passed, amused at the response of their guest and no doubt reliving their own amazement at seeing the same room for the first time.

"Welcome to the real *Oregon*," Juan said.

Raven recovered quickly from her shock and came to stand next to him, staring at the big screen relaying the drone feed.

"You people are full of surprises," she said. "Does Beth know about all this?"

Juan shook his head. "We like to keep things close to the vest. She probably thinks the artwork we buy with her help is kept in an airless vault. Most of it is, but we like to display some of it on board. Makes the *Oregon* seem more like a home, which for us it is."

"You must make a good living."

"The Corporation is a for-profit enterprise, but we're also patriots. We only take jobs that are in America's interests. The fees we charge are compensation for the dangerous work we do. The *Oregon* has taken some costly hits in the past, and we've lost good people along the way. I don't want to lose Beth, too."

Raven gave him a brief nod. "Then let's find Locsin."

Juan turned to Gomez. "Anything interesting yet?"

"Nothing so far. I started on the north side at the dirt airfield, and I'm traveling counterclockwise around the island. The drone is flying at a thousand feet, but if we notice something interesting, I can zoom in."

The quadcopter's camera was currently focused on Topside, where the island's main artillery batteries were located. Most of Corregidor was heavily forested, with only a few roads connecting the structures and displays making up the Pacific War Memorial.

Gomez narrated whenever he focused on a particular item. "That husk of a building used to be the island's hospital, at least the one that was above ground. The other hospital was underground in Malinta Hill, which we'll see in a few minutes."

The camera panned over to a quarter-mile-long, burned-out structure.

"That's the old barracks. Used to be the largest in the world. Next to it is the museum. Those little open areas at the ends of the roads are where the old cannons are. Some of them are still intact, but they were disabled long ago."

Tourists strolled around the attractions, and open-air trams trundled along the roads to shuttle them amongst the sites.

The drone circled around and flew east toward the tail end of the island. The flat area of Bottomside was where the Lorcha Dock was located, to the north. Another pier jutted from the south coast, and a small powerboat was pulled alongside it. "Tourist catamarans and other boats have been going in and out next to the old Lorcha Dock."

"What about the south dock?"

"Not used commercially, but it's used occasionally by private charters. There are enough people around that you'd be noticed if you docked there."

Juan looked at Max. "We may not want to disembark there and draw attention, but it sounds like a good place for a pickup to get off the island. What about the landing?"

"There's an unused airstrip at the tail end of the island," Max said. "The tourist trams don't go there, so we should have some privacy to come ashore. I'll have the techs get the Gator fueled and ready."

The drone kept going. Juan's eye was drawn to a fine cloud of dust rising from a spot on the south side of Malinta Hill.

"I'd say that qualifies as unusual," Juan said.

"I see it," Gomez replied. "Zooming in."

A narrow road could be seen hugging the steep terrain, ending where a dark hole punctured the hill. A van was parked outside, and cables led from a portable generator into the tunnel. A miniature bulldozer, commonly known by the brand name Bobcat, came out to add a load of rocks and dirt to a large pile. When it was finished dumping its load, the Bobcat went back inside.

"I think we have a winner," Max said.

"Do we have a map of the tunnel system?" Juan asked.

"Pulling it up now."

Gomez zoomed out, and Max overlaid the tunnel map over Malinta Hill. A twenty-four-foot-wide main tunnel bisected the hill from east to west along the central axis of the island's tail. Dozens of smaller lateral tunnels extended from the main tunnel, forming a herringbone pattern. Another herringbone went south toward the exact spot where the excavation was taking place.

"Those are called the Navy Tunnels," Max said. "The whole complex was dug out by the U.S. Army Corps of Engineers after World War One, since the Philippines was an American colony at the time. Some of the tunnels were intentionally blown up during the 1945 American invasion by suicidal Japanese Marines and were never reopened. They no longer connect to the main tourist tunnel."

"We have our destination, then," Juan said.

"Do you think Locsin is in there?" Raven asked, her eyes focused so sharply they seemed to be piercing the screen.

Juan stood. "Only one way to find out. Time to show you the moon pool."

 **NEGROS ISLAND**

Beth's eyes fluttered open. She had no idea how long she'd been asleep, but sunlight streamed through the tiny window in the room where she had been taken after the helicopter landed.

Everything about the trip had been a blur. The pain in her shoulder from the gunshot wound had been excruciating, and all they'd done to tend to it after dropping off Locsin somewhere in Manila was to wrap it with a cloth to stanch some of the bleeding. Then they'd put a blindfold on her for the remainder of the trip. All she knew was that she had to be somewhere in the Philippines.

When they'd led her from the helicopter into the building, she thought she'd seen the moon overhead, but she could only make out a circular area of stars around it as if the rest of the sky were blotted out by unmoving black clouds. It was such a strange sight, she thought she might have been hallucinating from blood loss.

Before she'd been left alone, she was forced to take two pills. At first, she refused, but the guard threatened to shoot her right then and there if she didn't. He examined her wound and declared that the bullet had gone in one side of the meat of her shoulder and out the other. Every time he touched it, Beth screamed in agony.

Finally, she could feel herself passing out, either from the trauma or the drug, and she assumed this was it. She was going to die. She accepted her fate and let darkness take her.

But here she was now, still alive. And, oddly, the pain had tapered off to a dull ache. She now realized they must have given her a narcotic or a sedative. She couldn't move her arm much, but at least the bleeding seemed to have stopped.

She was also famished. She lifted her head up from the thin mattress and saw that there was a tray of food set on the small table next to her. Normally, the spread of fish and strange fruits wouldn't be all that appetizing to her, but her stomach grumbled loudly when the aroma hit her nose.

She sat up and launched herself at the food, devouring every morsel on the tray as if she were a starving dog. She was so hungry that each bite tasted like the finest entrée from a gourmet restaurant. She washed it all down with a large glass of milk.

With her hunger craving satisfied, she examined the room more thoroughly, though there wasn't much more to see. The window was glass but too small to climb through. The door was metal. She got up and tried the handle quietly, but it didn't budge.

Then she heard talking outside. Someone was approaching.

She quickly went back to the bed and lay down, closing her eyes just as the door opened.

She tried not to flinch when she recognized the first voice to speak. It was Tagaan, the man from the Bangkok drug deal.

"It looks like the drug kicked in," he said to the guard. "She must have passed out again."

"I didn't think such a thin woman would be able to eat that much," the guard replied.

"It's her body repairing itself. It must be working. We'll check how she's healing later this evening."

Beth felt a charge of fear race down her spine, nearly causing her to shiver in disgust. She remembered now that the pills she'd taken had a cyclone symbol on them. They weren't given to calm her down. It was the Typhoon drug that Dr. Ocampo had told them about.

Beth normally avoided pharmaceuticals whenever possible, even taking aspirin only when she absolutely had to. And now she was their lab rat. She was terrified about what continued use of the drug might do to her, but what was her alternative? She believed the guard when he said he'd kill her if she didn't take it. Tagaan wouldn't be any more lenient.

She had to escape somehow.

"I have to go to the manufacturing building," Tagaan said. "But I'll be back later to take her to the paintings. Make sure she's fed again before then."

Fed. Like an animal.

Then the word *paintings* hit her. Plural. Now she felt a thrill at the implication. Was she going to see the missing Gardner paintings? That was definitely a reason to stay alive.

The door closed. She opened her eyes and saw that the tray was gone.

She stood and found her legs to be a bit wobbly. Escape would have to come later. For now, she could at least get a peek at what her surroundings were outside to help plan how she might get away.

She went to the window, and her jaw dropped now that she had a better view outside.

From her vantage point, she could make out only a few squat buildings around a central plaza. But what caused her to gape was the view high above.

Water streamed down from a circular hole at least five hundred feet in the air, where the midday sun was shining through. Her heart sank as the idea of escape was snuffed out with the realization that there were several huge stalactites hanging from the limestone roof that extended so far that she could see no walls.

There *was* no outside for her to flee into. She was being held captive in a gigantic cavern.

Gerhard Brekker sat in the driver's seat of the yacht, one hand resting lazily on the wheel as he massaged his neck with the other. It still
ached from the SUV wreck in Manila when he'd hit the air bag.
Luckily, all of his men had made it out of the fire truck chase alive,
but each of them was recovering from an array of cuts, sprains, and
bruises.

The busy ferry and shipping lanes between Manila and Cebu
were now five miles behind them, and a low uninhabited island lay
dead ahead, far from the normal tourist dive sites. No wonder that
the *Pearsall* hadn't been discovered until now.

The sea was calm, but the weather reports forecast that Typhoon
Hidalgo had a fifty percent chance of passing over this very spot in
two days, so they'd have to make short work of their recovery and
demolition operation. Since their negotiations with Locsin had fallen
apart, Brekker had decided to investigate the wreck himself. If there
was more of the drug on board, he'd take it and sell it to the highest

bidder. If he couldn't find any in the time he had, he'd wire the sunken destroyer to blow up and hold it for ransom after he reconnected with Locsin and told him where it was.

One of Brekker's men rushed into the cockpit and said, "We've lost Alastair Lynch."

Brekker whipped around and glared at the man who was supposed to be guarding Lynch's door. He'd kept the Interpol official around in case he provided any other info about Locsin's operations. So far, the only thing he'd given them was headaches from his periodic bouts of caterwauling during moments of consciousness.

"He escaped?" Brekker demanded.

"He's dead."

Brekker eased the throttle back to idle and went down to find the door wide open and two men milling around the cabin, looking at the body sprawled on the blood-soaked bed.

Brekker said, "What happened?"

The closer man shrugged. "Looks like his hand became so skinny that he was able to pull it out of the cuff. He found a pair of scissors in the drawer and slit his wrists with them. Guess we're not getting our damage deposit back."

Lynch's corpse was a mere shadow of the brawny man they'd captured in Bangkok. His ropey muscles had atrophied, and his shirtless torso was so gaunt that Brekker could count the ribs. Lynch's body had literally consumed itself. Even if he hadn't committed suicide, he would have been dead in a day or two anyway. The pain must have been unbearable.

"Wrap him up in the sheet," Brekker said.

"Same treatment we gave Polten and his friend?"

Brekker nodded. They'd disposed of the two American chemists' bodies by weighting them down and dumping them overboard during the trip from Manila.

He went up on deck. And, several minutes later, the men brought up the body with the bloody sheet around it. It was fastened with a nylon rope, and a kettlebell weight was lashed to Lynch's feet.

"With that much blood to attract the sharks," Brekker said, "they'll make short work of him."

He looked around to see if there were any witnesses but shouldn't have bothered. The only visible ship was a ferry on the horizon.

"Do it," Brekker said, and the men tossed the body into the water. It immediately sank from view.

"Get the dive gear ready," he told the men. Although it was late afternoon, they'd still have a few hours of daylight to do an initial reconnaissance.

Brekker went to the cockpit and put them back on course. NUMA had helpfully provided the longitude and latitude of the wreckage to Polten, and the GPS system was guiding him to that precise spot only five hundred yards from the islet.

Though fishermen had discovered the *Pearsall* weeks ago, the wreck was located far from the normal tourist dive spots, and recreational companies had been warned to stay away until NUMA had completed its survey to assess the danger from unexploded ordnance on board.

It looked like the warning had worked because when the yacht arrived, they had the place all to themselves. At the indicated location, Brekker motored back and forth over the coordinates, a sandy stretch of seafloor fifty feet deep. He kept an eye on the bottom-scanning sonar until he saw the angular shape of a ship's bow jutting from the sand.

After dropping anchor and shutting off the engine, he went back to the aft deck to find his four mercenaries already donning their wetsuits.

"How could the *Pearsall* have been undiscovered here for more than seventy years?" one of them asked as he checked his oxygen tank. "It's deserted right now, but we're not exactly in the middle of nowhere."

Brekker shrugged into his own suit. "It was probably covered by sand in a typhoon like the one that's approaching and then uncovered by normal erosion, which is why we need to get down there now. Hidalgo might cover it up again."

When they were ready, the five of them went over the side.

Brekker immediately spotted the prow of the destroyer in the crystal clear water. He could make out the top of the ship's hull number stenciled on the side: DD-542. The warship must have come to rest on the bottom with its stern lower than the bow. The top of the superstructure barely peeked above the surface of the sand. Most of the metal showed very little corrosion, supporting the theory that the entire ship had been buried in the sand until recently.

If they were going to explore the interior of the *Pearsall*, they'd have to find a way inside, but all of the visible port hull was intact. Brekker had acquired underwater cutting torches, but he hoped to find an easier way in.

He led his men around the ship and saw just what he was looking for: a jagged hole where the Japanese torpedo had hit. Most of the hole was filled with sand, but Brekker thought they could dig their way through.

And if they couldn't, carefully placed explosives would make sure no one else would be able to, either.

 **CORREGIDOR**

At the sound of a vehicle in the distance, Juan held up his hand to stop his team. Eddie, Linc, MacD, Raven, and Max all froze in their tracks. When it was clear that the vehicle was approaching, Juan motioned for them to take cover. They all dropped to the ground, shielded from the road by the island's thick woods.

Getting from the Gator onto Corregidor had gone as expected. No one had been at the unused airfield to see them come ashore. They'd been making their way through the underbrush to avoid being spotted along the road. All of them were equipped with M4 assault rifles, except for MacD, who had his crossbow. They wore green and sand colored camouflaged fatigues and helmets similar to those worn by the Philippine National Police Special Action Force. On their chests and backs were Velcro panels that would reveal the words PNP-SAF and POLICE when torn away. Around their necks were balaclavas that could be pulled up over their faces to conceal their identities, just like the police would wear on a drug raid.

Juan didn't know if Locsin was inside the tunnel, but the plan was to capture Locsin's men alive and then march them the quarter mile to the south dock, where the *Oregon*'s more spacious lifeboat would pick them up. By the time the actual Philippine police made it out to the island, they'd be long gone and would be able to conduct the interrogation in private to find out Beth's location.

The *tranvía* tram passed by without slowing, likely heading to the Japanese Garden of Peace, which they'd already passed. Juan gestured for them to get back up and keep moving.

They stopped again when they reached the base of Malinta Hill. Juan crouched with the rest of them and they watched another *tranvía* drop off a load of tourists, snapping photos, before they were escorted into the main tunnel for a guided visit of the attraction.

Juan then led his team along the south side of Malinta Hill. He could see the *Oregon* anchored in the distance. Linda, who was in command of the ship, would send the lifeboat as soon as she got word from Juan that he had Locsin in custody.

They reached the Navy Tunnels south entrance, where the excavation was in progress, and Juan positioned his team behind the trees and undergrowth in three sets of two—Juan with Max directly in front of the tunnel, Eddie with Raven to the right, where the dirt pile lay, and MacD with Linc to the left, where the dusty road led down the hill—so they had it covered from all angles. The Bobcat had to be inside the tunnel.

"Ready to see who's in there?" Juan asked Max.

"Absolutely." Max handed him a bulky set of glasses and put on a pair himself. Then he removed a remotely operated tracked vehicle the size of a paperback novel from his backpack, an ROV of Max's own design that he called the Crawler. He set it on the ground and flipped a switch. A tiny camera mounted on the top of the Crawler came to life and swiveled around. The view from the camera showed up on an offset screen in Juan's glasses. Max's grinning face filled the image.

"High definition isn't your friend," Juan said with a smile.

"Hey, I earned these wrinkles. Besides, most of them are your fault. One for every Plan C you concoct."

"Then let's stick with Plan A for today. Wouldn't want to break the camera next time."

Max chuffed good-naturedly but said nothing as he extended an antenna and set it on the ground. Then he checked that the audio feed was working, and Juan heard Max's voice echoing in his earpiece. Satisfied that everything was ready, he used the handheld controller to set the Crawler in motion. It silently glided away, only the occasional crackle of leaves betraying its location. Juan was impressed at how Max had eliminated the motor's whine.

"What's the range on that?" Juan asked.

"Since we have a direct line of sight into the tunnel, I'd say it could get two hundred feet inside before we lose the signal, depending on how many turns it has to make."

The Crawler reached the entrance and went inside, hugging the concrete wall as Max drove it over the smooth tunnel floor. For a moment, the screen went dark as the sensor adjusted to the change in light. Then Juan could make out a string of lights going down the tunnel, bare bulbs hung from the arched ceiling. Piles of debris and pockmarks in the walls were reminders of the intense World War II battle to retake the fortress.

When the Crawler had gone another twenty feet, Juan heard the sound of machinery and voices, but he still couldn't see anything but empty tunnel. The sound of a motor grew louder. The Bobcat came around the corner fifty feet away, its bucket trailing dirt that overflowed its sides.

Max maneuvered the Crawler into a small notch in the wall and let the Bobcat pass by. Seconds later, the Bobcat emerged from the tunnel and dumped another load on the pile before disappearing back inside.

"This is perfect," Max said. "We've got our own escort."

As the Bobcat passed, Max switched the Crawler into high gear, and it shot forward, racing after the Bobcat, until it was underneath the loader.

"Nice work," Juan said.

"Gotta earn my keep somehow."

The Bobcat made a left turn to go back the way it had come. Max deftly guided the Crawler to match course. A few seconds after that, Juan could make out people at the end of the tunnel. All of them, dressed in hard hats and colored vests like any normal construction crew, were digging or operating machinery, except for one man who stood off to the side directing their efforts. When Juan saw him, it confirmed that this was no ordinary archaeological dig.

"Is that Locsin?" Max asked.

"That's him," Juan said. "If he risked coming here himself, they must be close to breaking through."

The Bobcat stopped next to a man operating a hydraulic rock hammer that was pounding away at the collapsed heap of concrete blocking the way. Some of the men tossed what they had already loosened into the bucket of the Bobcat while the rest unloaded beams from a trailer to shore up the dirt walls of the tunnel that they'd already dug out.

"We'll lose cover once the Bobcat comes back out," Juan said.

"I'll move the Crawler under the trailer," Max said.

"You read my mind."

Max waited until all the men had moved away from the Bobcat and raced the Crawler across the open space to the underside of the trailer, the rock hammer masking the sound of the high-speed motor. Max switched it back to low gear and moved the Crawler around until it had a good view of the worksite while remaining in the shadows.

"If they get through, will you be able to move over that debris?" Juan asked.

"No, it's too jagged, but it won't matter," Max replied. "I'm getting a really low signal from the Crawler. If it goes in any farther, we'll lose it."

"Then all we can do is watch and wait. But, either way, we're taking them when they come out." Juan radioed the rest of the team to report what he and Max had seen so they could prep for the upcoming ambush. They'd wait until Locsin and all his men were clear of the tunnel.

Juan and Max settled in and watched their tiny monitors like they were catching a game on TV, the most boring one they'd ever seen. There wasn't even a good beer commercial to liven things up. The monotony, however, didn't last long.

Twenty minutes and two more Bobcat runs later, the man operating the rock hammer shut it down and yelled to Locsin. He pointed at a black hole in the debris.

Locsin climbed up and shined a flashlight through the opening. When he looked back at his men, he was smiling. They had broken through.

The quick view of the area past the blockage didn't show Locsin much, so he was eager to get inside and retrieve what they had come for. It took another ten minutes before the hole was wide enough for him to squeeze through. Without waiting for his men to shore up the hole, he climbed past the obstruction, leaving his men to widen the opening.

He shined the flashlight around and saw nothing at first. He walked several yards and then spotted a desk with papers and files piled on it and some lab tables holding a variety of equipment. All of it had corroded from the moisture leaking into the tunnel where the concrete had been blown away. A blanket of dust coated everything.

The Typhoon pills that they'd recovered from the other Japanese lab on Negros Island had been carefully packed in tins and sealed with wax, which was why the drug had maintained its potency. The records they found implied there was a much larger stash on Corregidor, which had been the primary laboratory facility during the World War II occupation.

Locsin yanked open all the desk drawers, looking for the same kind of tins, but all he found were more files. He desperately searched the rest of the tunnel, getting angrier and more frantic as he went. He tossed aside microscopes and smashed vials, shouting in frustration at the fruitless hunt.

When he reached the end of the tunnel without discovering the mother lode they'd been hoping to find, he had the urge to blow up the place all over again. He screamed for his Japanese translator to stop digging and come inside the tunnel.

The translator climbed through, shining his own flashlight at the mess Locsin had created.

Locsin pointed at the desk. "Examine those files. Tell me if the formula is in there."

The man looked at the pile of folders and said, "That may take some time with this many papers to go—"

"Then get started!"

The translator started with the top file and began skimming the pages.

Locsin examined the tunnel while he waited. Apparently, the Japanese had collapsed the passage in the hopes that the records would be destroyed as well. Locsin would have to excavate the entire pile of concrete and debris to see if any Typhoon pills had been buried in the collapse, but he didn't have high hopes they'd find any that hadn't been crushed. In fact, it was possible that it had all been transported back to Japan before the American invasion in 1945.

But Locsin was puzzled. The Japanese would have wanted to remove any trace that it was ever there. He wondered why this part of the tunnel had remained intact. Then he saw why.

Several plastic explosive bricks lining the ceiling had failed to detonate when the Japanese collapsed the tunnel. The cord connecting them to the rest of the bombs had never been tied together, as if they had been interrupted before they could complete the job.

"Well?" Locsin shouted at his translator. "Is the formula in there?"

"I don't know yet. It might be. But I did find something interesting." He handed a sheaf of papers to Locsin. The pages were written in English.

As Locsin scanned through them, he felt a surge of renewed confidence. There was another possibility of finding more Typhoon before their supply ran out.

He handed the papers back to the translator. "Gather up everything you can find. We're leaving soon." Locsin decided that staying to sift through the rubble was a useless effort.

He climbed back through the hole and told his men to stop digging. Instead, he instructed them to conduct a thorough search of the tunnel in case he missed anything. Then he walked to the tunnel entrance so he could get a phone signal.

Locsin dialed Tagaan.

"Did you find it?" Tagaan asked, as eager as Locsin was to discover another source of Typhoon.

"No pills," Locsin said, absently scanning the sea around Corregidor as he talked. "But we've found documentation that might include the formula. We also found some additional documents that we weren't expecting. They could lead us to Brekker and . . ."

Locsin's voice tailed off when he saw a sorry-looking cargo ship anchored to the south of the island. No, he thought. It couldn't have gotten here so fast.

"Describe the ship that sank the *Magellan Sun*," he said to Tagaan.

"About five hundred feet long. Superstructure aft of amidships. Five cranes, but some of them seemed broken."

Against all logic, Locsin was looking at the same ship.

He turned toward the tunnel entrance and quietly said, "It's here."

"What?"

"Juan Cabrillo's ship is here."

"Then the speed wasn't an illusion."

Locsin yelled down the tunnel for two of his men to get outside.

He hung up on Tagaan and dialed another number.

When it was answered, Locsin said, "We need to leave quickly. How soon can you be here?"

The voice on the other end replied, "Less than ten minutes."

"Good. We'll be waiting."

Locsin hung up but kept the phone at his ear as if he were still listening. He eyed the trees around the entrance, but he couldn't see anything unusual.

When his soldiers arrived, Locsin whispered, "I want you to go back and get your weapons, then do a sweep of the area."

"What are we looking for?" one of them asked.

"Anyone who shouldn't be here."

46

Juan and Max watched as Locsin ducked back inside the tunnel with his two men. They kept an eye on the camera feed from the Crawler to see what Locsin would do when he got back to the opening they'd widened.

"Something's up," Max said, peeking through the bushes. "You think they're getting ready to leave?"

"Depends what they found inside that tunnel," Juan said. They'd heard only snippets of Locsin's phone conversation, something about documentation but no pills.

"Wait, there are the men he was just talking to."

"But where's Locsin?"

The two communist soldiers leaned over the trailer so only their feet were visible to the Crawler's camera. Juan could hear them unzipping something. Then the men went back toward the tunnel entrance. Max moved the Crawler to the end of the trailer, but Juan could see only the backs of the men. They were each carrying something.

Seconds later, they emerged from the entrance holding Chinese-made Norinco QBZ-95 assault rifles.

Locsin was still nowhere to be seen.

"That's some high-quality hardware," Max said.

"And they brought it out for a reason," Juan said. "We've been made."

Juan looked over his shoulder and saw the *Oregon* sitting near Manila Bay's entrance.

"Locsin recognized the *Oregon*. Someone on his side must have seen it last night when we sank the *Magellan Sun* and made the connection."

"But how did they see it? Their trucks were gone by the time we came into the bay at Negros Island."

"Doesn't matter now," Juan said, watching Locsin's men cross the road where Linc and MacD lay.

"You're about to have some uninvited guests," Juan said to them over the radio.

"We see that," Linc whispered back. "ROE?" He wanted to know the rules of engagement.

"Take them out quietly, if you can. That might lure the rest of them out here."

"Roger that."

"Remember, act like they're wearing full body armor."

Linc didn't respond this time. Locsin's men were too close. Juan trained the red-dot sight of his own weapon on them.

Suddenly the head of one of the men snapped back, a crossbow bolt sticking out of his eye. At the same time, a Ka-Bar knife tumbled through the air, striking Locsin's other man in the neck. It was a beautiful throw from Linc, and any normal human would have gone down instantly, but the man ignored the mortal wound and raised his assault rifle.

Juan fired a single shot that went through his target's head, but not before he was able to squeeze off a fusillade of rounds in Linc and MacD's direction, shredding leaves and branches. The man went down like a marionette cut from its strings.

"Everyone all right?" Juan said loudly. No need for quiet after the gunshots that would have been heard all over the island.

"Thanks for the cover fire," Linc said. "No casualties here."

"So much for our ambush," Max said.

Juan sat up and shifted his sights to the tunnel entrance. "Where's Locsin?"

"He's coming back on the camera," Max said. "He must have been just inside the tunnel when he saw his two goons killed."

Locsin's men started pouring out of the hole, but he was waving most of them back into the excavated chamber after they gathered their weapons. He kept two men behind to cover him while he took a screwdriver and opened the hood of the Bobcat. The Crawler's view was blocked, so Juan couldn't see what he was doing.

"Where are his men going?" Max asked, incredulous. "I checked the map, and that tunnel doesn't have an outlet. Are they going to commit suicide?"

"Or they plan to make a last stand in there instead of out here," Juan said. "You didn't see any masks on them, did you?"

"Nope. And, luckily, I brought just the thing to get them to come to us." Max removed one of the canisters of tear gas he'd brought with him. "A couple of these through that hole, and they'll be shoving each other aside to get out."

Locsin backed away from the Bobcat carrying the loader's twelve-volt battery. He motioned for his men to come back and follow through the hole they'd opened.

"What's he doing with that?" Max asked.

"Let's find out," Juan said. He stood and waved for the rest of the team to move forward toward the tunnel.

When they were all together, he said, "I don't care about anyone else, but we want Locsin alive." He looked at Raven. "It's the only way we're going to find Beth."

She nodded at him, and they all went in.

Locsin had his men pull down the bricks of plastic explosive from the ceiling. He thought he had enough for what he was planning, assuming the RDX chemical still maintained its potency.

He knew Juan Cabrillo was coming. It had to be him out there who had killed his men. If it had been the Philippine National Police, he would have heard some idiot officer on a megaphone telling him to give up and come out.

Cabrillo was much more dangerous. He would know that Locsin would never willingly surrender and would come in after them.

And Locsin was sick of him. He wanted to finish Cabrillo once and for all, but that wasn't possible here. Besides, killing him wasn't enough. Locsin needed to destroy that ship of his as well.

He turned to his translator, who had gathered up all the files and papers, so many that another man had to help carry them.

"Where are the pages you showed me?"

The translator looked at him with a perplexed expression, then dug around in his armload and removed five sheets of paper. Locsin took them and tossed them on the ground. He even stepped on several of them, leaving dusty footprints. Now the scattered pages looked like they'd been dropped accidentally.

"But the Americans will find them," the translator said.

Locsin grinned. "Exactly."

When his men had the bricks of RDX in hand, Locsin took them and went to the end of the chamber. He pressed the plastique against the wall, shaping the charge so it would blast outward. Then he stabbed the wire ends of the detonation cord into the mass and backed up, unspooling it as he went.

The soldier at the hole said, "We've got movement outside."

"Fire some warning shots," Locsin said.

The soldier unleashed a volley through the hole.

At the same time, Locsin held the ends of the wire over the battery he'd taken from the Bobcat. He had his men flip the desk and lab tables over to use as shields.

"Get down," he said and ducked as he touched the ends of the wire to the battery nodes.

JUAN WAS PEERING around the corner, the sight of his assault rifle to his eye, when a massive explosion shook the tunnel. Everyone on his team instinctively flattened themselves to the floor and covered their heads.

Dust shot out of Locsin's refuge. Everyone raised their balaclavas to protect themselves. The sharp tang of pulverized concrete and chlorine aroma of burnt plastic explosive mixed with the smell of diesel exhaust from the Bobcat.

"Those idiots actually did kill themselves!" Max sputtered.

Juan wasn't so sure. It didn't fit Locsin's profile. "I'll believe it when I see it."

Juan got to his feet and crept around the corner, his rifle at the ready. He was still getting the feed from the Crawler and hadn't seen anyone coming through the hole.

The six of them kept low as they made their way down the tunnel. When they reached the Bobcat, they used it and the trailer for cover.

Max readied one of the tear gas canisters, but Juan put up his hand.

"I want to get a look inside first. Hand me the Crawler."

Max drove the Crawler to Juan, who picked it up. The area in front of the hole was too rough for the ROV to navigate, but if he could get close enough, he could place it on smoother ground near the opening.

He told the rest of them to cover him while he made his way forward. When he reached level ground, he put the Crawler down, and Max took over.

He maneuvered the Crawler to the hole, where the camera finally had a look inside the chamber.

The air was heavy with dust, and pitch-black except for a blurry trail of flashlights at the end of the chamber. One by one, they winked out as if they were being switched off.

"A trap?" he said, looking at Max.

Max furrowed his brow for a moment, then his eyes went wide.

"They're getting away!"

"Where?"

"They must have been blowing another hole at the opposite end of the chamber. I remember the schematics now. That's close to a lateral that leads to the main tourist tunnel."

Juan took a flashbang grenade from his belt and chucked it through the hole just in case Locsin had left any of his men behind to set up his own ambush.

The grenade went off and Juan dived through the hole, sweeping the tunnel with the flashlight attached to his assault rifle.

Just as he had expected, two men had been crouching behind overturned tables. Now they were staggering around as they clawed at their eyes.

Juan followed Julia Huxley's advice and didn't take any chances. He shot each of them in the head. They both fell to the floor, their guns clattering on the concrete.

He checked the remainder of the chamber before yelling, "Clear!"

The rest of them hustled through. Max was last and focused his attention on papers that were strewn about the floor.

"These might be important."

Juan said, "You collect what you can find and meet us at the Gator." The lifeboat extraction was no longer possible.

He didn't wait for an answer and waved for Eddie, Raven, Linc, and MacD to follow him as he raced toward the point where Locsin and his men had escaped.

Juan poked his head briefly through the fresh hole in the wall and didn't draw any fire, so he jumped through and ran toward a dim light he could see a hundred feet ahead.

He emerged in the main twenty-four-foot-wide Malinta Tunnel. People were running in both directions to the exits at either end of the tunnel while clusters of terrified tourists cowered on the ground, some of them nonetheless taking videos with their phones. When they saw Juan and the others dressed in police uniforms, several of them pointed toward the tunnel entrance that led to the tail end of the island and shouted.

"Men with guns!"

"Terrorists!"

"They went that way!"

Juan sprinted after them. He could see Locsin and the remainder of his men exit the tunnel into sunlight. Locsin leapt on a *tranvía* that had just delivered a load of tourists and threw the driver to the pavement. He took the wheel of the tram, as his men climbed aboard, then sped off down the road.

When Juan got outside, he saw another *tranvía* backed into a parking spot, its driver watching the fleeing tram with a stunned look.

Before Juan could order the driver to get out, Raven yanked his arm and pulled him off. She got into the driver's seat and, as if to ward off any questions, said, "I drove a fire truck last night. This is nothing. Get on."

She hit the gas, and Juan had to grab one of the handholds before she drove off without him. Eddie, MacD, and Linc all barely made it aboard.

The *tranvía*'s top speed wasn't impressive, but Raven did her best to keep Locsin in sight as they careened around the curves leading to Corregidor's tail. Whenever the Locsin's tram came into view, two hundred yards ahead, gunfire would rip into theirs, and Juan and his team would return fire. The windshield lasted about five seconds, then shattered in a hail of bullets, showering Raven with safety glass.

She averted her eyes for a moment to avoid the pellets but never took her foot off the gas.

After three more turns, Juan could see Locsin's *tranvía* through the trees as it reached the old airfield at the same time as a de Havilland Twin Otter touched down on the dirt strip. The propeller-driven plane was a favorite of bush pilots for its ability to land on short, unpaved runways. Locsin must have stepped outside the tunnel to call the pilot for retrieval.

It rolled to a stop and turned just as Locsin's *tranvía* pulled up to it.

"Come on, you stupid thing!" Raven yelled at the tram, vainly coaxing it to go faster.

The door to the plane popped open long enough for Locsin and his three surviving men to jump on. The trees prevented Juan from taking an effective shot. None of his bullets made it through the thicket of branches.

The Twin Otter's engines revved to full power, and the plane tore down the runway. Raven tried to give chase, but their tram was literally left in the dust.

Juan disgustedly pulled his balaclava down, knowing they'd just lost their best chance at capturing Locsin. He looked at Eddie, Linc, and MacD, in turn, and saw the frustration on their faces.

Raven stood on the brake and faced Juan, irate that their quarry had escaped.

"Can't you shoot it down?" she demanded. "I saw launch controls for surface-to-air missiles in your op center."

Juan was impressed. Not many people would have been that observant.

"We can," he said, "but we won't. Not in broad daylight, at the entrance to one of the busiest harbors in the world. The area around Manila Bay is home to eighteen million people. Thousands of witnesses would see the *Oregon* fire a missile."

"Then what *can* we do?"

"We can try to track the plane," Eddie said, "although I doubt it has a transponder. And the Filipino radar isn't sophisticated enough to follow it if they fly low, which that plane can do."

Raven beat on the steering wheel but said nothing.

"Come on," Juan said. "Let's get back to the Gator before the real police show up, wanting to find out why we just shot up a national monument."

They left the *tranvía* where it was on the runway and started marching back to the point where the Gator had dropped them off not far from there.

"Hey, guys," Max said over the radio. By the way he was huffing, Juan could tell he was retracing their hike through the trees on his way back. "I've been listening in on your conversation. I might have an idea where they're going."

"From the papers you found?" Juan asked. "I didn't know you read Japanese."

"They weren't in Japanese. They were in English. One of the pages says that the last known shipment of Typhoon developed during the war left on a destroyer called the USS *Pearsall*."

"An American destroyer? How is that possible?"

"Because we've had the wrong assumption all along," Max said. "The Typhoon drug wasn't created by some top secret Japanese research group. It was invented by the United States Army."

 **NEGROS ISLAND**

By the time Beth finished her next meal, it was nighttime in the communist rebel headquarters. She could make out a few stars through the open roof, even though the cavern was illuminated from below by enough lights for a small town.

She sat down on the bed and pulled aside the crude bandage that had been wrapped around her injured shoulder. She was prepared for the worst, possibly an infection that she couldn't feel because of nerve damage.

Instead, the wound was scabbed over as if she had merely suffered a scrape. The puckered skin around the bullet hole looked pink and healthy, not the angry red welt of septic bacteria eating away at her. The pain was completely gone, and she could move her arm normally, which seemed impossible given that she was shot twenty-four hours before. She felt her forehead, and it didn't seem like she had a fever.

The door to her room opened. It was Tagaan and the guard who had been watching her. Both were wearing holstered pistols.

"You will go with Dolap," Tagaan said, nodding at his comrade, who had a wisp of a goatee and a scar in the center of his lip.

Beth stood. "Why?"

"You have work to do."

Tagaan walked over to her and roughly looked under the bandage.

"Excellent," he said. "It's almost morning. You'll get another dose of Typhoon when you come back." He pushed her to the door. "Go."

Dolap took her by the arm and guided her through a large building, where they passed at least a dozen rooms with bunk beds, meaning this had to be the main barracks.

When she got outside, her earlier assessment that there were enough lights for a small town seemed right on. Scores of men, all Filipino and obvious Typhoon users, based on their musculature, moved about in a purposeful way. She counted more than fifteen buildings arranged around a central plaza dominated by a huge stalagmite stretching halfway to the roof. The buildings were separated into quadrants. Most of them were prefab structures like the ones she'd seen at the chemistry lab north of Manila.

The biggest building was three stories tall and fronted by several loading docks with trucks backed up to them. She could hear sounds of machinery coming from inside as if it were a factory. Next to it was another building, almost as large, with ten more trucks parked outside. Two men were wheeling a huge powered cart from the factory to the second building, its cargo covered by a tarp. She got a quick look inside the building when they briefly raised the overhead doors and she saw rows of sleek, black, bullet-shaped objects lined up inside.

A truck pulled away from the factory and drove down a road

leading from the plaza to the far end of the cave. It disappeared inside a tunnel that must have been the entrance to the cavern. Then she saw a helicopter parked on a pad big enough for two and realized that the opening in the roof above was wide enough to fly through. So, two ways out, not that it helped her in the slightest.

Tagaan said to Dolap, "Radio me when you are done." Then he walked toward the factory and disappeared inside.

"This way," Dolap said and guided her past the central stalagmite. She shuddered when she saw a set of manacles bolted to the rock. Blood stained the ground and the shackles as if someone had flayed themselves trying to get free.

At the opposite side of the central plaza, he took Beth into a smaller building the size of a mobile home. When she went in, she was surprised to find it air-conditioned, much different from her sweltering accommodations. He locked the door with a key, sat her at a long table, and went to the back of the building.

Beth wiped her sweat-stained brow on her shirt as she waited for him. The one window was shuttered and covered with iron bars, and the door looked solid enough, so escape seemed impossible. Besides, she had nowhere to go.

Dolap returned, holding six hard plastic tubes, and Beth's heart rate skyrocketed as she understood what they were.

He set them on the table and said, "You are to appraise these for sale. If you damage them, you die." He seemed bored and considered her no threat, which was probably true since he was built like a professional wrestler.

He went to the restroom, leaving Beth alone. She picked up the first tube and uncapped the end. Inside was a rolled-up canvas. Her heart fluttered with excitement as she carefully pulled it from the tube.

When she unrolled it on the table, she gasped, nearly fainting, when she recognized the three-foot-by-three-foot painting. It was the exquisite image of a girl sitting at a harpsichord with a man seated next to her. Another girl was standing and holding a sheet of music while she sang.

If authentic, it was *The Concert* by Vermeer, stolen from the Isabella Stewart Gardner Museum in 1990 and one of only thirty-four Vermeer works known to exist. On the open market it would be worth more than two hundred million dollars, the most valuable unrecovered painting in the world.

She could barely restrain herself from ripping open the other tubes and laying eyes on the bounty before her. But she had to safeguard the Vermeer. It seemed to be in good condition for having been in less than ideal conditions for all these years.

Dolap flushed the toilet and returned from the back of the building, holding a steaming cup of coffee. He pulled out his phone and sat in the other chair, idly playing with something on the screen. He set the full mug on the table, and Beth nearly knocked it away, afraid that a spill would damage the work of art.

But even though it made her cringe to leave it there, the coffee mug gave her the inkling of an idea, and she didn't object. She couldn't get away, but maybe there was a way to tell someone where she was.

"I need a pencil, a piece of paper, and access to the Internet to do my work," she said.

Dolap looked up, annoyed that he had to tear his eyes away from his phone. "No Internet."

"You mean you don't have Internet access here?"

"No Internet for you."

So they did have Internet service.

"Then how am I supposed to do my appraisal?"

He sighed heavily, raised the phone to his mouth, and clicked a button. It must have doubled as a radio because Tagaan answered, "You can't be done already."

Dolap relayed her request.

"I'll have someone bring a pen and notepad over," Tagaan said.

Beth interrupted. "Not a pen, a pencil. Pens might damage the art."

Dolap relayed her request.

"Fine," Tagaan said. "A pencil. She can't have Internet, but if there are any books she wants to download, we can give her a tablet computer."

Dolap looked at Beth questioningly. She nodded and said, "That will be fine." She recited the titles of several books, though she didn't really need them. The appraisals would be complete guesswork anyway. She just had to make it look legitimate.

When Tagaan signed off, Dolap said, "How long will this take?"

"An hour, maybe."

Dolap rolled his eyes. "What about for the other ten paintings?"

Beth looked at him, slack-jawed. "You mean there are more?"

He nodded, exasperated by her apparently stupid question.

"I'll have to see them" was all she could say.

"Fine," Dolap replied. "I'll bring them out when you're done with this." He took a sip of his coffee and went back to playing with his phone.

While she waited for the items she'd requested, she mapped out a plan in her mind, surreptitiously checking out her position in relation to Dolap's.

Beth decided that she'd have only one chance to make it work. Despite the risk, she had to try it if she wanted to get out of this place alive.

 **MANILA BAY**

With the Corporation's senior staff gathered in the boardroom, along with Raven, Juan nodded to Murph, who put Langston Overholt's craggy face on the main view screen. Because of the thirteen-hour time difference between Washington and Manila, they could see the rainy late afternoon outside the CIA windows even though it was almost dawn where the *Oregon* was. Maurice finished serving mugs of coffee and breakfast pastries before closing the door behind him.

"I see a lot of bleary eyes there," Overholt said in his gravelly baritone.

"We've had a busy few days," Juan said, stifling a yawn. "Rack time has been hard to come by."

"I don't think what I'm about to tell you will help you sleep any better." Overholt trained his eyes on Raven before saying, "By the way, Ms. Malloy, this conversation is strictly confidential, and you are bound by the security clearance you obtained while you were a military police officer."

"Understood," she said. She was the only one who wasn't eagerly downing coffee, preferring orange juice to wash down her Danish.

"Have you been able to confirm that Typhoon was developed by the Army?" Juan asked.

"I'm afraid so," Overholt said. "I pulled a few strings and obtained classified records from Dugway Proving Ground. They've been buried in a dusty storeroom for over seventy years. That is, until a chemist in an experimental lab out there found the file. Name's Greg Polten. He and a colleague named Davis are now missing."

"Do you think they sold the info to Salvador Locsin?"

"I doubt it. Apparently, using off-the-books wire transfers that we were able to track, Polten hired Gerhard Brekker to help him find more. Given what Ms. Malloy told us about his encounter with Locsin, it doesn't sound like they were working together."

Julia Huxley sat forward. "Mr. Overholt, what can you tell us about the drug?"

"The files are not complete, for reasons I'll get to in a minute. The military considered U.S. involvement in the war inevitable in 1941, so we were conducting all sorts of experiments to see what kind of edge we could give our soldiers in battle. The use of methamphetamine for some of our bomber pilots was one unfortunate result of that project. But Typhoon was on a whole different level. Some in the community considered it a superdrug until its full effects were understood. Its original code name was TYPE-400N, but the scientists started calling it Typhoon."

"Why was it developed out here?" Juan asked.

"Because that's where the plant that formulated its key ingredient was located. It was a rare variety of orchid, but its scientific name and description were not in the file. Its identity was so secret that only a few scientists on the project knew what it was."

"It's odd they wouldn't include such an important piece of information in the file," Julia said. "What happened to the scientists?"

"This is where we come to the reason for the incomplete info," Overholt said. "No one saw the Japanese invasion of the Philippines coming, of course. Corregidor was the location of the top secret laboratory where the drug was being developed and produced. When it was clear in early 1942 that the invasion would overrun U.S. forces, MacArthur himself ordered the scientists, the drug supply, and all their equipment to be evacuated by destroyer. It was called the USS *Pearsall*, and, according to Japanese war records, it was sunk with all hands somewhere in the Philippines by Sub I-38, which was itself sunk by the U.S. Navy before it could return to Japan and record the exact location of the *Pearsall*."

Julia looked puzzled. "Then how did the Japanese subsequently get the Typhoon formula?"

"We can't know for sure, but, from the documents you found, it looks like they rescued one of the scientists from the *Pearsall* and dropped him off at Corregidor after it fell. The Japanese might have tortured him to get him to cooperate, then killed him to hide the secret. What we do know is that they developed their own version of the drug and shipped most of it back to the homeland in 1945 when we retook the Philippines. Despite the terrible side effects, they were scaling up to mass-produce it in a large factory in Hiroshima. It could have turned the planned home island invasion into the bloodiest battle in history. I'm not saying that's why we nuked Hiroshima, but the A-bomb did obliterate any trace of it."

Overholt paused to let that sink in.

"I'm just glad we never ended up using Typhoon ourselves," Julia said.

"The Army agreed, which was why they buried all mention of

the drug when it didn't make it back to U.S. shores. After we saw the horrors that the Nazis and the Imperial Japanese Army's Unit 731 committed in the name of science, we didn't want to continue down that path."

"So if the destroyer sank," Linda Ross said, "then all traces of Typhoon must have been destroyed."

"Locsin may have found the formula in the Japanese files Juan saw them take," Overholt said, "but it's unlikely. They would probably have never left such critical information behind. Which is probably why he will be looking for the *Pearsall* right now, and why Brekker might already be there."

"But whatever supply Locsin found should be running out soon, and we know he didn't find any more on Corregidor," Eric Stone said. "If the *Pearsall* is on the bottom of the ocean, then the pills would have turned to mush long ago even if they hadn't been destroyed in the sinking. Even if the tablets were sealed in metal containers, they would have rusted apart in five to ten years, letting the salt water in."

Overholt shook his head slowly. "Earl Silas Tupper."

"Who's that?" Max said.

Mark Murphy rattled off the answer. "As in Tupperware. He was the inventor. Created it when he was working at DuPont. He started selling the products to the general public after the war, but he actually made non-breakable containers for the military during the war."

Max shook his head in amusement. "Why aren't you on *Jeopardy!*?"

"My application has been accepted twice," Murph said matter-of-factly, "but it wouldn't be good publicity for the Corporation for me to go on national TV."

"Mr. Murphy is exactly right," Overholt said. "The Typhoon was being shipped back to the U.S. in plastic, watertight barrels designed by Tupper himself."

"How much?" Juan asked.

"We don't have the exact figures, but the scientists produced two million pills before they halted production after seeing its long-term effects."

Max whistled at the astounding figure.

"Enough to supply an entire Army division for years," Juan said.

"Or a communist insurgency for decades," Overholt replied. "You need to keep both Brekker and Locsin from getting that supply."

"Do we know where the *Pearsall* is?"

"NUMA does. Divers reported finding the wreck in a small archipelago northeast of Negros Island." Eric noted the GPS coordinates that Overholt recited.

"NUMA hasn't excavated the wreckage yet?" Juan said.

"They have a ship on the way," Overholt said, "but it's not expected to be on-site for another week. It wasn't considered a high-priority mission."

"Because they didn't have access to the classified records about its cargo."

"Correct."

"And if we find the cargo intact?"

"I'm sure there are elements of the U.S. Army biochemical warfare division that would like to get their hands on it again, despite Typhoon's grievous reputation," Overholt said. He paused for a moment, then added, "But if the drug and its formula somehow got destroyed once and for all, they wouldn't know what they missed, would they?"

Juan smiled. "I suppose not."

"Then I will sign off here. Godspeed." The screen winked to black.

"You heard the man, Stoney," Juan said. "Anchors aweigh, and set course for Negros Island."

"Aye, Chairman."

"And Murph?" Juan said.

"Yup?"

"Be ready to counter more of those Kuyog drones in case Locsin left behind those papers on purpose."

Murph raised an eyebrow. "This smells like a trap to you?"

Juan nodded and patted him on the back. "It positively reeks."

 **NEGROS ISLAND**

Light from the cavern's roof opening was now streaming through the shutters over the window, and Beth's stomach was already grumbling for breakfast. She was almost finished appraising the paintings and still couldn't believe the incredible bounty of stolen artwork that Locsin and his group had amassed. It was like the best Christmas morning ever, despite her predicament. She could open one of the best museums in the world with what was inside this single room.

In addition to every one of the stolen Gardner paintings, she had seen works by Van Gogh, Raphael, Gauguin, and Cézanne that had been missing for years, as well as items by Renoir and Monet from an auction house theft. There were only three more to appraise out of the sixteen. The piece she was inspecting now was a small oil painting from Picasso's cubist period. It was the least valuable artwork she'd seen because it was so small, but it would still likely fetch a million dollars if it went back to auction.

She had been making notes on a pad with a pencil. She added up her estimates, and the total of all of the paintings ran close to half a billion dollars on the open market. However, because they couldn't see the light of day without being confiscated, they would be worth only a tenth that in the underground trade. Fifty million dollars was still a huge sum, but she'd bet there would be plenty of Russian oligarchs or Saudi sheiks willing to part with a bit of their oil money to get their hands on these masterpieces.

Dolap was still intently playing with an app on his phone, which she'd seen was a puzzle game when she'd gotten up to use the bathroom. His half-full coffee mug was on the table. She was ready to put her plan into motion, but she cringed thinking about what she had to do.

Beth had positioned the tube that had held the Picasso in exactly the place she wanted.

She nodded at it and said, "Can you hand that to me?" She watched him out of the corner of her eye as she continued to jot on the notepad.

Dolap reluctantly looked away from his game and leaned forward to pick up the tube. He handed it to her, and when she took it from him, she pushed it into the coffee mug, tipping it over. Coffee spilled across the table, splashing onto the Picasso.

Beth screamed at the same time Dolap leapt to his feet. She swung the tube around as if in a panic and slapped the phone out of his hand. He barely noticed because he was so concerned with the painting.

She dropped the tube and jumped out of her chair.

"What have you done?" she shouted.

"It's not my fault!"

"It was your coffee, wasn't it?"

He looked at her in terror when he realized what Tagaan would do to him if he found out that Dolap was responsible for ruining one of the valuable paintings.

He pleaded with Beth, "What can we do?"

"I think we can still save it, but I need some cloth towels right now."

Dolap charged toward the bathroom, but Beth stopped him. "Not the paper towels in there. Bath towels. Clean."

He would either have to take her with him and draw unwanted attention or leave her alone in the trailer to get them. He was paralyzed with fear and indecision.

Beth clapped her hands and pointed at the door. "We don't have much time before the coffee seeps into the canvas! Hurry! I want to save it as much as you do. I'm not going anywhere."

He nodded and dashed through the door, locking it behind him.

Beth picked up the Picasso and let most of the coffee drain off as she set it aside. She wasn't too worried about the damage, not only because she was willing to sacrifice the artwork if it saved her neck but also because she suspected the coffee would probably just run off the oil.

She got down on her knees and frantically searched for Dolap's phone. She spotted it in the corner and snatched it up. It was still unlocked, paused on the game.

The icons at the top of the phone showed no bars for a cell signal. She didn't know if that meant the cave didn't have cell service at all or just not in this part of the cavern, but, either way, she wasn't going to be able to call for help. There was, however, an icon for Wi-Fi service.

She checked the contact list for the phone's own number, then quickly opened the email app and typed in a message to Raven's address. Beth had no idea how much time she had before Dolap came back, so she kept it short.

Raven, this is Beth. In a huge cavern but don't know where. Track this cell number to find me.

She added Dolap's phone number to the end and hit SEND.

As soon as the message was gone, she went to the SENT folder and deleted the message. Then she opened the game up again and put it back in the corner just as she heard footsteps pounding toward the door.

Dolap yanked the door open and thrust a pile of towels in her arms before locking the door behind him.

While she patted the painting dry, he found his phone, looked at it briefly, and put it in his pocket. He watched her with concern.

"Well? Can you save it?"

"I think you were quick enough to salvage it."

He looked at her with a deadly serious expression. "If you tell Tagaan about this, I will kill you."

Beth shook her head. "Why would I want to tell him? He'd probably kill both of us."

That seemed to put him at ease. He picked up some of the tubes that she'd already looked through and went to the back of the building.

When she was satisfied that the Picasso was dry, Beth rolled it back up and sealed it in the tube, then wiped down the table so she could get back to work.

Dolap returned and took his chair again. Beth pressed her hands down on the table so that he couldn't see her shaking from the adrenaline rush of getting away with her plan.

Now all she could do was try to stay alive long enough for the cavalry to arrive.

THE BANTAYAN ISLAND ARCHIPELAGO

The process of digging through the hole in the side of the *Pearsall* had gone faster than Gerhard Brekker had anticipated and by mid-morning they were able to explore the interior of the sunken U.S. warship.

During the night, Brekker had downloaded the schematics for the Fletcher class destroyer from a website dedicated to cataloging World War II ships. That let them narrow their search to the rooms on the ship where cargo would most likely have been stowed.

The crew areas were divided roughly in half fore and aft, with the fire rooms and engine rooms in the center of the ship. They'd never reach the stern without significant work, but they could search the bow section fairly quickly.

Most of the organic material had disintegrated in the warm salt water, so Brekker saw no clothes or bodies, not even skeletons. Fish and crabs had found a way into the ship, but there was no sunlight for coral to grow in the interior.

They found a mess hall, with metal dishes and silverware rusted but still intact. They also happened upon the ammunition magazine for one of the forward guns. The steel casings of the shells were corroded, and some of the rounds had come loose from their bins, piling onto the floor. Brekker warned his men not to touch them in case the explosives inside were still active.

By the time their air was exhausted, they had made it through two storerooms, with no luck, marking doors with a large X if the room inside had already been visited.

The dive team had to surface twice more, during the tedious search, to exchange air tanks. By the afternoon, the clear skies were growing ominous as the first tendrils of clouds from Typhoon Hidalgo approached from the east. The gray overcast didn't deter the fishing boat in the distance, one of several they'd seen the past couple of days, and a ferry lumbered by, a few miles away, making one of its last trips before the storm arrived. If Brekker didn't find anything before sundown, they'd have to withdraw and seek calm waters out of the storm's way.

However, on the next dive they struck gold.

The most forward cargo room was one of the two boatswain's

lockers. Brekker forced the hatch open to find that it had been cleared of the tackle and rigging that would normally be stowed there. The room would have been easily isolated from the rest of the ship so that the crew wouldn't be able to see what was inside.

If any cardboard boxes containing files had been in the room, they had rotted away long ago.

But the real prize was still there.

Twenty orange plastic barrels the size of beer kegs were grouped along the bulkhead, although any ropes lashing them in place had crumbled away. Unlike contemporary Tupperware, these barrels were opaque, so it was impossible to see what was inside until they got them to the surface. One of them had overturned, and the lid popped off. If it had contained Typhoon pills, they had dissolved in the water.

But judging by the weight of the other barrels, they definitely held something. Brekker instructed his men to attach one of the neutral buoyancy floats that they had brought along to the barrel closest to the hatch. Once it was secured to the barrel, Brekker filled the float with air from his tank using his octopus regulator. When the barrel was floating, Brekker took it in tow and swam toward the exit hole. His men stayed behind to retrieve two more barrels.

When they reached the surface, the watchman on board the yacht hauled the barrels aboard with the minicrane usually used to transfer Jet Skis in and out of the water.

Brekker got out of the water and took off his gear while the men toweled off the three barrels. As soon as they were dry, Brekker carefully pried open the lid of the first one. It came off with a pop just like a tub of Tupperware straight out of the fridge.

The top of the barrel was filled with cotton batting, as white as the day it was vacuum-sealed inside. Brekker tore it away to reveal thousands of pills etched with the Typhoon logo. All of them were intact and looked as if they'd been packed away yesterday.

Brekker's men slapped each other on the back and let out a whoop. One of them said with awe, "How many do you think are in there?"

Brekker thought about the large bottle that held the vitamin supplements he took daily. "I'd estimate there are roughly a hundred thousand pills in here."

A cheer went up from the five men. With nearly two million of the pills to be brought up and sold to the highest bidder, they all knew they'd be very rich very soon.

"Should we still plant the explosives?" one of them asked.

Brekker nodded and looked at the acoustic trigger that would be used as an underwater detonator. It would send out an audio pulse that could be detected by the receiver miles away, allowing them to retreat to a safe distance before setting off the explosion.

"If anyone ever comes looking for the *Pearsall*," Brekker said, "we don't want them to know we took the barrels. Put most of the bricks in the ammo magazine. It should tear the entire ship apart."

LOCSIN WATCHED the yacht with a telescope while his men continued working the nets on the fishing boat as if they were hauling in a catch. From this distance, the image was fuzzy, but he could tell they had pulled something from the water. He had never seen Gerhard Brekker during the fight in the fire truck warehouse, but he could see which man was ordering the others around. Locsin recognized a fellow leader when he saw him.

After returning to Negros Island, his translator had skimmed the Japanese files and found nothing in the papers relating to a formula for Typhoon. It was mostly notations and data about the experiments that the Japanese had performed on Filipino captives who they'd been using for drug tests. If it hadn't been for the discovery of the *Pearsall*'s location, the dig on Corregidor would have been a complete bust.

He handed the telescope to Tagaan, who watched the activity on the yacht and asked, "Should we take them now?"

Locsin shook his head. "Not until we think they're finished. We might as well let Mr. Brekker do all the work."

"What about Juan Cabrillo's ship? Do you think they're really coming?"

Locsin grinned. "I know they are. Are you ready for them?"

"Fifty Kuyog drones are prepped and operational."

"And the bait?"

Tagaan nodded.

"Excellent," Locsin said, taking back the telescope and surveying the horizon. "Now all we need is a target."

Brekker surfaced with his men and another three barrels to haul aboard the yacht. It had been a long day, but they were almost done. Two more trips down and they'd be able to get out of there with all their loot. Brekker was already considering who would buy the treasure and how much he should charge. The Americans, Chinese, and Russians had the most money, but he wasn't counting out the Saudis or Iranians. All he knew was that Salvador Locsin had his chance and he blew it. Besides, with the meth shipment in police custody, Locsin didn't have the funds to pay for it.

Brekker threw his fins over the railing and climbed up the ladder to supervise hauling up the barrels. When he looked over, he froze, stupefied by the sight of Locsin and his men standing over the dead body of the watchman Brekker had left on board.

Five assault rifles were trained on him. He slowly finished getting out of the water. Locsin's fishing boat had been circling two hundred yards away to avoid being seen as Brekker's team surfaced. With their return, it now headed toward the yacht.

Locsin smirked at him. "Right now, you're wondering how I found you here." He obviously relished echoing the same line Brekker had used on him at the Manila fire truck warehouse. "The Americans left a record of the *Pearsall* at Corregidor."

"You killed my man."

"You and I both understand the need for force to make a point. We appreciate you bringing up the barrels of Typhoon for us. How many are left down there?"

"None," Brekker said, fighting back the bile in his throat. "This is all of them." He looked at the three of his men who were left. All of them were eyeing their captors for a chance to attack, but it would be a useless effort.

"I think you're lying," Locsin said. "The information we found said there were twenty barrels on board. I only see fifteen."

"Then why don't you go down and take a look for yourselves?"

"Because you're already dressed for the occasion. I may even let you live if you dive down and get the rest of them."

"And if I say no?"

"Then you die right here, right now. I may be a communist, Mr. Brekker, but I drive a hard bargain."

Brekker looked at his men and nodded. They would go back down to the wreck. In fact, it would be necessary for what he was planning.

"I need a fresh oxygen tank," he said.

Locsin waved his hand toward the equipment. "Of course. But remember that the water is crystal clear. We will be watching you."

"I'm sure you will."

He walked over and began the process of exchanging his old tank for a new one. At the same time, Locsin's men began transferring the barrels of Typhoon from the yacht to the fishing boat.

The acoustic detonator was still lying where Brekker had left it. As he picked up the tank, he palmed the small electronic transmitter, which was wirelessly linked to the yacht's sonar array. One push of the button would activate an underwater pulse that would set off the bombs they'd already planted on the destroyer below them. The bombs still aboard the yacht wouldn't be activated because they weren't yet in the water, but there were more than enough on the *Pearsall* to cause the ammo in the magazine to explode, taking both the yacht and the fishing boat with it.

But Brekker wasn't suicidal. He had something else in mind.

He shrugged into the tank harness and took his mask and snorkel. He climbed back down the ladder, and just before he sank into the water, he shoved the small detonator onto a ledge behind the ladder. He couldn't get the electronics in the transmitter wet because they would short out.

Accompanied by his men, he descended to the *Pearsall* and had them round up three more barrels. Meanwhile, Brekker went to the destroyer's ammo magazine and removed one of the bombs they'd placed amongst the piles of five-inch high-explosive shells.

When the barrels were ready, they went back up. Locsin was so eager to get more of the Typhoon pills that he barely looked at Brekker, who carried the bomb in a net cinched closed with a nylon rope. As he took hold of the dive ladder to climb aboard, he quickly knotted the bomb to the lowest rung.

While climbing the ladder, he snatched the acoustic detonator and held it high for Locsin to see.

"If you shoot me," Brekker said, "I will set off the bomb I just brought up and we will all die."

He pointed to the bomb dangling next to him. He knew that he needed Locsin to believe his threat. Merely claiming that there were bombs in the wreck below wouldn't have been convincing enough.

When they didn't lower their weapons, Brekker yelled, "I mean it!"

Locsin peered over the railing, saw the bomb, then said to his men, "Put down your guns and let him up."

Brekker slowly climbed up to the deck, watching for any sign they would try to kill him. He wasn't bluffing. He knew Locsin had no intention of letting him and his men live. If he was going to die, he might as well take them all with him.

All of the barrels except the ones they'd just brought up had been moved to the fishing boat. Brekker dropped the oxygen tank to the deck, eyeing Locsin warily as he did so.

"Now what?" Locsin said. "We have the guns and you have the bomb. Is there a solution where we don't all blow up or get shot?"

"As a matter of fact, there is," Brekker said, who had thought of a way out of the standoff during the dive. He pointed at a chest holding the remainder of the explosives they hadn't planted on the *Pearsall*. "We're going to take a bomb out of there and tie it to your fishing boat."

"Why? So you can blow us up as soon as we're out of range of your yacht?"

"No. There's also a backup detonator in the chest and it's also connected to the yacht's sonar system, which will send out a pulse at the push of the button. The sound wave will be received by any of these bombs that are underwater within three miles and activate the trigger mechanism. So as your boat leaves, we'll each have a detonator and a bomb ready to explode. If you press the button, we both blow up. If I press the button, we both blow up. If neither of us presses it, we both come out of this alive."

Brekker edged over to the chest and opened it. Locsin watched intently as Brekker bent down and removed a bomb and the second detonator.

"Which one do you want?" he asked Locsin.

"How do I know either of them work?"

"You want proof? If I push this button, that bomb lashed to the ladder will explode, and we'll all be dead a split second after you got that proof. So, what will it be?"

Locsin looked at both of them before answering. "I'll take the detonator you came out of the water with."

"That's exactly what I would have chosen."

Brekker tossed the bomb and detonator to Locsin, who handed the bomb to one of his men and told him to hang it in the water from the stern railing of the fishing boat.

"When we're five hundred yards apart," Brekker said, "we'll simultaneously lift our bombs out of the water, which will neutralize them. Fair?"

Locsin nodded. "Fair."

"Oh, and one more thing before you go. I want six of those barrels you already took."

"What?"

"It's our compensation for all the work we've done. If you want them later, you can always pay us market value."

Locsin hesitated, no doubt sick at the idea.

"My men and I are willing to die," Brekker said. "Are you?"

Finally, Locsin said, "We are, but not over this. I'll give you four since there are two more below. If that's not satisfactory, you can kill us all."

Brekker smiled. "You negotiate like a capitalist, Comrade Locsin. I accept your terms."

"We'll be watching. If you or any of your men try to remove your bomb before we reach the agreed-to distance, I'll detonate it."

"And I will do the same."

As promised, Locsin's men moved four of the barrels back to the yacht. Brekker's team hauled up the three that were still in the water.

Before he got onto the fishing boat, Locsin nodded at the horizon behind Brekker. "We need to get out of here now, and you may not want to stick around to get those other two barrels."

"Really? Why's that?"

"Because that ship rushing toward us knows what we found here today, and they won't like that you've taken the cargo."

Without fully turning around in case it was a trick, he glanced sideways and saw a merchant ship coming their way at high speed, far faster than he would expect for a vessel her size.

"Who is that? The Philippine Navy?"

Locsin shook his head as he climbed into the fishing boat. "Remember that Juan Cabrillo person you said you didn't care about, back at the fire truck warehouse? You should care about him now, because I'd bet that's his ship. A friend of his told me the name when she was in a daze from a gunshot wound. It's called the *Oregon*."

52

Juan leaned forward in his chair in the *Oregon*'s op center as he watched the yacht and fishing boat separate on the big screen. They had been butted up against each other right where NUMA had reported the sunken *Pearsall*'s position to be. A densely forested islet, no more than a mile across, was visible in the background under dark clouds rolling toward the late-afternoon sun. The fishing boat stopped for a short time a quarter mile from the yacht, then continued toward the north end of the islet.

Juan turned to Max. "Salvador Locsin doesn't seem to be the type to rent a fancy yacht like that."

"Not very communistic," Max replied. "He must be on the fishing boat."

"Do you think they made the deal they were talking about in the warehouse?" asked Raven, who was standing next to Max.

Juan looked back at the screen and shook his head. "It seems unlikely, after the fight they had, but it does look like it, doesn't it? And the destroyer hasn't been blown up like Gerhard Brekker threatened to do, so either they've brought up all of the barrels of Typhoon or they were destroyed when it sank."

"Maybe they just haven't found them yet, and we've scared them off," Max said. "Look, there goes the yacht."

Juan frowned. The yacht was making full speed toward the fishing boat, which was already halfway to the islet.

"I don't get it," Juan said. "Why is he taking off after the fishing boat?"

"Buyer's remorse?" Raven said.

"Whatever the reason," Eric Stone said from his position at the helm, "they'll catch up with the fishing boat before we do."

"How long until we close on them?" Juan asked.

"Ten minutes to the yacht. By that time, the fishing boat will be out of sight on the other side of the island."

"Do you think it's the trap we're expecting?" Max asked.

"You read my mind," Juan said. "Seems like a clear lure to me. Murph, how are you doing with the sensor analysis on those Kuyog drones?"

Murph spun around in his seat at the weapons controls. "Eric and I came up with a beacon that might fool the sensor, but it's a long shot. We can't really test out the idea without a working Kuyog. Gomez is working on mounting the beacon on one of our aerial UAVs. In the meantime, I'll be able to shoot any drones they send at us with the Gatling guns."

Juan didn't ask if he was sure. Murph could have been a professional video gamer, so aiming the Gatling guns remotely was a snap for him, using either the radar or the targeting cameras mounted on the guns.

Even if there were more Kuyogs than Murph could handle, the

Oregon would be able to outrun them with her magnetohydrody-namic engines at full throttle. They'd never close the distance before their small fuel tanks ran out.

"Our main target is the fishing boat," Juan said, "and then we'll board the yacht as well, just to be sure." He had Hali radio down to the boat garage.

"Linda here."

"Are you ready to launch?" Juan asked.

"Eddie, Linc, and MacD are suited up with their dive gear in the RHIB. We're just putting Little Geek on now. Set to go in two min-utes." Little Geek was their small remotely operated underwater ve-hicle, which Linda would be able to control from the rigid-hulled inflatable boat. Since Raven had told them about Brekker's plan to booby-trap the wreckage, he didn't want to send his people down there until he knew there were no explosives on it.

"Good, but there's a change of plans. Instead of diving on the destroyer, just do a quick inspection with Little Geek and then catch up with us in case we need you to board the yacht. We can always come back later and do a night dive on the wreck."

"Aye, Chairman," Linda confirmed. "Conducting a boarding party with this trio will be no problem. We've got enough weapons aboard the RHIB to take down Godzilla."

"We'll slow long enough for you to launch, then continue on our way. Good hunting. Chairman out."

When they reached the site of the *Pearsall* wreckage, Juan had Eric slow to a crawl. The door to the boat garage was already open, it took only a few seconds for the RHIB to shoot out of the *Oregon*.

As soon as they were clear, Juan ordered Stoney to take her back up to flank speed.

"Let's stay alert," he announced to everyone in the op center, his voice taking on a grave tone. He looked at each of his crew, in turn, as he talked.

"From our run-ins with Locsin to this point, he's shown himself to be ruthless and unpredictable. Don't make the mistake of underestimating him. He's a dangerous man even if we are able to capture him, which is what our goal is for Beth Anders's sake."

Raven nodded to Juan before his eyes finally settled on Max.

"Be ready for anything."

IT DIDN'T TAKE LONG for the RHIB to reach the *Pearsall*. The *Oregon* was already well on its way toward the islet when Eddie throttled back and idled at the designated coordinates. Linda peered over the side of the boat's inflated tubular gunwales. Even with the cloud cover dimming the view, the bow of the destroyer jutting from the seafloor sand was clearly visible.

She finished prepping Little Geek and had MacD and Linc lift it over the side and into the water. Linda tested the onboard camera to make sure she was getting a good feed through the fiber-optic tether connected to her handheld control panel. The high-definition signal was strong, so she started its descent.

When Little Geek reached the bottom, MacD pointed at the screen and said, "Ah think we know where they went in."

"I see it," Linda said, pointing the ROV at the hole ripped in the *Pearsall*'s side by the torpedo that sank her.

As Little Geek went inside the destroyer, she popped on its powerful LED lights. At the first room it reached, she saw a big X drawn on the open door.

"That looks new," Linc said.

When Little Geek went past it to the next room and another X, Linda said, "They must have crossed off rooms as they searched them."

MacD nodded. "No Typhoon cargo inside. Makes it easier for us."

She kept going forward until she found the only door not marked. Little Geek went through and broadcast an image of a single sealed orange plastic barrel against the bulkhead. Another was overturned on the floor, its lid gone.

"Typhoon?" Linc asked.

"Only one way to find out," she said. After circling the barrel and spotting no booby traps, she moved Little Geek forward and unfolded its small manipulator arm. Its claw reached out and gripped the lid. She tried lifting it up, but it wouldn't budge.

"Must be pressure-sealed," MacD said.

"In this case, brute force is a good solution." Linda revved the motors to full speed and yanked the arm at the same time.

The lid popped off, and water rushed into the container. White cotton batting floated out. Linda angled the ROV so they could see the interior.

The pills were already dissolving in the seawater, sending a cloud of white powder roiling through the boatswain's locker.

"No way there were two million pills inside these two barrels," MacD said, who had been told about Overholt's briefing about the *Pearsall*'s cargo and the implicit instructions to destroy the pills.

"Wait a minute," Linc said. "Back up and pan down."

"Did you see something?" Linda asked.

"Shapes on the floor."

She moved Little Geek to give them a better view and saw what he meant.

Algae had grown around the bottom of the barrels where they met the floor. She counted the bare circles.

"Eighteen missing," she said.

"That means one-point-eight million pills are gone," MacD said.

"I'll let the *Oregon* know," Eddie said and radioed Hali.

"Tell them we're done here and we're heading their way as soon as we get Little Geek back," Linda said.

Eddie nodded and told Hali. Linda maneuvered Little Geek back the way it had come. It was almost to the opening in the hull when a glint reflecting the ROV's lights caught her eye.

She turned Little Geek into the room and immediately saw stacks of shells for the destroyer's five-inch guns. Some of them had spilled onto the floor. But what had caught her eye was a shiny metallic object unsullied by years of corrosion.

She edged Little Geek closer until she got a good look at it. MacD must have recognized it at the same time she did because he said, "Uh, guys, that's a bomb."

"And it's got an acoustic detonator attached to it," Linc said.

At least six explosive devices were planted among the ammunition.

Linda swiveled Little Geek around and quickly set it to automatic guidance so that it would follow its original path, exit the ship, and head for the surface.

She yanked the fiber-optic cables from the controller and threw them over the side.

"Eddie, get us out of here now!"

Without hesitation, he jammed the throttle to its stop, and the RHIB took off like a rocket.

53

Brekker glanced back at the *Oregon* gaining on them from the direction of the *Pearsall*, amazed that such a large ship could move at that speed. But the strange cargo vessel wasn't his highest priority, so he turned back to focus on the fishing boat ahead. Locsin was his primary target. Once he'd done away with the Filipino communist leader, he'd take care of Juan Cabrillo. He'd lure the ship back over the sunken destroyer and break its keel in two with the explosives he'd put in the ammunition magazine.

Since both Brekker and Locsin had brought their bombs aboard as agreed, blowing up the fishing boat was no longer an option. Sporadic fire was coming from it, but few of the shots were connecting with the yacht. Brekker thought Locsin simply wanted to scare him off. That wasn't going to happen. Not when Brekker had an RPG at his disposal.

He'd acquired the rocket-propelled grenade launcher and ammo from a dealer he knew in Manila before heading out to the wreckage site. He hadn't wanted to take a chance that NUMA had moved up their schedule and arrived while he and his men were diving on the *Pearsall*. Now he'd use the weapon to take out Locsin and have the world's remaining supply of Typhoon to himself.

When Brekker's men brought up the weapon and unpacked it, he handed over the wheel and picked up the RPG, its grenade already loaded. He wanted to deliver the final death blow himself.

He went to the yacht's bow and knelt on the deck, the RPG on his shoulder. With the sight aimed at the fleeing fishing boat, he readied to fire.

Locsin must have seen what he was preparing to do because a fusillade of automatic rounds zinged past him, and Brekker hit the deck as the yacht swerved to avoid the shots. He'd have to fire from a prone position.

He turned back and waved to the man at the wheel, who looked at him through the bullet-riddled windshield.

"Closer!" Brekker shouted, and the driver nodded.

The yacht stayed on a steady course, and Brekker raised the RPG again, preparing to fire the kill shot.

LOCSIN WATCHED Brekker's yacht closing the distance.

"He's persistent," Tagaan said as he opened another barrel to inspect its contents. "We should get rid of him. Now."

"But he's carrying seven barrels of Typhoon pills," Locsin replied. He was hoping Brekker would simply make a getaway and Locsin could get the balance of the drug from him later, one way or the other. Killing him now would eliminate almost half their potential supply, and Locsin would rather concentrate on the pursuing *Oregon* that was looming close behind the yacht.

"Fire another volley," Locsin ordered. "See if we can at least injure enough of his men to get him to back off."

His men unleashed another torrent of bullets, downing one of Brekker's men, but the driver was uninjured, and the yacht continued its relentless chase.

"Comrade Locsin!" Tagaan shouted in an excited voice as he looked into the barrel he'd opened. "Come quick!"

Locsin hurried over and saw two pieces of cardboard pressed together under the remnants of the cotton batting that had been removed. He picked them up and pried them apart to find a dried flower flattened and taped to one of them. Locsin recognized it as a variety of orchid, though one he'd never seen before. Next to it was a label that read *Typhoon—Cephalantheropsis inviolabilem— Mindanao.*

There was no formula, but this had to be the plant with the key ingredient that Ocampo had been missing. It even gave him a lead on where to look for what must be a rare flower. The island of Mindanao in the southern Philippines was large, but with the surplus of Typhoon pills he now had, and enough new recruits, he was sure he could find more of the orchids. With the flowers in hand, Locsin could build a new laboratory and hire more chemists to create new Typhoon pills, perhaps even make it more potent than it was now.

"Do you realize what this means?" Tagaan said to him with awe.

Locsin smiled and nodded. "It means Mr. Brekker has become expendable. Then we can deal with the *Oregon.*"

He took the acoustic detonator from his pocket, then turned to the yacht and waved it over his head so that Brekker could see it.

When he had boarded the yacht, he didn't know the South African mercenary had stowed a second detonator on board the yacht, but he did find the bombs in the chest right away. In fact, from the very beginning he'd planned on using one to get rid of Brekker.

BREKKER WAS getting ready to fire the RPG when he saw Locsin waving something at him. It took him a moment to realize it was the second detonator he'd handed over to make their détente work.

Why would he be showing it to me? Unless . . .

An iciness suddenly chilled Brekker's stomach. The threat of the bombs should have been long behind them when they'd both tossed theirs overboard. Had he overlooked something?

Brekker leapt to his feet and raced back along the port railing, searching for anything that was out of place. When he didn't spot anything unusual, he did the same with the starboard railing and froze at the sight of a thin nylon rope knotted to one of the cleats.

He looked over the side and saw a bomb dangling in the water along the side of the boat, its submerged acoustic receiver ready to receive the signal.

He shot a savage look at Locsin and saw white teeth grinning back at him and a thumb over the detonator's button.

Brekker lunged at the rope in a frenzy, desperate to pull the bomb from the water before it could explode.

54

Twin camera feeds on the op center main screen showed the RHIB racing away from the site of the *Pearsall*, on one side, and Gerhard Brekker frantically reaching over the side of the yacht, trying to reach something.

"What's he doing?" Juan asked.

No one had time to answer before the yacht erupted in a fireball. Simultaneously, a massive water plume blasted hundreds of feet above the sunken destroyer's location. If the RHIB hadn't fled when it did, Eddie and the others would have been pulverized.

"Find out how they're doing, Hali," Juan said as he watched the RHIB slow down.

Hali radioed Eddie and put it on speaker. "Are you all still in one piece out there?"

"No injuries," Eddie replied. "Except for Little Geek. Linda says she saw it get thrown into the air by the explosion. We'll go see if we can salvage it and then head your way."

"Eddie," Juan said. "Hang back until we give you the all clear. I have a feeling Locsin has more tricks up his sleeve."

"Roger that, Chairman. We'll stay here until you call back. Out."

The fishing boat was just rounding the north end of the islet.

"We can't let them get away," Raven said. "We have to make us take them to Beth."

Max patted her on the shoulder. "We'll get her. There's no possibility that they'll outrun us in that thing."

The *Oregon*'s camera picked up a green flash from the fishing boat.

"That had to be a laser," Max said. "We've just been targeted."

The fishing boat disappeared around the islet's northern point. As soon as it was gone, small black shapes came racing at them across the water.

"Those are the Kuyog drones," Juan said. "I count ten. Prepare to take them out, Wepps."

"That's a big affirmative, Chairman," Murph said. "Gatling guns coming online."

The hull panels hiding the trio of 20mm weapons slid aside, and their six barrels whirred to life, spinning in preparation for the three thousand rounds per minute that would be fed by a belt from the mounted ammunition drum.

"Chairman, I'm not showing any of them on radar," Murph said. "That Chinese stealth technology seems to be working. I'll have to target them manually."

"Mr. Stone, come ten degrees to port. That should give us the best angle to take them out."

"Coming about," Eric said. "Ten degrees to port, aye."

"You may fire when ready, Gridley," Juan said to Murph, paraphrasing Commodore Dewey's order just before the Americans decimated the Spanish fleet in Manila Bay during the Spanish–American War in 1898.

"Firing." Murph let loose a torrent of tracer shells from the starboard Gatling gun. The chain saw buzz of the weapon resounded through the *Oregon*'s hull.

The first Kuyog was blown apart by the tungsten rounds. Murph kept firing as the gun swung to the next drone, and Juan could see the rounds kicking up a trail of water as they lanced their way to the target. It blew up in a satisfying gush of flame.

Murph systematically cut down the rest of the drones one by one. None of them got within a quarter mile of the *Oregon*.

"Good shooting, Murph," Juan said.

Murph shrugged. "Just call me Deadeye."

"Keep a deadeye out for more."

"They can try again, but it'll be a huge waste of hardware for them."

"As the wise Mr. Solo has said, Don't get cocky."

"*Moi?*" Murph said, turning to show off the black T-shirt he was wearing. The white letters on the front read *Once I thought I was wrong, but I was mistaken.*

"Glad to see I have a crew with their egos in check," Juan said with a smile.

"If you want to see a bruised ego," Eric said, "watch me kick his tail at chess."

Before Murph could respond, the fishing boat came into view on the big screen, cruising along the opposite side of the islet.

Another fishing boat appeared. It looked just like the first one.

"What's the double?" Murph said.

Then another one. And another. Soon, there were twenty similar boats on-screen, all motoring toward Negros Island eight miles to the west. Every one was the same color and model, though each had slight differences.

"Can anyone distinguish which was the one we were following?" Juan asked.

"Playing back the video," Hali said. The recording of their chase came on the screen next to the live feed. None of them matched the recording.

"Did it disappear?" Max said, incredulous.

Juan frowned. "Locsin must have changed the configuration of his boat while it was out of sight, just like we do. It means we can't tell which of the boats is the original since we don't know what changed."

"Can you disable all the boats with the Gatling guns?" Raven asked.

"Not without killing potentially innocent fishermen," Juan said, "which is probably what Locsin is counting on. We'll have to board them one at a time."

"Chairman," Hali said, "we're being hailed. It's Salvador Locsin. He wants to talk to us on a private channel."

"Put it on speaker."

Locsin's accented but articulate voice came through with a jaunty tone. "Is this Juan Cabrillo that I'm finally speaking to after all these encounters?"

"Are you calling to surrender?" Juan said. "It'll save us some time."

"It's hard to tell which boat I'm on, isn't it? The fishermen on board the other nineteen have no idea what's going on, of course. I was planning to use this tactic on the Philippine Navy, but I thought I'd put it to good use here. It seems to be working well."

"Just as long as it takes us to board every fishing boat in your fleet. Odds are, we'll get to you sooner rather than later."

"I could simply have all the boats take off in random directions," Locsin said. "That would slow you down." Despite his threat, all of the boats continued on a steady pace.

The obvious boats to start with would be the ones headed to Negros since it was the closest inhabited island, but Juan didn't mention that. "The search would take longer, but we'd find you eventually."

"That was my conclusion, too," Locsin said. "So I have a surprise for you. Look toward Negros Island and a little north."

Juan nodded to Hali, who panned the camera around until it was aiming northwest. A white ship was motionless five miles away. Juan's stomach knotted when he recognized it as a passenger ferry.

"What have you done, Locsin?"

"You have a dilemma on your hands, Captain Cabrillo. I know the type of man you are. I saw it when you rescued Dr. Ocampo and his scientists from my laboratory, despite the fact that they meant nothing to you. You can't understand that sometimes you have to sacrifice innocents for a larger purpose."

"Most would call it a virtue to value the lives of innocents."

"I call it a weakness. That ferry has over twelve hundred passengers aboard. My men have killed its crew, disabled its radio, sabotaged the lifeboats, thrown all the life vests overboard, and opened the sea cocks. I estimate it will sink within the next twenty minutes. What you may not know is that many Filipinos can't swim. Strange, for an island nation like ours, but true. Most of them will die within sight of the shore." He paused, then said, "Unless you do something about it."

Juan seethed at hearing Locsin so casually talk about killing men, women, and children who were simply in the wrong place at the wrong time. What he would do if Locsin were in the room right now . . .

"The clock is ticking, Cabrillo. I know you'll 'do the right thing.' You've been a challenging enemy, but I have to go now."

With a click, the line went dead.

Juan knew it was no choice at all. He couldn't take the chance that Locsin was bluffing.

He looked at Eric and said, "Stoney, give me all available speed toward that ferry."

Remembering the ruse he'd read about Locsin using to escape from the police transport boat, Juan knew they would need to tread carefully. As the *Oregon* raced to the sinking ferry, he had Hali send out a distress call to the Philippine Coast Guard, but he knew it might be an hour or more before help arrived. If there really were passengers on board, they would have to carry out the rescue themselves.

When the *Oregon* neared the ferry, which was already riding low in the water, Juan ordered Eric to come up beside it but not too close. The sight that greeted them was disturbing.

Lining the railings were hundreds of people, including a large proportion of women and children, many of them terrified and crying. There was no doubt they were civilians. Juan could not imagine the mind of someone who would put in motion the atrocity that would occur if the ferry actually went under.

"We'll have to take Locsin's timing at his word," he said. "That means we have fifteen minutes before that ferry sinks. Options?"

"We can start bringing them over," Murph said, "but the deck of the *Oregon* looks to be about twenty feet higher than the deck of the ferry. With twelve hundred passengers, it would take at least half an hour for the evacuation even if everything went perfectly. And we're starting to get a lot of chop out there from the coming storm."

With the *Oregon*'s advanced stability systems, only large waves would be discernible to the crew, so Juan hadn't noticed the swells. But the ferry was an older boat and rolling viciously and no longer under power. Many of the passengers were getting sick. Even if they could get a gangplank connected between the ships, bringing people across safely would be difficult.

"What about going aboard and seeing if we can close the valves flooding her?" Max suggested.

"Chairman," Hali said, "the RHIB is pulling into the boat garage." Eddie and the rest of his team had rendezvoused with the *Oregon* after recovering a severely damaged Little Geek.

Juan nodded to Max. "Get over there and see what you can do. Maybe you can slow the flooding long enough to get people over. Take Eddie, MacD, Linda, and Linc with you. Hali, make sure they're armed in case Locsin left some of his soldiers on board."

Hali nodded and relayed the order to Eddie.

"On my way," Max said as he grabbed a handheld radio and hurried out of the op center.

"I'm going, too," Raven said, but Juan put up a hand to stop her.

"My people have got this."

"But—"

"Stay right here. They know how to work together. Stoney, pull us alongside the ferry."

Raven grumbled but didn't move.

The *Oregon* edged up beside the ferry. A minute later, Juan could see Max and the others latch a ladder over the railing and begin climbing down to the stricken vessel.

"We could tow her," Eric said. He nimbly kept the *Oregon* butted up against the side of the ferry. There was a screech of metal as the ferry's rocking hull scraped up and down against the *Oregon*'s.

"Where's the nearest port?" Juan asked.

"Fifteen miles plus," Murph said. "Our speed will be severely limited if we're towing a sinking ship. It could take us an hour or more to get there."

While Juan was watching the ferry bob, he could see Negros Island in the background every few seconds. The waves crashing on a wide, sandy beach less than three miles away gave him an idea.

"We don't have to go that far," Juan said.

Eric and Murph followed his eyes.

"Beach the ferry?" Murph said.

Eric nodded. "If we get it to shallow water, that would at least keep it from going under until the Coast Guard could get here to evacuate the passengers."

"Chairman," Hali said, "I've got Max."

"Put him through." When Hali nodded, Juan said, "Max, how's it looking over there?"

"We had a hairy time getting onto the ferry. It would be a mess trying to get people off in a hurry. One of the English-speaking passengers confirmed that the crew is dead."

"Change of plans. We're going to tow you. Get ready to tie up some lines."

"Roger that. We'll go to the bow and get ready to receive them."

Juan had Eric pull the *Oregon* ahead until the stern was next to the ferry's bow. The deck crew tossed over three weighted nylon lines that let Max and the others pull three heavy ropes over to the ferry. These were lashed around the forward capstans, and Eric eased the *Oregon* ahead until they were taut. The ferry was one hundred feet directly behind them.

"Start increasing your speed, Mr. Stone," Juan said.

The magnetohydrodynamic engines hummed as the *Oregon* strained against the ferry's load. Eric was careful not to accelerate too quickly for fear of snapping the ropes. Soon, they were at ten knots, and steadily increasing.

Max called in and said, "It looks like the lines are holding at our end. I'm going to the bridge, and Linda and the others are going to check the flooding to see if they can close the valves manually."

"What about the time?"

"I think Locsin was right. At the rate we're settling, I'd say ten more minutes might be generous."

Juan glanced at the clock and then at Negros Island on the screen growing slowly in the distance. "See what you can do."

Eric didn't take his eyes off the controls, but he said, "Chairman, at this pace of acceleration, we're going to need all ten of those minutes to get to the beach."

"Maybe more," Murph said.

Juan frowned at the clock again. "I know. Right now, time is the enemy."

LINDA RACED to keep up with MacD as they descended the port stairwell to the ferry's lower decks to figure out if they could close the valves flooding the ship. Max was headed to the bridge to see if he could close them from there, while Eddie and Linc tried to calm the passengers, to keep them from jumping overboard.

Since it was a passengers-only ferry, there was no vehicles deck. Locsin's men must have instructed all of the passengers to go topside because there was nothing but an eerie silence below, punctuated by Linda's and MacD's footfalls. The only light was provided by the faint, battery-powered emergency lights.

Five decks down, they reached the water and waded in. A sheen of oil on top meant the engines were at least partially flooded. The water level was already waist-deep on Linda and rising.

"This isn't the bottom deck," MacD said. "I can feel more steps going down."

"Then there's no way to get to the valves," Linda said. "Maybe there's still enough power for Max to do it remotely."

She was about to radio Max when they heard faint cries.

"Those are coming from this deck," MacD said.

Linda turned and pointed to the starboard side. "It sounds like they're coming from that direction."

They splashed through the water into a corridor running the length of the ferry. The meager emergency lighting punctuated the darkness every thirty feet.

The pleas for help were more distinct now, and accompanied by repeated pounding. Linda and MacD went down the hall until they reached an unmarked door.

MacD knocked on the door, and the response came in two different languages—English from a woman, and some kind of Filipino language from a man.

"Don't kill us! Please!"

"We're not going to kill you," Linda called through the door. "We're here to help."

"Oh, thank you! Thank you!" The woman inside translated for the man, who let out a cry of joy, then began speaking quickly in his native tongue.

"We saw some men killing other crew members, so we hid in here," she translated. "Now we can't get the door open, and water is seeping under it."

MacD examined the door and said, "It opens out. There's too much pressure on this side."

"Then we need to equalize it," Linda said. "I didn't see any axes on the way down."

"The door looks pretty flimsy. We'll try it the old-fashioned way." He reared back to give himself some room to kick. Though the water was above Linda's waist, it wasn't quite above his.

"Stand back from the door!" Linda shouted, and gave MacD space.

MacD lashed out with a hard kick, but the door held. He tried again, with the same result, but Linda thought she saw the door buckle a little at the jamb, so she said, "Keep going."

He gave it three more kicks. On the third one, the door caved in. It happened so suddenly that it swept MacD and Linda inside with it.

Linda swirled around and finally came to rest against the far wall. She stood and wiped the oily water from her eyes. She saw the two crew members help each other to their feet while they spit out the nasty mixture.

"Are you all right?" Linda asked them.

They both nodded. Linda told them to join the rest of the passengers on the deck, where they could get more info about what was going on. The woman said, "Thank you," again, and she took the crewman by the hand as they waded out of the room toward the relative safety of the upper decks.

Linda turned to see MacD kneeling, the water lapping at his chest and dripping from his head. He grimaced in pain.

She went over and helped him up. "What happened?"

"My ankle got twisted when the door gave way," he said through gritted teeth. "Feels like it was cranked in a vise."

"We need to get topside."

Even though MacD towered over her, Linda put one of his arms on her shoulders so she could help him hobble to the stairs. When they got there, he hopped up to the next landing with her assistance, then stopped so Linda could radio the situation to Max.

"Linda, give me good news," he said.

"Wish I had something nice to say," Linda replied, "but MacD injured his ankle saving a couple of the crew. And there's no way to get to the valves. They're underwater, maybe a deck below us, so we're on our way up to you. Can you do anything from the bridge?"

"Not a chance."

"How bad does it look up there?"

"Really bad."

MAX STOOD in a slaughterhouse.

The ferry's bridge was littered with half a dozen corpses, all of them shot and left where they dropped. Footprints of Locsin's killers were stamped into the blood that was already congealing on the linoleum. The distinctive coppery smell was nearly overpowering.

The crew wasn't the only thing that had been laid to waste. All of the instrumentation was blown to bits. Radio, helm, engines, ballast control—all of it was completely destroyed. They had made sure that no one would be able to save this ferry, condemning twelve hundred people to their doom if the *Oregon* couldn't save them.

To the south, Max could see the fleet of fishing boats chugging along as they headed west toward their home port. They'd soon be out of view, shielded by the peninsula jutting from Negros Island. Max knew that just as soon as the ferry was safe, Juan would chase the boats down and carry out his plan to board each and every one of them to find Locsin.

He stepped out onto the flying bridge to get some fresh air. Passengers milled about on deck below, but the information that Linc and Eddie were passing along to those who spoke English had seemed to quell the panic.

He looked at the *Oregon*, its stern frothing with white water as it dragged the ferry toward the safety of Negros Island. Eric was doing an admirable job keeping the trajectory steady in seas that were getting choppier by the minute.

The beach, however, was still a long way in the distance. Max didn't want to think about what might happen if the ferry foundered before it got there.

With the engines stopped and all of the ship's equipment silent, Max was surprised to hear the whine of a small motor from the rear of the ferry. He turned to see something black bouncing along the water at high speed as it approached the stern on the starboard side.

With horror, he recognized one of the Kuyog drones. It wasn't bothering with the ferry. It was heading straight for the *Oregon*.

"Juan, you've got a drone coming!" he yelled into the radio. "Starboard side!"

Murph was lightning quick. The Gatling gun came to life, rotating quickly to find the drone. With a teeth-rattling buzz, it fired and blew up the Kuyog just before it reached the *Oregon*.

The massive explosion caused many of the ferry passengers to scream and drop to the deck. But the cries of terror didn't mask the noise of more approaching motors.

Max turned to the chilling sight of dozens more Kuyogs coming at them like a swarm of hornets.

Though Murph was the best at what he did, he wouldn't be able to shoot them all before they hit. And if enough of them made it through, not even the *Oregon*'s armored hull could withstand that kind of punishment.

Then two more ships would join the USS *Pearsall* on the ocean floor.

56

While Murph struggled to fight off the Kuyogs, Juan glanced at the fishing boats disappearing one by one behind the Negros Island peninsula. Locsin must have targeted the *Oregon* with a laser when they were distracted attaching the tow lines.

Since the attacking drones were shielded from view by the ferry, Max spoke to Murph on a private channel to tell him whether they were coming along the port or starboard side.

Murph couldn't set the Gatling guns to automatically fire with the radar targeting system because of the stealth technology, so he had to switch back and forth between cameras on either side of the ship to see what he was aiming at. Both of the gun camera feeds were up on the big screen, along with the view dead ahead. Murph destroyed the first five Kuyogs, but he had only seconds to hit each one when it came into view.

The sixth one got through.

It struck the starboard side of the *Oregon* right at the waterline. Juan felt the ship rock as the explosion reverberated through the hull.

Juan looked at Hali. "Damage report!"

"We've got flooding in the starboard ballast tank," Hali said. "Watertight doors are sealed and holding."

The *Oregon* began to tilt to starboard as the tank filled. Murph continued to fire away as more drones came into range.

"Let's get this list under control," Juan said. "Flood port ballast tanks. It'll slow us down, but we need the stability."

Hali said, "Aye, Chairman," and initiated the flooding procedure. The listing stopped, and the *Oregon* began leveling out, though it was now riding lower in the water.

"Our speed has been cut by twenty percent, Chairman," Eric said.

"Push the engines as hard as you can," Juan said. The beach was growing on the view screen, but too slowly.

"We're already at one hundred percent power output."

"Take us to one hundred and ten percent, and keep an eye on the coolant temperature."

Juan could hear the objections from Max in his head, that the supercooled magnets that accelerated the water through the Venturi tubes would fail if they operated above the red line for too long. They might even melt, irreparably damaging the engines.

"Stoney, Murph said you and he had a possible way to decoy these drones away from the *Oregon*."

"I also said that we needed a working Kuyog to test out the theory," Murph said, the strain in his voice obvious, as he blew away another drone. "This wasn't what I had in mind, but now might be a good time to try it out."

"As long as Gomez has the UAV ready," Eric said, "the beacon is set to go."

"Hali, tell Gomez to get it into the air ASAP."

"Aye, Chairman."

Juan watched as two Kuyogs came in from both sides simultaneously. Murph hit the first one but missed the second, which was aimed directly at the *Oregon*'s stern.

"Incoming!" Juan called out.

The drone went out of sight of the camera and detonated in a huge blast that echoed through the op center. The aft end of the *Oregon* momentarily lifted up from the impact.

"Speed falling," Eric said. "It must have damaged one of the engines."

Juan didn't want to distract Max from his duties helping out Murph, so he got Linda on the line. She was now on the ferry's flying bridge with Max and MacD, who was propping himself up on the railing to take the weight off his injured ankle.

"Linda, did that explosion sever any of the tow lines?"

"No, they're still intact," she replied. "But it looks like the starboard Venturi nozzle was hit. It's spewing water upward, so it's doing nothing for propulsion. I recommend shutting it down."

"Do it, Eric," Juan ordered. "Linda, what's the ferry's status?"

"It's just a matter of time before she goes under. The passengers are scared stiff, but Linc and Eddie are doing a good job keeping the situation from melting down. Everyone has been moved to the stern of the ferry to keep them away from the explosions."

"Good work."

Juan hated having his people on the sinking vessel. But there was no way to bring them back over now. And if the *Oregon* detached to fight off the Kuyogs, the ferry would sink before they could tow it to safety or evacuate the passengers.

They were all getting to the beach. Or none of them were.

FROM LINDA'S VANTAGE POINT, she could easily see the results of shutting down the *Oregon*'s starboard tube. Water no longer jetted up at an odd angle, and the froth on that side subsided.

She felt useless as she watched the *Oregon* struggle to pull the ferry to dry land. Max and MacD were beside her, noting the positions of the speeding Kuyogs and passing the information on to Murph, who continued to deftly take them out one by one. By this point, however, the Gatling guns had been spitting out 20mm tungsten rounds for far longer than normal, and she could see steam rising from the overworked barrels. If they overheated, the guns would jam, and there'd be no stopping any more drones.

The sea was being churned by waves from the approaching typhoon, making the progress of the two ships that much more difficult. Because they'd been able to modulate the closing of the watertight doors, the ferry was no longer in danger of capsizing, but the bow was dropping closer and closer to the surface, with some of the bigger whitecaps now breaking onto the deck.

Linda glanced up at the sky, but, judging by the cloud density, it didn't look like the worst of Hidalgo itself would be arriving before the ferry could be off-loaded by the Coast Guard. Assuming, of course, that there was a ferry left to off-load.

A black dot caught her eye as it danced in front of one of the ominous gray clouds. At first, she thought it was a bird, but the way it moved was more like a fly buzzing around a kitchen.

She nudged MacD and pointed at the darting object. "Do we have a UAV in the air?"

MacD peered at it and said, "Let me check." He passed the question along to Max, who got a quick response from Hali that it wasn't theirs.

"Then tell the Chairman we've got a spy in the sky," she said.

Max called it in and got a confirmation that Juan would take care of it since Eric and Murph were busy.

Seconds later, a deck plate near the stern of the *Oregon* slid aside, and a large rectangular block mounted on a rotating armature rose above the Iranian flag fluttering on the jackstaff. On the front of the block was a grid of one hundred holes, which were actually the ends of the barrels of the Metal Storm gun.

Unlike the six rotating barrels in the Gatling gun that fired a stream of rounds fed by a belt, the Metal Storm antiaircraft/antimissile system was completely electronic, so there were no moving parts, making jams impossible. Rounds were loaded into the grid of barrels so that the projectiles lined up nose to tail. The electronic control allowed for a precise firing sequence that made the Gatling gun's rate of three thousand rounds per minute seem pokey. With each barrel of the Metal Storm gun firing simultaneously at a staggering rate of forty-five thousand rounds per minute, the weapon could pump out its entire load of five hundred tungsten slugs in six milliseconds.

The Metal Storm gun swiveled around and tilted up until it was pointed at the unknown UAV, presumably Locsin's observation drone watching his Kuyogs trying to finish off the *Oregon*.

The gun fired with a thunderous boom. The rounds flew out of the barrels so fast that it seemed like a single flash of light.

The UAV didn't stand a chance. The heavy tungsten rounds formed a wall of shells that would be impossible for even the most dexterous operator to evade. In a fraction of a second, the UAV simply ceased to exist.

The Metal Storm gun then disappeared back into the deck for reloading in case it was needed again. At the same time, the Gatling guns continued their buzz saw howls as they picked off more Kuyogs. Linda counted more than fifteen destroyed so far, either by the guns or by the drones hitting their target.

A moment later, a large UAV emerged from the bowels of the *Oregon* on a deck elevator. This one was the Corporation's heavy supply drone. Slung underneath it was a device Linda recognized as the decoy beacon that Murph and Eric had showed her. The supply drone's eight propellers whirred to life, and it took off from the deck, flying low over the ferry.

Linda followed its flight path and paled when she saw what was behind her.

She hoped Eric and Murph's decoy beacon was going to work because more than twenty Kuyogs were heading toward them in a side-by-side formation to deliver the coup de grâce. The *Oregon* didn't have nearly enough firepower to take them all out before they ripped it to pieces.

"NO!" Locsin screamed when the feed from the observation drone cut out. He grabbed Tagaan by the shirt. "Get it back! I want to see the *Oregon* die!"

Tagaan shoved the hands away. "I can't. There was a flash on the ship's deck before we lost it. They must have shot it down."

"Then turn us around!"

He lunged for the fishing boat's pilothouse, but Tagaan stepped in his way and pushed him back.

"Comrade!" he yelled. "We have what we came for! The *Oregon* will be destroyed. Even if it isn't, it's severely damaged. We need to get this supply of Typhoon to safety before the storm comes."

Locsin was shocked by Tagaan's pushback. He had never defied an order before, and the insubordination threatened to send Locsin over the edge. He very nearly grabbed one of the assault rifles to shoot Tagaan where he stood, until his right-hand man continued.

"You have your victory," Tagaan said. "You outwitted Juan Cabrillo. Savor it. And when we take over the country and have factories churning out Typhoon pills, you will have whole armies at your disposal. No one will be able to stop us."

Locsin took a deep breath and saw that Tagaan was right. The Typhoon pills he had in hand and the search for the orchid used to make it were the highest priorities. He straightened up and told the man at the wheel to keep heading for home.

Besides, he'd seen the last two dozen Kuyogs racing in for the killing blow. The *Oregon* would sink, he was sure of it. Cabrillo himself might survive the attack if he was too cowardly to go down with his ship, but if he wasn't killed, he would have to live with the fact that Locsin had beaten him.

But Locsin knew it was even worse than that for Cabrillo. The former CIA agent was pointlessly bound by an overdeveloped sense of ethics. He didn't have the unflinching long-term vision that Locsin possessed. That vulnerability had been Cabrillo's undoing, and the memory of these events would haunt him for the rest of his life. It would always be the day that he'd failed to save the lives of twelve hundred souls.

57

From the supply drone's camera feed, Juan could see that it flew mere feet above the whitecaps lapping at it from below. Gomez Adams, now at his remote flight station in the op center, was doing a remarkable job keeping it from being swamped while Murph picked off the last few Kuyog stragglers that preceded the final wave of twenty-four that were nearing the ferry's stern.

"You've got to keep it right above the water," Murph said to Gomez. "Otherwise, the sensors might not pick up the supply drone's beacon."

"Easier said than done," Gomez said without breaking his concentration on the controls. "How close do I have to get to these Kuyog things?"

"I'd say less than a hundred yards. More than that and they might not break the lock they have on the *Oregon*. Think of it like the countermeasure flare a fighter jet uses to fool a heat-seeking missile into diverting from the jet's hot engine exhaust."

Gomez shook his head. "Except this fighter jet weighs over eleven thousand tons and is towing a huge ferry."

Murph shrugged. "I didn't say the analogy was perfect."

"How long until we are in danger of beaching ourselves, Stoney?" Juan asked. He was happy to see that Raven Malloy was watching everything in silence, letting them do their work without interrupting.

"We're less than a mile away," Eric said. "Then we'll have to disengage from the ferry."

Juan looked at the ferry they were dragging. Its gunwales were perilously close to the water. They'd have to time this perfectly to have a chance of succeeding.

"Once the Kuyogs have locked onto the beacon," Murph said to Gomez, "no jerking movements or they'll break away and head back for the *Oregon*. Right now, they're all grouped together, so this is our best shot at having them all follow the supply drone together."

"If this works," Gomez said, "just remember what happened when they didn't pay the piper."

"If this *doesn't* work," Juan said, "I have a feeling the annual bonus will be sharply reduced this year."

"Living is better than dying," Gomez said with a sly chuckle. "Got it."

When the Kuyogs were less than a football field's length from the supply drone, the ones at the outer edges turned toward it. Gomez matched their speed and began flying backward in the direction of the ferry.

"It looks like they have a lock on the beacon," Murph said. "They're following you past the starboard side of the ferry. Now you're going to have to fly the supply drone right past the *Oregon*. Otherwise, their sensors might detect they're being redirected away from the real target."

"How close?"

"Close enough to give it a high five as it goes by."

Gomez said nothing further, keeping his entire focus on the drone's flight path. With the breeze picking up, Juan could tell that Gomez was having to use all of his flying skills to keep the supply drone in front of the Kuyogs without hitting either the water or the *Oregon*.

Everyone in the op center sat in silence as the Kuyogs approached the stern. If the sensor lock was lost, two dozen high-explosive warheads would impact the *Oregon* before they could do anything about it.

The rusty hull of the *Oregon* dominated the supply drone's camera feed as it flew by. Juan breathed a sigh of relief when he saw the first Kuyog skim past the ship in pursuit of the drone. Then the second and the third followed. Within seconds, all twenty-four had whizzed by.

Murph jumped up and fist-bumped Eric before returning to the weapons station.

"Now what?" Gomez asked.

"We need to get rid of them," Murph replied.

"There," Eric said, pointing at the screen showing the view in front of the *Oregon*. "Five hundred yards off the starboard bow. See those waves breaking on the rocks?"

"That must be a barrier reef," Juan said. "You have your destination, Gomez."

"That I do, Chairman," Gomez said with a smile and gently arced the supply drone toward it. The Kuyogs raced after it.

When the supply drone reached the rocks, Gomez brought it to a halt a hundred yards beyond them, hovering like a tempting piece of bait on a hook.

The first Kuyog didn't even slow as it hit the rocks. It detonated in an impressive fireball. The other Kuyogs followed suit, dashing themselves on the rocks in a futile attempt to reach their target. The combined explosions sent a huge black mushroom cloud into the sky that would be visible for miles. If Locsin still had eyes focused in this direction, he might see it rising above the peninsula between them and conclude that the *Oregon* was destroyed.

Gomez and Murph both slumped back in their chairs for a moment, spent from the adrenaline surge. Then Gomez went back to the controls and began flying the supply drone back to the *Oregon*.

"I'll buy you two a beer later," Juan said, "but we're not out of the woods yet." The beach was approaching rapidly. "Hali, tell the deck crew to prepare to cut the tow lines."

"Aye, Chairman."

"Stoney, what do the depth charts say?"

"We can get within two hundred yards of the beach without grounding ourselves. If they're accurate, that is."

"Let's give ourselves some maneuvering room," Juan said. "Tell me when we're within three boat lengths of the beach." Getting the 560-foot-long *Oregon* stuck in the sand wouldn't help the ferry passengers.

Juan leaned forward as the jungle beyond the beach became unnervingly close. A minute later, Eric called out, "Three boat lengths."

"Cut the ropes to the ferry," Juan ordered.

When Hali got confirmation from the deck crew that they were disconnected, he said, "Tow lines cut, Chairman."

"Hard aport, Stoney." The *Oregon* was so agile that she could stop and turn on a dime, but the same couldn't be said for the ferry behind them. It would keep plowing forward on inertia alone and would hit their stern if they didn't get out of the way.

The *Oregon* heeled to port, her heavy ballast tanks and damaged engines keeping her from moving as quickly as usual. In a few more seconds, she was parallel to the beach and still turning.

The ferry kept coming, though it was slowing rapidly now that it was no longer being dragged forward. Max reported that it missed the *Oregon*'s stern by mere feet.

The *Oregon* made a wide circle until she was directly behind the ferry.

"Get our bow right up against the ferry," Juan told Eric. "We need to give it one final push."

"Tugboat maneuver, aye," Eric replied. He nudged the *Oregon* forward until she touched the wide stern of the ferry. When he was sure he had good contact, Eric revved the engines, and the *Oregon* shoved the ferry forward until it ran up onto the sand, lurching to a stop with a grinding noise audible in the op center. The ferry's metal stern was slightly crushed in by the *Oregon*'s armored bow, but Eric had timed it so that he threw the engines into reverse at the last second to minimize the damage.

The passengers watching at the stern railing were thrown off their feet by the sudden grounding. When they picked themselves up off the deck, they began cheering wildly.

"Are we stuck as well, Mr. Stone?" Juan asked.

"We may be touching bottom at the bow, but I think I can get us free."

"Then please do so."

Eric pushed the engines to maximum reverse power. The *Oregon* resisted at first, but the remaining operational Venturi tubes must have acted like enormous dredges and scoured the sand out from under them. The *Oregon* moved away from the beach until Juan felt they were in safe waters. He ordered Eric to maintain position. Everyone relaxed and waited for Corporation crew members in the RHIB to retrieve Max and the others from the ferry.

By the time the RHIB returned to the boat garage, passengers were already scrambling down makeshift ladders from the bow into the surf and wading ashore, grateful to be on dry land again.

When Max got back to the op center, he began assessing the damage to his engineering systems. He looked at Juan and shook his head in disgust.

"Not good?" Juan asked.

"You've done a number on my ship while I was gone."

"Yes, a lot has happened since you left us twenty minutes ago. Now, can we get out of here before the Coast Guard arrives?"

"Yes, but we can't go far."

"What do you mean?"

Max held up his fingers as he ticked off the problems one by one. "We've got a rupture in the starboard hull that we can't repair until we get to a service dock. Our starboard Venturi tube is damaged and will need a refit. And the magnets have overheated, which means that they'll have to be completely overhauled and recalibrated. I can do the last part myself, but it'll take time, and, until then, we'll risk a full system shutdown if we travel any appreciable distance."

Juan had Eric put up the weather map tracking Typhoon Hidalgo. "You see the problem, right? Hidalgo is heading straight for us. According to the latest projections, it will pass directly over Negros Island."

"And I would love to get out of its way," Max said. "But if we try to outrun it, we could be stuck in the middle of the open ocean without operational engines during a Category Five storm. Doesn't sound very appealing to me."

"I hope you have an alternative."

"As a matter of fact, I do." Max replaced the weather map on the screen with a detailed coastal map of Negros Island. He zoomed in on a bay only twenty miles away.

"That's not a shipping harbor because the area around it is marshy," Max said, "but it should provide us some protection from the storm surge. By the time the full brunt of the typhoon arrives, I'll have the engines in good enough shape to ride it out."

Juan didn't like the idea of sitting in a bay during a storm like

Hidalgo, but the notion of being stranded at sea in mountainous waves was even worse.

"Stoney, set course for that bay," he said. "Top speed that Max allows."

"Aye, Chairman," Eric replied, and the *Oregon* began moving away from the beached ferry. Since the passengers had been moved away from the bow during the firefight between the Kuyogs and the Gatling guns, all they'd be able to report was that a mysterious ship and its crew had saved them from certain death amid dozens of explosions from unknown watercraft. Juan would have his people reconfigure the *Oregon* while it was idling so that even if the Coast Guard did subsequently come across them, they would look like a completely different ship.

"Congratulations, Mr. Cabrillo," Raven said now that they were out of harm's way. "I've never seen such a remarkable display of teamwork."

"We only bring on the best. Every corporation says that, but we really mean it."

"I can see that. But Locsin is still out there, and so is Beth."

"I know. We'll have to wait out the storm and plan our next step once it's passed."

Raven held up the temporary phone they'd loaned her to replace the one taken by Locsin. "I don't think we have to wait that long. While we were recovering from the battle, I was finally able to check my email and found a message from an account that I've never seen before. It says, '*Raven, this is Beth. In a huge cavern but don't know where. Track this cell number to find me.*' I checked the number in the message, and it has a Philippines prefix based on Negros Island. If this is legit, Beth might have found a way to lead us right to Locsin."

 **NEGROS ISLAND**

By the time night had fallen in the cavern, Beth was lying on her bed going crazy from boredom. Besides her meal breaks, she'd had no human contact, and there was nothing to read or do in her cell. Because of the double doses of Typhoon, she felt better than ever. Her wound was healing well, but she also had the periodic urge to smash everything in the room from frustration at her predicament.

She wondered if her email message had been received. It was possible that it had gone straight to Raven's junk mail because it came from an unknown number. And Beth had no idea if they really could track Dolap's phone, nor did she know if the phone was actually broadcasting, especially given the depths of the cavern. She had a feeling that this is what Purgatory would be like.

The exquisite masterpieces she'd examined were the only thing keeping her sane. She could have kicked herself for assessing the value of the paintings so quickly. She should have said it would have taken days, not only so she could revel in their beauty but also to stave off the inevitable moment when she was no longer useful to Locsin.

She heard voices in the hallway and got up. They were approaching her room. If she was going to get out of here, she might as well try anything and everything. She really didn't have much to lose.

A key rattled at the lock, and she picked up the metal nightstand with ease. To her surprise, she was able to hold it over her head even with her injured shoulder.

As the door opened, she swung the table at the first person she saw, delivering a strong blow to the man's shoulder. It was Dolap, who shrugged it off as if it were just an annoyance and wrested the table from her hands. With a look of fury, he raised the table as if to strike her with it, but a voice behind him yelled, "Stop!"

Locsin stepped into the room with Tagaan. Both of them started laughing, and Dolap joined in after a moment, putting the table back down. Beth wouldn't give them the satisfaction of being cowed, so she sat on the bed and checked her nails with disdain. They actually weren't too bad, given the circumstances.

"Ms. Anders," Locsin said after the laughter ceased, "you're looking well."

Beth didn't even look up, concentrating on a chip in her thumbnail.

"I hear you've had a healthy appetite. It must be helping your wound."

Out of the corner of her eye, Beth saw him nod at Dolap, who walked over and yanked aside the bandage on her shoulder.

Locsin peered at it. "Excellent. This has been a very interesting experiment. And thank you for the appraisal of the paintings. Tomorrow I would like you to show me how to verify their authenticity."

"I doubt I could teach anything to someone like you."

"You might be surprised," he said with a sickening smile. "I spent three years at university in Manila before I came back here to carry on the struggle for my people."

Beth looked Locsin in the eye and laughed derisively. "Every murderer like you thinks he's a freedom fighter."

Locsin shook his head. "It's pointless to get into a debate with you about whether the ends justify the means. Today I had a similar discussion with your friend Juan Cabrillo, and it didn't go well for him."

Beth shot to her feet. "What did you do to him?"

"Him and his whole ship, actually. They're gone. If you were holding out some pathetic hope that he would come rescue you, you might as well forget about it."

Stunned, Beth collapsed back onto the bed.

"Now get some sleep," Locsin said. "I want you rested for my lesson tomorrow. Even if you think I'll be a slow learner, we'll have plenty of time. There's a typhoon coming through. By tomorrow afternoon, we'll be socked in for several days. Good night."

They left, and Dolap locked the door behind them.

Beth was in shock. She didn't know whether to believe Locsin or not. But it was likely that Raven had teamed with Juan after Beth was abducted, which meant that if he was really dead, Raven probably was, too.

It felt like there was a hole in Beth's stomach. Normally, she would sob uncontrollably at the loss of her friends and at the true hopelessness of her situation. But right now there was nothing inside her but anger. She wanted to kill Locsin, Tagaan, Dolap, all of them. She wanted to make them suffer, but she couldn't. At least she could let them know she wasn't going to take this quietly.

Beth picked up the nightstand and beat it against the door until her fingers ached.

AS HE STOOD with Tagaan and Dolap at the end of the hall, Locsin could hear the bang of metal against Beth Anders's door.

Dolap made a move toward her room, but Locsin put his hand up to stop him.

"Let her vent," he said. "It shows that the Typhoon is working."

They continued talking as the banging went on.

"Are we ready for Hidalgo?" Locsin asked.

"We need to bulk up our food stores before the storm arrives," Tagaan said. "We don't know how long the roads may be out after that. We also need ingredients to keep our meth lab in operation." The meth lab was in a remote corner of the cavern because of the noxious chemicals required.

Locsin turned to Dolap. "Since you've done such a good job with Ms. Anders, I'll give you some time in Bacolod tomorrow morning to get the supplies. Pick a man to take with you. You shouldn't require more than one truck."

"Thank you, comrade," Dolap said, obviously pleased with the reward. "She has been difficult at times."

"You won't have to deal with her much longer. We'll test the Typhoon on her for one more day. If the effects are still positive, we'll dispose of her before Hidalgo has passed. No sense in wasting any more of the drug on her."

He dismissed Dolap, who went back to his post outside Beth's room.

"What about the Typhoon and the flower?" Tagaan asked. All of the barrels were still inside the truck in which they'd arrived, under armed guard even inside the cavern. "Where should we store them?"

"Once the storm has passed, I will drive them to our hiding spot outside the cavern. Only you and I will know the location of the bulk of the pills. The temptation of theft by our men will be too high here. Since we should be in full production of the drug soon, I want to move up our timetable to take over the Philippines. How is Kuyog production proceeding?"

"With half the parts shipment destroyed by Juan Cabrillo and his people, and with fifty of them used to sink the *Oregon*, we're down to one hundred and thirty-eight either complete or in production. We can order more components from the Chinese supplier that we addicted to Typhoon, but it will take time to manufacture and ship them here."

Locsin thought about their planned attack on the Philippine Navy. Now that they'd annihilated the ultra-sophisticated *Oregon* and had refined their tactics, he felt confident that they could wipe out the more conventional warships of his own country's navy with the remainder of the Kuyogs.

"Continue our production at maximum capacity," Locsin ordered. "I want them all completed in a week and prepared for use. Then we will begin our campaign to conquer the Philippines. After that, we set our sights on the rest of Asia."

Tagaan frowned. "Comrade, we should wait until we have Typhoon in production. It is reckless to move against the government before we have our supply secured."

Locsin stared at Tagaan. This was the third time that his number two had questioned his judgment. "Do you think you're smarter than I am?"

Tagaan hesitated only a moment before answering, but it was enough for Locsin to notice. "Not at all."

"But you're saying I'm reckless. Am I stupid, too?"

Tagaan averted his gaze. "Forgive me for being unclear. I meant that we have time now that we have more than a million Typhoon pills at our disposal. We should use them to take over the government from the inside. Then we can use the Kuyogs against any country that opposes us."

Locsin balled his hands into fists, then released them and smiled. "Excellent. You are a wise man, my friend. I don't know what I would do without you."

"Thank you, comrade."

"But I also think it's wise to complete production of the Kuyogs as quickly as possible in case something unforeseen happens. Don't you agree?"

"I do, comrade."

"Then go make sure our production is continuing as projected. I'll take the lead on finding more chemists to develop the drug from the orchid."

Tagaan nodded, and Locsin glared at him from behind as he left.

Locsin then called to Dolap, who rushed to his side. Dolap was Locsin's cousin and one of his most trusted men, which was why he'd been put in charge of Beth and the paintings.

"Yes, comrade," Dolap said.

Locsin put his hands on Dolap's shoulders and looked him in the eye. "When you're in the city, I have a special mission for you. Make up some excuse for whoever you take with you that you need twenty minutes on your own. This is just for you and me. No one else is to know. No one."

On the deck of the *Oregon*, Juan was buffeted by the steadily strengthening winds as he walked toward Max at the stern. The black clouds made it look like daybreak even though the sun had risen an hour before. A small river fed the wetlands that were protecting the ship from the brunt of the waves crashing onto the shore, but they wouldn't completely mitigate the effects of the storm surge when Typhoon Hidalgo arrived. For that, they would need propulsion from the engines, which were currently shut down.

Standing beneath the jackstaff, Max peered over the railing at crewmen working on the Venturi nozzle below. He had to yell at the top of his lungs to be heard over the howling wind.

"No! Just rip it off!"

When Juan reached the railing, he looked down and saw three men in the water tugging at a bent piece of metal. A fourth crewman was using a blowtorch to cut apart the jagged remnant of the Kuyog explosion.

"Are you scrapping my ship?" Juan teased.

Max turned to him with bloodshot eyes from working straight through the night. "We might as well if we can't get that nozzle functional in the next few hours. An anchor isn't going to keep us in place. What's the latest forecast?"

"We should be seeing hurricane-force winds before dark. It's been downgraded to a Category Three, but the center of the storm is still on track to pass right over us, so we'll get the worst of it. Do you think we'll be ready for it?"

"Fingers crossed. There was nothing I could do about the ballast tank flooding. That will take some heavy-duty welding on the exterior hull. But I've finished recalibrating the cooling system, and the damage to the magnets wasn't as bad as I first thought. If we can get this Venturi nozzle at least somewhat operational, I think we can get us to three-quarters power output. But even if that happens, the ride is going to be pretty rough for the next thirty-six hours."

"I have faith in you," Juan said.

"I'm glad someone does, because the thought of doing maintenance work outside in a gentle one-hundred-mile-an-hour breeze isn't my idea of fun."

Juan left Max still yelling and went to the nearest hatch, which looked as if it were jammed shut with a broken handle. He pressed in three spots simultaneously on the hatch, and it sprung open, revealing the luxurious secret interior.

He took the teak-paneled stairway down to the Magic Shop, the *Oregon*'s workshop and storehouse for any gadget, costume, or makeup needed for a mission. He found Kevin Nixon hunched over one of the many workbenches tinkering with an electronic device. Dozens of clothes racks were behind him, as was a makeup counter worthy of a movie set, a metalworking table, a woodshop, and shelves full of electronics, tools, and assorted gear.

Kevin was an award-winning Hollywood special effects master

who had joined the Corporation after his sister was killed on 9/11. Any time someone on the *Oregon* needed a disguise, a uniform, or an unusual piece of equipment, such as Juan's combat leg, Kevin would put his considerable expertise to work. Unlike the athletic veterans, former special forces operators, and CIA agents that made up the bulk of the crew, Kevin's sedentary job and rich food provided by the chef meant that he was constantly at war with his weight, though right now he was looking more svelte than usual and seemed to be winning the battle of the bulge.

When he saw Juan enter, Kevin looked up, pushed the pair of magnifying glasses back onto his head, and sighed.

"You're not going to blow up this tracker, too, are you?"

"Me personally?" Juan said. "No. But, then, I'm not going on the mission. Besides, technically I didn't blow up the last one, either. That was Tagaan's fault."

"Who's going to destroy it this time?"

"Eddie, Hali, and Raven. They'll blend into the Philippine crowds better than Linc and I would."

"I met Raven when I was outfitting you all with those Filipino police uniforms. She seemed quiet, but extremely competent."

"She's performed well even though she hasn't worked with us before," Juan said.

"She's highly motivated. The few times she talked, she had some choice words for this Locsin guy. Sounds like it's personal."

"It is. She was on protective detail for Beth Anders. We think this mission will help find her."

"You said she sent a phone number to home in on?"

Juan nodded. "I have a request in to Langston Overholt to track it down, and he passed it on to the NSA. I figured they owed us for the Vietnam job. Lang says they agreed to find it, but apparently the phone isn't transmitting right now. It may be off or unable to get a signal. As soon as it comes back online, he'll let me know. Then I'll send the team in to plant that new tracker of yours so we can find out where he's going. Unless, of course, Beth is with the phone's owner at the time. Then they'll snatch her back right there."

Kevin handed the tracker to Juan. "Since you gave me a second shot with this one, I decided to add a few features."

The device was a little larger than the previous tracker that Juan had planted on the truck holding the Kuyog components. It was cylindrical and painted black.

"One end is magnetic," Kevin said. "Just stick it under the chassis of any vehicle you want to follow. If the satellite signal is blocked because it's in a building, it will use any cell phone or Wi-Fi signal available to continue transmitting."

Juan noticed a thin seam near the end opposite the magnet.

"What's this?"

"Good eye." Kevin turned to a laptop and typed in a command. The cylinder telescoped out to reveal a tiny camera suspended from a gimbal. "I repurposed this from one of our drones. You'll be able to control the camera sightline remotely. There's even a mic for audio feed. Just make sure the cylinder is placed somewhere that the telescope can extend past the vehicle's frame."

Juan smiled. "You're a genius. And to think your talents could have been wasted winning an Oscar for designing some monster in the latest superhero movie."

"If it helps save Beth, I don't mind missing out at all. Award shows are overrated anyway."

Juan's phone buzzed, and he answered it immediately when he saw it was Overholt.

"Did you find it?" Juan asked without preamble.

"The NSA reported that the phone came online a few minutes ago," Overholt said. "Who knows how long it will be active, so I advise sending in your team immediately. I'll relay the coordinates to you."

"Where is it?"

"Just like you thought, the signal is coming from Negros Island. It's a city called Bacolod not too far from your present position. Good hunting."

He hung up and called Hali, who was waiting with Eddie and Raven in the boat garage ready to take the RHIB up the river to a small town where they could "borrow" a vehicle for the morning.

"Hali," Juan said. "We just got the coordinates of the phone signal. Tell Eddie the mission is a go."

60 BACOLOD, NEGROS ISLAND

Finding an isolated car to hotwire took longer than Eddie thought it would, but according to the NSA, the phone that Beth had told them to track was still in the city when he, Hali, and Raven arrived. With over half a million people, the modern city of Bacolod was a major hub for the processing and shipment of the sugar grown in the vast fields they'd passed on the drive. If they didn't intercept the person with the phone before it turned off again, they'd never find him.

Although none of them looked Filipino, Raven's and Hali's caramel complexions and dark hair meant that they could more easily disappear into the crowds of people preparing to ride out the coming typhoon. And since people of Chinese ancestry made up a significant portion of the population, Eddie looked like he could be a native. Most of the inhabitants spoke English, so language wouldn't be a problem, though they'd have to fake the accent.

The NSA guidance led them to a plaza crowded with shoppers

getting last-minute supplies before the storm. The nearest building had a sign on it that read *Visayan Wholesale Foods.*

Eddie parked the car, and the three of them walked toward the building, which had trucks lined up outside loading crates of food to replenish the rapidly emptying grocery stores. There was apparently no thought of evacuation, but Eddie wasn't surprised. There was simply no way to clear out an entire island of more than four million people.

Rain showers were coming in bursts now as the outer edges of Hidalgo approached Negros, so all three of them wore hooded windbreakers. Many of the workers wore no protective clothing and were getting soaked, while the shoppers carried umbrellas. The bustle of activity made it difficult to tell who their target was.

They stopped at the building, and Eddie turned to Hali. "Can't the NSA get more precise than the signal is coming from the vicinity of this food supplier?"

Hali nodded. "A half-block radius is the best they could do."

"Raven, keep your head down but let me know if you see anyone familiar."

"If it's Locsin himself," Raven said, "he'll recognize me immediately. Getting the tracker onto his vehicle will be tricky."

"We'll deal with that if we need to," Eddie said. "Right now, we need to find out who owns that mobile phone."

Eddie scanned the shoppers while Hali eyed the workers. Raven switched back and forth between the groups. Five minutes later, Hali tapped Eddie's shoulder and nodded at two muscular men walking out of Visayan Foods, each pushing a handcart full of produce boxes. They began loading them into an unmarked white truck with surprisingly knobby tires.

"Those guys seem like the kind of meatheads we're looking for," Hali said.

"Do you recognize either of them?" Eddie asked Raven.

She shook her head. "Neither was in the Manila warehouse."

"And I don't remember them from the gunfight on Corregidor. Still, Hali's right that they fit the profile of Typhoon users. Let's find out if we're right."

He took out a burner phone he'd gotten from the Magic Shop. He'd asked Kevin Nixon to program it with a Negros Island number for this very possibility.

He dialed the number they were trying to find.

Seconds later, they heard a phone ringing in the pocket of one of the men loading boxes. He had a scar on his upper lip like someone who'd had a cleft palate repaired. The man answered the phone, and Eddie hung up without saying a word. The man shrugged and put the phone back in his pocket.

"Looks like we've got our man," Eddie said.

"Now we just need to wait until they go back inside to plant the tracker," Hali said.

"They may not go back inside before they leave," Raven said. "Look how full the truck is. They may be getting ready to head out."

"We may never get a chance like this again," Hali said.

Eddie frowned at the men. Everyone else was giving the truck a wide berth, as if they knew not to approach it. Even if the two communist soldiers standing nearby didn't notice him attaching the tracker, somebody else in the crowd might alert them. They wouldn't have a second try. Eddie dismissed the clichéd idea of sending Raven in to use her feminine wiles to distract the two men. Besides, it probably wouldn't work in this kind of weather.

But he had an idea that would work in any conditions.

He handed the tracker to Raven. "Get ready to put this under the truck by the rear wheels. Wait for the distraction."

She narrowed her eyes at him. "What distraction?"

One of Locsin's men was closing the rear door of the truck while the other wheeled the handcart back to the door and gave it to one of the employees. They were preparing to leave. It was now or never.

"You'll know when," Eddie said to Raven and put his arm around Hali's shoulder, pulling him toward the rear of the truck.

"What are we doing now?" Hali asked in confusion.

"Get ready to hit me as hard as you can," Eddie said in a low voice.

Hali looked at him like he was crazy. "What?"

Eddie staggered like a drunken idiot when they got close to the truck and loudly slurred his words into Hali's face. "I said, your sister invited me over to her place. What was I supposed to do? I think we'll have a storm party today."

He glared at Hali, who finally got what he was going for. Hali reared back and sent a solid punch into Eddie's gut. His tightened abs absorbed most of the blow, but he was impressed with Hali's punch. The lessons Eddie had been giving him were paying off.

Eddie went down on his back, then sprung up and grabbed Hali by the neck and wrestled him to the pavement. A cheering crowd surrounded them, eager to have a good fight to distract them from the coming storm. While they exchanged softened blows, Eddie stole a glance at the people around them and saw that Locsin's men were among the spectators, exactly as he had hoped.

Raven wouldn't need long to snap the tracker's magnet into place. Eddie put on a show with Hali for a few more seconds, just long enough to make it look respectable. Then he rolled away and acted like he was catching his breath. Hali didn't pursue, much to the groaning dismay of the crowd.

They looked at each other as if they were grudgingly conceding the fight and got to their feet.

"Okay. I won't go to her place if you don't want me to," Eddie said reluctantly. He extended a hand to Hali, who shook it. With that, the crowd dispersed as quickly as it had gathered.

Eddie watched the two men get in the truck and drive off.

Raven walked over to them and said, "You fight like girls, and I mean that in the best way."

Hali rubbed his chin and smiled at Eddie. "You got me pretty good on one of those punches."

"Sorry about that, but we had to make it look real," Eddie said. He turned to Raven. "Is the tracker in place?"

"Exactly where you wanted it. Nobody saw a thing."

"Then let's return that farmer's car and get back to the *Oregon*. If there weren't such long lines at the gas stations I'd fill it up on the way back."

He didn't need to text Juan that the tracker was operational. It went active the moment the magnet connected to the truck. Seconds later, Eddie got confirmation on his phone. The *Oregon* was already receiving its signal.

Because the tracker was planted underneath the rear bumper of the truck, the big screen in the *Oregon*'s op center could only show lateral and rear views as Kevin Nixon's camera panned around. Still, Juan thought it was much better than simply following the blinking dot on the map next to it.

After leaving the city, the truck took the northern highway. For most of the trip, fields of sugarcane on both sides waved in the steadily worsening weather. The highway ran right along the coast for two miles before the truck turned off and headed inland on a narrow paved road.

After another few miles, the truck turned again, this time onto a muddy road toward one of the island's central mountains. Almost immediately, the farms were replaced by a thick jungle as it started going uphill. The truck bounced so much on the bumpy road that the broadcast from the camera looked like it was coming from the back of a hyperactive kangaroo.

"I play a lot of video games," Murph said, "but even my stomach isn't going to be able to take much more of watching this."

"I'll help Kevin build an image stabilizer into the next camera," Eric said.

"That doesn't look like a public road to me," Linda said. "If it is, their tax dollars are going to waste."

The truck stopped abruptly. They could hear a few voices over the burbling exhaust, as if the driver was speaking to someone at a gate. Seconds later, the truck started moving again and was engulfed by darkness as it entered a tunnel. Just before it went inside, Juan noted that the road continued on along the hillside.

Receding into the distance at the tunnel entrance were two guards closing two chain-link gates that were covered with vegetation to disguise the opening. As soon as the gates were closed, they returned to their posts at seats inside. The positioning would give them a clear field of fire at any vehicles that approached.

"Does this remind anyone of the Bat Cave?" Murph asked.

"Locsin is pretty much the opposite of Bruce Wayne," Juan said.

After a hundred yards, the tunnel opened into a much larger cave. Locsin was apparently so sure that the cave entrance was undetectable that he hadn't bothered to post any guards where the tunnel entered the cave.

"This must be the cavern Beth mentioned in her email to Raven," Linda said.

The camera's limited view didn't show how high the cave's ceiling went. But the cave floor around them, leveled and compacted with crushed rock, was well lit by arc lamps powered by a huge diesel power plant. A tanker semi-trailer was parked alongside feeding it fuel, indicating Locsin's headquarters complex was much more than simply a few men huddled in a dank cave.

The delivery truck moved through a cluster of low-slung buildings. Right now, Juan was just trying to get a feel for the overall layout of the place, but the recording from the camera feed would give them detailed intel they could review when planning the mission to infiltrate the cave and rescue Beth.

The truck continued on through a central plaza with a stalagmite in the center. For a split second, Juan saw a strange sight beyond it, unexpected for the interior of a cavern.

Eric saw it, too, because he said, "Was that a helicopter?"

"Looked like it to me," Juan said. "Linda, I want the highest-resolution satellite photos you can get of this area. There must be another opening that we haven't seen yet."

"On it," she replied.

The truck kept driving and did a three-point turn almost like they were giving a three-hundred-sixty-degree tour of the place. Juan counted at least a dozen buildings and twice as many trucks and Humvees. Beth was right in saying the place was huge.

The men they saw were all muscle-bound. Definitely long-term Typhoon users. There were enough of them to populate a small town, which meant a full-on assault was out of the question. Juan was already formulating a plan for getting in and out without being seen.

At one point in the truck's turn, he saw a large cart being wheeled from a large three-story-tall building to one just as big but only two stories high. The tarp covering the object on top slid aside briefly before it was put back into place. It was the exact same type of black drone that had damaged the *Oregon*.

"I guess we know where they're manufacturing their Kuyogs," Murph said. "Judging by the size of those buildings, they could have hundreds of them in there."

Given that each of the Kuyogs was packed with high explosives, Juan noted that could come in handy if the need arose.

The truck backed up to a long one-story building where the largest number of the men were entering or leaving, which meant it was likely the barracks, mess hall, and kitchen.

The driver and his companion shut down the truck, came around the back, and began unloading it. For fifteen minutes, they shuttled food crates inside with dollies. While they did, Juan had Linda pan the camera as much as she could to focus in on whatever was in view so they could construct a map of the place.

Then a female voice made Juan sharply say, "Quiet!"

Everyone in the op center fell silent. The driver and his pal were noisily chatting while they removed boxes from the truck, masking the woman's voice.

"Turn up the gain on the audio," he said to Linda. "See if you can find the source of the voice."

The camera turned until they saw Beth's flaming red hair. Her clothes were filthy, but she was walking normally, and there was no apparent pain on her face even though she had a bandage on her left shoulder.

Salvador Locsin was walking next to her, yanking her by the arm so that she would keep up with him.

"I told you, I'm not going to help you anymore," Beth said, her voice full of bluster.

"You will if you want any more Typhoon," Locsin said.

"I don't care what you do to me."

"You'll change your mind in a day or two without your dose."

They entered the same building where the food was being taken and went out of range of the microphone.

"They've been making her take that stuff?" Linda said with disgust. "Didn't Langston Overholt say it's addictive?"

Juan nodded. "Very. According to the World War Two records, the addiction becomes permanent in just a few days, maybe a week at most. We need to get her out of there as soon as Hidalgo finishes passing or she might be irreversibly hooked on it."

Then Juan heard one of the men inside the truck say Beth's name and he held up his hand for quiet again, but the conversation was brief and in Tagalog. The men were silent as they went inside with more boxes.

"Play that back, Linda," Juan said. "I want to hear them again."

When the recording rewound to the point where Beth and Locsin entered the building, Linda began playing it forward, and Murph ran it through the computer interpreter to convert it to English. The translation wasn't perfect, but they got the gist of it.

"He is right, Dolap," one of the men said. "She tells him anything. Remember the thing that happened to that administrator, Alonzo? I wanted to throw up all the times I saw him chained to that rock out there."

"It doesn't matter," Dolap said. "Locsin and Tagaan tell me we kill her tomorrow. They already see the effects of the Typhoon they want to. I will ask them to allow me do it. Beth Anders is a big pain in my side since she arrived here."

Linda gasped. "That's long before Hidalgo will be gone. It'll still be near full strength tomorrow. The eye is forecast to pass right over us at four in the morning."

Everyone in the op center was quiet again, this time from the shock of the death sentence they'd just heard. Juan didn't want to admit defeat, not when they were so close. But mounting a mission in the middle of a Category 3 typhoon seemed beyond even their capability. In fact, he was worried that Eddie, Raven, and Hali wouldn't make it back before the brunt of the storm hit.

Then he sat forward in his chair as something Linda said resonated.

"Linda, put the predicted storm track up on the screen and lay it over the map of the truck's route."

She did so, and the center of Hidalgo was not only predicted to go over the *Oregon* but the cavern as well.

"How wide is the eye of the typhoon and what's the speed?" he asked her.

"The eye is twenty-three miles across, and the wind speeds could be up to one hundred and twenty-five miles per hour when it makes landfall."

Juan shook his head. "Not the wind speed. The forward speed of the entire typhoon."

She furrowed her brow at the odd question. "About ten miles per hour."

"Then that gives us a little more than two hours to work with." The cavern was only seven miles from their present position.

Both Eric and Murph turned to him at the same time with incredulous looks on their faces.

"Are you seriously thinking of going out in the middle of a typhoon?" Eric asked.

"Technically, the middle of a typhoon is very calm," Murph said. "There could even be blue sky inside the eye during daytime hours."

"So, technically, we *can* do it," Juan said.

Eric looked at Murph, who shrugged and then said, "I guess so. But if you get stuck out there when the eye finishes passing over, you won't be able to get back to the *Oregon* for a long time."

"Then we need to have a good plan. Have Eddie and Raven join me, Linc, MacD, and Gomez when they get back." He checked the clock. It was nearly two in the afternoon. "We've got fourteen hours to put together the mission."

Linda shook her head in amazement at the idea of venturing out of the *Oregon* during a major storm. "Max is going to have a heart attack when he hears this one."

"Then you get to tell him," Juan said. "And maybe have Hux with you when you do just in case she needs to revive him."

62

Juan didn't know if this was the craziest thing he'd ever done, but flying in a helicopter in the literal center of a typhoon had to be up there. Even though it was four in the morning, the towering eye wall of Hidalgo was brightly lit by a nearly full moon. The roiling clouds just a few miles in the distance were a stark contrast to the eerie calm around them.

Nobody aboard the *Oregon* had gotten much rest since the typhoon arrived. Max's repairs to the ship's engines had been completed in time to weather the storm, but the ride during the tidal surge in the bay was pretty rough.

Despite the menacing conditions, Gomez lazily chewed gum like he was piloting a routine recon mission. Behind Juan were Eddie, Linc, and Raven, who had taken the last seat in place of MacD. Julia had ruled him out for the op as soon as she saw his swollen ankle and diagnosed it as a severe sprain.

All of them were dressed in jungle camo gear and carried M4

assault rifles equipped with flash suppressors and 40mm grenade launchers under the barrels. If everything went according to plan, they wouldn't need to use them. Their objective was to get in unde-tected, spring Beth, plant explosives to take out the Typhoon pills recovered from the *Pearsall*, and get back to the helicopter before anyone besides the guards on duty woke up. Though the helicopter had only five seats, the high payload capacity meant they could squeeze Beth in as well.

To aid their silent infiltration, all of them except Linc were car-rying Smith & Wesson M&P 22 Compact pistols threaded with sup-pressors and loaded with subsonic rounds. MacD had entrusted his faithful crossbow to Linc.

The MD 520N, the *Oregon*'s onboard helicopter, was launched from an elevator platform that rose from the internal hangar near the ship's stern. It had no tail rotor, steering instead with the turbine exhaust routed through the finned tail. This feature not only made it safer to be around because it didn't have a vertical spinning blade of death, it also made the helicopter much quieter, which meant they could land relatively close to the cavern without betraying their presence.

Their destination was a clearing a mile up the dirt road from the cavern. Gomez circled to make sure it was still clear, using his night vision goggles to verify that no trees had fallen into the landing zone. Then he touched down on the soaked grass as gracefully as a hummingbird.

While Linc, Eddie, and Raven got out and lowered their night vision goggles, Gomez shut down the engine and looked at his watch, then at Juan. "Linda estimates that we've got to take off in forty-eight minutes if we want to reach the *Oregon* before the oppo-site edge of the eye wall does."

Juan nodded. His original time estimate had been too rosy be-cause they had to wait to fly until the eye of Hidalgo was over both the ship and the cavern.

"If we lose the comm link and the go time comes before we get back," Juan said, "your orders are to fly back to the *Oregon*. There are plenty of trucks and Humvees in the cavern to provide us alternate transportation."

"I wouldn't risk it," Gomez said. "You'll be lucky to find clear roads all the way to a safe shelter. Better to fly the friendly skies."

"We fully intend to. See you soon."

Juan joined the team and set his own goggles in place to see through the deep shadows cast by the jungle. They hoofed it double time down the road toward the cavern entrance.

Juan was impressed by the resilience of the jungle flora. Although many large branches had been torn down by the gale-force winds, none of them were big enough to block the road. If they needed to commandeer a Humvee to get back to the chopper quickly, they wouldn't run into any major obstacles on the way.

Fifteen minutes later, they reached the location where they'd seen the truck enter the hillside. Juan checked his GPS twice to make sure they were in the right place because the entrance was so well hidden by the foliage covering the gates. Even the tire tracks of the truck leading inside were invisible, disguised by artificial turf layered over solid pavement.

Careful to maintain absolute silence, the four of them crept up to the gates. Without disturbing the camouflage, Juan looked through one of the only spots with a tiny gap left for the guards inside to see out.

Two guards lolled on chairs, obviously unconcerned that anyone would be approaching the hideout in this kind of weather in the middle of the night. Ensconced safely in the tunnel, Hidalgo was no threat to them. One of them was nodding off, and the other was watching something on his phone. The lack of discipline was appalling but suited Juan's purposes.

He nodded to Linc, who had MacD's crossbow at the ready. Linc shouldered it and lined it up with another gap so he could aim at the man distracted by his phone. Juan drew his suppressed pistol and aimed it at the ear of the dozing guard.

He whispered, "Now." With a barely audible twang, Linc fired the crossbow. At the same time, Juan fired a single round, which sounded no louder than the snap of a rubber band.

Both men slumped in their chairs and collapsed to the ground.

Juan waited a moment to see if any alarm was raised. No Klaxons, no warning bells, no shouted commands.

He found the hidden handle and twisted it so he could pull open the gate just wide enough for them to slip inside. The well-oiled hinges made no sound.

They propped the dead guards back on their chairs in case anyone happened to look down the tunnel. Juan took one of the radios and gave the other to Eddie. They both attached earpieces to the audio jacks so they could hear incoming calls without being audible to anyone else.

They slowly made their way down the hundred-foot-long tunnel, their pistols and crossbow in hand to take out any other patrolling guards. When they reached the central cavern, each of them knelt and gawked at the majesty of the natural wonder that had been sullied by the communist terrorists.

It had to be one of the biggest caverns in the world, rivaling the recently discovered Hang Sơn Đoòng caves in Vietnam, and large enough to hold at least ten city blocks of forty-story buildings. Gigantic stalactites dangled from the ceiling high above. Several waterfalls, fed by the downpours from Hidalgo, cascaded from the limestone. They rushed into a swollen river that streamed along one side of the cave and disappeared in a huge pool.

The dozen or so buildings comprising the rebels' headquarters covered only a small portion of the cave. That section was well lit by lamps powered by the diesel generator, but the rest of the cavern was swallowed by darkness.

As Juan gaped at the soaring ceiling, he spotted the huge hole that had been hinted at in the satellite photos they'd examined in the pre-mission planning. Vines lined the rim so that, from above, it would simply look like a sinkhole. That was how Locsin's helicopter got in and out. Only during a low-altitude night flight directly above the opening would anyone have a chance of seeing the interior lights.

Juan scanned the cluster of buildings and saw no movement. He pointed to the nearest structure, which housed the noisy diesel generator, and they dashed over to it for cover. They could talk quietly here without fear of being overheard.

He checked his watch, then said, "It took us seventeen minutes of hiking time to get here, plus the time we spent taking out the guards, so we've now got sixteen minutes to find Beth and leave. Eddie and Raven will check out the long building to look for her. Linc and I will head to the Kuyog manufacturing plant on the far side. We'll make this our rendezvous point. Remember, sixteen minutes. Then we'll blow the cavern and the tunnel entrance and let the Philippine National Police dig them out. Understood?"

Juan was sure that Eddie and Linc knew their jobs, so he looked at Raven. She gave him a curt nod of her head.

"I wish I could see Locsin's face when he realizes we were here," she said.

"If everything goes according to plan, that realization will last about one millisecond," Juan said. "He won't have time to twitch an eyebrow. Let's go."

They checked once more for roaming guards but saw nobody. Eddie and Raven took off for the barracks while Juan and Linc skirted the miniature town as they circled around to the manufacturing facility.

A minute later, they were beside the larger of the two buildings, a three-story structure with no windows, with large garage doors on the front for truck deliveries and a smaller personnel door. There were also a small door and a larger cargo door set into the side facing the building next to it, which was identical except that it was only two stories tall. The only other feature on the outside of each building was a ladder leading up to the air-handling system on the roof.

Juan and Linc went to the side door of the three-story building, where Juan pressed his ear to it. There was no sound coming from inside.

He eased open the door and peered in. It was completely dark, so he lowered his night vision goggles. He spotted no movement and nodded for Linc to follow him in.

Just as they expected, it was an enormous factory for manufacturing Kuyog drones. Each was on its own cart for easy maneuvering to the next workstation, though there was also a mobile crane for lifting them. Dozens of the drones were lined up in various stages of assembly as if it were an auto plant. Parts were stored on the far side of the building, and the most complete Kuyogs were located closest to the side door, though they all looked to be missing the critical sensor housed on top.

In one corner of the building was a room encased in cinder blocks. Juan pointed at it, and he and Linc stepped toward it in standard recon formation.

The door to the fortified room was heavy steel. Juan yanked the handle and pulled it open. When he looked inside, he realized why it was reinforced.

It was the depot holding the high explosives to be put in the Kuyogs. The Semtex was stacked on shelves all the way to the ceiling.

Juan shook his head. "Sloppy. This should be an entirely separate building far from any of the others."

"I know," Linc replied, pulling out a brick of C-4. "They're just begging for an unfortunate industrial accident."

Just as Brekker had done on the *Pearsall*, Linc and Juan scattered blocks of C-4 among the ammo in the backs of the shelves where they wouldn't be seen. Each of the timers was set to go off five minutes after they were supposed to be out of the cavern.

Linc set the timer on his last brick of C-4 and nodded to Juan, who went to the open door to make sure they were still alone.

That's when the building's lights came on.

On their way to the barracks, Raven and Eddie had seen only two men. They were guarding a truck near the front of the factory building that Juan and Linc had entered. Everyone else seemed to be asleep. Raven was watching Eddie's back as he used an endoscope attached to his phone to look into the barracks windows. She understood that it was better than charging into the building, guns blazing, but the search was tedious. So far, they'd found a dozen rooms with bunk beds full of snoring communist insurgents, but none with Beth.

"We've got movement inside the factory," Juan whispered over the comm link. "Going silent."

Raven and Eddie quickly shared a concerned look, but there was nothing they could do to help, so they kept searching. Two rooms later, they hit the jackpot. This room was different because it had just a single bed. Beth was sound asleep on it, a tray of dirty dishes next to her on a nightstand.

Raven counted the rooms from the entrance and nodded to Eddie, who put away the scope.

They went to the front door and entered with their suppressed pistols in hand. No sounds except for a few snorts from the sleeping men.

They went down the hall as fast as they could while staying quiet. As they approached the correct room, Raven saw that there was an empty chair outside as if someone had been guarding it. Either the post had been abandoned or the guard would be back at any moment.

The door was locked with a key. Eddie knelt and took out a set of lockpicks from his pocket. In seconds, he turned the unsophisticated lock. Raven was duly impressed by the skills he'd acquired in the CIA.

He eased the door open, and Raven slipped quietly inside to find Beth about to swing the nightstand at her. Raven put up a hand to stop her and held a finger to her lips.

Beth dropped the nightstand on the bed and launched herself at Raven, grabbing her in a surprisingly strong bear hug.

"You got my message," Beth whispered through a choked sob. "I thought Locsin killed you."

"He tried," Raven whispered back. "Didn't work."

Eddie had his eyes on the hallway. "Hate to break this up, but we need to go. Juan has already set the charges."

Beth's eyes widened. "He's blowing up this place?"

"That's the plan."

"The paintings are here. We need to save them."

Eddie shook his head. "Sorry. We're cutting this close as it is. Let's go."

Beth crossed her arms and didn't budge. "I'm not letting them be destroyed."

Raven looked at Eddie. "Believe me, it'll be faster if we do it her way."

Eddie sighed and looked at his watch. "All right. I'll give us five minutes." He radioed Juan that they had Beth.

They stole back out of the building. Beth pointed across the compound to a trailer-sized building. The guards by the truck were no longer visible. They must have been the ones Juan was dealing with inside the factory.

They dashed to the building and went inside. Instead of turning on the lights, Eddie lowered his night vision goggles. Raven did the same and led Beth by the hand.

"They should be in the back," Beth said. "They'll be in sixteen tubes."

"Sixteen paintings?" Raven asked.

"They've amassed an incredible collection."

"We can't carry that many," Eddie said.

"The tubes are large in diameter, so we can take them out and roll up some of them together. We won't need more than six tubes."

"Will that damage the paintings?"

Beth shrugged. "It's better than leaving them here to burn. The tubes have straps, so we can carry them easily."

"These paintings better be amazing," Eddie grumbled.

"You have no idea."

At the back of the trailer, there was a large metal cabinet. It was secured by a heavy padlock.

"This is a tough one," Eddie said. "Might take me a little longer than that door."

He crouched down next to it and got to work.

JUAN DIDN'T DARE close the door of the explosives storage room or make a move for the exit. The acoustics of the quiet factory meant that he and Linc could easily hear what was being said all the way on the other side. Tagaan was talking to four other men. All of them were armed with Chinese assault rifles.

"Comrade Locsin has become a threat to our movement," Tagaan said. "We have almost a million Typhoon pills in the truck, but he wants to waste our advantage and risk everything before we are ready."

One of the men protested, "But he will kill us all if he finds out that we are going to betray him. So will all the others who are loyal to him."

"That's why we need to act now. His guard is down because of the storm. When he's dead, they will see that I'm the one who should lead us."

Linc raised an eyebrow at Juan. "We should let them off each other," he whispered.

Juan nodded. "If only we had the time."

"Locsin will begin his daily factory inspection at dawn," Tagaan said. "Two of you will wait in the Semtex storage area. When he enters, make sure you shoot him in the head. The other two and I will kill Dolap and his most faithful men. Then we will take the truck to secure the Typhoon supply. Understood?" They nodded, and two of the men started heading toward the storage room.

"I understand that we better get out of here," Linc whispered.

Juan readied his pistol. "Wait until they're close. We'll try to take them out silently."

Linc raised the crossbow.

As they were walking, one of the men walking toward Juan and Linc called back over his shoulder, "Comrade Tagaan, why is the door to the storage room only partly closed?"

Tagaan turned around, alarmed. He gestured for the other two men to join the first two.

"That plan failed in record time," Juan said. He holstered his pistol and swung the assault rifle around. With a nod, he kicked the door wide open and shot the closest man through the heart. Linc got his companion through the eye with a crossbow bolt.

"MacD's going to have to fight me for this," he said.

With their presence revealed, Juan and Linc ran for the factory's side door. A few shots came their way until Tagaan ordered his men to avoid hitting the Kuyogs. Then they raced out the front entrance.

Juan and Linc burst through the side door, but Tagaan was waiting for them to appear. From the cover of the building corner, he let loose a wild volley with his assault rifle. The other men would be coming out the side door any second, and it was a long way to the far end of the factory, so Juan sprinted to the building next to them and charged through the door. He and Linc made it inside just as bullets slammed into the closed door behind them.

The lights in this building must have been connected to the ones in the factory because they were all on. It was apparently a final assembly facility and warehouse. Long rows of Kuyog drones were arrayed nose to tail in a pristine white environment. The ones at the front of the building looked complete and ready for shipment while those at the back were just missing the all-important imaging sensor.

Juan and Linc ducked low so they wouldn't be seen over the Kuyogs and put some distance between them and the side door.

"I don't see a back exit, do you?" Linc asked. "And I don't think we want to go out the front."

"Not with everybody wide awake now. It looks like I've got us boxed in."

"You have a Plan B, right?"

"Plan B was the one where we leave by truck if we need to."

Dozens of shouts and pounding footsteps outside the building made it clear that they had an army coming at them.

"Then I hope you have a Plan C," Linc said.

Juan looked at the nearest Kuyog and nodded. "As a matter of fact, I do. But you're not going to like it."

"Why?"

"Because it means getting as many of them in here with us as possible."

64

Locsin was out of his bed in the barracks the moment he heard the first gunshots. He snatched up his rifle and his radio and shouted, "What's happening?"

"We've got intruders in the warehouse," Tagaan replied. "It's Juan Cabrillo and the black man who was with him at the shipping dock."

During a typhoon? Locsin couldn't believe it. "Here? He can't be."

"They just killed two of my men."

"How did they get in here?"

"I can't reach the guards at the front gate."

Locsin went out into the corridor and saw men racing down the halls, weapons in hand. "How many are there?" If it was a full invasion, he could slow it down by blowing the tunnel entrance.

"I don't know. So far, just these two."

"Don't let them out of the warehouse," Locsin ordered. "Do you understand me?"

"Yes, comrade."

Locsin stopped Dolap, who was running from the direction of the mess hall.

"What are you doing away from your post?" he demanded.

"I was just gone for a minute," Dolap replied.

"Check on Beth Anders."

"Yes, comrade." Dolap ran off.

Locsin exited the barracks and stopped one of his top soldiers. "Take ten men and sweep the compound. Make sure no other intruders are here."

Locsin didn't wait for an acknowledgment. He sprinted toward the warehouse.

DOLAP'S HEART was pounding at getting caught away from his chair outside Beth Anders's room. During his guard stints in the middle of the night, he usually went off to find some food when everyone else was asleep. This was the first time anyone had seen him, and he hoped his punishment would be light after carrying out Locsin's mission in town as ordered.

When he got to the room, he fumbled with his key in nervousness. When he inserted it, he realized with dread that it was already unlocked. He flung the door open and was aghast to find the room empty.

Now he was in a panic. If he didn't find her, Locsin would surely take away his Typhoon dosage. And Dolap definitely couldn't let Locsin know she was missing until he found her.

He hadn't been away from his post for long, so she and her rescuers couldn't have gotten far. Given her love of those stupid paintings, there was only one place she could be.

He checked his assault rifle and made sure there was a round in the chamber before going to find her.

USING A MULTI-TOOL, Juan rapidly unscrewed the housing on the nearest Kuyog while Linc kept Tagaan's men at bay. The only reason they weren't under constant attack was Tagaan's desire not to damage the drones.

With the screws out, Juan pulled the housing off and carefully removed four bricks of Semtex that had been packed inside.

"Juan Cabrillo!" a voice yelled from the far end.

"Salvador Locsin!" Juan yelled back as he pressed the Semtex against the back wall. "I see you figured out I'm not dead."

"Not yet, anyway. But you will be soon."

"That's big talk coming from a man who can't even sink a ferry right. By the way, the Philippine National Police are eager to talk to you about that. They should be here anytime now."

"Now who's talking big?" Locsin said with a laugh. "I don't think they sent out an assault team in the middle of a typhoon. No, it's just you."

"You have more enemies than you think. Ask your good friend Tagaan."

That shut Locsin up for a moment. Juan could hear lowered voices but not what they were saying.

Gomez called on the radio. "Chairman, I've got bad news. Hidalgo's course is shifting."

"That's the only kind of news we're getting right now," Linc mumbled.

"How long have we got until the eye wall is here?" Juan asked Gomez.

"Ten minutes, tops. You need to steal one of those trucks you were talking about and get back here pronto."

Linc rolled his eyes and shook his head at Juan, who said, "We'll work on that."

"I've already got the engine spooled up. Let me know when you're on your way. Out."

Locsin must have gotten an answer he liked from Tagaan because he called out again. "Cabrillo, I'm done talking to you. You're going to die either way, but if you don't come out right now, I'll torture Beth to death in front of you. Your choice."

Juan nodded to Linc and they crabwalked as far from the Semtex as they could, pushing the Kuyog on the handcart so that it stayed between them and Locsin's men.

When they reached the opposite wall, Juan yelled out, "Locsin, if you want us, you'll have to come and get us!"

That did the trick. Locsin angrily ordered his men to make their way forward. He wanted Juan and Linc alive.

When Dolap was close to the trailer where the paintings were stored, he saw the door open. He quickly ducked behind one of the Humvees parked nearby. A Chinese man poked his head out and looked around before waving two women out with him—Beth Anders and a dark-haired woman carrying an assault rifle. All three had plastic tubes slung over their backs, while Beth carried another tube in her hand. Dolap immediately recognized the man as one of the two who'd gotten into a fight in Bacolod the day before.

It was like an electrical shock to his spine when Dolap suddenly realized that he must be the reason these intruders had found the cavern headquarters that had remained hidden for so long. They followed him back here somehow.

He had to atone for his mistake. He raised his rifle, flicked the safety to full auto, and indiscriminately emptied his magazine at the three of them, not caring if he hit any of the precious paintings.

Beth went down, clutching her side, and dropped the tube. The other two instantly hit the ground and returned fire, clipping Dolap in the shoulder as he dropped down behind the Humvee to reload. The wound was no more than a bee sting to him, and he slapped another mag into the assault rifle.

When he rose again, he saw the dark-haired woman drag Beth around the building while the Chinese man laid down suppressing fire. Then they were out of sight.

Dolap charged forward and picked up the tube. It was marked *Picasso* in Beth's handwriting from when she had appraised each painting. He opened it to quickly check and saw that there were at least three paintings inside.

With Beth injured, he considered continuing the pursuit, but he needed to inform Locsin that there were more intruders. He went into the paintings storage trailer as he called on the radio.

"Comrade Locsin, this is Dolap. Two more people have infiltrated the cavern and have taken Beth Anders."

"Where are they now?" Locsin demanded.

"On the other side of the compound from your location. They broke into the paintings storage trailer and took them. I'm in pursuit."

Locsin sounded uncharacteristically panicked when he asked, "Did they take all of them?"

Dolap looked around him at the discarded tubes all over the floor and then checked the storage cabinet and found it empty. Even the eagle finial was gone. Blood dripped from his arm, but it was already starting to clot.

"Not all of the paintings," he said into the radio. "I have the Picasso and a couple of others in one of the tubes."

"You're sure it's the Picasso?"

"Yes, comrade. The intruders are armed, so I'll need more men to help me search for them."

"No! Bring the paintings to me at once. I'm in the warehouse."

"Yes, comrade. I'm on my way."

———

JUAN HAD BEEN listening to the conversation between Locsin and Dolap over the radio he'd taken from the dead guard. He didn't know why the paintings were so important to Locsin, but the communist leader seemed desperate to get them.

But Juan and Linc had more pressing problems. Specifically, the forty or so men who were currently inching their way through the rows of Kuyog drones. None of them had a clear shot yet, but it wouldn't be long before they did.

As they crouched behind the partially dismantled Kuyog they were using for cover, Juan said to Linc, "You ready?"

Linc had the crossbow on his back and now held his assault rifle. He snapped the 40mm grenade into the under-barrel launcher, took a breath, and nodded. "Let's cause a mess."

Juan smiled and aimed his own M4 at the bricks of Semtex against the rear wall on the other side of the warehouse. It was a common mistake in movies that rifle rounds could set off extremely stable plastic explosives, but he wasn't going to shoot bullets at it. He had his own grenade launcher.

They needed an escape route, and all their breaching charges were back in the Semtex storehouse, which was why Juan had raided the Kuyog for its payload. He squeezed the trigger, and the grenade hit the pile of Semtex dead center. The grenade itself wasn't powerful enough to blow a hole in the wall, but its explosion acted as a detonator for the plastique.

The resulting blast knocked the wind out of Juan's lungs and ripped a huge hole in the building's exterior, but the job wasn't done yet. Linc quickly recovered and leaned over the Kuyog to aim at the Kuyog closest to the front of the warehouse.

He fired, and the grenade lofted over the heads of the men interspersed amongst the dozens of drones filling the warehouse. Then he and Juan ran for their newly created exit route.

The shell hit the Kuyog dead center and exploded, setting off the Semtex inside the drone. It blew up in a fiery eruption that began a chain reaction, with one Kuyog after the other exploding like a synchronized fireworks display.

Locsin's men, horrified to realize what was happening, ran for their lives, but the efficient arrangement of the Kuyogs meant they had no chance. The last thing Juan saw as he plunged through the exit was the insurgents disappearing in the white-hot flames and deadly shrapnel.

Linc and Juan ran toward the empty vastness of the cavern, trying to put as much distance between themselves and the warehouse as possible.

The explosions from the warehouse were coming so fast now that they seemed to meld together until finally the whole building blew apart, tossing girders and pieces of metal high into the air before being reduced to rubble. The concussion was so powerful that it knocked them off their feet, and, as he was falling, Juan really didn't know if this was his last moment on earth.

66

Tagaan blinked his eyes as he regained consciousness. For a few seconds, he didn't know where he was. Then he saw that he was close to the truck with the Typhoon supply inside. He must have been thrown far from the warehouse in the explosion.

Now he remembered that he had been right by the entrance with Locsin, trying to deflect the suspicion that Cabrillo had cast upon him. Knowing that Locsin would interrogate him further when the situation was under control, Tagaan had been backing out of the building as the first Kuyog exploded. His shirt was full of tiny holes where bits of the building had pierced his skin, but none of them seemed to have done real damage.

He pushed himself up and felt a sharp cramp in his calf, the first time he'd felt any significant pain since he began taking the drug. He looked down to see what could have caused it and went cold when he saw that his left foot was gone below the ankle.

Although it throbbed, the pain was manageable, but he had to get out of the cavern. His future here was over. If Locsin didn't kill him, the police would no doubt be raiding the place as soon as Hidalgo had passed.

He looked up to see the first hint of daybreak through the hole in the cave roof. They were still in the eye of the storm. If he could get out now, he could get to a safe hideaway and tend to his leg. With the huge supply of Typhoon in the truck, maybe his foot would even grow back. He'd heard of salamanders regrowing lost limbs, so it might be possible.

He didn't worry about putting on a tourniquet. The blood was no longer gushing from his leg and would soon stop flowing completely.

He crawled over to the truck and pulled himself up. He opened the rear door just to make sure the Typhoon was still inside. He counted the barrels and saw that all nine were there. He quickly opened the closest one and saw the cardboard piece holding the pressed flower. He took it and closed the door, then hopped to the driver's seat.

The keys were in the ignition. He started the truck and patted the remote detonator in his pocket.

Sure that he had everything he needed, he shifted the automatic transmission into drive and accelerated toward the entrance tunnel.

JUAN SHOOK HIS HEAD as he sat up. Linc was doing the same.

"You all right?" Juan asked him. He worked his jaw to try to get the ringing in his ears to stop.

Linc winced. "I'll need about four hundred ice packs when we get back to the *Oregon*, but I'll live."

Then two noises added to the sounds of the burning warehouse. One was the exchange of gunfire echoing through the cavern, which made it difficult to tell where it was coming from. The other was the sound of a truck speeding away.

They turned to see the truck that had been parked near the front of the still-intact factory tearing across the compound. Tagaan was driving, and he wasn't waiting for anyone else.

"That's the one with the Typhoon inside," Linc said.

Three nearby Humvees were in flames, but one looked undamaged. Juan pointed to it and said, "We can't let him get away with the drug. Tail him, and stay in touch. We'll intercept you after we get back to the helicopter."

Linc nodded and sprinted to the Humvee.

Juan stood. "Eddie, what's your status?"

"Juan, this is Beth" came the reply, amid intermittent three-shot reports of assault rifles in the background. "Eddie and Raven are busy right now shooting people."

"How many?"

"A lot. I don't think they're real happy about you blowing up the place. Are you all right?"

"Tell Eddie we're fine. Where are you?"

"I don't know exactly. I think we're on the other side of this complex from you."

"I'm on my way."

"I don't think we're going anywhere. Just follow the gunshots."

Juan picked up his M4 and ran along the side of the burning warehouse as Linc got the Humvee started. He gunned it just as Tagaan disappeared into the tunnel.

IN THE REARVIEW MIRROR, Tagaan could see a Humvee giving chase. That might be one of his men, but he couldn't take the chance.

When he got to the entrance, he didn't even slow down. The

guards didn't move as he sped toward them and he realized it was because each had a hole in his head.

He rammed the gates and they went flying into the jungle as the hood of the truck crunched from the impact. It had been modified to travel muddy roads, with a more powerful engine and bigger tires, so Tagaan knew it could take the punishment.

Once he was clear of the entrance and speeding down the road, he fished the detonator from his pocket and pushed the button.

LINC HAD HIS FOOT mashed to the floor as the Humvee rocketed into the tunnel. Then the light at the end of the tunnel vanished.

A split second later, the roar of an explosion rattled the Humvee, and Linc stood on the brakes. He came to a stop, and a roiling cloud of dust soon enveloped him.

He activated his comm link. "More bad news, Chairman."

"Don't tell me that explosion was you."

"Almost. Tagaan blew the front entrance. We're stuck in here."

"Not necessarily," the Chairman said. "But, first, Eddie, Raven, and Beth are pinned down. We can give them an advantage with the night vision goggles for at least a few minutes before dawn comes. Remember the diesel generator?"

Linc did indeed. He threw the Humvee in reverse. "I'll help contribute to the mayhem."

He backed out of the tunnel. When he was in the clear, he had a good view of the huge generator and the diesel tanker feeding it fuel.

He picked up his M4 and loaded another grenade into the launcher. He rammed it closed and fired at the tanker.

When the grenade hit the truck, it went up with a satisfying boom of thunder. A second later, the generator next to it blew up as well, and all the electric lights in the cavern went out.

"GOOD JOB, LINC," Juan said over the radio. "I'll meet you where Eddie and the others are."

He stopped at the center stalagmite pillar and called Gomez.

"This is the Chairman," Juan said. "We need immediate extraction."

"Gotcha. Where?"

"Inside the cavern. We're locked in."

"Sorry, Chairman, did you say 'inside the cavern'?" Gomez asked with disbelief.

"There's a hole in the roof. Plenty big for you. We'll be on the side of the cave that isn't burning."

"Sure! Landing inside a cave? I do it all the time. This should be interesting. See you soon."

The gunshots were more sporadic now, so killing the electricity must have slowed down the attackers. The only remaining light was from the warehouse and truck fires. Juan was about to join the fray when he spotted a beaten-up plastic tube lying on the ground.

The Picasso.

He was bending to pick it up when he was tackled from behind. The night vision goggles were knocked from his head, the assault rifle went flying. Juan rolled to avoid being pinned to the ground. He leapt up into a fighting stance and was confronted with a bloodied and bruised man. It had to be Dolap. It looked like he'd been caught on the fringes of the warehouse explosion.

Dolap, backlit by the fire, didn't bother looking for the assault rifle. He drew a wicked-looking knife the size of a bayonet and launched himself at Juan.

Juan fell back, as if off balance, and put his prosthetic leg up in a defensive posture as Dolap landed on him, reaching out with the knife until the blade was only inches from Juan's neck. Juan gripped

Dolap's wrist and pushed with his foot against Dolap's chest, but he couldn't budge the powerfully built man. The knife edged closer.

Juan reached to his combat leg and found the hidden trigger that controlled the single-shot slug in his heel.

Just as he felt the blade digging into his skin, he activated the secret gun.

The shotgun shell blasted from his artificial foot and into Dolap's chest. It must have pierced his heart, although it took a moment for the brain to register. Dolap went limp and toppled to the ground.

Juan stood, picked up the Picasso tube, and slung it over his shoulder. His goggles were toast, from hitting the ground, so he began to search for the assault rifle in the deep shadows.

Movement from the warehouse caught his eye, and he saw a figure climbing out of the ashes of the demolished building like a phoenix rising. Locsin's skin was charred, and his clothes hung in tatters, but he seemed to shrug off the severe wounds and raised a radio to his face.

Instantly, Juan heard the sounds of shouting and footfalls coming his way from Eddie's direction, far more men than he could take on by himself.

He couldn't wait to find his weapon, and he couldn't afford to get stuck inside a building he didn't know. But Juan remembered the ladder on the outside of the factory building. If he could get up there, Gomez could land on it and pick him up before the charges they set went off and blew up the building underneath him.

Juan drew his pistol and ran.

67

Although Locsin had drawn most of his men away from Eddie, Raven, and Beth to go after Juan, four men still had them cornered at a curtain of limestone that formed a natural barrier at this side of the compound. They were crouched behind some rocks with nowhere to go.

"I'm low on ammo," Raven said as she took another shot. The battle was maddening because she knew she'd hit at least a couple of them, but they simply wouldn't go down if they weren't shot in the head or the heart.

"Me too," Eddie said. "Last mag for me. Conserve your shots."

Then they heard the roar of an engine coming their way.

"Don't shoot," Linc said over the comm. "It's me. Get ready to hop in."

The Humvee screeched to a stop between them and their attackers. While they scrambled into the passenger side, Linc stuck his weapon out the window and fired a grenade at the building shielding Locsin's men. When it exploded, they heard a single scream. It didn't kill them all, but it at least bought time for Eddie and the others to climb in.

"Go!" Eddie yelled and fired the last of his rounds as they took off.

Instead of heading toward the factory, Linc took off for the dark nether reaches of the cave, his headlights off. He used his night vision goggles to drive.

"Why aren't we getting Juan?" Beth asked.

"I just heard from him. He ordered me to take you all as far away from him as possible while we wait for Gomez to get here."

They reached the edge of the paved part of the compound and bounced onto smooth rock that felt like it had been scoured by an ancient river. Raven didn't know how far this cave went on, but in the briefing before the mission she'd found out that Vietnam's Hang Sơn Đoòng cave extended more than five miles.

Soon, the occasional shots that chased them ceased. They were now invisible.

"We have to go back and get him," Beth protested.

Linc stopped the Humvee. "We're not leaving the cave without him. But, right now, they have the advantage in numbers. When we have the high ground in the chopper, we'll have better odds."

"Well, where is he?"

Linc pointed to the largest building. It was the factory, still lit by the burning warehouse next to it.

"He's going to be on top of that one." He checked his watch. The timers on the charges he and Juan had set in the factory continued to count down. "And it's going to explode in five minutes whether we get him off or not."

THE LIGHT FROM the hole in the roof was growing as morning dawned. For a moment, Locsin lost Cabrillo's trail, but one of his men soon spotted him climbing to the roof of the factory. The former CIA agent was an excellent shot, even with the small-caliber pistol aimed from midway up the ladder, and Locsin lost several men until Cabrillo ran out of ammo. Then he pulled another pistol from what looked like an ankle holster and used that to pick off a few more men before he got to the roof, though by that time the second one was empty as well.

Locsin was famished as his body tried to repair the damage from the explosion. His skin tingled as it grew new dermal layers, and his muscles were tight where shrapnel had ripped through sinew. He would need several days of recovery after this battle, but the emergency supply of Typhoon he kept in his quarters would be more than sufficient to get him through it and he could track down the traitor Tagaan.

He used the durable Chinese radio that had survived the Kuyog blast to call his pilot and tell him to collect the drug supply and ready the helicopter while they still had a chance to fly out through the eye of the storm. The pilot balked at such a risky mission until Locsin threatened to cut off his Typhoon doses.

When Locsin reached the bottom of the ladder, he told the remaining men who'd gathered there to make sure no one else followed him up. He had to show that he was still the leader and could conquer their problems. Besides, he had to get that Picasso back from Cabrillo.

His men kept their weapons trained on the edge of the roof as he climbed up, an assault rifle slung over his shoulder. At the top, he quickly peered over the edge and saw Cabrillo standing on the opposite side, the tube held out at arm's length.

"You don't look so good, Locsin," Cabrillo taunted. "You'll probably feel even worse if I throw this tube over into the burning warehouse."

Locsin understood and dropped the assault rifle to the ground below. He subtly looked down and gestured for two of his men to go to the other side of the building. Then he held up one hand, then the other, as he climbed up onto the roof.

"I just want to talk," he said.

"No, you want to kill me," Cabrillo said. "I have to say, the feeling's mutual."

Locsin began to slowly walk toward him. "I don't want to kill you, Mr. Cabrillo. You're already dead, but you just don't realize it. You're a *multo*, which in my culture is a spirit that has come back from the dead to finish unfinished business. Except I know how to banish you back to the underworld."

"Please," Cabrillo scoffed, "you're a communist. You believe religion and individualism are plagues to be wiped out."

Locsin smiled. "Well, at least one individual."

Cabrillo must have heard the men below who had circled around because he turned and ducked just before bullets raked the roof's edge.

Locsin used the distraction to sprint toward Cabrillo. Locsin hit him in the gut with his shoulder, and Cabrillo went down with a woof of air. The tube went skittering across the roof, teetering on the edge.

Cabrillo was fast, backhanding Locsin in the jaw. Pain or no pain, the blow was strong enough to knock Locsin over.

He shrugged it off and jumped to his feet. Cabrillo was already up in a defensive stance used by practitioners of the Israeli combat discipline Krav Maga. Locsin, however, was skilled in the Philippine national sport of Arnis, particularly the mano a mano, empty-handed component, which considers the hands and feet as weapons to be wielded.

They exchanged blows while they searched each other for weaknesses, though Locsin was feeling stronger by the minute even without food to refuel himself. Cabrillo would be an interesting sparring partner but not a real match.

Then Cabrillo jabbed with one hand while launching a haymaker with the other, which caught Locsin by surprise. The strike to the side of his head made his ears ring, but he didn't go down. Instead, he spun in a roundhouse kick and smacked Cabrillo in the back.

He staggered to the side but came back almost immediately, and they traded punches. Locsin was enjoying this, and he was amazed at what a beating Cabrillo could take.

JUAN WASN'T GOING to last much longer, but he wasn't going to give Locsin the satisfaction of seeing him falter. He just had to distract him long enough for Gomez to arrive.

Then he heard it, the throbbing pulse of helicopter rotors coming from the roof of the cavern.

He and Locsin took a moment to watch the MD 520N descend carefully through the hole. When it was clear, the chopper flew into the ebony depths of the cavern to pick up the Corporation team.

Locsin grinned wickedly at Juan. "Enough of this, Cabrillo. You've been a tough opponent, but—"

Juan didn't wait for Locsin to finish his monologue. He sprinted for the tube with the Picasso and snatched it up. He could feel Locsin directly behind him, trying to chase him down.

Juan whipped around, and Locsin grabbed for the tube.

They began a tug-of-war for it.

"What's so important about this painting?" Juan asked as his fingers struggled to maintain their grip.

"It's the key to everything," Locsin answered cryptically. "I had to hide it from him. Now, give it to me."

Juan maneuvered himself around so that he was facing the fires, which were beginning to die out. Then he pulled even harder on the tube. When he felt Locsin pull back with all his strength, Juan suddenly pushed instead.

The effect was similar to a master playing tug with his dog and abruptly releasing the toy. Locsin immediately lost his footing now that his center of gravity was pitching him backward. His feet stumbled, and since Juan had angled him right to the roof edge without him realizing it, one of Locsin's feet hit nothing but air before he understood what was happening.

Naturally, his instinct was to grab for something more solid than a plastic tube, so he let go. But Juan kept pushing, and Locsin fell back, flailing as he fell.

At first, the men below were stunned to see their leader slam into the ground from three stories up. But they had momentarily forgotten about the extraordinary powers of Typhoon.

Locsin was dazed from the impact but recovered remarkably quickly. He pointed at Juan, staring down at them. Juan stepped back before more shots rang out.

As Juan watched the *Oregon*'s chopper lift off in the distance, he hoped he'd timed this right. Because he was all out of weapons, and Locsin would now be sending every man he had up to the roof.

LOCSIN WAS IRATE at getting tossed off the roof and not only losing the Picasso but failing to kill Cabrillo.

He saw the chopper approaching and ordered several men to go after Cabrillo and the others to retrieve the cache of RPGs. As soon as they had them in hand, they were to keep firing until the rogue helicopter was lying on the cavern floor in pieces.

Locsin was going to take out that helicopter one way or the other, so he raced to his own chopper. The rotors were already spooling up.

"Get this piece of junk in the air now!" he screamed at the pilot as he jumped in the back.

This helicopter already had the minigun mounted on the floor. He flicked the switch to on and was ready to cut the other chopper to ribbons.

"THERE'S GUNFIRE coming from the base of that building," Gomez said as he cranked the MD 520N to full speed.

Linc sat in the front passenger seat while Eddie and Raven took the outer seats in the back with Beth squeezed in the middle with the pile of painting tubes. The doors of the chopper had been removed prior to the flight just in case they needed to fire weapons in flight. As soon as Eddie saw that Juan was under attack, he knew they'd made the right decision. His assault rifle was now fully rearmed with one of Linc's magazines.

Juan was pointing to the opposite side of the building and said over the radio, "There are unwanted guests coming up the ladder."

Gomez circled around the building, and Eddie and Linc each took out two men scrabbling up the ladder. They fell to the ground, and no more tried to go up, though they did take potshots at the helicopter as it came in to land on the roof.

Gomez touched down, and Juan handed the Picasso tube to Beth as he heaved himself into the helicopter on Raven's side. Beth gleefully added it to her collection, which she cradled like they were her newborn children.

Since there wasn't another seat, Raven slid up and let Juan take hers. With nowhere else to go, she sat on his lap. Eddie noticed that Juan didn't seem to mind the discomfort of the close quarters. Juan leaned his head back for a moment as he put on a headset.

"You okay?" Eddie asked as they lifted off. "You look like you had the snot beat out of you."

"And a bunch of other stuff," Juan replied.

"Hey, guys," Gomez said, "we're not out of the woods yet." Then he banked wildly, and Juan had to grab Raven around the waist to keep her from falling out.

Punctuating Gomez's words was the streak of a rocket-propelled grenade as it flashed by and exploded against the cavern roof.

"There's more where that came from," Gomez said. "Not only that, we have company."

Eddie looked back and saw a chopper in hot pursuit. Jutting from its left door was the nose of a minigun.

Two more RPGs simultaneously lanced up at the *Oregon*'s helicopter, but Gomez maneuvered out of their path, and the rockets went right past toward a stalactite. They smashed into the hanging rock formation and blew it in half. Juan watched as it fell hundreds of feet and crushed one of the compound's buildings.

To avoid more of the RPGs, Gomez flew beyond their range into the far reaches of the inky cavern, using his night vision equipment, but the other chopper stayed on their tail. Three flares were sent up from below, lighting up the massive cave.

"What's the ETA on the eye wall?" Juan asked.

Gomez was too busy flying to answer, so Linc replied, "Estimated to arrive in two minutes."

"Then I suggest we get out of here."

"Working on it," Gomez said as he yanked the stick again to dodge minigun fire from Locsin. Its tracers added to the illumination from the flares.

Although he was now belted in, Juan struggled to keep Raven in his grasp as Gomez weaved back and forth. If Locsin were a skilled tactician, he would simply have his pilot hover sideways and provide a stable platform for the minigun, which had sufficient range to reach a thousand yards. But because Juan had outwitted him, Locsin was too enraged to think clearly and so he had his pilot stupidly chasing them from behind.

Gomez swung around in a wide turn so Locsin wouldn't get a clean angle on the helicopter and headed back toward the hole in the roof. More light from the rising sun was streaming through, but darkness would be coming soon.

"I hate to tell you this," Gomez said through gritted teeth, "but I'm going to have to go straight up to get out of here. No yanking and banking during that time, so it's going to leave us exposed for about ten seconds."

He meant they'd be vulnerable to both the minigun and additional RPG fire. It would be a lethal combination for a hovering helicopter.

They needed a distraction. Then Juan remembered they already had one coming.

He checked his watch. They had sixty seconds. The timing would be close.

"Gomez," Juan said, "can you time your flight so that you are over the roof of that large building in about fifty-five seconds?"

"Sure. I'll have Linc count it down. But why?"

"It's going to blow up."

"I generally like to stay away from that kind of thing, but I see what you're going for."

As they came around, Juan momentarily got a glimpse of Locsin's face twisted in anger as he loaded another belt into the minigun. They locked eyes for a moment, and Juan cheerfully waved, taunting Locsin into maintaining his pursuit. Then he was out of sight as the MD 520N made its turn for the factory.

Gomez dived the helicopter down, almost like it was a suicide run. He skimmed the tops of the compound buildings and flashed by so fast above the heads of the RPG wielders they didn't have a chance to fire.

They crossed above the factory, and Gomez pulled back on the stick as he continued heading forward, away from the building and toward the roof.

They made it halfway up before a blinding flash lit up the entire cave.

LOCSIN'S HELICOPTER was tossed around like a toy by the blast, and the pilot fought the controls to keep them from crashing. Locsin, connected by a single strap, fell out the open door and was bashed against the skid. Shards of the disintegrated building battered the chopper, but they didn't seem to hit anything critical. Two seconds later and they would have been blown apart along with the remainder of the Kuyog drones.

When the pilot got it under control again, Locsin was able to climb back inside, seething at the colossal failure handed to him by Juan Cabrillo. Tagaan had the Typhoon supply, the Picasso was gone, most of his men were now dead, and his plan to wipe out the Philippine Navy was over. Once he found Tagaan and killed him, he would have to start over from scratch.

Locsin looked up and saw Cabrillo's chopper rising through the hole in the roof. He ordered his pilot to follow. Out in the open sky, he would have a much better chance of blowing them away with the minigun.

The pilot protested, but Locsin shut him down.

"Either we go up or you die!" he screamed.

The pilot nodded, and the helicopter began to ascend. Locsin finished reloading the minigun and prepared for the final battle. It was only when they were nearly out of the hole in the roof that it registered in Locsin's mind that the bright sky had become as black as sackcloth.

JUAN LEANED OUT of the helicopter to look behind them as Gomez raced to keep ahead of the approaching eye wall. The clouds churned like a devil's brew as it passed over the cavern sinkhole they'd just risen out of.

Locsin's helicopter appeared above the jungle that was getting slammed by the intense Category 3 winds. It seemed to be pushed one way, then the other, by some unseen giant's careless hand. The pilot made a valiant effort to battle the gale-force beating, but the chopper's fragile tail snapped in half from the incredible pressure.

The helicopter spun three times, then nose-dived toward the jungle, before it was swallowed by the raging typhoon.

Juan pulled his head back inside and said, "We're clear. Locsin's helicopter just crashed."

"So will we if we don't have somewhere to land soon," Gomez said. "*Oregon*, Gomez here. What is your current position?"

Juan heard Max say, "Northwest of you and enjoying a lovely sail through typhoon-roiled waters."

"What about Tagaan?" Juan asked.

"We're just about to reach the coastal road where we think his truck will make an appearance. The only question is whether he got there first."

Although the winds were calm in the eye of Typhoon Hidalgo, the *Oregon* bucked like a bronco through the heavy seas in the narrow strait between Negros and Panay islands. Max, whose hands clenched the arms of the Kirk Chair in the op center, would have been shocked if any other ships were foolish enough to be out in these kinds of swells, and Linda confirmed that they were alone. The few roads they could see were deserted, as would be every building still standing along the shore if the residents valued their lives.

Max could see on the map that they were almost in visual range of the shoreline highway that had been used the day before by Locsin's truck. They were taking a chance that Tagaan hadn't chosen a different route, but it seemed likely he would be heading away from the eye wall, not toward it.

The road hugged the shore for only two miles, so they had a brief window for the intercept. If they missed Tagaan before he turned inland, they'd never find him again.

When they came around the next point, the highway came into view. The palms lining it were eerily still compared to the looming storm clouds behind them.

The big screen showed a single truck speeding along the road away from the direction of the cavern. It matched the description Juan had given them and was already halfway to the curve taking the road away from the shore.

"Murph, ready the cannon to fire," Max said.

Murph worked his weapons control panel and said, "Cannon coming online."

The hull plates covering the 120mm smoothbore cannon at the bow of the *Oregon* slid aside.

"Steady as she goes, Eric," Max said.

"Steady, aye," Eric replied from the helm as the *Oregon* slammed into another deep trough between waves.

"Your definition of *steady* needs work," Murph cracked. He would need to time his shot like an archer on horseback at full gallop. "Ready."

Max leaned forward. "Fire at will."

TAGAAN HAD TO slow considerably when he was in the jungle to go around fallen branches, but now that he was on the highway and had it all to himself, he could more easily stay ahead of the storm. He knew of a concrete parking garage in Bacolod where he could outlast the rest of Hidalgo and plan his next steps. If he was lucky, he'd be there long before the edge of the eye wall reached him.

The stump of his leg still stung, but the bleeding had stopped. That was another thing he'd take care of in the city.

Now that he could pay less attention to the road, he had been able to open the cardboard sheets holding the pressed flower. As he looked at the secret ingredient of Typhoon, he considered how he could search for more of it. Finally, he would be the one with all the power.

But something about it wasn't right. It was a white orchid, all right, but he didn't remember the yellow petal in the center when he'd seen it on the fishing boat. The scrawled name was there, but it read *Ceratostylis incognita.* He thought the second word should be something more like *inviolable.*

Before he could make sense of it, the sugarcane field to his left exploded, throwing dirt high into the air.

Tagaan jerked the steering wheel in surprise but stayed on the road. Was someone bombing him? But surely no one was idiotic enough to fly in this weather. Then he glanced in the passenger-side mirror and saw the *Oregon* plunging through whitecaps.

A flash erupted from her bow. It was followed seconds later by a towering geyser of water erupting from the waves offshore.

The gunner now had him bracketed. Tagaan stamped the pedal to the floor. If he could get inland, he'd be out of visual range of the gun and home free.

When he saw another flash, he slammed on the brakes. A shell blasted a crater in the road where he would have been if he'd kept up the same speed. He swerved around it and accelerated back to full speed.

He could see the curve ahead. At this firing rate, they had two more shots at best.

Another flash. This time, he didn't let up on the gas.

But the gunner hadn't aimed at the truck at all. A hundred feet in front of the truck, he landed the shell right at the base of a palm tree next to the road. Severed from its newly created stump, the tree fell across the road, blocking the truck's path. Tagaan stood on the brakes, but it was too late. The truck struck the tree, catapulted over the trunk, and flipped onto the driver's side.

Tagaan's front teeth were knocked out when his face smashed into the steering wheel, and he tasted blood as he tried to push himself out of the seat. Then he realized that the immobile truck was now an easy target.

He looked up to the passenger-side mirror and saw the *Oregon* relentlessly coming toward him.

From the bow, he saw one more flash.

THE SCREEN in the op center was zoomed in on the truck lying in the road. One second it was there, the next it was gone, blasted into a million pieces by the exploding shell.

"Say good-bye to Typhoon," Max said with a smile. He turned to Murph. "That was genius taking out the tree to stop him."

"The guy was getting on my nerves," Murph said with a shrug as he closed up the plates over the cannon. "Pretty good shot, though, right?"

"You did miss him three times," Eric reminded him.

"*Fourth time's the charm* is therefore my new motto."

"Right," Max said, chuckling. "Put it on a T-shirt. Now, let's get our people back before we run out of maneuvering room in the actual typhoon."

HIDALGO'S COURSE was taking the eye over Panay Island, so Gomez had to get the helicopter back inside the *Oregon* as soon as possible. As they hovered over the ship, he told Juan and the others that the landing might be a little dicey.

They had to wait until the pitching deck came to them. As the skids touched the *Oregon*, Gomez shut down the engine, and the helicopter dived into the next trough along with the ship. Eddie and Linc jumped out and lashed the chopper to the tie-downs as the helicopter was lowered on the elevator platform.

"That was some gutsy flying," Juan said to Gomez.

"All in a day's work," he replied matter-of-factly.

"Thanks for keeping me from dying," Raven said as she hopped off Juan's lap.

He nearly replied, "My pleasure," but thought that wouldn't come out right. "Happy to" was almost as bad. He just said, "Of course." A soft snicker came from his right, and Beth put a hand to her mouth.

Juan got out and was met by Max and Julia Huxley as the deck closed above them.

"You look like you need a thorough checkup," Julia said to Juan.

"I'll be okay," he said and nodded to Beth. "There's your patient."

When Julia saw the bloody bullet wound in Beth's side, she called for the waiting stretcher. Juan helped Beth out and onto the gurney.

"Take care of the paintings," she said with a beatific smile. She didn't seem to be feeling any pain. But when she saw Maurice suddenly appear next to Juan to deliver his traditional celebratory cigar, she barked, "Absolutely no smoking around the paintings!"

Juan handed it back and said, "Please leave it in my cabin, Maurice."

"Along with a full breakfast and a Bloody Mary," Maurice said and glided away.

"Satisfied?" Juan asked Beth, who relaxed again. "I promise you will get as much time as you want with them once you've recovered."

Beth clapped her hands in glee, ignoring the injury. "I can't wait." Then she took Raven's hand. "Thank you for rescuing me."

For the first time that Juan had seen, Raven's lips turned up in a tiny smirk. "Wait until you see my fee."

"Believe me," Beth said, "with the reward we're going to get from those paintings, I can afford it."

Raven turned to Juan and got so close to his ear that he could feel her breath on his neck. "I'll go with her. From what I understand about the effects of Typhoon, she's going to have a rough few days as she goes through withdrawal." She didn't add that Beth might die if she had become fully addicted to the stuff.

Juan nodded, and Raven kept hold of Beth's hand as Julia and the med techs wheeled her to the medical bay.

He looked at Max and grinned. "I'm glad you got Tagaan. I wasn't looking forward to another mission to find him. I think I need about twelve hours of shut-eye."

"We all do," Max said. "Eric has the *Oregon* headed to a harbor on Panay, where we can ride out the rest of the storm. The ship will rock you to sleep."

Juan handed a couple of the tubes of paintings to Max and took the rest himself.

"Before I turn in, I want to see what we've got here."

They went to the boardroom, where Juan opened the tube marked *Picasso*. He carefully pulled the paintings out and unrolled them on the conference table.

"Wow," Max said when he saw the masterpieces lying there. "I can't wait to hear what the reward is for returning these." The top one was a Rembrandt that Juan recalled from the Gardner Museum heist. The one below it was signed by Gauguin.

"I know how we're going pay for repairs to the *Oregon*," Juan said.

"And maybe a few upgrades?" Max asked with a cocked eyebrow.

"Not a bad idea."

The third painting was a small cubist oil instantly identifiable as a Picasso.

"Beth said this one is available for purchase since it was stolen from an auction."

"Picassos always make a good investment." The Corporation already had one in its possession, currently in a bank vault in Monaco. "This one might look good on the walls in here."

As Juan lifted it up for Max to get a better look, he suddenly understood why Locsin had wanted it back so badly.

He nodded appreciatively and grinned at Max. "I'll take it."

EPILOGUE

Juan found Max in the starboard ballast tank, which also doubled as an Olympic-length lap pool. Juan's preferred method of exercise was swimming in its dual lanes, but he hadn't been able to use it since the Kuyog blew a hole in the side of the ship, which was why they were now docked at a maintenance depot.

The hull had since been patched up on the outside, appearing as slipshod as possible of course. On the inside, Max was inspecting the welds, making sure that the new armor plating was seamless.

"When can I go back to doing laps?" Juan asked, his voice echoing off the marble-clad flooring. A week's worth of algae had been scrubbed away, revealing the gleaming surface.

"When I'm sure that all the damage has been repaired," Max said. "Should take another hour. Then, remember, we head out for beer and nachos at eighteen hundred."

"Should I invite Hux?" Juan teased.

Max shot him a look that would melt steel. "Don't you dare."

"I was about to talk to Raven. Do you want to be in on the conversation?"

"No, it's your call. A good one, by the way. You can tell me how it goes at the bar."

"I'll meet you on deck."

Juan left Max muttering to himself and went up to the boardroom, where Raven was waiting.

He took a seat next to her as she put down the Jane Austen book she was reading.

"*Persuasion*," Juan said, reading the title. "I haven't read that one."

"Everyone thinks I'd want to watch war movies or read about military history," Raven said. "It's nice to get away from all that once in a while."

"I'm glad you've been taking advantage of our library. It's nice that you've stuck around during Beth's recovery."

"I've been there. A familiar face helps you get through it. Besides, the facilities on your ship are incredible, and my little apartment in San Diego isn't much to look at."

"You don't have anyone back in the States?"

"My parents, but I don't see them all that much." She ran her fingers through her hair. "I don't have a boyfriend, if that's what you're asking."

"It was, actually. But not for the reason you're thinking."

She tilted her head and gave him an amused look. "I'm listening."

"Everyone in the Corporation, myself included, was very impressed by your skills and composure in the Philippines. You may not realize how difficult it is to find someone with your set of abilities."

"Very difficult, I'd guess. They're aren't many women out there like me."

Juan laughed. "At least you know your worth."

She shrugged. "False modesty isn't one of my flaws."

"Then you'd fit right in with us. What do you think about join-ing the Corporation? As you can tell, it's dirty work sometimes, but you'd be surrounded by people just like you, people who are the best at what they do."

"I'm assuming the job isn't open because someone retired."

Juan's eyes clouded with Mike Trono's memory. "It's also dan-gerous work, as you've seen."

"Being a bodyguard is, too. And from what I've heard, the pay isn't nearly as good as it is for your crew."

"You'd be well compensated. We can talk numbers, if you're in-terested."

She paused. "Let me think about it."

"Absolutely," Juan said, rising from his chair. "Max tells me we'll be ready to set sail in two days. We hope you'll still be here when we cast off."

Raven never took her piercing brown eyes off him as he left.

Juan smiled to himself as he walked to the medical bay, since he thought he already knew her answer. It would be fun having her around.

When he got there, he found Julia helping Beth from her bed into a wheelchair. She looked much better than she had while going through the depths of Typhoon withdrawal. Julia had told him it was touch-and-go for a while, especially with the added complica-tion of the gunshot wound, but Beth hadn't become fully addicted in the short time she'd taken the drug. Still, Julia had been tending to her round the clock to keep her from succumbing to its effects.

"You're looking good," Juan said. "Ready for our outing?"

"Are you kidding?" Beth said with a voice that remained weak. "I've been getting claustrophobic in here."

"Not too long," Julia warned him. "She's still regaining her strength."

"Just a spin around the block and we'll be back," Juan assured her.

As he pushed her into the corridor, Beth said, "Now, what's this surprise you promised?"

"Boy, talk about impatience. You'll see soon enough."

"Sorry. I'm still getting over that drug they forced on me. I hope every single one of those pills was destroyed forever."

"We think that's the case," Juan said. "NUMA is currently diving on the *Pearsall*, but most of the destroyer was wrecked in the blast created by Gerhard Brekker. If there was any still aboard, it's gone now. The police are still excavating the entrance to the cavern, but I doubt there's any left in there after that explosion."

"What about the load in Tagaan's truck?"

"Vaporized. And I don't think Dr. Ocampo has any reason to keep trying to synthesize it. He and all the other scientists have been returned safely to their families, by the way."

"That's good to hear. I don't want anyone else to go through what I've experienced over the last week. And with Salvador Locsin dead, the last link to Typhoon is gone."

Juan frowned. "No one told you?"

"Told me what?"

"I guess they didn't want to bring it up when you were in recovery. They found Locsin pinned in the wreckage of his helicopter two days after it went down."

Beth turned in her chair to look at Juan with concern. "He's not dead?"

Juan shook his head. "Not yet, anyway."

MANILA

Locsin writhed in agony, chained to a bed in a prison infirmary. He begged for death that wouldn't come.

The doctors tried to pump him full of morphine and sedatives to ease his suffering, but nothing worked on his now skeletal body, his muscles atrophied beyond recognition. The medical staff didn't know how long he'd survive, but they told him it wouldn't be long. His body was literally consuming itself.

The dozen Special Action Force soldiers outside his room in full riot gear were woefully unnecessary. Locsin was in no condition to get out of bed, let alone make an escape, and this time no one was coming to spring him from captivity.

The pain was so unbearable that he went in and out of hallucinations. One minute he was thrashing against his shackles and screaming in a sweat-soaked bed, the next he was back in the cavern switching out the cardboard pieces holding the dried orchid with a fake using a flower he made Dolap acquire for him in Bacolod.

He could picture Tagaan's face when he realized he'd been duped, that Locsin had hidden away the real name of the flower in a safe place so that only he knew where it was. Locsin had been right to do it, too. His right-hand man had betrayed him.

He'd heard that Tagaan had been killed in a mysterious explosion that consumed the entire supply of Typhoon. But he felt no satisfaction in that knowledge. He felt only envy at Tagaan's quick death.

As his mind returned to the horror of the hospital bed, he realized there was something else besides the excruciating pain and overwhelming envy. There was hatred of Juan Cabrillo for putting him here. No, not hatred.

Fury.

GUAM

Beth's jaw dropped open as Juan wheeled her into the *Oregon*'s dining room. Virtually every table had been transformed into a display with a painting lying atop it. Even the eagle finial that had started the whole thing was there.

"This is the last time all of these paintings will be in one place," Juan said, "so I thought you'd want to take one last look at them before we return them to their rightful owners. Sorry we couldn't bring the Manet you recovered in Bangkok. The Gardner Museum has it under lock and key in Thailand until it goes back to the U.S. They're ecstatic that you found their stolen art, as are the other museums. The discovery has made worldwide news."

Beth wiped the tears streaming down her cheeks. All of these magnificent masterworks had been thought to be gone forever and now they'd be preserved for future generations. She felt an enormous sense of pride for having a part in their retrieval.

She took her time appreciating each and every one until she got to the last. Then she realized there were only fifteen.

"Where's the Picasso?"

Juan went over to a rectangular object draped with a cloth. He carried it to her and removed the cloth with a flourish.

It was the Picasso. set into an elegant gold frame.

"This belongs to the Corporation now," Juan said. "We made a generous offer to the insurance company that paid off the owner and they gladly accepted. Maurice thought it would look good in here. Would you like to hang it?"

"I'd be honored."

He gave her the small oil painting and she checked out the stellar framing job. She turned it over and gasped when she saw that the back had been marred by writing that looked like it had been done with a Sharpie.

It was a crude drawing of a flower along with the words *Cephalantheropsis inviolabilem*. Beth recognized it as scientific plant name. The first word was the Latin for the flower genus. The second was the species. The word meant *invulnerable*.

"This wasn't here when I first inspected the painting," she said. "Believe me, I would have seen it."

Juan nodded. "I think Locsin wrote it there for safekeeping. Can it be removed?"

"Not without risking damage to the canvas."

"That's what I thought. Since it's not visible from the front, we'll leave it as is."

He helped her secure it to the wall fasteners that had already been installed. She had to admit it did look beautiful there.

Juan put his hand on her shoulder and said, "It's done."

Beth knew what he really meant. The hateful drug was finally gone for good. As long as the Picasso stayed on that wall, no one would ever again see the name of the flower used to make Typhoon.

And she believed him. From what Beth had seen, there was no better place on earth to keep a secret than the *Oregon*.